P9-CKO-166

The Marvelous Journey Home

The Marvelous Journey Home

By John Simmons

The Marvelous Journey Home

Edited by Bruce Call

Cover Design by Laura Ashby and Zack Luther, Interform Group, Centerville, Utah

Photo of Author (casual) by Interform Group, Centerville, Utah

Photo of Author (semi-formal) by Dave Labrum, Busath Photography, Salt Lake City, Utah

Library of Congress Control Number (LCCN): 2007923049
ISBN: 978-0-9725916-1-4

01 – 06 – 07 – 001

Published in Kamas, Utah, in 2007 by:
White Knight Printing and Publishing, LLC.
187 E. 670 South, Kamas, Utah 84036
www.whiteknightpublish.com

Printed In India

Dedication

For Marina, Svieta and the girl in the blue bandana. Three beautiful young women who saw past the shards of their own shattered dreams, to find joy in the fulfillment of hope for a beloved younger sister in tribulation, who they would never see again in their lives.

You will trouble my thoughts and dreams as long as I live.

Acknowledgements

First and foremost I must thank my wife, Amy. She is the stability in my life, as she also is for my children, all nine of them. She lives a comparatively obscure life, doing the hard work, caring for my home and family, my life's most important dreams, while I set my sails, roam the world and continue to chase additional ones. At times it must seem overwhelming when I bite off more than she can chew, but Amy's abilities as a wife and mother are unsurpassed.

I must also thank my children for their patience with a father whose time is spread too thin. Fortunately, they do not measure my love for them merely by the individual attention that I give them. But I need to say that I am proud of them for all of their individual accomplishments, which in so many cases happen in spite of their father rather than because of him.

It would be very wrong to pass over thanking my team at White Knight, and in particular my siblings who I have the privilege of working with. My successes in business come from my team. I am not just a dreamer, I am also compulsive, and that is a volatile combination. I usually stay on task just long enough to get a new idea rolling. Theirs is the job to organize, create, correct, rework and follow through, turning my garbled meanderings into success upon success.

Though they created a monster, I need to thank my parents for teaching me that I could accomplish anything that I put my mind to. Also for teaching me that integrity was important in success and failure, in poverty and in wealth, and on good days and bad days alike.

I would like to thank those who traveled to and from Russia with Amy and me and assisted us in bringing five of our children home. It was incredible to watch our children bond with my parents and Bill and Joan Jenson who have been kind enough to serve as surrogate grandparents for my children. These incredible people have also been more like another set of parents to me than just friends.

Stas and Anya, our adoption coordinators in Russia are miracle workers. It would be not only wrong to overlook them in these acknowledgements, it would be immoral. I must also remember those who helped, protected, and raised our children before we got them home. Though I don't know all of their names, I must thank social workers, orphanage workers, directors, doctors, surgeons, prosecutors, and all of those who work behind the scenes in providing for the overwhelming number of children in the orphanages. I am grateful to the Department of Education of Primorski Krai for making our adoptions possible. Perhaps most important in my thanks for those in Russia, I must remember the judges, who, while stoic in their duties, obviously love these children. They removed my children from a home that endangered their lives and wellbeing, and even though there are public concerns about too many children leaving Russia, decided for the best interest of the children, and allowed them to have a family.

After about six months at home, Sarah, then five, in an effort to show loyalty, told me that she didn't love Russia, she only loved America. I told her that made me sad because I loved Russia. When she wrinkled up her forehead and asked me why, I told her; "I love Russia because Russia gave me you." Then Sarah saw that she could love Russia too. But our family doesn't just love Russia, we love all of the people there who worked so hard to make our family possible.

Thank you to Tatiana, Olga, Erina, Valentina and Galina, directors at our children's various orphanages, and also to Marina, Valentina and Zoya, our children's assigned social workers at the time of their respective adoptions. And, in a place where bus drivers make more money than doctors, thanks to our friend, Dr. Valentina, who did the required physicals for all five of our adopted children from Russia.

My most tender thanks goes to my little Russian friends who loved me even though I didn't choose them. Thank you to Jenya, Maxím, Dasha, Marina, Jula, Ksenya, André, Sergei, Lilya, Lidia and scores of others whose names I never knew, or forgot before I was able to record them. Though your names are not in my mind, your faces will never leave.

I am thankful to all of our friends at the Vlad Motor Inn, the only hotel in the world that I stay at which I consider my home away from home. While all of the workers there are our friends and did all that they could to help us on good days and bad days alike, I must especially thank Nellie and Tanya who provided hours of interpreting as well as encouragement for us and our teenaged daughters as we tore down walls and set about constructing a foundation for our new relationship.

One of our teenaged daughter's orphanages provided one of their workers to stay with us and our daughters at the hotel over our almost three-week stay. Tania provided help and support that only she could give, knowing our daughters, and what they had been through. An incredible and compassionate woman and caregiver, we are proud to call her and her son Artúr (Arthur) our friends.

There are two communities that also must be thanked. During our first foreign adoption experience we lived near Owosso, Michigan. The community was incredible at getting behind us and making it work. Our children were accepted, looked after and loved. Thanks to family friends, neighbors, workers at the schools, doctors, nurses, eye doctors, dentists, as well as students and their parents who realized the difficulties that our children would have in adjusting, and set out to make it as easy for them as they possibly could. Our second international adoption experience involved two teenaged daughters and a new community: Kamas, Utah. These girls had been hardened by years of abuse and neglect and could not adapt as easily as their younger siblings did. South Summit schools have been incredible at providing for their needs, up to and including an aid who speaks Russian. Again, in our new community, there are teachers, administrators, other school workers, neighbors, doctors, nurses and other medical and emergency personnel, dentists, and eye doctors who deserve our thanks. In our community, a very special thanks also goes out to the youth of the Kamas Valley, who have not only accepted our children, but have embraced them. These young adults, wise beyond their years, don't expect our children to behave as if they have lived their lives in a supportive family. Our daughters' friends are supportive, patient and compassionate. If these youth are reflective of the generation that will lead our country when I am old, then I am extremely confident in our future as a nation.

Thanks also to Svetlana Zachek, our dear friend and neighbor. Svieta comes from Kiev and speaks Russian as her native language. She spends countless hours in our home and with our daughters, at school, translating, teaching, encouraging, counseling, clarifying, and supporting. Her abilities and assistance go far beyond her language abilities. Spaseba.

I am thankful for family, immediate and more distant who along with family friends, help us and support us, particularly when we are feeling overwhelmed. They make sure that "mom and dad" get some time alone and that our children have all that they need, even though their parents have spread themselves quite thin.

I am also grateful to about fifty friends who read the pre-edited version of this book, waded through the parts that rambled, proofread, and made suggestions. Thanks for the praise and encouragement, but more importantly, thank you for honest opinions and constructive criticism. Your help has assisted in making this work something that I am happy with. I must also thank my editor, Bruce Call, who has the difficult job of taking a fun story and turning it into a readable book from a framework that resembles technical writing more than the writing of a novel that must keep the reader's attention. Metaphorically speaking, I feel like I handed Bruce a pretty and quaint little house that I wanted him to do the finish carpentry on. Bruce, rather than stopping at finish carpentry, handed me back a mansion.

Thanks to those who encouraged me to write the stories that we told and who prodded me to finish the novel. Your encouragement has made this book a reality.

It is impossible to do a list of acknowledgements without inadvertently missing someone who deserves to be recognized. In such instances, I ask forgiveness for my failure and offer my sincerest thanks.

Table of Contents

The Marvelous Journey Home

1

I Didn't Even Tell Her Goodbye

"Get up, Katya." Anastasia Lebedeva could be quite abrupt and emotionless. Ekaterina wished that she was more like Sofia. Sofia always cared how Katya felt, and went out of her way to make sure that she knew she was loved. Today, of all days, little Katya needed to be loved.

"You heard me, child. You know the rules here. Get out of your bed and make it this instant." Mrs. Lebedeva, like so many other Russian women, still went by her childhood nickname, Nastya. She briskly pulled the warm blankets down and Katya felt the cool draft which seemed ever-present, no matter how warm buildings got during the frigid Far East Russian winters. Katya turned her eyebrows down and wrinkled her forehead as much as she could. Her scowls were as intense as her smiles could be. She half groaned and half whined as she jerked the covers back up over her, and brusquely turned her back to Nastya.

"I won't ask you again, Katya. Get up." She pulled the blankets down again, grabbed Katya by the arm and firmly pulled her from the bed, standing her next to it.

Katya stood silently next to her bed, deepened her scowl, and wiped the sleep from her eyes as Nastya walked away. Slowly she pulled the blankets up over the bed and tucked them tightly into place. She walked around to the other side and pulled out all of the wrinkles. Nastya would settle for no less, and Katya didn't want to hear any more from her. Not today, anyway.

"Good morning, *Zaichunook*. How did you sleep?" The soft voice of Sofia Pavlova made Katya's heart warm; she loved it when Sofia called her by the popular Russian pet name "Baby Bunny." But as a smile complete with dimples tugged at the corners of her mouth, she immediately pushed the smile and the feeling away. Not today.

"Let's wash your face and comb your hair," said the pleasant young woman. "You'll feel better after breakfast."

Sofia quickly brushed through Katya's hair. It didn't take long. Her hair was short now, the way all childrens' hair was kept in the Russian orphanages. It wasn't ugly; Katya could never be ugly, but she did miss having her hair longer. *Babushka,* Grandmother, had always told her that she had the most beautiful hair of any child in the world. But that was no more. The orphanages were overloaded and understaffed and no one had the extra time to spend on something as frivolous as long hair on a child.

"What's the matter, Katya?" asked the soft motherly voice, "You always talk to me. Why so somber this morning?"

Katya burst into tears. "Why does Tanechka have to leave? I want her to stay here with me. She is my best friend in the whole world! Why does she have to leave?" Katya started to sob. "Why? Why?"

"I'm surprised, Katya. I thought that you would be happy for Tanechka." Sofia soaked the wash cloth with warm water and began to wash Katya's face. "Tanechka is happy and we should be happy for her too. You met her new mommy and poppy when they came here last month. They are such nice people. They have always wanted children and have prepared for years to make a good home. Tanechka will be well cared for. I needn't remind you either of how excited your friend is to begin her new life with her family in Amérika."

Katya had heard much of this faraway place called Amérika since entering the orphanage. Amérika had been the sworn enemy of Russia until less than a decade before Katya's birth. But now, people from Amérika came to the orphanage several times a month to adopt little Russian orphans to take back with them. Most of the mamas and papas from Amérika seemed to be very friendly. Often they would bring candy for the orphans, and usually they would leave some toys, books, or necessities as gifts for the children who remained in the orphanage when they returned to their fairytale land. Little Tatiana hadn't stopped talking about Amérika since her adoptive parents first visited, and though Katya was happy for her, the incessant talk of this land far away was beginning to get on her nerves.

"My new mommy said that there is an ice skating rink near our home in *Chee-kah-go* and my new poppy said that he will buy me my own ice skates so that I can learn to be an ice skater! I want to be a figure skater when I grow up," she had said dreamily as she spread out her arms and twirled in circles. Tanechka was so caught up in her new adventure that she couldn't possibly have seen how her excitement affected her friend, and Katya just wanted things to go back to the way they were before Tanechka's new parents arrived.

"Off you go, Zaichunook. It's time for breakfast."

"But why can't I go with Tanechka? Why can't Tanechka's new mommy and poppy be *my* mommy and poppy too? Why can't I go to Amérika with them?" Katya was no longer crying, but her face and eyes were still red and her voice was cracking.

"You know that it cannot be, Katya. The Bronsons are only qualified to adopt one child. Even if they wanted it differently, the documents are not in place. The court would never allow it. Now go. Eat your breakfast. Tell Tanechka goodbye." The thin young worker patted the child on the head and nudged her on her way.

Katya pulled her chair up to the table in her usual spot next to Tanechka. "Did you know that my new mommy and poppy are coming to get me today?" squealed the beautiful blonde five-year-old.

"Yes," came the short, abrupt reply. Katya's eyebrows turned down and pointed inward again.

"Mommy and Poppy are bringing me all new clothes for our trip home! On their last visit, Poppy promised to bring me a special present when he came back. Oh, I hope that he brings me ice skates! Katya, do you think that he's bringing me ice skates?"

"I don't know." The response was even more curt than the first, and the scowl deepened. Katya picked up her spoon and quietly poked at her porridge.

"We are going to go on an airplane to Moscow! We will see all of the beautiful places, the museums and the churches! Oh, I can't wait! I wonder if we'll see President Putin. Do you think that we'll see President Putin, Katya?"

Finally, it was more than Katya could take. "I don't know if you'll see President Putin!" she screamed. "I don't know if you'll get ice skates. I don't know and I don't care. I hate hearing about your new mama and papa, and I hate you!"

"Silence!" Nastya barked as she stomped toward the girls. "Katya, we'll have none of these tantrums. Return to your bed at once! You know the rules. Sit there with your hands on your lap and feet off the edge of the bed until you are told to do otherwise."

Katya wanted to push her chair to the floor and run from the room, but she dared not do it. Nastya was quite stern, and such behavior would certainly merit more severe punishment than a skipped meal and a short session of sitting on the edge of her bed. So she quietly stood up, slid her chair back under the table and walked briskly off to her bed as all the other children quietly returned to their porridge. All that is, except for Tanechka.

She remembered the day the social worker brought Katya to the orphanage. Katya had a cast on her arm and a big sore on her chest from a burn. Katya was afraid of everyone. Sofia had asked Tanechka if she would be her special friend and help her.

"Katya comes from a home where her mother beat her," Sofia had told her. "She has no friends and she is afraid." The tender caregiver held Tanechka's chin in her soft hand. "Will you be her friend?"

Tanechka, lonely for a friend herself, was eager to do it. She helped timid little Katya learn the ways of the orphanage. They ate together, played together, and slept in beds that were next to each other. The two children became each other's family. They were inseparable.

One day, several weeks later, the doctor came and removed the cast from Katya's arm. "Does your arm still hurt?" Tanechka had asked.

"No," came the reply. "But it itches really bad."

"Does the scar on your chest still hurt?"

"Not any more. But it used to hurt a lot. I would cry every time they changed the bandages. It felt like they were pulling off my skin." Katya shuddered at the memory.

"How did you get the burn?" Tanechka had asked.

Katya hesitated. Remembering seemed to make the large red scar on her chest throb.

"We hadn't eaten for two days, but Mama finally got some money so she bought some food and some vodka. Mama started cooking soup, but then she just sat at the table pouring the vodka into a glass and drinking it." Even though the girls had become best friends, Katya kept her eyes downcast as she told the story. "Mama fell asleep, and I was so hungry. I didn't want to make Mama angry by waking her, so I took the pan by the handle. But it was so heavy that it tipped over and spilled on my shoulder and chest."

Tanechka winced at the image in her mind.

"It hurt so bad that I screamed. Mama woke up and saw the soup all over the floor. She was angry because now we would have no food. When she hit me and I fell, I heard my arm crack."

Tanechka felt her eyes beginning to fill with tears as Katya's voice hushed almost to the point of a whisper.

"I couldn't stop crying. Mama said if I didn't stop, the police would come and take me away. But I couldn't stop; it hurt so bad."

Katya looked so little and small at that moment, small and afraid. Choking back her own emotions, Tanechka asked, "Did the policemen come?"

Silent now, Katya nodded.

There was nothing else to say, and so Tanechka reached over and held Katya's hand in both of hers.

The thought of that day filled Tanechka's mind as she stared into her bowl of porridge.

"Eat, Little One," Nastya said brusquely. "You're traveling today and there will be little time for eating. The car ride through the mountains is three hours before you reach Vladivostok. Eat your meal now or you'll be hungry for the rest of the day."

Tanechka took several bites, but she still had a lump in her stomach.

"Fine, fine. I see that you won't eat. Well don't let it be said that you had no warning." Nastya gathered up the dishes, all eaten clean except for Katya's bowl, which was still full, and

Tanechka's. But the food would not be wasted. It would go back in the pot for tomorrow. "Come, child. It's time we prepared you to leave."

Nastya led her off to the office to prepare the final paper work needed before sending Tanechka on her way.

"Nastya told me you had quite an outburst at the breakfast table," Sofia said softly.

Katya remained silent.

"It's always hard to lose a friend. Sometimes it seems unbearable to lose a best friend. But life is like that. Friends come into our lives and friends leave our lives. But friends never leave our hearts, and best friends always get to stay in the best places in our hearts."

"It's not fair!" Katya sobbed. "First the policemen took me away from my mama because I cried too much. Now Tanechka is going away to Amérika. It's just not fair."

"Oh, child," Sofia gasped. "Is that why you think that you were taken from your mother? Because you cried too much?"

Katya didn't say a word.

"It's not so, Zaichunook. You had no blame! Your mother couldn't take care of you and you aren't yet old enough to care for yourself. The policemen brought you to us so that we could help you to get better and so that you would have enough to eat."

"I'm sorry I cried." Little Katya didn't understand, couldn't understand, and it was breaking Sofia's heart. "I won't cry any more. Will you please let me go back to Mama?"

"Katya," Sofia said tenderly, but firmly, "if you never remember anything else I tell you, understand me now and never forget what I am about to say. Your mother could not even care for herself. She certainly couldn't care for you. Every minute that you lived in that home your life was in danger. You were taken from your mother for your own protection, not to punish you. You did nothing wrong."

Katya sat quietly staring at the floor. Sofia stroked her head softly for a moment. This child needed so much. But time was limited, and with Nastya handling the final adoption arrangements for Tanechka, Sofia couldn't neglect the other children.

"Why don't you lie down and take a nap, child? I know you didn't sleep well last night. You must be exhausted."

"I can't," Katya replied, her pain turning to stubbornness, the scowl returning to her face. "Nastya told me that I had to sit on the edge of the bed with my hands on my lap."

"You lie down and take a nap, and I'll talk with Nastya."

Sofia pulled back the covers and after several seconds of hesitation, the little girl climbed underneath. The loving caregiver pulled the blankets way up around Katya's neck and tucked them tightly around her. Katya loved it when Sofia tucked her in like that. It didn't happen very often. There wasn't enough time. Katya liked to imagine that the warm blankets tucked around her were Sofia's arms holding her while she went to sleep.

"So, how did it go?" Sofia asked. "Is Tanechka on her way?"

The older, stout orphanage worker wiped a few beads of sweat from her head and pulled back the bangs of her orange-dyed, salt and pepper-rooted hair. "The Amerikáns gave me a nice pair of leather gloves as a going away present. The gloves are very nice, but a bit extravagant for me. They should fetch enough on the black market to feed me for a week." And then, as an afterthought, "Yes, Tanechka is off to Moscow on her way to live the Amérika dream." She said it with a snort. She always spoke of the Amérika dream with a snort.

"Tanechka's life will be good in Amérika," Sofia responded. "Perhaps even better than they say."

"Better?! How could it possibly be better than the propaganda that comes from Amérika? Don't be naïve, Sofia. Every country has hunger, has poverty. Life in Amérika is not a fairytale."

"No life is a fairytale, Nastya, but these children are hardly going into poverty. Just to adopt one child, these parents pay more than you or I make in five years! Look at those gloves they gave you! No, the days of hunger and poverty for any child lucky enough to go to Amérika are only a bad memory. Thank heaven above that it is so."

"Heaven? Oh Sofia, now really. You want to bring heaven into this? Such superstition is hardly what I expect from someone as bright as you."

Sofia wanted to reply that it wasn't superstition, that since attending church, for the first time in her life she felt hope. Hope for herself and for all God's children. That even for those who suffer throughout their entire lives, there is hope in the life to come. But such language would only bring anger to one so hopeless as Nastya.

Sofia decided to change the subject. "Any new blankets?"

"Oh, yes. I told the Amerikáns that the old thin orange blanket was Tanechka's favorite."

"Well, it was," Sofia countered. "You did not lie."

"Yes, yes, but at any rate, I told them that we would like to let her keep her favorite blanket, but that we had none to spare. They offered to buy a new one in its place. Really, I should be a horse trader."

Sofia saw her opportunity to heap praise on her coworker and moved swiftly. "You truly are brilliant when it comes to providing for these children. I don't know what we would do without you."

"Of course you don't. The blanket is in the office. Put it to good use."

"I will. Perhaps a nice new blanket will cheer up Katya a bit."

"Katya? She hardly deserves it. Such a tantrum at the breakfast table! That reminds me, is she still sitting on her bed as I sent her to do?"

"She was when I checked on her but I told her to lie down. She wasn't feeling well, poor thing."

"Really Sofia, you let these children push you too far." It was Nastya's honest belief. "But as long as she is behaving herself, I guess I have no complaint. There is a stuffed animal, a bear I think, with the blanket. Tanechka's parents brought it for her from Amérika. Something about a promise and a special present. Tanechka was excited of course. She squealed and hugged it for the longest time. But then the strangest thing happened."

"Strange?" Sofia asked.

"Yes, quite strange. She asked if she could leave the bear for Katya. The translator started to cry. It took her a moment to compose herself before she could even ask the father. When she finally got it out, the father started crying. He's a big man. I didn't see that coming. These people from Amérika are soft and weak."

Sofia was ready to cry, herself. She couldn't wait to hear the rest of the story. "What did he say?"

"Oh, of course he said it would be alright. He promised to buy Tanechka one *twice* that size when they got back to *Chee-kah-go*. Hmph! Twice that size!"

Sofia was bubbling with excitement. This would be exactly what Katya needed. Her silent prayer to know how to help had been answered. "I'll take the bear right to Katya," she said, hurrying to leave.

"Sofia!" The command brought the younger woman to a halt. "Perhaps after lunch. You said the child wasn't feeling well. Maybe she should rest, as you recommended. Besides, she hardly deserves it after her performance this morning. For the life of me, I can't figure out why Tanechka would do such a thing after being treated that way. Anyway, for now we have other responsibilities at hand. Katya is not the only child in this orphanage with needs."

"Yes Nastya, of course," Sofia said submissively. "I'll tend to my other responsibilities first."

"Wake up, sleepy head." Sofia gently shook Katya's shoulder. "Wake up. It's time for lunch."

Katya rolled over on her side and pushed up on her elbow. She squinted her eyes while they adjusted to the light and began to focus. Had it all been a bad dream?

"It's lunch time, Zaichunook. Soup is on the table. Get up, let's make you presentable." Sofia spoke as she quickly combed through Katya's hair. "There's a new blanket for you at the foot of your bed. Tanechka's parents brought it to us from Amérika. Help me make your bed with it and I'll have your old one laundered and put with the others."

Sofia pulled the old blanket to the floor and quickly threw the new blanket out over the bed. Katya walked around the bed with her and helped her tuck it in.

"Let's go, child, you must be hungry." She put her arm around Katya's shoulder and they started off to the cafeteria.

Katya sat down at the table and began to eat. She felt guilty for her outburst at breakfast and sensed the eyes of the other orphans on her, though she didn't look up. She was hungry, and the thin chicken soup tasted good. She finished it off in no time, then looked down at her hands and waited for the others to finish so that they could be excused from the table. She didn't look at Tanechka's chair, but she could feel the emptiness of it. Silently she sat and wished that Tanechka had not gone away.

The clacks of spoons on bowls gradually diminished, and soon all the orphans sat quietly. "You may now be excused," said Nastya. Then she and Sofia began to clear the dishes.

The children scurried to the other room to play with their favorite toys. Katya walked slowly behind them, not knowing what to do. Until now, she and Tanechka would have taken turns being Sofia and taking care of a worn baby doll. Today, Katya could have the doll all to herself, but she didn't feel like playing.

The other children had removed the toys from the boxes and Katya stood alone, unsure of how to occupy her time. Finally she picked up a book of Russian fairytales. She recognized the book as one that Babushka had read to her on several occasions. Babushka wasn't her real grandmother. Katya and Mama had lived with one of Mama's boyfriends at his mother's home for a while. The old woman had grown attached to Katya, and had insisted that she call her Babushka. Katya liked having a grandmother and she loved the extra attention. But that, just like every other family relationship in her short life, soon came to an end; this time when she and her mother moved away.

Katya didn't like the fairytales much. They were always so scary, with some bad person always trying to hurt someone else. But she had loved spending time with Babushka and the fairytale book brought back the fond memories of sitting on her lap and listening while her hoarse voice brought the stories to life.

Katya couldn't read words yet, but she recognized the pictures as Babushka's voice told the stories again in her mind. This book was old and worn. Perhaps that's how it ended up at the orphanage in the first place. Many of the pages had been torn and some of Katya's favorite pictures from the fairytales were missing. But she didn't feel like playing with other children, so she continued to sit quietly with the book.

Days at the orphanage would be long without Tanechka.

"Come with me, Little One." Sofia held out her hand to Katya and pulled her to her feet. "It will soon be time for everyone to go to bed, but I want to talk to you first."

Katya was exhausted. Her eyes still felt swollen from crying and her face felt like it does when you spend too long out in the wind on a cold day. But inside, she just felt numb. The rest of the day had been uneventful, but it had dragged on forever. Katya had never felt more alone, and she held Sofia's hand tightly as they walked to the dormitory and along to the side of her bed.

"Sit, child. I have a very special surprise for you." Sofia was beaming. She had been waiting all day for this very moment.

Katya wasn't in the mood for surprises, but she didn't feel like arguing either. She just wanted this day to be over, and she wanted to go to sleep. So in an effort to have this event end as soon as possible, she sat on the edge of the bed and folded her hands in her lap.

Sofia stooped down and pulled the stuffed bear from under Katya's bed. "I have a special friend for you. Perhaps you would like him to sleep with you and keep you safe."

The dark brown stuffed animal was soft and beautiful, with deep brown glass eyes. But Katya wanted nothing to do with it. She spun her head and shoulders away. Did Sofia really think that this stuffed bear could replace Tanechka?

"Come, Zaichunook, it's such a lovely bear. I've never seen its equal." She softly placed the bear on Katya's lap and lifted her little arm up onto the soft fur.

Katya jerked her arm back and used the other hand to firmly push the animal away. "I don't want it. I don't want anything. I just want to go to sleep." She turned even further away.

"I know how you must feel, Katya. But this is a special bear. He comes from a land far away to be here with you." Katya pretended to ignore her. "This bear comes from Amérika. In fact, this bear came all the way from *Chee-kah-goh*. You remember, where Tanechka's new home is? I thought that he might help you to remember your friend so you wouldn't feel so lonely."

How was this silly stuffed animal supposed to make her feel less lonely? Katya, offended as only a five-year-old could be, folded her arms firmly over her chest, still refusing to speak.

"There's something that you should know." Sofia moved around so that she would be in the girl's field of vision. Katya watched her from the corner of her eye but did not attempt to move further. "Remember how Tanechka's new father promised to bring her a special gift? Do you remember how excited she was to get it?"

Remember? Remember?! Who could forget? Tanechka hadn't shut up about that stupid, special gift for a full six weeks.

"Katya, this is the special gift that Tanechka's father brought for her all the way from *Chee-kah-goh*. She loved it. But she thought that you would be lonely here at the orphanage. She thought that you needed a special gift more than she did. Tanechka asked her new father if she could give the bear to you. He said that he thought that would be good. Your friend hoped that the bear would make you less lonely and that it would help you to remember her always."

Katya burst into tears and she reached for the bear, pulling it close to her chest. She squeezed the bear hard as if she were clinging to her best friend as she cried harder and harder.

"Oh Sofia, I was so bad." Katya continued to cry. "I was so mean to Tanechka. I yelled at her and told her that I hated her. But I don't hate her. She just made me mad. But she thinks that I hate her, and now I can't tell her that I don't. She's gone, and I didn't even tell her goodbye." Katya started to sob as she clung ever more tightly to the bear.

"There, there, Zaichunook. Tanechka doesn't believe that you hate her. We have all said things that have hurt our friends and we wish we could change that. But our true friends know that we love them even when we are angry. Our true friends forgive us even if we don't ask them to. I know that Tanechka loves you. Otherwise, she wouldn't have given you such a special gift. She wants you to be happy, just like I know you want her to be happy."

Katya stopped sobbing and sniffed her nose. Sofia wiped off her face with a clean rag used for a handkerchief and then helped her to blow her nose. She hugged Katya and held her tight.

"But I didn't even tell her goodbye," Katya cried. Sofia squeezed her tighter as the girl took a deep, quivering breath and let out a long sigh. "I didn't even say goodbye."

The tenderhearted caregiver searched her mind, trying to find the right thing to say, but it just wasn't there. Then suddenly it came to her.

"Listen, Katya. Sometimes we get to say goodbye, and sometimes we don't. Sometimes we are able to prepare our thoughts and speak our feelings, and sometimes we can't. But it doesn't really matter. Our true friends know the feelings that we have deep in our hearts even if the feelings don't make it out in words."

Sofia gave Katya another squeeze to conceal her need to glance at the clock on the wall. A caregiver's time in the orphanage was extremely limited. It was time to put the other children to bed and she had spent so much time on Katya, far more than she should have. Nastya wouldn't tolerate this. And,

Nastya's opinions aside, this was the way of things. Other children needed her too.

"It's bed time, Katya." Sofia pushed the little girl back and looked deep into her eyes. "Tomorrow will be a better day, but now it's time to sleep." She pulled back the covers and Katya scurried underneath. Sofia pulled the new pink blanket from Chicago over the child and tucked the covers tightly around her.

"Good night, Zaichunook," she whispered. "I'll see you in the morning." She walked slowly to the door and then hurried off to her other responsibilities.

Katya reached up to pull the new blanket to her face. The new blanket had satin on it and Katya loved satin. She grabbed the silky fabric in her hand and began to rub it back and forth against her cheek. In no time she drifted off to sleep.

2

Never Lose Hope

Two months had passed since Tanechka left the orphanage for the fairytale land of Amérika. Katya had adjusted well. She no longer had a best friend at the orphanage, but she played well with all of the other children. One of the adopting couples from Europe left several puzzles for the children to play with and Katya loved to put them together with her other friends. Her favorite puzzle was of a large white castle with a green roof, perched on a mountain. She liked to imagine that she was being adopted by rich parents from Amérika who would take her away to live there and to be a princess.

Katya had just finished putting together the puzzle of the castle when Nastya walked into the room.

"Soup is ready, children. Off to the table." She turned to walk from the room when Katya grabbed the hem of her faded green dress. Nastya didn't have time for such annoyances, but she turned to see what the little girl wanted. "What is it, child? And be quick. Soup is on the table."

"Do you think that a rich mama and papa from Amérika will come to get me to take me to a new home?" Katya looked back down at the puzzle as the husky woman scoffed.

"Don't get your hopes up, child. It's more likely that your life will be one of orphanages, until it gets worse."

"But Sofia says that we always have hope. She says that the right mommy and poppy are looking for me, but they just haven't found me yet." Katya didn't look up from her puzzle, but she felt her optimism beginning to crumble.

The gruff woman grunted. "Foolishness, child. You have had tuberculosis and you have that hideous scar on your chest. You're hardly the perfect child that these vain people from Amérika are looking for." It was harsh, but it was the truth. Better that the child learned early. "It's best not to get your hopes up. There's less disappointment that way. One day you'll see that I am right. I am always right. Now off with you. Off to the table. Soup is ready. Be glad that you have something to eat. Now there's something to hope for. Hope for enough to eat."

Nastya walked away, the hem of her dress pulling loose from Katya's fingers. The little girl's hand dropped to her side.

A much sadder and more cynical child hesitated for only a second before following the orphanage director into the small cafeteria where she sat and ate soup in silence.

"There you go, Zaichunook. You have such beautiful hair. It suits a girl like you perfectly." Sofia gave two more quick brush strokes through Katya's hair as she tapped her shoulder to signal that she was finished with the very short morning grooming session.

"No mommy and poppy are coming for me. My life will be in the orphanage, until it gets worse." Katya folded her arms across her chest.

Sofia was so shocked that she almost dropped the brush.

"Why, child! Why ever would you say such a thing?"

"Nastya said that the parents who come here from Amérika are looking for perfect children. She said that they wouldn't want me because I got sick. And my burn is ugly. No one from Amérika wants an ugly child. My life will be in the orphanage until it gets worse."

Sofia felt her blood boil as anger coursed through every vein in her body. How could the director be so cruel? She felt her face turn a brilliant red as she tried to control her feelings in the presence of the crushed child.

"Katya, you know how Nastya is. Sometimes she says things that hurt. Nastya thinks that if you never hope, you never get hurt. But that isn't so. People who don't hope hurt more than people who do." She stooped and took the young girl's shoulders, turning Katya to face her. "You must never lose hope, Katya. Hope is something that can never be taken from you unless *you* allow someone to take it. Family can be taken from us. Friends can be taken from us. Even our health can be taken from us. But hope only leaves us if we *allow* it to be taken. Never let anyone take hope away from you. If you never lose hope, Zaichunook, you will never truly be poor."

At that moment, Sofia wanted more than anything in her life for Katya to understand what she was saying. But how much can a five-year-old comprehend? Perhaps more than she realized, Sophia thought. This five-year-old had understood pain, had understood betrayal, had understood loss. Certainly she could understand love, and faith, and hope. The caregiver looked deep into the little girl's eyes. Yes. Yes, perhaps she does understand.

Once more Sophia smoothed the child's hair with her hand.

"Now, go and eat your breakfast."

And Katya did understand. A new world opened to the little orphan as she walked quickly down the hall. She could hope for anything that she wanted to. She could hope for a family, she could hope for love. She could hope for things even as silly as puppies, and toys, and pretty dresses. Nothing, not even Nastya could stop her from hoping. She would never stop hoping again.

"How dare you crush the hopes of that child!" It was all Sofia could do to keep from completely losing her temper.

"Be careful, Sofia. You forget your place. Or am I mistaken? Are jobs now easy to come by in Russia? Perhaps you have a rich poppy from Amérika now and you no longer need this job."

As much as she hated hearing it, Sofia knew that the director was right. She needed this job. Even if she didn't, the children needed her. To overstep her bounds with Nastya would destroy any chance of helping the children to discover what had taken her so long to find. Communism, ineffective at so many things, had been quite effective at destroying faith and belief.

Faith and belief. The very heart of Sofia's life now, the very core of her newfound religion. But it came at a cost. Even her family and closest friends had called her naïve when she began searching for truth, for meaning, at church. All around her, people still clung tightly to the hollow, yet familiar, emptiness of cynicism; it was far less frightening than hope. She had quickly learned that it did no good to force her beliefs on others. Against all reason, nobody likes to be told their life could be better. The best that she could ever do was to live a life that caused others to wonder where her happiness and fortitude came from. When people asked questions, they were prepared to listen.

Nastya, Sofia knew, was not prepared to listen. But maybe, if the approach were right, she could be influenced.

"I'm sorry, Nastya. I don't mean to be disrespectful." Sofia bowed her head meekly. "But there was a time when I felt no hope. Even though I had friends and family close to me, the loneliness that came with hopelessness was unbearable. Please don't take hope away from the children."

Nastya almost laid into the younger worker again, but when she saw that Sofia had submitted, she saw no reason to continue. *People are like animals*, she thought. *They must be made to submit. But this can be done without instilling unwarranted fear or hostility.*

"That will be all, Sofia." The stocky, brusque woman stood her ground and waited for the humbled young subordinate to retreat.

Sofia didn't quite know what to feel as she walked away. She did still feel anger, but it was anger overwhelmed with sadness. If only people could find the hope that she had found, their lives would be better. The difficult would become possible, the excruciating would become tolerable, and the unbearable would become endurable. And when dreams came true, the hope that had been sustained was made exquisite. Each improvement in life became a gift, and each day was a newfound opportunity. If only she could get others to understand.

Of course, the path to understanding was never easy. Her own path was painful and tragic. How she missed Aleksander! How she longed to see her husband one more time, to touch his face, to feel his kiss on her forehead as they embraced. How she hated God when he was taken from her! Why Aleksander? Why not one of the others so deep within the earth that cold January day? Why not one of the coal miners who had lived his life, raised his family, held his grandchildren?

But anguish can be like a red-hot sword, cauterizing even as it cuts. And her anguish, even while it left scars, planted the seeds of recovery, for it led to a determined search for truth. A kind priest offered friendship and comfort, and, eventually, a knowledge of God's plan for his children. But the journey was a long one, with Sofia resisting much of the way.

Now she remembered why she loved working with the orphans so much. The children almost never refused help. They could always be led to hope. Walking away from her confrontation with her supervisor, Sofia understood that now, more than ever, she needed to be here to lead them. To lead them on, to hope.

3

The Decision that Changed Lives

A half a world away Laura pulled a frilly pink dress from a rack at the local department store.

"Look, Sweetheart, it's Emma's size. You know how much she likes pink. Wouldn't she just look adorable in it?"

"Sure she would," Mike replied.

"It's twenty-five percent off. I can't pass up a deal like that. The dress probably won't be here by the time I tell Dawn about it, so I think that we should just pick it up for her."

"You're the boss," Mike said, knowing that her heart was set on it and that it wouldn't do much good to protest. Besides, secretly, he liked buying dresses and other girl things for his nieces as much as Laura did.

Laura held the dress up, turned it around in front of her, and then held it facing her—just off the floor at Emma's height—one last time before nodding approvingly and placing it in the cart.

"Do you know what? I don't think Emma has shoes that will match this, at least not ones that fit her anymore. We should pick her up some new shoes, and some tights. That's what we should do."

Mike just smiled. They'd been down this road many times before. He knew that this would never end with just a dress. Laura wandered through the aisles, carefully inspecting several pairs of shoes before deciding on tan suede ones with a pink and purple flower embroidered on the top of each shoe. She grabbed a pair of white tights nonchalantly as she passed the display and they headed for the checkout line.

The two were silent driving out of the parking lot. Both were thinking the same thing quietly to themselves, but Laura was the first to speak.

"I really do wish that we could have had a little girl. I love our boys and I wouldn't trade them for anything. But I do wish that we could have had a little girl, too."

"I know what you mean. My siblings are great about sharing their girls with us, but I've always wanted a little girl of my own." They drove on silently for another moment until Mike finally said what they were both thinking. "Have you ever thought about adoption?"

"Oh Mike, could we?" Laura's eyes lit up and she grinned from ear to ear.

"Sure, why not? People do it every day. Take some time tomorrow. Do some checking online and make a few phone calls. Find out what we need to do."

"I can't wait!" Laura squealed. "Finally I'll have a little girl to take shopping, to teach to play the piano, and to have tea parties with. Oh, Mike, I can't wait!"

It had been a busy day at work when Mike finally walked through the door. Production had a machine down and promised orders kept being pushed out further and further. He had spent the entire day on the phone, fielding one frustrated call after another, calming his customers down and reassuring them that this was only a short term glitch. *Things will be back to normal in a couple of days.*

Mike had a splitting headache and planned on making the medicine cabinet his first stop before plopping into the easy chair. Laura met him as soon as he walked through the door.

"Welcome home, Good Lookin'," she beamed as she jumped up and threw her arms around his neck, kissing him on the cheek. It was all Mike could do to keep from tumbling over backwards with her on top of him. He put his hands around her thin waist, boosted her up, and kissed her quickly on the lips.

"What's with the warm welcome? I think you quit giving me welcomes like that before our first anniversary."

"Oh, silly, I did not. You still get a warm welcome every night when you come home."

"Yeah, right," was all he could say before she grabbed him by the hand and pulled him through the kitchen and down the hall towards the den where the computer was kept.

"I have been busy all day! I have the names of adoption agencies, government organizations, support groups... We have lots and lots of options. Come on. Help me decide what we need to do next."

"Oh yeah, the adoption." It was all coming back to him now. He shouldn't have been surprised that Laura hadn't wasted a minute now that a daughter was within the realms of possibility.

"Of course *the adoption,* silly! What did you think I was talking about?"

Mike just smiled back at her and tried to keep up as she bounced down the hall.

Laura pushed Mike gently into his high-back office chair while she tucked her right leg under herself and sat on the chair next to him.

"Here are eight adoption agencies," she said as she plopped a stack of papers in his lap, each bundle separated by a different color paper clip. "I emailed them and asked them to send us more information to get us started."

"You asked *eight different* adoption agencies to send us more information, *to get us started*?" Mike asked, bewildered.

"Well, yes. What's wrong with that?"

"Oh, nothing. Nothing's wrong with that. But I'm sure that eight of them will get you plenty of information." He chuckled to himself as he compared the situation to work; the thought of throwing blueprints at eight different machine shops and asking them for quotations. *They won't let her off the phone for weeks,* he thought. She might as well have filled a thimble with a fire hose.

"What's so funny? Are you laughing at me?" She smiled as she poked him in the ribs and tickled him just a little.

"No, no. It's not that. I'm just glad to see you so happy and excited. I haven't seen you this bubbly in a while." He grabbed her hand mostly to make sure that the tickling didn't resume, but then he gave it a gentle squeeze and he leaned over and kissed her again. "You never let me forget why I love you."

"Well, what do we do next?" Laura asked excitedly.

Mike chuckled again. "Oh, I don't think that we do anything *next*. I think that the adoption agencies will make the next move."

"How long do you think it will take for them to get back to us?"

Mike smiled, but caught himself before laughing, again thinking of the hungry machine shops beating each other to pieces for a shot at a new contract. "Oh, don't worry. I think you might have some response by tomorrow," he said. "Now, what's for dinner?"

"I just got so involved in this today that I wasn't even hungry. I'm sorry, I didn't even think about it until a half hour ago." Mike tried not to show his disappointment. "But don't worry. It won't be long. The Dominos guy should be..." *Ding-dong*. "And there he is!"

"Come and eat, boys!" Laura yelled up the stairs while Mike settled the bill with the pizza deliveryman. Jeff, fifteen, and Stephen, thirteen, bounded down the stairs and into the kitchen.

"Mom said we're getting a sister," Stephen said after the blessing on the food. He was pulling a piece of the pizza to his plate with strings of cheese still connecting it to the box. He hooked the strings next to the box with his index finger and twirled them around it until the coil ended next to the slice. He pulled the saucy cheese ball loose, lifted it to his mouth and stripped it off his finger like a pitted olive.

"We're looking into it," Mike said cautiously. "Don't get too excited yet. I've heard that these things can take a while."

"A while on a calendar, or a while on a clock?" Jeff asked, stealing a line that his father used regularly when trying to get a more specific answer from production crews at work.

Laura responded. "We don't know at this point, guys. But I've asked some adoption agencies to send us more information. We should have a better idea in a couple of days. But don't be surprised if the whole thing takes several months."

Mike looked up quickly, ready to add something, but thought better of it. Lynn, from the office, and his wife had been trying to adopt for three years now with no end in sight.

“It will take some time,” Mike said. “We may all learn what patience is about before this is over.”

“Yes, but we have plenty to keep us busy in the meantime,” Laura added, a smile of anticipation spreading across her face. “We need to move the things from the storage room into the attic and turn it into a bedroom. We need to paint it and put in new carpet and curtains. Oh, and we’ll need to childproof the house again. There’s so much to do. We’re going to need a lot of help from you boys.”

“You seem a little less chipper tonight,” Mike said as he peered over Laura’s shoulder at the computer screen.

“Oh! You startled me. I didn’t know you were there,” Laura said as she turned in the chair to meet him. She reached up and hugged him as he bent over to get his welcome home kiss. “Boy, this adoption stuff is a mess! I heard back from five of the agencies today, two of them twice.” Mike grinned. “They are all sending me a bunch of information on their agencies and why we should use them. I got email packets from several of them today. I just got them all printed off. They’re in the folder over there.” She pointed at the far corner of the desk.

“So, what are you finding out? Has somebody got a little girl they can FedEx out to us?”

“Hardly. In fact, it’s way worse than I thought. They’re telling me that if we want an infant, we’re in for a long wait, particularly since we already have two biological children. I guess that kind of puts us at the end of some mysterious list. The agencies that I spoke with today all recommended that we go with a special needs child if we want this to happen in any kind of reasonable time frame.”

“Special needs…what exactly do they mean by that?”

“A lot of things, really. Mostly it means children who will be more difficult to find a home for than a healthy newborn. It can mean anything from a child being a little older, to being from a minority race, or even mentally or physically challenged.”

"So, what do you think about that?" Mike asked, not knowing quite what he thought about it himself.

"I don't know. I just don't know. The Wilsons, whose kids go to school with Stephen, adopted the cutest little black twins a couple of years ago. Things are going great with them. But I've always imagined having a little girl that looks like me. I feel almost racist for saying that, though. Do you think I'm being selfish?"

"Yeah…I mean, no! Not that you're racist, or selfish. I'm just thinking. I'd never really thought about anything but a newborn little girl that looks just like us coming home from the hospital wrapped up in a new pink blanket."

"But they're telling me that it will take years to do that. There are situations where potential adoptive parents can pay for the medical care of expectant mothers—you know, the delivery and stuff—but there are no guarantees. I guess if there are guarantees it's considered buying the child, and of course, that wouldn't be right."

"What does that mean, no guarantees?" Mike asked. His business mind didn't like the sound of this option one bit.

"It means that at any time before the adoption is final, even after the child is born, the birth mother or father can change their minds and decide to keep the child rather than allowing it to be adopted. And since the payments were considered 'gifts' there would be no reimbursement."

"You're kidding!" Mike felt his face grow red. "They con you into paying for the pregnancy and then keep the kid themselves? What kind of lowlife does that?"

"Calm down, Honey. Of course, in *theory* that could happen, but we would screen the possibilities. You know, look for a young unwed mother who doesn't have insurance and who really needs to finish high school anyway. We *can* stack the odds in our favor."

Mike scowled. "I don't know, maybe it's just the business in my blood, but I don't like it. Even if it's a young unwed mother, how many women do you know who, after giving birth, wouldn't strongly consider changing their mind? Even if there wasn't malicious intent, I don't like the odds. Call me cynical, but I hardly think that could be our best option."

Laura slowly nodded her head. "There are other options. We could consider adopting a child with mental or physical challenges."

"What do you think of that? Before we found out that we couldn't have more children naturally, all you could talk about was the things that you wanted to teach your daughter when you finally got her. Playing the piano, cooking, gymnastics, dance…I mean you would be giving up a lot of what you wanted a little girl for. How would that sit with you?"

Laura felt uneasy, like it was all falling on her. "This is something that we have to decide together, Sweetheart. It has to be based on what we both decide is *best* for our family, not just what I *want*. You know, we could have had a child with special needs naturally. We both know that we would have dealt with it like any other challenge that we have had. It's not something that we couldn't do. I mean, I guess at least at this point, I think we should leave it open as an option."

"Yeah, okay. So what are the other options?"

"We could consider adopting an older child. But if we decide to do that, I don't want to adopt one older than Stephen. It might sound weird, but I wouldn't want him to feel that we have given away his place in line, if you know what I mean."

Mike nodded. "What about international adoption? My cousin in Atlanta adopted her two children out of Uzbekistan."

"That was the next option. I saved it for last. There are children available in Eastern Europe, Russia, and other countries from the former USSR. Most of these children look European. But the cost would be quite a bit more."

Mike gave a slight shrug. "Well, I don't think that makes it undoable. This family could live with a little belt tightening. We've been pretty fortunate with work the past few years. I don't think that the kids even remember the good old days when you and I used to sit at the table and decide which bills to pay."

"No, of course they don't," Laura agreed. "But, you know, if this is the way that we think we should go, we should involve the boys in the decision. This is their family, too. They're good boys, Mike. They take after their dad. I'm sure that they'll be willing to give up whatever it takes if they're allowed to participate in the decision right from the start."

"You're right. They have their mom's soft heart, even though Jeff doesn't like to let it show. Either of them would do anything to help someone in need. Let's think about it for a couple of days before we talk to them and make sure that we still think we're on the right path."

"Boy, there is a lot to consider when you start looking at these adoption agencies," Laura said as she turned down the stereo and sat down next to Mike on the couch.

"What are you finding out?"

"Well, some agencies only work in the U.S., while others specialize in particular international areas. But, in reviewing information on the internet and from a couple of chat rooms, just because an agency can handle international adoptions doesn't mean they can do business everywhere. Even in Russia, agencies that are certified to adopt out of one region may not have access to other regions."

"So, what's the big deal with how many regions they can adopt from? We only want one kid."

"Yes, but the greater the number of regions, the more we have to choose from and the more likely we are to find what we're looking for, and in Russia, finding a child we want might be tough. Even just finding a healthy child."

"Really?"

"Yeah. I mean, it gets weird. Some Russian officials are concerned that all the healthy orphan babies were going abroad, and all of the sick ones were staying in Russia, so some laws were passed to make it more difficult for non-Russians to adopt. But there just aren't enough Russian homes that are able to adopt. So now they have healthy kids that need homes, but nowhere to send them. Because of that, there are Russian doctors who overstate or even fabricate medical conditions so that it looks like it was an unhealthy child that left Russia."

"Yeah, but how do you know what the *real* condition of the child is?"

"I guess you never do. Sometimes a big long medical name will be used to describe 'dry skin,' or 'needs glasses.' A lot of times they will put that the child is developmentally delayed, when really nothing is wrong. I mean, what child in an orphanage would not be a little bit behind? I am hearing that there are doctors here in the U.S. who are experienced with reading these Russian medical reports. They can help us to understand whether there is a real problem or if the report is just a smokescreen."

Mike started shaking his head. He was not a man who dealt well with chaos. Things should be orderly and correct. "Why, then, would we even consider Russia? Why not just adopt from another country?"

"Believe it or not, Russia's adoption program has historically been more stable than most. The Eastern Block countries and former Soviet states often have more difficult issues. Some of these countries occasionally shut down international adoptions, for no reason at all, and leave the families who were planning to adopt to wait until they decide to start up again."

"You have got to be kidding! So what about adopting from a place that is more reasonable?"

"Some countries are more reasonable, but then we're talking about children who don't look like us. But still, we might want to consider it. With the population control in China, most people want to have a son to carry on the family name. Little girls are easy to come by in China."

Mike shook his head in exasperation. "So, back to the adoption agencies. How do we decide which one to use?"

"We're better off with a local agency. Home visits and studies have to be done both before and after placement, and an out-of-state agency would just subcontract that work to a local one, so why not cut out the middleman? We should look for a local agency who has a broad base in areas we would consider adopting from. Lastly, like you said, we need to check references."

"Sounds like I'll be a Tylenol poster child before this is all over," Mike said as he leaned forward and began rubbing his temples in circles.

Laura laughed as she reached over and began to rub his back. “It’s alright, Sweetheart. It will all be worth it by the time we’re finished. I’ve already gathered up information on some adoption agencies with local branches, and I’ve already eliminated a couple of them based on reviews from other families. I think that I can have it narrowed down to two or three in the next couple of days.”

4

The Adoption Agency

"We are pleased that you have chosen Miracle Child Adoptions to represent you," Kristin said as she escorted Mike and Laura into a small meeting room in the branch office. "Can I get you a cup of coffee?" she asked politely as they took their seats.

"Just water for me," Mike replied.

"Water sounds great," Laura echoed. "Thank you."

"Sure, I'll be right back," said the sharply dressed professional woman as she slipped back out of the room.

She returned minutes later with two glasses of ice water and one cup of coffee. "I hope you don't mind," she said as she took her seat. "If I don't get my afternoon fix, you'll probably have to revive me before our meeting is over. My little girl was up most of the night with a cold, so don't mind the bags under my eyes."

"A little girl! How old is she?" Laura gushed.

"She's three and a half."

"Is she your only child?"

"No, she has an older brother who is eight and a sister who is five." Kristin removed a picture holder from her wallet and handed it to Laura. The first picture showed Kristin with her husband and three children next to a paddleboat on a pond.

"What a lovely family," Laura commented as she handed the photo to Mike.

"So you've adopted, too!" Mike blurted as he quickly looked back up at Kristin, divining the obvious from the youngest child's appearance.

"Mike!" Laura gasped as she shot him the glance designed to help him remember his manners.

"I'm sorry," Mike said sincerely. "It's just that we're so excited about adoption and it all seems so confusing. I'm just glad to know we'll be working with someone who has experienced adoption from our side of the table as well."

"Oh, that's quite all right," Kristin chuckled as Mike handed her back the photo. "That's one secret that you don't keep when you adopt interracially. And you're right. I have sat on your side of the table. We adopted Lee from Korea a year ago."

"How wonderful," Laura responded as she sat forward in her chair and leaned lightly on the table. "So, what are we in for?"

Kristin laughed. "A little bit of everything, I'm afraid. Excitement, anticipation, frustration, hope, exhaustion, happiness, anger, surprise…you name it, you're in for it. But when you finally sign the last paper and you pick that child up in your arms knowing that no one can take her from you, it will finally all be worth it."

"How long will it take for all that to happen?" Mike asked. It was the engineer in him wanting to get the ball rolling.

"It really depends. I know that's the last thing that you want to hear right now, but there are so many variables."

"This is tougher than having kids conventionally," Mike added. "With the others we just made the decision and waited nine months."

"Easier for *you*, maybe!" Laura exclaimed. "It's obvious which one of us was pregnant for nine months and in labor for twelve hours!"

Kristin laughed again. "You know, Laura brings up a good point. No matter how you have children, there are difficulties and challenges. Some people spend years trying to conceive and go through a fortune on medically assisted fertility. Others have great difficulties with pregnancy and child bearing. With adoption, the difficulties are still there. They are just different in nature. I guess it's best just to realize that there is no easy way to get a child. You know, maybe that's the way it should be. I think that the difficulties help us to appreciate them more."

"Can you give us any idea of how long it might take?" Mike asked once more, this time almost pleading.

"First of all, due to the varying circumstances, I can't say with any degree of certainty, but I can tell you that most adoptions we do here take anywhere between six and eighteen months from the application to the child being placed in the home."

"So where do we go from here?" Mike asked, never being one to delay progress.

"Well, first of all, I'd like to know a little bit more about what you're looking for so we can get going in the right direction. Laura tells me that you're looking for a little girl. So what are the other specifics?"

"We want a one day-old little baby in perfect health, that looks just like us, wrapped up in a pink blanket, with a bow on her head, waiting for us at County General Hospital," Mike said in jest, but halfway hoping that such a thing might be possible.

Kristin chuckled. "Well, you're not alone. In fact, I can put you at the end of a long and distinguished list. I just hope that you don't mind being there for a while. You should know that many people who aren't willing to compromise a request like that stay on those lists for years and never do have that wish come true."

"I was just being facetious," Mike said, though a disappointed tone was distinguishable in his response.

"Most people who consider adoption have heard that there is a disproportionate relationship between newborns awaiting adoption and parents waiting to adopt them," Kristin continued. "But few realize how disproportionate the numbers are. In the United States, approximately 51,000 newborn children are placed for adoption each year. For those children, there are about two million parents waiting to adopt them. If those numbers aren't bleak enough for you, then consider that this is *all* infants placed for adoption. Now Mike, you mentioned adopting a child that looks just like you. I assume then, that you are looking to adopt a Caucasian child. The proportion of Caucasian children, without special needs, to couples who want them, is far more extraordinary. It's something in the neighborhood of 800 couples waiting to adopt each child. I hate to burst your bubble, but you seem like a numbers sort of a guy, so I think that you would understand that the odds in this scenario are against you."

"We have heard that we can get closer to what we're looking for if we adopt out of Russia or Eastern Europe," Laura offered as Mike sat bewildered, crunching the numbers for the actual odds in his head.

"Yes, that is true. You can get *closer*. But most of the countries where children have a more European appearance, including Russia, require that a child be available for adoption by their own citizens for a certain number of months before making them available for international adoption. You would most likely be looking at a child of six months or older. You should also know that an international adoption, though providing more options, also adds more complications. Now, I'm not trying to steer you away from a foreign adoption, but it does become more involved and it is typically more expensive. Just remember, it's my job to help you understand all of your options and the advantages and disadvantages that each of those options pose."

"We understand, and we do appreciate that," Laura said sincerely. "So, just for a starting point, let's say that we have access to sufficient money to adopt from any country, that we want a Caucasian girl, as young as possible, and in good health. What direction would you recommend that we pursue?"

"Definitely Eastern Europe; Russia or other former Soviet States," Kristin replied firmly.

"Which one?" Mike asked.

"The difficulty with many of these areas is that they tend to open and close for no apparent reason. We might be able to get children out of a particular area for a certain amount of time, and then a new government comes in, or laws change, and the area closes indefinitely. So, unless you decide on Russia, we recommend that you apply with several areas simultaneously in case your first choice closes before you adopt."

"So, why is it different with Russia?" Laura asked.

"Russia tends to be a lot more stable program. It's pretty much open all the time."

"So why would we look anywhere else?" Mike and Laura asked simultaneously.

"Russia has its own set of difficulties. First of all, they will be more expensive. Second, they now require two trips by the adoptive parents, one to formalize the process, meet the child, and get the ball rolling, and the other to retrieve the child. Also, the second trip requires a ten-day stay in the country after a positive court decision, and usually before you get the child. Sometimes we can get a judge to waive the ten-day waiting period, but you definitely can't count on it."

Mike's head was swimming with all of this craziness. Efficiency and clarity were high on his importance list and this definitely didn't fall within the comfort zone of his engineering mind. "What is the deal with these guys? These children have no home, no future, and no hope without adoption. Don't they want these kids to be adopted?"

"Honestly, probably not."

"Oh come on, you've got to be kidding. Of course they would want the children to have homes."

"Let me qualify my last statement," Kristin replied, backing up just a bit. "They want the children to be adopted, but not internationally. Any country views their children as treasures. They would like these children to remain in their homelands. This is particularly the case in that most adoptive parents want children in near perfect health, or at least with as few medical conditions as possible."

"Naturally," Mike interjected.

"Well, you can see the problem. The healthy children go out to foreign adoption and the mother country is left with the most difficult cases to handle on its own. So, it appears to them that all of the orphans with potential leave to contribute to another country, and all those who will be a drain on resources stay. The reality is that even the most promising of these orphans, if not adopted in-country, will be turned out on their own at as early as fifteen years of age."

"I can't believe that!" Laura gasped. "Fifteen? Those poor children! They don't have a chance!"

"Sadly, Laura, you're right. Many will turn to crime or prostitution and will eventually end up as drug addicts and suicide cases, or even murder statistics. And the ones who do better are hardly looking at a life of ease and comfort."

"You'd think that understanding those facts would make those countries want to be more cooperative," Mike noted.

"There are other difficulties," Kristin continued. "The economic predicaments in these regions are embarrassing to them. They *want* to be able to be self-reliant and they don't want people from other countries thinking they aren't. Additionally, they still feel some competition with the U.S."

"I guess there's no sense in looking for reason in any of this, much less in trying to fight it," Mike relented. "So how do we do this?"

"Well, we have a packet for you. There is a lot of reading here that should help you to have a little better idea of the things you need to do, things the adoption agency needs to do, time frames, and the like. There is an application that will need to be filled out before we can get started on our end. After that, we'll need to have you sign a contract. Our agency also requires the reading of at least three specified books on adoption. You'll find the list of them in the packet. We also recommend you getting to know the culture and history of the area that you intend to adopt from. There will be lots of reading. I hope you like to read."

"So much for your ritual of reading medieval histories and thrillers in the bath tub!" Laura laughed.

Mike wrinkled his forehead. He didn't like others knowing that it was he rather than his wife who was guilty of two-hour baths. "Yeah, I like reading. That won't be an issue."

"Good. Great. Then this packet will get you started. There is a list of all the documents you'll need for the dossier we'll send out. Most of those will need to be notarized and then taken to have the notary stamp verified by appostille. As you fill out the application, keep in mind that you really need to put what you want. For instance, if you put maximum age of child at six months, a child who is six months and one week will not be sent out for a referral. Also, if you would even consider taking more than one child, you need to put the maximum number in the application. Later on, we cannot increase that number without starting over. But, for instance, if you put two children down, it doesn't mean that you intend to adopt two. It just gives you the flexibility to do that without starting over. I always recommend that families put two children even if they intend to only do one. There are just so many instances when the parents get into the country and wish they had the option to do more. But, that is your decision."

"Okay, well, that sounds good. Do you have any questions for us?" Laura asked.

"Oh, we will. We will ask plenty of questions. In fact, the application will ask a lot of questions. The answers you give will be a good starting point for our next meeting. After we review your application we'll really roll up our sleeves and get to work."

"So, is that all for today?" Mike asked.

"Yes, that's about it, unless you have more questions for me…"

"Not yet." Mike replied.

"Yes, I'm sure that we'll have plenty of questions during our next meeting." Laura added.

"Well then," Kristin said while pushing back her chair and standing up, "I look forward to working with you. This will be fun." She extended her hand first to Laura and then to Mike as they got up to leave. "The next time I see you will be when I come to do your home study. Have a safe drive."

Within days Laura had completed the paper work and returned it to Miracle Child. Two weeks after their initial visit, Kristin visited them for the home study. Laura had gone to great extremes to have the house ready for a white-glove inspection, though it was hardly necessary.

The questions about the home and family were quite personal, and, although things went smoothly, Mike resented the intrusion of privacy. Even Laura felt that some things were getting ridiculous.

"How do you and Laura discipline your children?" Kristin asked.

"For what?" Mike asked.

"Oh, I don't know. For anything."

"Well, did the kid neglect turning in a school assignment, or did he use a hand gun to knock off a 7-11?"

"Let's say it's not as severe as armed robbery."

"Okay, so has the child done it before? Has he been warned? What type of punishment does the child respond best to? Is it the child who is most affected simply by Dad and Mom being disappointed, or is it the one that challenges authority and needs more than that?"

"Okay. I see where you're going with this." Kristen responded.

"Well, those are some things that I'd like to know before I decide on a punishment."

Laura joined in, using monotone and spacing her words evenly. "We-have-a-time-out-chair. Every-time-a-child-needs-to-be-punished-they-sit-in-the-time-out-chair-for-fifteen-minutes. Is that what you want to hear?" she mocked.

Kristin sighed. "I think what we're looking for here, particularly in dealing with Russia, is that you don't use corporal punishment. Russia is very much against it, particularly with several high profile cases of late where children adopted from Russia have been abused. Several were even beaten to death."

"You're kidding!" Mike exclaimed exasperatedly.

"I only wish I was. You can see now why these home studies are so involved and so important."

"I'm sorry. We had no idea," Laura responded meekly.

"So, do you use corporal punishment?" Kristin asked.

"No," Laura responded. "We take away privileges most of the time for older kids. When the children were younger, we used time-outs or had them stand for a little while with their face in the corner."

"That sounds great," Kristen replied.

The home study lasted about two hours and involved Kristen questioning each family member individually. Finally she finished up with the family all together.

"I think that's about all I need," She said as she put her notebook back in the brief case. "If I have missed anything, I'll just give you a call on the phone for any more questions. Barring that, you should receive a written copy of the home study from me within a couple of weeks.

5

Under Katya's Care

"Zaichunook, I need to speak with you," Sofia said while touching the child on the head.

Katya smiled and looked up. "What?"

"Mrs. Petrova is talking with the authorities right now. Two new little girls are coming to live here today."

Nastya had been transferred to a new orphanage, and Mrs. Petrova, Polina, was now the director. She was much more happy and friendly than Nastya was, and the atmosphere at the orphanage had changed accordingly.

"What are their names?"

"Their names are Anya and Marishka. Both of them are just a year or so older than you. They have both been taken away from their homes, and they will be very sad and scared. Anya and Marishka will need a special friend to help them. You have grown up so much since you first came here. I think that you are big enough to help them. Would you please be a special friend to them? Help them to know what to do here at the orphanage and try to help them be happy?"

"Yes. When are they coming?"

"They will arrive this afternoon. After they get cleaned up and checked in and get their bed assignments, I will bring them to meet you. Please be very nice to them so that they will know that you want to be their friend."

"Okay!" the child responded happily. "I like to have friends. Marishka and Anya will be my best friends!"

"Wonderful. I'm sure that they will. Thank you, Katya."

"Anya, Marishka…this is Katya. Katya, these are my friends that I told you about, Anya and Marishka. Katya has lived here with us for a while and she understands how things work here. She said that she will help you. Why don't you three go out and play with the others until dinner time?"

"Okay! Come on!" Katya said grabbing Anya's hand with her right one and Marishka's with her left. "We should go out and play on the swings. We can take turns pushing each other really high."

Katya hurried toward the door dragging her two new friends along. Marishka quickly caught on and kept up, but Anya looked back bewilderedly at Sofia with one good eye and a lazy one turned inward. Within minutes the three girls were walking across the yard to the playground. Other children were strewn about the yard, the older teenaged orphans mostly stood in groups talking, while the younger ones chased each other around, playing various types of tag games. The dirt-covered yard was dusty and had only an occasional clump of grass or short weeds. The playground was located at the center of the yard and was made up of old but brightly painted makeshift equipment. There were worn car tires fastened together and stacked, with other ones on edge and partially buried. They protruded from the ground, in line, to make a small tunnel. There was a slippery slide, a swing set, a teeter-totter and several simple sets of monkey bars. Most of the equipment was whatever could be welded together from scrap pieces of pipe.

"Do you have a mama?" Marishka asked Katya as they walked across the yard.

"Yes. But I don't see her anymore. Sofia said that Sasha is trying to find a new mama and papa for me. Do you know Sasha?"

"No."

"She brings people here from Amérika who want to be mamas and papas. Sometimes they take children home with them to Amérika. My friend Tanechka got a new mama and papa from Amérika and she moved to a place in Amérika with a funny name."

"Did she have to go away?"

"She wanted to. Her new mama and papa were really nice. They brought her presents and told her that she could be an ice skater if she wanted to."

"When will Sasha bring a new mama and papa for you?"

"I don't know. Sofia told me that it might take a long time. I will ask Sasha to find a mama and papa for you the next time I see her. I will ask her to find a mama and papa for Anya, too." Anya, who still hadn't said a word, smiled brightly.

"I already have a mama," Marishka replied. "But maybe Sasha could find a papa for me."

"Did your mama bring you here?"

"No. Elizaveta, the social worker, came to my house and brought me here. Do you know Elizaveta?"

"Yes. Sometimes she comes here with Sasha and the new mamas and papas."

"My mama was really mad at Elizaveta. She said that she couldn't take me away. But Elizaveta had papers from the judge, and she told Mama that she had to talk to the judge if she wanted me to come back home. Mama screamed a lot at Elizaveta and she also cried. I was really afraid, and I cried, too. I told Elizaveta that I didn't want to go, but she made me go anyway. But Mama will talk to the judge so I can go back home."

"Do you have a mama and papa, Anya?" Katya asked.

"I have a mama," Anya mumbled almost inaudibly.

"Did your mama bring you here?"

"No." It was all the child mumbled before turning quickly and bolting for the slippery slide.

The three girls spent the next hour playing with each other on the playground. Serious talk, at least for that day, was over.

6

Wrangling with the Sheriff's Office

"Mike, I don't know what to do," Laura said through sobs of frustration over the phone. She tried not to call him too often at work, but she really didn't know what to do next.

"What's wrong?"

"You know how we got our criminal background checks for the dossier the other day?"

"Yeah, what about them?"

"I took them to the state office in Lansing today to have them appostilled. The appostille officer said that the date for the commission of the notary at the police office was wrong."

"Look, Honey, I know that you've been back and forth having documents notarized and appostilled three times already, but the adoption agency warned us that might happen. We don't have much choice but to go back to the County Sheriff's Office and have the notary redo her thing and then go back to Lansing again."

"I know. That's not the problem. I already went back to the County Sheriff's Office and talked to the notary. She got mad at me and told me that there was nothing wrong. She said that no one had ever complained before and that what she had done was all I was going to get. So I went home and called the Appostille Office and they told me that the date on the commission for the notary was absolutely wrong and that they would absolutely not appostille wrong information. They told me that's what an appostille is all about. Its only purpose is to verify the notary, and the information for the notary at the County Sheriff's Office is not correct. They said that she has to correct it before they can do anything. It's not like we can go to another notary—the personal background checks have to come from the County Sheriff's Office."

"So, what did the notary say when you called her back?"

"She is refusing to take my calls."

"You've got to be kidding. I'll call the County Sheriff's Office and I'll call you back in a few minutes."

"Thank you, Sweetheart," Laura said, her voice still skipping from crying. "I'm sorry I had to bother you at work. I just didn't know…" She began crying again.

"It's alright, Honey. It's no big deal. I'm glad that you called me. I'm sure that it is something that can be worked out pretty quickly. Let me give them a call and I'll get right back to you."

"Okay. Thank you. Good luck."

Mike smirked as he hung up the phone. He didn't need luck. He knew how to deal with obstinate loudmouths. You don't even need to deal with the intransigent worker; you simply intimidate their superiors. Everything goes smoothly from there.

"Hello. I need to speak with Sheriff Oldham," Mike said after dialing the number.

"I'm sorry. Sheriff Oldham is very busy. Is there someone else who can help you?"

"No. And Sheriff Oldham isn't half as busy as he's going to be if he doesn't take my call."

"Just a minute, sir," the assistant replied rudely as she put him on hold.

"This is Sheriff Oldham. How can I help you?"

"I'm sorry that I had to bother you, Sheriff. If your staff were doing their jobs, this would have been something easily resolved without involving you and taking you away from more important issues." Mike paused waiting for a response but none came. "My wife was in there this morning and picked up background checks for our family for an adoption that we are working on. This is for a Russian adoption, so they needed to be notarized and appostilled. When my wife took the reports to Lansing to have them appostilled, the office there told her that your notary's commission date was incorrect and that it needed to be re-done. My wife talked to your notary who denied that anything was wrong, and then refused to redo the letter." Again Mike paused for a response but even after ten seconds, none came. "I'm just wondering what I need to do to get your notary to conform to state law."

"Just a min-" Mike heard the phone click on hold before the sheriff even finished the word 'minute.' Five minutes later the sheriff picked up the line again.

"You still there?"

"Of course," Mike replied trying to echo the rudeness tit for tat.

"I talked to the notary and she told me your wife said that her information was wrong and needed to be corrected. She said that there has never been a problem before, and that she was sure that everything was fine. She also said that when she tried to explain that, your wife became rude, so she decided to wait until your wife calmed down. My people don't have to put up with folks who are rude and unreasonable. I would suggest that your wife calms down and listens when someone tries to talk to her."

"I'm sorry. Did I hear you say that my wife was rude?" There was no response. "My wife doesn't know how to be rude. That's my department. And listen, it's not my wife complaining that something is wrong. It is the government of the State of Michigan. They say that the stamp your notary is using has the wrong dates of commission on it, which makes it invalid. Now that's not my wife's fault, nor is it mine. But it is something that your office needs to correct."

"Well, if that's the case, then I guess we'll start looking into it. If what you have isn't good enough, then give us a call back in a couple of months and we'll let you know what we found out."

"That isn't going to be acceptable. It sounds like I might need an attorney."

"Don't threaten me. It won't work."

"Sure it will. I think I'll call every attorney in the county. I only need one, but I'll call them all. What do you think? I'm betting when they hear my case, each one will realize that everything that your notary signed in cases opposing the County Sheriff was illegitimate. I wonder if those attorneys, knowing that they can go back and reopen cases on technicalities, might cause you a little more work than simply correcting a letter that your staff should have done right the first time." Mike waited again for a response. It was a long time coming, but he wasn't giving in this time. The sheriff would eventually speak. He was backed into a corner.

Finally, after a full two minutes of silence, the sheriff barked back. "So, what exactly do you want?"

"My wife will stop by your office at ten tomorrow morning to pick up the corrected letter. Your notary knows what needs to be done. As long as it is there and correct by ten, then we don't have a problem, and I'll know that I won't need an attorney."

Mike heard the phone slam down on the other end. He hung up the phone, picked it up again and called Laura.

"What did the Sheriff's Office say?" Laura asked anxiously.

"Not much. They should have everything waiting for you at ten tomorrow morning."

"Is that what they said?"

"No, not exactly. But if you stop by tomorrow morning, I don't think that you'll have any trouble."

"Were you rude to them? Because, for once, if you were, I think they had it coming."

"Oh, let's just say that Sheriff Oldham and I had a mutually stimulating conversation. Stop by the office tomorrow at ten and I think that you'll get what we need."

"Alright. Thanks, Sweetheart. I'll see you tonight."

"What did you say to the Sheriff's Office?" Laura asked as soon as Mike picked up the phone.

"Why? Did they give you any trouble?"

"No, none whatsoever! I went there at ten and the receptionist handed me the packet before I even asked for it. She was really nice but she told me that the notary was busy and just asked her to give me this. I saw the notary sitting back at her desk doing nothing, but obviously she didn't want to talk to me."

"Is everything right?"

"Yes. I'm just leaving Lansing right now. I thought I'd call to congratulate you. We finally have everything we need to complete our dossier. I'm stopping at the FedEx office on the way home to send this to Miracle Child. Kristin said as soon as she gets this, she'll send our dossier to Russia!"

"Great! I guess that now we just wait, huh?"

"I guess so. Kristin is saying that with what they have been seeing lately, it will be somewhere between three and four months before we get a referral on a baby girl."

"Well, that's a little better than we thought, isn't it?"

"Yeah. Earlier it was looking like six to eight months."

"Well, that sounds great. Congratulations. It looks like I have a call holding, though. I'd better take it, so I'll see you later."

"See you soon. I love you."

"I love you, too."

7

The Referral

"How much longer is it going to be before Russia sends information on our sister?" Stephen asked Laura as the family cleared the dinner table.

"I've been on the phone with Miracle Child once a week since they sent out our dossier. They must be tired of me calling them all the time. But I called them again today, and they told me that we're second on the waiting list for a six to twelve month old girl."

"What does that mean in real world numbers?" Mike asked.

"I asked Kristin, and you know how it is. They never commit to time frames, but she guesses that it will be another sixty days or so."

"So, that will put us about the first of the year. How nice, Honey! We'll be able to go to Russia in the winter! That must be the absolute opposite of hell in the summer!" Mike quipped.

"Our sister won't be home for Christmas, then?" Jeff asked.

"Not much chance of that, buddy," Mike responded. "If we get a referral at the first of the year, it will probably be summertime before we actually get her home."

"Mike! We're getting a referral today!" Laura blurted into the phone. It had only been two days since she had told him and the boys that they were second in line.

"How could that be? I thought it was going to be a couple of months!"

"I don't know. But Kristin just called. She's emailing some pictures and a medical and social report. We should have them within an hour! You aren't working late tonight, are you?"

"No, of course not. In fact, I'll send out a couple of pressing emails and I'll be right home. You'll see me within an hour."

Mike rushed through the several emails and then let his assistant know that he would be out for the rest of the day. He drove home quickly and burst through the door.

"Where is everyone?" he hollered after entering the house.

"We're in here on the computer." Laura yelled back. "Come here!"

Mike hurried in and found Laura sitting in the chair with Jeff and Stephen peering over her shoulder at the screen. "So, what do we have?"

"Oh, Mike! She is simply beautiful!"

Mike rushed to the computer and squeezed in between Jeff and Stephen to see. Laura scrolled through the three pictures that had been sent of the seven-month old infant. "Isn't she adorable?" Laura commented.

"She is. She is just beautiful. What's her name?"

"Valentina."

"What a beautiful name. What do we know about her?"

"I don't know. They sent the medical and social file, but I haven't opened them yet."

"Well, let's get on it," Mike urged. Laura had already accepted the child in her own mind, but Mike wanted to see the medical file before getting too attached. He wanted to make sure that everything was within the acceptable limits they set. Mike knew that if, in one day, they had moved past the first family in line, chances were that someone had rejected the referral of this child.

A few clicks of the mouse later, Laura had Valentina's medical report open.

"Medical Report on a Minor Child" was written in bold letters across the top of the page. The child's name followed; Bukreeva, Valentina Selezneva, born, 01-06-2004.

Laura began to read the report out loud. "Biological anamnesis: The child comes from a family leading a socially unacceptable lifestyle. The girl was born of 3rd pregnancy, during which the mother was not under medical supervision, smoked, used alcohol. Third delivery at term, at home. Weight at birth: 2940 g., height at birth: 50 cm., head in circumference: 32 cm., chest in circumference: 33 cm. The girl was transferred from Khankaisk Central Regional Hospital into Baby Home of Vladivostok on 07-27-04 with the diagnosis: perinatal encephalopathy of mixed genesis, motor disorder syndrome."

"What does that mean?" Mike queried.

"I have no idea. But let's go through the rest of the report."

"HIV, Syphilis, HBS Ag, all show negative. The child was examined by the following specialists: Oculist, Otolaryngologist, Surgeon…prognosis: Healthy. Neuropathologist, prognosis: perinatal encephalopathy of mixed genesis, motor disorder syndrome. Whatever *that* means. Past illnesses: acute respiratory infection. Prophylactic inoculations: age appropriate. At present, the child's health condition is satisfactory. Weight at present: 5300 g., height at present: 55 cm., chest in circumference: 37.5 cm., head in circumference: 37 cm. Skin and visible mucous are clear. Normal constitution. Under-skin tissue is sufficiently developed. Clear pulmonary respiration, no rales. Heart sounds are clear and rhythmical. Soft, painless belly. Stool and diuresis are normal. The girl is active. She smiles when someone speaks to her. She supports her head well, babbles, rolls herself over from back to belly. She takes toys from various positions, examines them, hands them to her mouth. Diagnosis: Perinatal encephalopathy of mixed genesis, motor disorder syndrome. The child was examined by the Board of Medical Examiners of Vladivostok city on 09-10-04."

"So, what does all that medical jargon mean?" Mike asked again.

"I don't know. I'll call Kristin right now."

Laura picked up the phone and dialed Kristin's number while the others stood by. She was only on the phone for a couple of minutes before politely closing the conversation and hanging up the phone.

"Kristin says that they recommend that we send the pictures and medical report to a doctor who is accustomed to dealing with adoptions from Russia for an evaluation. But, she says that the undesirable conditions described are those they see misused a lot. You know, what we talked about before. She says that there's no way to know for sure, but with the conditions described in the medical report, and then viewing the pictures of the child and seeing that she's progressing at a pretty normal rate for a child in an orphanage, she thinks it's just smoke and mirrors."

"I can't believe all of this. It drives me crazy," Mike steamed. "Does our family doctor have any experience with Russian adoptions?"

"Actually, yes. I talked with him a while back. He has been involved with several kids adopted from Russia."

"Why don't you give him a call and see what he thinks. Why don't you boys get on your home work. We'll have a family meeting tonight and decide what we're going to do."

"The doctor had good news," Laura said as she took her place at the kitchen table for the family meeting.

"He finally called you back?" Mike asked.

"Yes. His receptionist tracked him down on the cell phone and had him call us. I just got off the phone with him."

"What did he say?" Jeff and Stephen blurted. Both had been going crazy, still not knowing how to react after Mike had been so guarded on seeing the medical report.

"He thinks the same thing that Kristin does. He told me that the descriptions in the medical report are stereotypical of the ones used by Russian doctors when little or nothing is wrong. He told me that we know what healthy kids look like, and that he thinks that we should move forward with the trip to meet Valentina. If there really is a lot wrong, he said it would be evident and we could back out then. I called Kristin and she confirmed that we can move forward and back out later if something is really wrong."

"Oh, boy," Mike said, not knowing what else to say. He knew that once Laura got that baby in her arms there was going to be no backing out.

"What do you mean, 'Oh boy?'" Laura asked accusingly.

"I'm sorry. I don't mean anything by it. It just seems surreal. I can't believe that after all this time and effort it's really moving forward."

"So are we going to adopt Valentina?" Stephen asked.

"I don't see any reason at this point to say no," Mike replied, "but I'm not the only one in the family. What do you think, Stephen?"

"I think we should do it."

"How about you, Jeff?"

"I think we should move forward, at least" he said mirroring his father's cautiousness.

"Alright then," Laura started merrily, "I'll call Kristin and tell her that we'd like to get things moving. She said that it will probably take several weeks to get an invitation to travel from the Department of Education in Vladivostok, but there's plenty to do before then. Well, Mike, shall we take the pictures over and surprise your mom?"

Again, Mike felt like they might be getting a little too attached, a little too early in the game, but he just couldn't burst Laura's bubble.

"Alright. Everyone grab your coats. Let's go to Grandma's house."

"Oh, she is adorable!" Grandma cooed as she thumbed through the pictures. "It will be so nice to have another little girl in the family! When do you get to bring her home?"

"We don't know yet," Mike replied. "There are still a lot of things that have to happen. The Minister of Education in Vladivostok still has to issue a formal invitation to travel. Then we have to go over there and meet her for a week or so. Then we come back for a couple of months and wait for them to invite us back to finalize the adoption. We could end up in Russia for a month on the second trip if they don't waive the ten-day appeal. Our best guess is somewhere between three and four months before we get her home."

"So we might have her home for Christmas!"

"Oh, we sure hope so, Mom!" Laura chimed in.

"Yes, we all hope so. But nothing has gone the way that we thought it would in this adoption. Let's not get our hopes too high." Mike cautioned.

"Oh, don't be such a spoilsport, Mike," Grandma scolded him. "We can hope that she's home for Christmas if we want to, can't we Laura?"

"Yes, we can."

Mike's mother was always careful to make sure that Laura felt like she was her mother, too. Laura didn't have any contact with her biological parents, and after a year of her foster parents trying to break up her marriage, she had not had any more contact with them, either. Mike's mom was the only mom she considered hers anymore, and Grandma was more than happy to have it that way. She made sure that Laura knew that she was there for her, as well as for Mike. At times, she even went out of her way to side with Laura. Mike was strong enough to carry on whether or not she sided with him in any given circumstance, but Laura really needed a mom. It worked. Laura finally had a mother she could trust.

"I need to get busy making a baby blanket for her. I make one for all of the grandkids. Could you take it over to her on your first trip?"

"We can take it and give it to her, Mom, but it's doubtful that we'd ever get it back when we brought her home. They are limited on resources, and we've heard it's all but impossible to get anything back. They usually say it's lost. Why don't you just give it to her when we bring her home?"

"Nonsense! I want her to have it now. I'll just make two of them the same. Then you can take one with you on this trip, and the other one to give to her on the second trip when you go to pick her up. I'd better get busy, though!"

"Mom, really," Mike started, "you don't need to do this. I think you'd better save your strength."

"Oh, for Pete's sake, Mike! How much strength does it take to make a couple of baby blankets? How soon before you leave?"

"We don't know," Mike relented. "Probably two to three weeks."

"Okay, I can do that. I'll get busy. Do you want the boys to come and stay with me while you're gone?"

Laura looked at Mike, concerned.

"No, Mom. You just take care of yourself. Mark and Dawn are going to stay with the boys at our house."

"Oh, Mike. I could handle it, you know. 'Remission' means getting better, not worse."

"I know, Mom. But you know that right now, we want to you to focus one hundred percent on yourself." Mike smiled. "And those baby blankets, too, of course."

Grandma smiled back, understanding. "Then I'd better get started!"

"So, guys, are we going to leave Valentina's name the same, or are we going to choose an American name?" Laura asked as they drove home.

"I think Valentina is a pretty name," Stephen ventured.

"It is, but it's not very common," Jeff added. "I wonder if she'd feel out of place, or different as she got older."

"What do you think, Honey?" Mike asked.

"I agree with both Jeff and Stephen. My initial thought is to keep Valentina for a middle name and then choose a new first name."

"What did you have in mind?" Mike asked.

"I want to know what you think first," Laura replied.

"I think you're right. Sarah for a first name and Valentina for a middle name."

"What?" the two boys and Laura blurted out together.

"I'm sorry, I meant…what I mean is, I think that choosing an American first name to go with Valentina is a good choice."

"But you said *Sarah*," Laura replied.

"I did?"

"You did. Is that what you want to name her?"

"No. I mean…not necessarily. I want you to choose her name. I mean, I think that you should."

"I think that we should choose it together. What made you think of Sarah?"

"I'm sorry. I didn't mean to do that. Please, choose some names and then we'll go through them together and decide."

"You've obviously been thinking about this, Mike. Tell us why you thought of that name."

"Well, I've dreamed for years about us having a little girl. I wanted our little princess for a long time. Sarah means princess in Hebrew. Somehow that name always stuck in my mind for our little girl. But that doesn't mean that's the way to go. Please, decide on a few names and we'll go from there."

"What do you boys think?" Laura asked. "Do you like Sarah Valentina?"

Both boys spoke over each other with affirmative answers.

"I like it, too," Laura added. "Sarah Valentina. It has a ring to it."

"Okay, let's consider it, then," Mike conceded. "But I don't want it to be that just because it was my idea. I want it to be something that you like, too."

"Then Sarah Valentina it is." Laura and the boys cheered.

The next two weeks dragged on, waiting for news from Miracle Child on when they would travel. The family spent the time moving items from the storage room to the attic and giving it a fresh coat of paint and new carpet. Laura and Mike spent the two Saturdays shopping for clothes, cribs, toys, and everything else they could think of, but the anticipation was driving them all crazy. At the end of the two weeks, Laura couldn't take it any longer. She finally called to see what the status was.

"Hi, Kristin. It's Laura."

"Hello, Laura. How are you doing?"

"We're pretty anxious here. We just thought we would have received travel plans by now. Is anything wrong?"

"Not that I know of. Sometimes it takes a little longer than two weeks. The Russians kind of do things at their own speed. I'll check on it and get back to you in a couple of days."

"Thank you."

"How is everything going there? Are you all ready?"

"Oh, we kind of went overboard. We already went and bought all the clothes and toys and bedding and stuff. We're just so anxious. At least while we were getting stuff, we felt like we were moving forward. Now we just kind of feel stalled again."

"It'll be okay. That's how adoption is. Hurry up and wait. I'll check on things, though, and call you back in a couple of days."

Predestined Heartbreak

"Mike! They won't let us go to Russia to see Valentina!" Laura sobbed over the phone. She was all but hysterical.

"Calm down, Honey. What's wrong?"

"Kristin called. Russia changed the law! We can't have Valentina now! Oh Mike, I can't take it!" she sobbed.

Mike felt his own stomach tighten. "What law changed? Why won't they let us take Valentina?"

"Up until now, the law in Primorski said that only Russian parents could adopt a child during the first four months after being made available for adoption, you know, before foreign parents would be considered. But they just changed it to six months. Valentina's only been available for a little over four months. They took her off the foreign adoption register! Oh Mike, someone could take our baby!"

Mike shuddered. "I'm sorry, Laura. I don't know what to say. What did Kristin tell you?"

"She said all we can do is wait. She feels bad for us, but she says there's nothing that we or the agency can do except wait and hope for the best."

"Does she think that Valentina will be adopted by Russians over the next month and a half?"

"She doesn't know. She said that Valentina made it through the first four months, so that's a good sign that she could make it the full six, but really, nobody knows."

"I'm sorry, Sweetheart. I really am. But I don't know what we can do besides sit back and wait. If there was anything that I could do, I would. But Kristin has warned us on several occasions that that if I ever tried to push the Russians, it would only make it worse."

"I know, Mike. I don't want you to do anything. I just needed to talk to you."

"Okay. Have you told the boys?"

"No. They're not home from school yet."

"Why don't you wait until I get home, then. We'll have a family meeting."

"Okay. Thank you. I'll see you in a couple of hours."

The boys didn't take the news any better than their parents had. Jeff became angry at the unfairness of the change in law, and Stephen was devastated. Mike had been afraid of counting their chickens before they hatched; so even though he was as devastated as the rest were, he silently felt like he had it coming. He knew better. He should not have let them become so attached. He should have forced them to be realistic about the possibilities. This whole situation was his fault for letting them ignore the possibilities, and for beginning to ignore them himself. He tried to be strong for them, though he was heartbroken, too.

Four weeks later, Kristin called Mike at work. "I'm sorry to bother you at work, Mike. Is now a good time to talk?"

"Yeah. Sure. As good as any."

"I know that Laura has kind of spearheaded this adoption and I usually talk with her. But this time I thought that I should talk to you first. I'm afraid that I have bad news. Valentina has been adopted by a Russian couple."

"I'm not surprised," Mike said, his voice quivering. "Well, the Russians must be happy. One more adoption for the home team and one less to leave the country."

"I'm sorry, Mike. We were praying for you. This one just didn't work out. I can imagine how hard it must be."

"Thanks. But we knew it was a possibility."

"Do you want me to call Laura and tell her?"

"No. She'll take it better from me."

"Are you sure? I know how hard it must be for you. I'll tell her if you want me to."

"No. Thanks. It's my responsibility. I'll take care of it."

"Okay." Kristin paused. "Listen, I'm not going to say anything to Laura yet. We'll allow her some grieving time, but our coordinators in Vladivostok are moving quickly to find another solution. We'll let you know as soon as we hear anything."

"Yeah. Thanks for letting us know. We'll be in touch."

Mike debated on calling Laura, but decided against it. He'd need to be right there for her. He spent the rest of the day holed up in his office, trying to get up the nerve to tell his wife the news that would crush her.

The drive home was longer than ever. It seemed gloomy out, even though it was a beautiful evening. His heart began to race and his hands started to sweat as he pulled into the driveway and parked the car in the garage. He sat in the car for several minutes, trying to get his emotions under control before going into the house.

"Family meeting," he said as he walked into the house. Jeff and Stephen were seated at the table doing homework and Laura was finishing up dinner. "Let's go sit down in the living room where it's comfortable," he added, and then he left the room.

The others followed him. Laura took her place next to him on the love seat and Jeff and Stephen plopped down on the couch.

"Kristin called me at work this afternoon. Valentina has been adopted by a Russian couple."

"NO!" Laura shrieked. "My baby!" She broke into hysterical sobs.

Stephen started to cry, too. Jeff just folded his arms tightly across his chest.

Mike put his arm around Laura to comfort her. "No!" she shrieked pushing his arm away. "My baby!" she sobbed. "Why, Dear Lord, Why? My baby!"

Mike sat silently and let Laura cry. Finally, after several minutes of crying, she wrapped her arms around him and sobbed into his shoulder. "Why, Mike? I had been praying for God to help us so that this wouldn't happen. Why didn't He answer my prayers?"

At once, Mike finally understood. "Obviously, the Russians don't think that it matters which child we get to bring home. But, do you think it matters to God?"

"What do you mean?" she asked between sobs.

"Do you think that God has in mind a particular child for us? Or do you think that He doesn't care?"

"I know He cares about us!"

"Of course, but do you think that there is one particular child that God has planned to place in our home?"

Laura paused before speaking. "Yes, I do. The Bible says that He notices even when a bird falls from the sky. So I think He knows which child He wants to send to us."

"Laura, you said that you've been praying so that something like this wouldn't happen. But what if we had decided to adopt a child that God didn't intend for us? How could He answer your prayer and still send us the right child? Wouldn't we expect God to intervene if we were going in the wrong direction?"

"I guess so," Laura said, looking up at Mike.

"What do you guys think?" he asked Jeff and Stephen. "Do you think that maybe our Heavenly Father knew that it was better for us to go a different direction?"

"Yes," Stephen replied immediately. But Jeff remained silent. Mike knew better than to press the issue with him. With Jeff, it would take some time.

"You're right, Mike," Laura said, looking at him through swollen, bloodshot eyes. "I can feel it. There is another child who is *supposed* to be here. God answered my prayer the only way He could."

"I know that this might be difficult to understand right now," Mike began, "But when we finally get that child home, we will be thankful to a loving Heavenly Father who intervened and brought the right child to us."

Even with new understanding, no one ate much at dinner that night.

The next night, as Mike walked into the house, he noticed that the picture of Valentina had been removed from the mantle. It was a bad idea to put it up when Laura did, right after it came, but he hadn't said anything.

"Hi, Sweetheart. How was your day?" Laura asked as she walked up and gave him a big hug and a kiss on the cheek.

"Not too bad. I've had worse."

"Mike, I want to apologize for how I acted last night. It was hard for you, too. I shouldn't have acted that way. I called Kristin today and she said that she offered to tell me, but that you wanted to do it so you could be there for me. Thank you."

"You're welcome. Sorry I couldn't have been the bearer of good news rather than bad."

"I guess it's all in the perspective. I've thought a lot about what you said last night. I'm sure that there is a special little girl who is supposed to be here. Looking at it from that perspective means that you *were* the bearer of good news. The right little girl is on her way. We just don't know who she is yet."

"So what else did Kristin have to say?"

"She said they feel as bad about the situation as we do, and they are really sorry. She also said the Russian coordinators are working on finding a little girl for us, but it's going to be difficult right now."

"Why?"

"Well, with this new law, it backs up availability by two months. Also, with babies being available longer to Russians, more of them will be adopted by Russians. So everyone who was waiting to adopt a baby is bottlenecked."

"Wait. We heard that we were number two on the list and then the next day we were given a referral. That must mean that we're at the top of the list."

"Yes, at the top of the list for Miracle Child, but there are dozens of other agencies involved."

"So how long does Kristin think it will take?"

"She has no idea. They've never had a situation like this before."

"So now what?"

"Kristin said that we are more than welcome to wait it out. But, if we were to raise the age of the child that we are willing to accept, she's sure it would move a lot faster."

Mike considered this, then looked at his wife. "How do *you* feel about that, Laura?"

"I feel good about it. Since I calmed down, I'm trying to listen to what God wants for us rather than what we want for ourselves. I think I feel really good about it, but I wanted to know what you think, too."

"I don't know. I hadn't really considered an older child before. But I can't say that I feel bad about it. What did you tell Kristin?"

"I just told her we'd talk about it and that I'd call her back within a couple of days."

"Have you talked with the boys?"

"Of course not. I wanted to talk to you first. But if you're okay with it, I think we should talk to them."

"Sure. Let's talk to them and start moving a different direction. It seems like the right thing to do."

Mike and Laura spoke with the boys later on that evening. Stephen was all for the change if it would move the process along. Jeff was defiant. "What is the point if they can take them away any time they want?" he had asked pointedly. "Do whatever you want. Don't ask me."

9

A Change of Plans

The Knights changed their age requirement to "five years old," but it was still an agonizing three months before they got the next referral. The old storage room had evolved into a beautiful bedroom for a little girl, complete with swarms of butterflies coming out from behind the headboard of the bed and winding up across the ceiling.

Knowing that the right little girl would eventually come to them, they made preliminary travel plans. They wanted to travel with their new daughter to Moscow, and they decided to stay at the Marriott Royal, only half a mile from Red Square. The Royal looked like a Russian palace, and Mike wanted his little princess to have a chance to play the part.

He even arranged for a friend to travel with them. Jim Christensen was the father of Mike's friend Brian, and the father-in-law of Jennifer, his travel agent. Jim, retired from the travel industry, knew Russia like the back of his hand, and had graciously offered his travel experience to help bring Sarah home. But it wasn't just Jim's experience that Mike wanted. Jeff and Stephen had pretty much adopted Jim and his wife, Patty, as grandparents, and Mike wanted Sarah to experience not only parents on her trip home, but also a grandfather.

It was the Monday after Thanksgiving when Mike answered the page and picked up his phone. "You ought to check your emails once in a while," Laura chided.

"What makes you think that I haven't checked my email?" he quipped back.

"If you had checked it in the last four hours, you would have called me back by now. But I guess you're too busy," she joked. "Call me when you're not too busy!" Then she hung up the phone.

Mike laughed to himself as he opened up his email and started to download the files. He loved to get information that Laura wanted, and then call her up saying; "I know something you don't know!" then hang up the phone. It drove her crazy. No matter how hard she tried, she could never hold out and wait until he finally told her on his own. Curiosity always forced her to call him back and beg for the information. Now she was paying him back. Usually, it didn't work. Mike could hold out until she wanted to tell him more than he wanted to know. But today, Laura had sounded way too sure of herself. This had to be about the adoption.

Sure enough, there was an email forwarded to him from Miracle Child earlier in the day. Though his analytical mind told him to open the medical file first, he couldn't do it. He opened the pictures. A beautiful little girl with hazel eyes and short, dishwater blonde hair filled the screen. In the first picture, she had the softest complexion and smile he had ever seen. Her hands were clasped in front of her stomach nervously while she posed in a beautiful jumper and turtleneck sweater that he guessed were only used by the orphanage for taking pictures. The second photo showed her sitting on a bench in a quaint traditional Russian dress, her hands beside her. She had huge dimples and a smile from ear to ear. Mike was in love.

But the next picture horrified him. The child's dress was held up for a picture of only her chest. A huge triangular burn scar started at the bottom of her sternum. It moved upward, along the line of a V-neck sweater, ending at her collar bone on the right, but extending upward onto her shoulder on the left. Whatever had caused that burn had been excruciatingly painful. Mike shuddered.

He opened up the medical report. "Bekher, Ekaterina Victorovna" was the name listed at the top of the report. He skimmed through it, and while the scar was mentioned, there was no more information about it. The child had been exposed to tuberculosis, but it was under control and there didn't appear to be any permanent effects. There was the usual notation about delay in motor skill development, fully expected now and easily dismissed. This could be the one!

Mike immediately called Laura. The answering machine picked up after the fourth ring. "Come on, Baby! I know you're there! I need to talk to you!"

"Oh, I thought that you were too busy!" she chided as she picked up the phone.

"Okay. You got me."

"Admit that I'm superior in these mind games," she joked, knowing that it couldn't be further from the truth.

"Alright, you win, Your Majesty!"

Laura laughed. "Isn't she beautiful, Mike?"

"She is. I'm in love."

"So, I can tell the boys?"

"Sure. Go ahead and tell them. You might as well call Kristin, too. Let's get the ball rolling."

"I'll call her as soon as I talk to the boys. They just got home from school. I'll see you in a couple of hours. I love you."

"I love you too, Sweetheart. Congratulations."

Adopting a five-year-old would require different preparations, but of course, the reading Laura and Mike had been obligated to complete for Miracle Child had made them very aware of that. Laura had spent countless hours on the internet reading everything posted by families with experience adopting older children. She wanted to make sure the waiting time between the first visit and the trip home was a bonding time, rather than a time of distance which could cause a child to be more cynical or anxious. While it wouldn't be easy, there were things that could be done to help the situation.

"We need to make two soft books," Laura announced as she plopped a stack of papers into Mike's lap the night after accepting Katya's referral. Mike muted the TV and picked up the papers.

"What do you mean, soft books?"

"You know, the ones people sometimes bring to church for their kids. They're made from cloth and have buttons to do up, or felt shoes to tie, anything quiet for the child to do."

"So, an activity book?"

"Well, most soft books are activity books, but I have something else in mind for Sarah."

"Like what?"

"You know how you can get iron-on T-shirt kits for inkjet printers?"

"Sure."

"If we made picture books with fabric, she wouldn't tear them and they would last the whole time between the first visit and when we go back."

"Sounds great. What do you have in mind for the books?" Mike asked as he looked down at the papers, which he now recognized as Laura's first drafts.

"We need to do one on our family and our home." Laura pointed to the first page of the first book. "We will put a pretty cover on it, but the first page will have a picture of the family and say; 'This is my family. We are a forever family.'" She turned the page to the next one that said; "My Daddy." On the page were several pictures of Mike. "'This is my daddy,'" she read. "'My daddy likes to ride horses. My daddy likes to go fishing. My daddy likes to read. My daddy likes to work. My daddy loves me.'"

"By having someone read her this book, or even just by looking at the pictures, she can get to know you and kind of get used to how you are. I've done pictures of each of the family members so that Sarah isn't just fantasizing, but really bonding," Laura explained while thumbing through the other pages. "I also included a page for Sarah. I want her to feel like she is a part of the family."

"Hang on…"

"Look, Mike, I know what you're going to say. I know that things could still happen and that Sarah's adoption could fall through. But I feel good about this. I think it is what we should do." The hair stood up on the back of Mike's neck. "But I will also do a second copy of the book without Sarah in it, to take with us, just in case. Is that okay?"

"I'm good with that."

Laura continued to go through the printouts. "Then I've done a page on pictures of the house during the different seasons and a description of the place. There are pages for each of the main rooms in the house, like the kitchen, the living room, the boys' bedroom, our bedroom, her bedroom, each with a description. I've got a page on the horses and one on the dog. Let's have her spend the time getting used to what she will be coming home to, rather than fantasizing about something that isn't correct."

"This sounds great. But Honey, I think that you're forgetting that Sarah speaks Russian. The workers in the orphanage speak Russian."

"I'm already on that. In the packet Miracle Child sent us in the beginning, there was a list of people who could perform translations. I called one of them and he said that he could do something as simple as these books for a couple of hundred dollars. It's pretty simple stuff. He said that I could just send him a Microsoft Word Document and that he could do the Russian translation under each phrase. Then we could just copy and paste the text into the book document. That way, we can put Russian at the top of the page and English at the bottom. Then, as the orphanage workers read the book to her now, and when we read it to her later, it could even help with language skills."

"That's brilliant! So, if the first book is about the home and family, what is the second one about?"

"I've been thinking a lot about this one. Russia is so far away from here. Even though she must be excited, she has to be apprehensive. She'll be leaving everything that she knows and loves. She'll be leaving friends, too, to go with people that she has barely met, and she's only a child. There have to be concerns about getting lost, or not making it home, or anything else that could be imagined by a five-year-old. I want to explain the trip home so that she knows what to expect. I also want to somehow make the world seem like a smaller place so that when we come back home and she has to wait, that we don't seem so far away. Then when she comes home with us, maybe it won't feel like her friends are so far away. Read through this book and tell me what you think."

Mike opened the second book to the first page which showed a beautiful sunset in Vladivostok, and began reading.

"When the sun goes down in Primorski," he turned to the next page, a picture of a sunrise near their home, "The sun comes up in Michigan!" He looked up at Laura with a little tear building up in his eye and smiled. She had accomplished her first goal in two pages. The sun made the distance between Russia and America seem short. Both places could see the sun at the same time.

"Where did you get the picture of Vladivostok?" Mike questioned.

"I did searches online. Some guy who got an online bride from Russia had this on his site. I got other pictures I needed from airline web sites and hotel sites. Several people had web sites that shared their adoption stories, so I was able to borrow some pictures that should apply. Like the ones of the Vladivostok airport and a Russian judge."

"That's great! I can't believe this!" Mike continued to leaf through the pages which each contained pictures and a simple caption. He read them one by one.

"Sweetheart, this is unbelievable. Where did you get this idea?"

"I don't know. I just wanted to be able to help Sarah prepare. As I started putting some ideas down on paper, this just kind of came together."

"Well, I can't think of anything that could help her more. Are you going to be able to get these done by the time we travel? Has Kristin given us any idea of when that might be yet?"

"I can get them done, that won't be a problem. I did talk with Kristin about getting out before Christmas, but it doesn't look good unless we're willing to be in Russia for Christmas, and I don't want to do that to the boys."

"No, you're right. Me neither."

"Kristin said that the adoption process pretty much comes to a standstill between mid December and the first several days of January. I guess most of the government offices pretty much shut down for holidays. She said there would be a bottleneck right after the first of the year with everyone trying to get moving again, but that they would get us out as soon as they could."

10

Packing Up

"Oh, good. I thought that you might already be on the plane," Laura said anxiously into the phone.

"Well, I am on the plane, but we're still on the ground and they haven't shut the door yet. I can talk for a minute. So, what's up?"

"I just got off the phone with Miracle Child Adoptions. They got our invitation to travel from Russia!"

"That's great, Honey. When do they want us there?"

"Next Monday."

Mike's head was swimming, first because of the excitement of finally being able to meet his new daughter, and then from trying to run down the logistics of getting to Russia on such short notice. "Next Monday? You've got to be kidding! That's only five days away! Let's see, first of all, Vladivostok is about fourteen hours ahead of us. That means we lose one day to begin with. Detroit to Tokyo is a thirteen hour flight by itself. Then there's a two hour flight to Seoul, with at least a two hour layover in between. When I spoke with the travel agent a couple of weeks ago, they told me that there's only one flight into Vladivostok from Seoul every day. That means that we'll have to spend the night in Seoul or Tokyo before going on to Vladivostok. Unless we go east instead of west, but I really don't think that it would make much difference. If we go east, we'll get stuck in Moscow overnight, and I'd be more comfortable in Seoul or Tokyo anyway. At least I've been there before. My guess is that we'll have to leave on Saturday. I hope that we can get visas that fast."

"My, aren't you just a travel encyclopedia," Laura joked.

"A hundred thousand air miles a year for eight years running will do that to a guy. You forget. I travel for a living."

"I could never forget how much you travel. I'm just surprised that you've already got the whole thing figured out. So, what do you want me to do?"

"Call Jennifer at the travel agency and have her start

checking on tickets. Ask her to see if they have any special rates or discounts for adoption. With only three days advance notice, these tickets will be expensive."

"I'll call her as soon as I get off the phone with you. What time do you get home tonight?"

"I get home about five-thirty. But hey, I've got to hang up. They've shut the door and if the flight attendant signals me one more time to shut off the phone she'll probably throw me off the plane. I'll see you tonight. I love you. Goodbye."

"See you soon. I love you." Laura hung up the phone and took a deep breath. It was hard to believe this was finally happening. Christmas had come and gone, and so had the entire month of January. And just when they had grown numb from waiting, the phone call came.

There was so much to do! It wasn't just the travel arrangements that had to be made. She had to arrange for someone to stay with the boys, there was last-minute shopping to do for the trip, and she would have to restock groceries before leaving. The house had to be cleaned and…she stopped. First things first. She picked up the phone and called Jennifer.

"How exciting!" Jennifer's voice resonated after hearing the news. "You must be so thrilled!"

"Oh, we are! I just have so much to do before we leave. I don't know if I can get everything done!"

"Don't be silly," Jennifer chuckled. "You'll get everything done that needs to get done. Anything that you don't get done will wait until you get back. But let me worry about the travel. I'll call you back with your options in an hour or two."

"Okay. Goodbye." Laura couldn't believe how talking to Jennifer calmed her nerves. Jennifer had such a fun voice and she was always so upbeat and happy. They had known each other from church association since before they had each married. Jennifer's husband, Brian, had been among Mike's closest friends since before their grammar school days. Their relationship was one of those few lifetime friendships that survived the trial of time and distance. *Jennifer is right*, she thought to herself. *Whatever doesn't get done before we leave will wait until we get back.*

"Barbecued steaks in the middle of winter? What's the occasion?" Mike asked while walking through the door and dropping the small carry-on and laptop bag in the corner on the kitchen floor.

"I know that you like a nice home-cooked meal, and it is a special occasion. It's not every day that we get an invitation to go and meet our daughter!"

Mike did like home-cooked meals. He remembered back to a time when he and Laura were at dinner with some friends who also traveled a lot for work. The woman talked about how much she just wanted to go out to dinner when her husband came back from traveling, just to get out of the house. The man said how much he hated going out for yet one more restaurant meal after a trip, and how he just wanted to sit in front of the TV with a plate of anything home-cooked. Even macaroni and cheese would do it for him. On the drive home, Laura asked why he had never told her that he felt that way. He always took her out to dinner as soon as he got home from a trip. He told her that it was no big deal, and that he was happy to get her out of the house after spending a week alone with the boys. But ever since then, she always had a home-cooked meal waiting for him as soon as he got back. Then, within a day or two, he'd take her out to dinner. He thought about how much he and Laura enjoyed their marriage, and how much that enjoyment was based on simple little things they each went out of their way to do for each other.

"Well, if adopting one daughter gets us barbecued T-bones, then maybe we should consider getting a couple more."

Laura laughed. "I got travel arrangements worked out with Jennifer today. We do have to leave on Saturday."

"Did I tell you?" Mike asked smugly.

"Yes, you did tell me, but Jennifer also asked me to make sure that you ordered the visas."

Mike felt his stomach sink. "Oh, no! I knew I forgot something! I should have called the agency handling the visas today. We don't have much time to spare. I hope that they can still get the visas in time." Visas to Russia were not the item to forget.

"Jennifer and I were pretty sure that you didn't get to it with all your plane hopping today, so she called the agency. They told her that since you already sent them passports and passport pictures, getting tourist visas by Friday shouldn't be a problem."

"Tourist visas? Not adoption visas? Is that allowed?"

"Technically, no. But I guess that they do it all the time. The agent doesn't think that there will be any problem."

"I guess I dropped the ball on that one. Thanks for bailing me out." Mike said while shaking his head in dismay. It wasn't like him to miss a detail like that.

"Even you are entitled to mess up once in a while, Mr. Perfectionist."

"So, what else do we have to do by Saturday morning?"

"I called Mark and Dawn and they will come and stay here with the boys while we're gone."

"Good call." Mark was Mike's younger brother by twelve years. He and his pretty wife, Dawn, were still young enough to be, act, and dress cool, and were the favorites of all the cousins. Furthermore, Dawn was a stay-at-home mom with two young preschoolers; so in trying to disrupt lives as little as possible, they were not only preferred by the boys, but the logical choice.

"We still need to pick up the other set of luggage that you were talking about. My set has had it. Also, we need to buy all of the little gifts that we're supposed to give people," Laura reminded him.

"That's right. I'd forgotten." The adoption agency had explained to them the Russian custom of giving small gifts of appreciation to translators, drivers, orphanage directors, and others. The recommended gifts seemed a little cheesy to Mike. Things like car window ice scrapers, spatulas, American make-up, and American music. But he had learned long ago to follow counsel when told how to behave in another culture. If the rumors were true, most of the gifts would be sold on the black market anyway, for cash to buy necessities. "I can take some time away from work tomorrow and pick up the luggage and door prizes."

"Good. That will help. I haven't done bulk grocery

shopping for almost a month, so I'll take care of that tomorrow. I'll make sure that there's plenty of stuff for Dawn to use for meals that are easy to prepare. Also, you had better get a hair cut."

"Yeah, I know. I'll take care of that tomorrow, too."

"Fortunately, the boys have a day off from school on Friday; so that ought to allow us to get the house pulled together and the packing done. We'll get the tickets, passports, and visas by FedEx to your work, so you'll just have to make sure that you throw them in with your portable office," she said nodding toward his laptop case in the corner.

"Sounds like you've got it all under control. Anything else?"

"Yes, there is one more thing." Laura's mood changed just a little, became a little more serious. "I want us to make time to visit Mom. I'm worried, Mike."

"Laura, Laura. The worst is behind her. Remember what she always says? 'Remission' means getting better, not worse." Mike paused for a moment. "Look, Mom's not going to die. Our faith and prayers saw to that. Our faith kept her with us through the chemo and the radiation. She got better. She's fine."

Mike could see that simple words weren't going to do it. "But of course we'll go visit her. We'll make time for that. Now, what about the adoption? Are you ready for this?"

Laura's mood brightened. "I've been ready for this since we first decided to adopt. The only thing that I'm more ready for is bringing her home. Oh Mike, we finally get to meet her." Laura threw her arms around his neck and gave him a big hug and kiss. "By the way, welcome home."

"There you go! Everything is packed and I still have one bag to spare! Looks like we'll be traveling lighter than anticipated," Mike said while zipping the last bag shut.

"You're the king of packing luggage," Laura acknowledged.

"It's all in how you cram socks and underwear in the

corners," Mike said proudly.

"Did you get the teddy bears out of the bed?" Laura had read on the internet that a psychologist recommended sleeping with a stuffed animal, then leaving it with the child on the first visit so that the child grew accustomed to the smell of the parents and came to recognize it as a sign of comfort. She had brought home matching pink and purple teddy bears that had been their bed partners ever since. Mike had asked why they needed two bears wadded up in bed with them and she had told him that she thought that they were both so cute that she couldn't decide, so she wanted to let Sarah choose which one she liked best. "Well, did you remember the bears?"

"No. I forgot them. I forgot the cassette tape and headphone player, too. But there is still room in one of the big suit cases." Laura had also learned about an adopting mother who had recorded a cassette tape of her singing lullabies and reading stories, and then left it with a headphone player for the child on the first visit. When the mother came back for the little girl, she had become accustomed to her voice.

"Okay. Don't forget them, and make sure that you pack your cologne, too. If that psychologist is right about smells, you should wear that when we go to see Sarah. I'll do the same with my perfume. Do you think that will all fit in one of these suitcases?"

"Yes"

"So, we still have room for more stuff?"

"Oh, no. I don't like where this is going," Mike said nervously. "What more could you possibly want to take with you for a one-week trip, two days of which are spent in the air?"

"It's not like that. I was just thinking."

"Thinking what?"

"Well, when we thought that we were adopting a baby, we went out and bought that entire wardrobe. We always thought that we'd just wait until someone in the family had a baby girl and then we'd give it all to them."

"What's wrong with that?"

"Nothing is wrong with that. I'm just wondering if there is anyone in our family who could ever need those clothes as much as the orphanage where Sarah lives. What do you think about taking those clothes and giving them to the orphanage?"

"I'm surprised that we didn't think of it sooner. I can't think of a place where those clothes would be more appreciated."

"So you don't mind loading them into the extra suitcase?"

"Nope. Not at all."

"Do you think that they'll all fit?"

"Oh, they'll fit alright. I'll make them fit. Little girl's clothes are like socks and underwear. I'll just keep filling up the corners until it all fits."

11

Rushing Off to Russia

"I can't believe they're actually holding this flight to take on more passengers," Mike fumed as they and all the other passengers sat anxiously in their seats. "We're an hour late already. We'll never make our connection in Tokyo!"

"Calm down, Honey. It will all work out," Laura said soothingly.

"Yeah, you think it will all work out. But if we miss our connection to Seoul, we won't make our flight to Vladivostok, and remember, there's only one flight a day from Seoul to Vladivostok."

"It will be alright one way or the other," Laura said. "Getting all worked up is not going to make this airplane move any quicker."

Mike shook his head and pulled a paperback from the laptop case. Laura put her arm up over his shoulder, twirled a finger in his hair and then started rubbing his neck. If that didn't calm him down, nothing would.

"Good morning, Handsome Prince," Laura said after lifting up the ear piece of Mike's noise canceling headphones and kissing him on the cheek.

Mike snorted and stretched as he opened his eyes and remembered where he was. He moaned as he tried to straighten out the kink in his neck.

Laura giggled. "Sorry to interrupt your beauty sleep, but the captain came on the intercom. We'll be landing in about forty-five minutes, just an hour late. He said he's never had a two hundred mile per hour tailwind traveling west like this. He joked that somebody on this plane must be living right."

"That's great news, but I hope you're ready for the mad dash to the next plane. It'll be crazy."

"Always a pessimist, aren't you?" she teased.

"Realist," Mike corrected.

Laura reached up and tried to straighten his hair, snarled and kinked from rubbing against the seat as he'd slid down during the uncomfortable nap. "I think it's hopeless without some water," she said. "I guess you're just going to have to have a bad hair day."

It was almost twenty-five minutes after touchdown before they actually got off the plane. Mike headed quickly up the jet way with Laura following close behind. He expertly directed them through the security and passport check points, but still they had to rush to the gate connecting them to Seoul.

Two gate agents waited anxiously next to the podium in the otherwise empty waiting area. "Yes. Mr. and Mrs. Knight. We've been waiting for you," one of the gate agents said politely as she checked the tickets against the passports. "Please hurry and we'll have you on your way as soon as is safely possible."

Mike and Laura moved quickly down the jet way and then hurried down the aisle toward their seats at the back of the crowded plane. Mike popped open the overhead bin, only to see it full to overflowing. "Yeah. I didn't see that coming," he said sarcastically as he glanced at Laura.

"I have some space back here that's still open," said the male flight attendant who had hurried up the aisle. "Let me take those."

He thanked the flight attendant and they quickly took their seats, Mike stuffing his long wool overcoat under the seat in front of him.

"Well, you were right," Laura said as she fastened herself in. "That *was* a mad dash."

The flight to Seoul was uneventful, and both Mike and Laura felt relief for the first time in hours, knowing that they would now easily make the morning flight to Vladivostok. Actually, it was the first time since the call from the adoption agency that neither of them felt hurried. Even during the flight to Tokyo, they had joked about going to the front of the plane to push, just to see if it could get them there faster. Now, with the plane on the ground and at the gate, they waited for all the other passengers to disembark before they grabbed their carry-on bags and made their way through customs.

Exiting the airport, they breathed in the fresh night air.

"You need taxi. I give you ride!" The abrupt little man grabbed hold of the handle of Mike's suitcase and started walking next to him, though a little faster, trying to break Mike's grip from the handle. But Mike kept his grip and slowed down even more.

"Sorry, Chief. We don't need a taxi."

"Sho! You need taxi. I give you ride. Where you stay?"

"We're staying here at the Hyatt, Partner. We don't need a taxi. We'll take the shuttle." Mike had experience with these poachers before, men who tried to steal business from the licensed taxi drivers. But the pursuer was unrelenting. Seeing that he was getting nowhere with Mike, he let go of his luggage handle, grabbed Laura's and pulled it from her hand while starting to walk away. Laura was startled as the handle tore free, letting the persistent little man hurry a few steps further.

"Hold on, Chief!" Mike said, elevating his voice for the first time.

The eager hunter, now ten steps away, stopped and turned toward Mike. "You stay at Hyatt. You need taxi. I take you to Hyatt. Special price for you."

"I said we'll take the shuttle."

"Sho! Sho! You need taxi. Hyatt Namsan have no shuttle. I give you ride. Make special price."

"We're not staying at the Hyatt Namsan. We're staying here at the Hyatt Incheon."

"Oh no! Hyatt Incheon too close. I no give you ride." The eager but dejected driver dragged Laura's luggage back to her and hurried off to find another victim.

"These guys used to beat the heck out of me," he explained to Laura. "First the unlicensed poachers at the airport, and then the real cab drivers. You give them the name of a hotel and where it is and then they take off to another hotel of the same brand name at the other end of the city. When they get you to the wrong place, they apologize and blame it on the language barrier. They're more than happy to take you to the right place after that, but by the time you get done, you've paid them three times."

"I can't believe that just happened!" Laura exclaimed.

"You live and learn," Mike replied. "In the meantime, you pay."

"It feels so good to finally be in a place where I can lay down," Laura said after falling backwards onto the bed.

"I know what you mean," Mike replied while rearranging the luggage against the wall. He pulled one of the carry-ons from the pile and tossed it on the chair next to the desk and began to empty its contents, toilet kits, snacks, fresh clothes for the next day and the like. "That was a long day," he continued as he plopped down on the bed next to Laura. "I'll give you first shot at the bathtub."

Laura slowly got up and went in to fill the tub while Mike lay in the bed, pondering meeting his new daughter and bringing her home. He wondered what it was like in the orphanage, if she got enough to eat, and if there were adults who spent time with her. He wondered if her past life from an abusive home had caused her to be afraid, angry, shy, or cynical. She looked happy in the pictures. He wondered how that could be. Maybe it was true that we make our own happiness, the way we make our own future.

Mike let himself be carried away, daydreaming of all the good that this daughter might accomplish, his thoughts drifting further and further from the Korean hotel. In the back of his mind it amazed him that his hopes, dreams, and aspirations for success for this child were no different from the ones that he had for his sons when Laura was pregnant with them. He could only imagine a perfect future, one laden with success and accomplishments for his new daughter.

Mike had no idea how long he had been laying there daydreaming when Laura slipped under the covers. "The bathtub is yours. Don't ask me to wait up. I'm so tired that I'll be asleep in no time and nothing could wake me up until morning."

"Except jet lag," Mike mumbled as he got out of bed.

"What was that?"

Mike just smiled as he made his way to the bathroom.

"Mike? Are you asleep?"

Mike rolled over to face his wife.

"I'm sorry. I didn't mean to wake you," she said. "It's three in the morning, and I'm wide awake."

"No problem. Same here," Mike said as he stretched.

"I was so tired when I went to sleep I thought I'd never wake up. And here it is in the middle of the night and I'm wide awake!"

"No sense fighting jet lag. It might say three a.m. on the clock, but your body thinks it's five in the evening."

Laura smiled. "So that's why you always get up in the middle of the night after returning from trips overseas. And I thought you were addicted to home repair shows and infomercials!"

Wide awake and propped up in bed, Mike read his book while Laura got out the list of Russian words and phrases from the adoption agency. The Russian was spelled out phonetically in English to make pronunciation easier, but she and Mike both feared they were butchering it. She sat on the bed and began drudging through the words. "*Zdras*-tvoy; Hello. *Da*-svi-*da*-nia; Goodbye. *Dob*-ro-ye *oot*-roh; Good morning. *Da*; Yes. *Nyet*; No. *Ya* tib-*ya* lou-*blue*; I love you."

"So, have you got Russian figured out?" Mike asked as he put his book back in his carry-on.

"These words are too hard," Laura said in frustration. "They put too many consonants together. Do you think that Sarah will be able to understand anything I say?"

"I'm sure that she'll understand the last one, whether or not she understands your Russian. Love doesn't need words. The rest will all work out."

"Oh Mike! Look at the beautiful mountains," Laura said as the plane descended toward the Vladivostok airport.

“It is beautiful, alright. But boy, that looks cold. See the snow blowing up over the peaks and trailing off?”

“Is that what that is? It must be freezing!”

Mike continued to look past Laura and out the window as they both admired the stunning snowy landscape until the plane touched down. The plane was barely off the runway when anxious passengers bolted from their seats into the aisle and threw open the overhead bins.

Within a couple of minutes, they taxied to within a stone’s throw of the terminal. An old truck with a staircase pulled up to the aircraft loading door and the passengers began to exit the aircraft and took their places, mostly standing, on a shuttle bus waiting next to the plane.

“This is bitter cold!” Laura chattered as they walked down the steps. “What’s the deal with the bus? The terminal is just right over there,” she commented as they squeezed their way onto the bus.

“Maybe we’re going to a gate on the other side of the terminal or something,” Mike wondered out loud. But then the bus door closed, the engine revved, and the driver pulled forward fifty feet, stopping at the nearest terminal door. The bus door opened, disgorging its passengers.

“I guess we get off here?” Mike laughed.

Laura shrugged her shoulders and followed the other passengers through the terminal door.

Mike shook his head as he walked along side his wife. “In a million miles of traveling, that’s about the strangest thing I’ve ever seen.”

A wave of heat hit them as they entered the building. They crowded toward the end of one of six ill-defined lines waiting to go through passport control. “It must be eighty-five degrees in here!” Laura gasped as they unbuttoned their coats.

They stood in line for about twenty minutes before the agent waved Mike forward. Laura followed, as she always did when they traveled together. “One person only,” the agent said coarsely to Laura. “You go back. You wait. Wait behind line.”

The agent looked at Mike’s passport and checked to make sure that he resembled the photograph. He then thumbed through the pages until arriving at the Russian visa pasted on its own page. He stopped reading several times, and looked skeptically up at Mike before inking a series of stamps on his visa and passport. He handed them back to Mike and pointed toward the hall leading to the exit. Mike took several steps until he rounded the corner, then stopped and waited for Laura. Several minutes later she joined him and they headed for the exit. At least they were through with that!

"Why you are here in Roshah?" a husky, brusque woman in a uniform asked, walking up behind them. Mike and Laura stopped and turned to face her.

Mike hesitated briefly. They were in Russia on tourist visas. Should he lie? He calculated the odds in his head. Tourists? To Vladivostok? In the middle of winter? Not a likely story. All the woman would have to do was open their luggage and find the ring binders loaded with adoption information. There wasn't much sense in lying.

"Sir, I ask you. Why you are here in Roshah?" she queried again in her thick Russian accent.

"For adoption," Mike stated flatly.

"Why den you here on tourist visa?" she questioned without missing a beat.

"It's our first visit. We're not really adopting on this trip. We're just here to meet the child. We aren't really adopting until we come back on the next trip."

"Dis no matter. You must have adoption visa because you here for adopt."

"Really? Our agent told us that a tourist visa would be alright."

"Dis not true. Your agent, he know this. You must have adoption visa." The woman paused for a moment to observe their reactions.

"I'm sorry," Mike said meekly while Laura remained quiet, but unnerved. "I didn't know how much it mattered, even if my agent did."

The Russian official paused for a moment longer. The American did seem sincere, and it did appear that he respected her authority. It was also obvious that the American woman was bewildered. "Dis time only I let you come wid tourist visa. You tell agent next time he make adoption visa *only* for adoption. No more tourist visa. Next time you come back, if not adoption visa, I no let you in."

"Yes Ma'am. I understand. Thank you for your understanding," Mike said as he lightly nodded his head in a semi-formal bow.

The woman turned and walked away.

"That was scary!" Laura gasped as they started back down the short hallway toward the exit.

"Shhh," Mike said firmly. "Not here. Not now. Keep walking." He had no idea if anyone was listening, but he could feel that things were far different here than anywhere else he had ever been.

After retrieving their luggage they stepped through a door to face a throng of people waiting for the passengers.

"Hello! You are Mike and Laura?" a petite and pretty young blonde asked as they moved toward the crowd.

"Yes. Sasha?" Mike quizzed.

"Yes. I am Sasha. This is Marik," she said, nodding toward her male companion. "It's nice to meet you. Did you see the Ericksons on the plane?"

"I'm sorry, who?"

"Doug and Michelle Erickson. Were they on your flight?"

"Gosh, I don't know." Mike paused as he tried to remember if he had seen anyone on the flight that fit the adoptive parent stereotype. "We didn't meet them. I don't *think* there was anyone else on the flight that was adopting."

"Okay," Sasha responded. "Maybe they aren't going to make it today."

"Wait," Marik said while peering through the door towards customs as other passengers came out. "I think that's them coming now."

Sure enough, another American couple came through the door several seconds later. Marik and Sasha greeted the Ericksons, and then introduced them to the Knights. "The Ericksons are here on their second trip," Marik reported. "They have a court date set for the day after tomorrow."

"Oh! Congratulations!" Mike and Laura blurted out simultaneously.

"Are you adopting a girl or a boy?" Laura asked.

"A girl," Michelle replied excitedly.

"How old is she?"

"Ten months."

"How fun! A new baby!" Laura squealed.

"Well, yeah, at least as young as you can get them here. She was seven months old when we came on our first visit. I was hoping that she wouldn't be walking by the time we came back!"

"Oh! I'm so excited for you!"

"Thanks. So, is this your first trip?"

"Yes."

"Boy or girl?"

"A five-year-old little girl."

"Oh, that will be fun for you! She'll be old enough to understand what's going on."

"Yes," Laura answered nervously. "We're hoping that's a good thing."

"Oh, of course it is. Everything will work out fine. I'm sure she's excited to meet you."

"So, are we ready to get going?" Marik interrupted politely.

Affirmative answers came simultaneously from all four in the group.

"Doug and Michelle, you go with Sasha and she will take you to the hotel. Mike and Laura, you come with me."

The two couples said their good-byes and wished each other well.

"How tired are you?" Marik asked as he loaded the luggage in the SUV.

"We're good, I think," Mike said glancing at Laura to make sure that she felt the same.

"Yes. We slept part of the night last night in Seoul and caught a nap on the flight."

"Okay. Then if you want to, we can go and meet Katya."

"Katya? Is that what she goes by?" Laura asked. "I mean, all of the documentation says Ekaterina; but from time to time, like on the video label, we see the name Katya."

"Yes. Katya is her nickname. Most Russian children, especially the girls, usually have at least one nickname.

Ekaterina goes by Katya."

"We would love to see her today!" Laura exclaimed. "How far away is she?"

"Today, and for the time you are here, we are in luck. Usually, it takes about three hours to drive to her orphanage. But now Katya is at winter camp. It's only fifteen minutes away."

"Winter camp?" Mike asked in a puzzled voice. "The orphans go to camp?"

"Yes. Just like American children might go to camp for the summer, Russian children do that too, sometimes in the summer, sometimes in the winter."

"Really? So the kids in the orphanages get to do that too?"

"Yes. The government pays for it. Some of the workers from the orphanage bring the children and they spend a couple of weeks staying at a different place, doing arts and crafts, playing outside and doing other activities. The kids really enjoy it."

"Does Katya know we're coming?" Laura asked, changing the subject slightly.

"She knows that you will come some time this week. But she doesn't know we are coming today."

"So will this be a good surprise for her, or a bad one?"

Marik laughed. "Of course it's a good surprise. She will be happy to see you. Katya is a very happy child. She is looking forward to having parents."

The threesome continued to make small talk during their drive to the winter camp. They pulled off the main highway and down the driveway several hundred meters to a large, two-story stucco building with a sign on the front with Cyrillic lettering: ВОЛНЫ.

"What does the sign say?" Laura asked.

"Volny," Marik replied. "It means *Waves*. The bay is just beyond the building there. Right now it is frozen, but that's the name of the camp. Waves." Marik coasted to a stop and turned off the engine. "So, are you ready to meet your daughter?"

"Yes! Let's go!" Laura was out of the SUV before the other two even had their doors open. "Hold on, Mike. We need my perfume and your cologne out of the overnight bag."

Marik raised one eyebrow curiously as he looked at Mike.

Mike rolled his eyes just a little as he looked at Marik, though he took care to make sure that Laura didn't notice. "Laura has done some reading. Apparently good smells will help the child bond with the new parents. Is it okay if we pull out one of the suitcases?"

"Sure, that's a good idea," Marik responded brightly, to Mike's surprise. He opened the back of the SUV and Mike got the appropriate piece of luggage. He pulled out the toilet kit and he and Laura both applied their fragrances.

"Okay, now we're ready," Laura said, straightening her coat and fixing Mike's collar. They turned toward the building, so common on the outside, but holding something very precious on the inside.

12

The Meeting

Laura and Mike anxiously followed Marik through white-painted double metal doors into a hallway where a stern-looking woman in a security guard uniform sat at an old metal desk. Marik spoke to her in Russian for several seconds before turning back to Mike and Laura.

"You should wait here," he said pointing to a bench between the entry doors and security guard. "The camp director is not here. She should be here when you meet Katya. I know this director very well, though, and I think it will be okay if you meet her, but first I need to double-check with the other worker who was left in charge and make sure it will be alright."

As Marik hurried down the hall, Mike and Laura sat nervously on the bench with the security guard watching them. Ten agonizing minutes later, Marik returned and began speaking with the security guard in Russian. Then he turned to Mike and Laura. "She says if the workers say it is okay, you can go in, so it will be alright. The workers are very excited for Katya. They want to surprise her with your visit. They will wait for us to be outside the door of the room the children are playing in, and then they will tell her there is a surprise for her out in the hall. Let's hurry down to the room."

The couple followed Marik quickly down the hall until they arrived at a door. "Wait here," Marik said quietly as he stepped inside the door and shut it behind him.

"I'm so nervous…" was all Laura could get out before the door re-opened and Marik walked out with two female workers and a beautiful little Russian girl behind them.

Laura gasped. She couldn't believe that the moment was actually here. One of the workers spoke to Katya in Russian. Mike and Laura only recognized three words in the sentence: *Mama*, *Papa*, and *Amérika*. But that was all they needed to understand.

Katya's eyes lit up, and a smile, complete with dimples, filled her whole face.

She quickly took two steps toward them and then she stopped. The smile left her face and she looked down at the floor. It seemed that Katya didn't know what to do any more than her adoptive parents did. This was uncharted territory for all of them, and no one knew exactly how they should act or react. But Laura, like all good mothers, understood that love bridges all gaps. She squatted down and held out her arms. The child looked up and her radiant smile immediately returned. She ran to Laura as fast as she could and threw her arms around her mother's neck. Laura wrapped her arms around Katya and the two remained there squeezing each other, though motionless, for nearly two minutes. The attention of everyone present was transfixed on the mother and child, and it seemed as if time itself had paused to witness the moment. Finally, Laura moved her hands to the child's shoulders and pushed her back just far enough to get a good look at her.

"Oh, Katya! You are beautiful!" she said as she embraced the child again. Marik translated while Mike, standing behind Laura, saw the child's smile grow even brighter and dimples go even deeper. It was clear that both mother and child had worried whether or not they would be acceptable to each other, and now both had received even more than their wildest wishes.

Marik spoke to Katya again in Russian. This time the Americans only understood one word: *Papa*. The little girl didn't stop smiling as she pulled back from her mother and scurried over to Mike. He bent over and scooped her up as she threw her arms around his neck. "*Preens-yessa*," he whispered in her ear. It was one of the few Russian words that he had taken the time to learn. *Princess*.

They hugged for several seconds before she turned to face the others, still perched in Papa's arms. There was rapid speech in Russian; the adults, directed toward Katya. But Katya didn't talk. She just sat there on her father's arm with her fist in front of her mouth, nodding affirmatively at the questions posed to her by the workers. But even the shy act of covering her mouth with her fist couldn't hide the enormous smile and those enchanting dimples.

"The workers said that we can go to the dormitory if we would like to have some private time to visit," Marik offered.

"That would be great," Mike replied, his voice still tight with emotion.

Marik spoke to Katya in Russian and she nodded excitedly. She wriggled in Mike's arms and he put her down on the floor. "I asked her if she wants to show you where she sleeps, and she said that she does," Marik said.

Katya grabbed Laura by the hand and began leading her up the stairs. Mike and Marik followed closely behind. Upon arriving at the top of the stairs, Katya walked across the hall to the first door and pushed it open. It was a large, pale green room and it was crammed full with twenty-four twin-sized beds. The beds were arranged side by side, in four rows, with about a foot between each bed. The aisles between the beds were a bit more spacious, at two feet, except for the two middle rows of beds, which were butted up against each other head-to-head.

"Which bed is yours?" Laura asked. Marik repeated the question in Russian and Katya pointed to the second one from the end, against the wall.

"Why don't you guys sit on this bed with Katya," Marik suggested. "I can sit on this one across the aisle and translate," he offered. He repeated the suggestion to Katya in Russian and the three sat together on the bed, Katya between Laura and Mike. Laura seized the opportunity before Mike could, and boosted the child up on to her lap. Mike slid over next to them.

Mike and Laura made small talk with Katya through the translator for a few minutes. Mostly Katya just smiled and nodded in affirmation, or shook her head when the answer was no. Every once in a while Marik could get a word or two out of her. But after a few minutes, the conversation lagged. Still, there was no awkwardness; silence communicated more than speech ever could. The four of them sat there for several minutes in silence taking it all in. Then suddenly, without warning, Katya spun on Laura's lap, threw her arms around her neck and started to sob. Laura held her tight and let her cry for a couple of minutes before asking Marik if she was alright.

"I think she's fine," he said. "I think it's just emotions." He asked Katya several questions in Russian to which she either nodded or shook her head while still crying, cradled on her mother's lap. "Yes, she's fine. She is very happy. It's just emotions."

"Oh, you poor baby," Laura cooed soothingly again and again as she held her little girl against her and stroked her hair. Marik didn't bother translating. Katya knew what was going on. After several more minutes of tears and cuddling, Katya sat up again and wiped her eyes with her hands. She smiled her beautiful smile again, no doubt concerned that her new parents might not approve of an unhappy child.

Not wanting to get into an uncomfortable silence again, Marik moved quickly. "Didn't you bring some treats or presents for Katya?"

"Sure, of course. They're out in the car," Mike replied.

"Maybe now would be a good time to get them. Why don't you come with me and we'll leave Laura and Katya here to wait for us."

Mike agreed and Marik quickly explained to Katya what was going on. She smiled and nodded and the two men left the room.

Mike and Laura had not intended to see Katya before a stop at the hotel, so Mike had to do some digging through the luggage before finding the candy necklace, Rice Krispy Treats, a baby blanket, and the stuffed bears. Just before closing the suitcase, he had an idea. He pulled out the toilet kit and lightly splashed the bears with his cologne and the blanket with Laura's perfume. They re-entered the building and Marik went through a ritual check-in again with the security guard, who wanted to know what they were bringing back into the building. As Marik was making his explanation, Mike saw a blur of a child shoot down the stairs and across the hall through doors into another room.

"I think that was Katya," Mike said to Marik as the security guard let them past.

"Where was Katya?"

"It happened so fast. I'm not positive, but I think it was Katya who ran down the stairs and across the hall into that room. She was really moving. I wonder if she got scared?"

"Oh, I don't think so. It must have been another child. We'll go up to the dormitory and if she's not there, I'll check it out."

The two men climbed the stairs and entered the dormitory where Laura sat alone on the bed where they had left her. "Where's Katya?" Mike asked, worried.

"One of the workers came in and said it was time for her to go and eat. She didn't want to go, but the worker told her she could come back as soon as she finished, so she took off like a shot."

"Oh, then she should only be fifteen minutes or so," Marik said as he sat on the edge of one of the beds. The three of them visited for another two or three minutes when the door burst open and Katya—smiles, dimples, and all—came rushing back into the room. She ran straight to Laura, who picked her up and plopped her down on her lap.

"She can't be finished already!" Laura commented to Marik. Just then one of the workers poked her head through the door. She spoke in Russian with Marik for a minute, both of them laughing, and then she left.

"The worker said she has never seen a child eat so fast before in her life! She said she ate everything, but she wanted to hurry so she could get back to her mama and papa."

"What did you have for dinner?" Mike asked Katya, waiting for Marik to translate.

"Chicken soup," Laura laughed before Marik could respond. "I can smell it on her breath. I don't know if the poor child even took time to swallow, let alone to chew!"

Marik spoke to Katya in Russian and she nodded. "You guessed it, chicken soup." The three adults laughed and Katya joined in, though not knowing for sure what was so funny.

"Mama and Papa have some presents for you that they brought from America," Marik told Katya in Russian. "Do you want to see what they brought you?"

Katya's eyes danced as she held her fist in front of her mouth and nodded shyly. Mike pulled the candy necklace from the bag and put it around her neck. She thought that it was beautiful and found it strange when Marik told her that it was candy and that she could bite off pieces to eat. She lifted the necklace to her mouth and put several beads inside. She pulled hard on the elastic, trying to separate the beads from the string.

Mike was sure that the string would snap and the beads would go flying, if she didn't tear a tooth out first! Marik laughed and explained to Katya how to bite the pieces off without pulling, which she did, mostly to humor the adults. She liked wearing the necklace more than eating it. Then Mike pulled a Rice Krispy Treat from the bag. Katya was excited by the blue foil package. Anything in a package that pretty had to be good to eat! Mike unwrapped the treat and handed it to her. She took a quick nibble to see if she really would like it and then smiled and took a large bite. She rattled off something in Russian to Marik and he laughed.

"She said she really likes this kind of biscuit," he translated for Mike and Laura.

"Do you think your mama and papa have anything else in the bag for you?" Marik asked Katya in Russian. She nodded vigorously.

"Do you have anything else, Papa?" he asked.

"Yes, I do." Mike stalled and waited for Marik to translate, which he did.

Katya was going out of her mind with anticipation as Mike reached deep into the bag and pulled out the pink and purple stuffed bears and the baby blanket. "Mama said that you get to choose which bear you want," he said holding them out, knowing that she would get the other one at a later date, anyway. Marik translated, and the little girl quickly grabbed the purple one and hugged it tight. Then she paused, held the bear away just a bit, looked at it curiously, and then buried her face in it and took a deep breath, inhaling the scent of Mike's cologne and smiling.

"What are you going to name the bear?" Mike asked as he put the other bear back in the bag. Marik repeated the question in Russian. Katya didn't answer at first, and it took some coaxing from Marik before she finally had a name come to mind for her new pet.

"Lilya," she replied confidently. Lilya was a good name for a bear.

Mike then handed the baby blanket to Laura, who wrapped it around Katya. The child sniffed, and then buried her face in the new blanket and took a deep breath of her mother's perfume before she dropped it back around her and spun into Laura. She flung her arms around her mother's neck and took another breath of perfume. Then she pulled back and smiled at her before turning to shyly smile at Mike.

The new family visited for another hour through the translator. There were no awkward silences or tears, just parents and child getting to know each other and savoring the moment they had all waited so long for. Laura pulled out family photos and showed Katya pictures of her brothers and her grandma. Marik translated everything. "I now have a grandmother?" Katya squealed in Russian as she took the picture from Laura and stared at it just inches from her face, trying to memorize every feature.

The view out the second story window to the west was beautiful that evening as the sun was setting, casting shades of orange, pink, and purple against the frozen snow. It was about halfway down the horizon when Laura pointed it out to Katya.

"Do you know where the sun is going?" she asked through Marik.

Katya shook her head.

"When the sun goes down in Russia, it comes up in America." Marik explained to Katya what her mother was saying. "So, when the sun is going down, we can blow kisses to the sun and it will take our love to our family in America." Katya's eyes danced at the possibility. "Would you like to blow kisses for the sun to take to your brothers and grandmother?"

Katya nodded shyly. Mike took her by the hand and helped her to slide off Laura's lap. Father and daughter walked hand in hand to the window, where they stopped and he stooped down next to her. Then the two of them raised their fingers to their lips and blew kisses for the sun to take to America.

"Now," Laura explained through Marik, "when the sun goes down in America, the sun comes up in Russia. When you get up in the morning and the sun is coming up, it will bring love and kisses from your family in America." Katya understood. Suddenly the world seemed like a much smaller place and Amérika seemed not so far away. Her family had been right there all along. She just needed to get their love from the sun. Of course, it had always been there!

Katya continued to visit with her mama and papa until the sun was all the way below the horizon. Then Marik told her that it was time for them to go. He promised her that they would return the next morning for another visit, but she was still sad. Seeing her drooping face, and wanting to make her happy, Marik asked if she had a favorite candy.

"Chupa Chupee" came the reply.

"Her favorite candy is Chupa Chups," he told Mike and Laura. "Do you have this candy in America too?"

They both nodded.

"We can buy some of these Chupa Chup suckers on the way here tomorrow and bring them to her, don't you think?"

"Yeah, sure!" Mike responded.

Marik looked back down at Katya. "How many Chupa Chups do you want them to bring you?" he asked. "One? Two? Three?" He held up the appropriate number of fingers with each increase.

Katya hesitated for only a second. They all laughed as she held up all ten fingers.

Laura grabbed Katya's hand and the group walked down the stairs to the playroom. Marik stuck his head through the door and summoned the workers who graciously came out to say goodbye and to take Katya back with the other children. The workers both spoke through the translator and expressed their excitement and pleasure that Katya was going to such good parents. It was very obvious that she was going to a home where she would be well loved and cared for, they said.

"*Desvidania*" the workers said cheerfully as Mike and Laura started to leave. "*Pah-ká pah-ká.*"

"Goodbye! See you tomorrow!" they replied.

"*Pah-ká pah-ká, Mama. Pah-ká pah-ká, Papa.*" Katya was telling her new parents that she would see them soon.

"*Pah-ká pah-ká, Preens-yessa*" Mike called back. But it was too late. Katya had already disappeared behind the door, eager to tell her friends all about her exciting day.

"Good night, Darling," Laura said softly as they turned and walked toward the painted metal doors.

13

Nothing is Certain Until it Happens

"So, do you like Katya?" Marik asked before the SUV had even left the camp driveway.

"Of course we like her!" Laura exclaimed. Both she and Mike were taken aback that he would even ask such a question.

"And you, Mike, you like her too?"

"Yes, of course! She's everything I ever imagined. She's a little princess."

"Good. Good. Then you both like Katya. So, you still want to adopt Katya?"

"Well, of course we want to adopt her!" Laura said. Both she and Mike were puzzled with Marik's questions. They had agreed to adopt Katya long before being invited to visit her, and the way that Marik probed made everything seem less certain, less complete. Mike took a moment to think. The reality was that nothing in Russia was certain. Nothing was certain until it actually happened. With a pit in his stomach, he realized that Katya would not really be theirs until the plane touched down somewhere outside of Russia after their second trip.

"Marik, somehow I must have misunderstood something. Laura and I were under the impression that we had already agreed to adopt Katya before we left the United States," Mike said, strongly enough to let the translator know that he was uneasy with the conversation.

"Oh, yes. You did agree to adopt her. But you can change your mind. Parents must meet the child and see if the child is what they really want. If not, then changes can be made. You can change your mind any time you want."

But what bothered Mike was what was *not* being said. No commitments already made from *either* side held water. Anyone on the Russian side could also change their mind, and a different child could be substituted. *The Russians could change their minds any time they wanted to, as well.* Mike was becoming agitated. It reminded him of Japanese business negotiations. He remembered how miserably he had failed in his first experience in that land; he actually thought people said what they meant. But no. People said what they assumed the other person wanted to hear. It was the job of the listener to understand that the speaker would do whatever was in his best interest, whether or not it was consistent with the agreement.

"Marik, please forgive me for being so forward. But if I understand this conversation, it seems like you are saying that the adoption is not a sure thing. It seems to me that if you are saying that we can change our minds, you are also saying that others can change their minds, too. Please be honest with us and help us to understand. Have commitments been made? Is it a sure thing that we can adopt Katya?"

"It is pretty much a sure thing," Marik replied. "Of course, if the orphanage or social worker does not like the parents, they would recommend against adoption. But I can tell. The workers really like you. You have no worry about that."

"I feel so relieved," Mike said with just a slight note of sarcasm. "We don't have to worry about the orphanage workers stopping this. So tell me Marik, what exactly do we have to worry about?"

Marik was used to working with Americans and he understood their uneasiness when things were not in their control. He had become very good at telling the truth while steering away from all the things that could go wrong. Americans would never be able to understand the uncertainty with which Russians lived their everyday lives. Russians were accustomed to expecting the worst and being happy if it turned out better. They didn't *hope* for the worst, but they were prepared to deal with it if it came. Americans, on the other hand, had a different, often foolish, philosophy: don't just hope for the best—*plan* on it. But, Marik noticed, Mike was a little different than most Americans; different even than his wife. He could deal with the truth even if he didn't like it. That is, as long as he knew what the truth was.

"Okay," Marik said, adopting a businesslike tone. "I will tell you the truth. I will tell you what you have to worry about. It is very likely that you will adopt Katya, but there are still things that could go wrong. First, remember that the judge has the final say. Until the judge makes a decision in your favor, it is not a sure thing."

"We understand that," Mike said quickly. "What else?"

"You are not going to like what I tell you now, but I think that it will help you to understand better. It is the regional Minister of Education that oversees adoption. Each region has its own Minister of Education who determines adoption regulations in that area, and the minister's office can change regulations at any time. You have already had a bad experience with this." In his rearview mirror, Marik noticed Laura wince at the memory of their first adoption effort. "Things like this happen in Russia. I wish I could change that. But it is just a fact. Part of the problem is that the minister's staff does not deal directly with the parents or children. As difficult as it may be for you to understand, they really don't think it matters which child goes home with you, as long as you get one that fits your description. If you don't get the child you have chosen, then you can have a different one."

Mike and Laura were clearly having a hard time with this. Marik could see it in the way they looked at each other. He went on: "But I can tell you that it is very unlikely that anything will go wrong. Sasha and I work with adoptions every day. I am certain you will adopt Katya. But understand that there may be delays. Things never move as quickly as everyone wants. Sometimes there are delays for small reasons. Sometimes there are delays for no good reasons. But for the most part, the system works."

Mike looked over at Laura, whose wide eyes made her look like a deer caught in headlights. "Thanks for your honesty, Marik. It's still difficult, but now at least it makes a little bit more sense to me."

Laura didn't know what to say. Maybe this brutal honesty was Mike's way of dealing with it, but she always did better hoping for the best and then working toward her goal. For her, knowing all of the things that could go wrong only made climbing a mountain seem impossible. She did better focusing on one step at a time, always assuming that the summit of the mountain was reachable. This way, when she reached the top, she could look back, amazed at the accomplishment. Mike, on the other hand, had to see the whole mountain from the beginning. He had to know everything that could go wrong. He had to be aware of every crevasse, rock slide, and dead-end ledge, even if they weren't in his intended path. To Laura, this seemed crazy. Knowing all the pitfalls, seeing the whole mountain, how could you even begin to climb?

But she and Mike were complementary, not identical. That's what made them such a great team. Where one was weak, the other was strong. It had always been that way. Knowing about the instability of the Russian adoption process didn't help Laura in any way, but she could understand that, for some strange reason, Mike needed to know. If it helped Mike deal with the situation, she could allow that. But for herself, she wished Marik would have kept his mouth shut.

Marik felt good about giving Mike straight answers, even though it would cause uneasiness for the rest of the trip. But there was no reason to dwell on what might or could go wrong. It was time to find another topic of conversation. "We have you staying at the Hyundai Hotel in Vladivostok. It is a very nice hotel. I'm sure that you will like it. I had them reserve a room overlooking the bay. The view will be incredible."

"Thank you," Mike replied. "We look forward to it. So, is Vladivostok's economy built on shipping?"

"Shipping is a very big part of the economy here. Our geographic and political situation here is unique. You see, we are very near North Korea and China, and we have free trade with both countries. But we also have free trade with Japan and South Korea. We are about the only ones who deal with everyone. But during the cold war, things were different. Vladivostok was the main port for the Soviet Pacific Fleet. It was a top secret place with the most advanced Soviet weaponry, ships, and submarines. During those times it would have been unimaginable to have you and Laura—Americans—staying in a top floor of the Hyundai Hotel overlooking the bay!"

"Yeah, I guess!" Mike exclaimed. "Fifteen years ago I never would have guessed I would be in a city that was home to one of the largest Soviet Naval bases. What a time to live, huh? I think the world has changed more in my lifetime than during any other lifespan in history."

"I think that's true," Marik agreed as he bypassed a line of cars waiting to turn left at an intersection. "We are only a few minutes from the hotel." He pulled up next to two other cars also waiting to turn left, then he took the first opening and surged left across the highway while the other cars continued to wait.

Mike raised one eyebrow as he looked at Laura. She just shrugged her shoulders. Marik caught the exchange in the rearview mirror. "That turn wasn't exactly legal. But you could wait forever for these people to make left turns. It's better to bend the law and get to where you're going in a reasonable amount of time."

"Do they have very many traffic police here?" Mike asked.

"Oh yes, of course they do. But usually you can just pay them."

"Really? There's no penalty if you try to bribe them?"

"Technically, it is not legal to offer them money. And if they pull you over, they don't exactly ask for money and you don't exactly offer to give them money; but both sides know what is expected. You see, I can get the ticket and then spend a day at the court paying the ticket, or I can spend the same amount of money and not waste a whole day. It's better for me and it's better for the policeman. Everyone here knows that the government doesn't pay the police enough money to survive, so they have to do things like this to make enough money." Marik shrugged. "Even the government knows it. A while back, the government decided to prosecute a person and a policeman for bribery, but there was a huge public outcry. It was all over the news. They said that everybody knows that the police have to take money and everybody knows that there isn't enough time for people to go to traffic court, so the government should just leave it alone."

"So what happened?"

"I don't know. After a while we just stopped hearing about it. I guess they must have dropped it."

They drove over a hill and the bay came into sight. The lights of the city, built on hills surrounding the bay, reflected off the water. It was a spectacular sight. "The hotel is just up the road. See, I told you it's a beautiful view."

"It's incredible," Laura concurred.

Marik helped the Knights get their luggage into the lobby and waited to make sure that all was well as they checked in. "So, you have your room alright?"

"Yes, everything is great. Thanks so much for all of your help, and thank you for such an incredible experience today," Mike added as he extended his hand to shake Marik's.

"Yes, Marik," Laura added. "Today was one of the most wonderful days of my life. Thank you."

"You're welcome," he smiled. "It's just what I do. Don't worry too much. Everything will be fine with Katya. You will be able to take her home before you know it. Just wait and see." Laura brightened as she shook his hand. "How about if I pick you up at nine tomorrow morning so we can go to visit Katya again?"

"Sure. Nine o'clock is great. We'll see you here in the lobby," Mike replied. With that, Marik gave them a friendly nod and headed out the revolving door.

14

The End of a Long Day

"Whew! What a day!" Mike said as he fell backwards, spread-eagle on the bed.

"Oh, my gosh! That was just too much stress for one day!" Laura added. "I thought that woman at the airport was going to make us go back home because we had the wrong visa. Didn't you think she was going to make us go back?"

"Well, I didn't think she was going to be as easy on us as she was, but I was pretty sure that she wasn't going to make us go back."

"Why not? She looked pretty serious to me."

"Oh, she was serious, there's no doubt about that. But remember what Marik told us about the police?"

"You mean the bribes?"

"Yeah. It's just a way of life over here. I think the woman in the airport wanted a sincere apology. She got one. If it wasn't sincere enough, I'm sure that she would have taken us to a more discrete place where we could have made a more sincere apology. Two hundred bucks probably would have been sincere enough, but I was willing to be at least five hundred sincere."

"This is just so strange."

"I know what you mean. I've done a lot of traveling and every place has its own little peculiarities. But I've never been anywhere that feels like this."

Laura plopped down on the bed next to Mike and they both looked up at the ceiling. "Wasn't Katya wonderful?"

"It was a dream," Mike said softly. "No one has stolen my heart like that since you did. She's just so perfect, so happy, such a pleasant child. How could she still be like that after everything she's gone through?"

"I'm sure it has a lot to do with her personality. But I also think she's responding to her earlier abuse. I know about these things, Mike. Children blame themselves for the abuse. They think that if they could just be good enough, or smart enough, or pretty enough, the abuser wouldn't want to hurt them anymore, or the neglectful parent would finally have enough reason to pay attention to them."

"So she's being nice so we won't hurt her?"

"She's just trying hard to be good enough. I'm sure she doesn't think that we're going to hurt her, ever. But she wants to be good enough for us to accept her. If she is pleasant enough, and pretty enough, and happy enough, and if she smiles enough, maybe we will like her enough to want her for a daughter."

Tears welled up in Mike's eyes. "She shouldn't have to feel like that. No one should."

"They shouldn't have to, but often they do. It's sad, but true. That's how it affected me."

Mike wiped the tears from the side of his face. "I just want Katya to be happy because she's happy."

"I think she is, at her core, a happy child. But just realize that there *are* effects of abuse. There will come a day when she tests us to see if our love is really unconditional. It won't be because she's disobedient, or because she doesn't love us. She will just find it hard to believe that we really love her for who she is and not just for what she does."

"That should be enjoyable," he replied sarcastically. "How long will that bliss continue?"

"It's hard to say. Everybody is different. But Katya is young. I'm sure it will involve tantrums and pouting. But I know we'll get through it. She truly seems to be a happy child. I'm sure that she'll be a joy to have in the home."

"Well, if she comes out of the abuse as well as you did, I can't imagine a daughter that I would rather have."

"Thanks!" Laura said as she rolled over and kissed him on the cheek. "I'm going to grab a shower before we go down to dinner, if it's okay with you."

15

Tell Me about Your Mama

"Come, Zaichunook," Sofia said pleasantly as she held out her hand. "I want to talk with you before it's time to go to bed."

Katya beamed as she took Sofia's hand and followed her up the stairs and into the dormitory. Sofia sat on the edge of Katya's bed and boosted the child onto her lap. "So, now you are a princess, are you?" Sofia teased.

"My papa calls me princess," Katya said excitedly. "Do you think that he really thinks that I'm a princess?"

"I'm sure he *knows* that you're *his* princess. But my, what an eventful day you have had. Tell me about your mama."

"She is so pretty! And she's nice, too!"

"And your papa, how do you like him?"

"He's nice, too. He gave me candy, and a biscuit, and look!" Katya dove under her pillow and retrieved the stuffed bear and blanket. "Mama and Papa gave me this bear and blanket. The bear smells like Papa and the blanket smells like Mama!" She alternated her face between the two items, taking a deep breath from each. "I named my bear Lilya!"

"Lilya is a fine name for a bear. Did you name her after your friend at the orphanage?" Lilya was a fifteen year-old girl at the orphanage who had taken little Katya under her wing. She loved to teach Katya how to dance and to act like a teenager. Katya really loved her.

"Yes, I named her after Lilya," Katya replied.

"What a wonderful gift! So, what did you talk about with Papa and Mama?"

"Papa didn't talk very much and both of them only speak the funny talk from Amérika. But Marik would tell me what they said."

"Well tell me, little one, what did your mama have Marik tell you?"

"She said that I have two brothers in Amérika, and a grandmother. I have a grandmother, Sofia! And lots of cousins and aunts and uncles!"

"How wonderful! What a fine family you will have!"

"And we have a dog named Dasha and two horses!"

"Horses? How fascinating! What are the horses named?"

"I don't remember. They have strange names from Amérika. But one of them is very old. Mama said that the old one likes to let little children ride on his back!"

"How exciting! Not only are you now a princess, it looks as if you will be a cowgirl, too!"

"Mama showed me pictures of our house. My bedroom is blue and white. It has butterflies on the walls and ceiling!"

"Butterflies? How beautiful!"

"Yes!" Katya squealed. "Mama showed me a picture of the kitchen where she cooks and where we will eat. There is a basket on the table with all kinds of fruits in it. Mama said I can have fruit from the basket any time I want! Marik asked me what my favorite fruit was and I told him pears. He asked Mama if there were pears in the basket and she said that there would always be pears there for me!"

"Well, who could ask for more than all of that? It sounds like a fairytale come true!" Sofia loved watching Katya beam as she squeezed her new bear to her chest. "So, what else did Mama and Papa have to say?"

"Mama said that when the sun goes down in Russia, it comes up in Amérika!"

"Yes, dear one, this is true."

"And Mama said that when the sun goes down in Amérika, it comes up in Russia. She said that we could blow kisses to the sun and that the sun would take our love to my brothers and grandmother in Amérika!"

"So did you blow kisses to the sun?"

"Yes! Papa and I went to the window and we blew kisses to the sun, so now my brothers and my grandmother can get my love for them!"

"They must be so happy!"

"Mama said that when I go to Amérika, I can blow kisses to the sun, and it will bring my love to my friends in Russia!" Tears began to well in the young caregiver's eyes. She tried to hold them back. "I will always blow kisses to the sun for you, Sofia."

Just then the door burst open and twenty-three other children came barreling through. Sofia turned toward them just in time for Katya to miss the tears leaving her eyes and rolling down her cheeks. "Calm down, children," she said as they ran to their beds. She wiped the tears from her face before turning back to Katya. She smiled brightly and said: "I will always blow kisses to you, too, Zaichunook. Good night."

She got up and quickly made her way to the door. Tears started streaming down her face again. "I'm sorry," she said sincerely to the other worker who had just walked into the room. "This is silly. I shouldn't be like this. But would you please take care of getting the children to bed without me tonight?"

"But of course, Sofia," her colleague responded. "I'd be happy to. Have a good night. I'll see you tomorrow."

"Thank you," Sofia said as she slipped past her friend into the hall.

Sofia was very happy for Katya. She was a good judge of character and she sensed that the two Americans would be wonderful parents for her little friend. She knew that this was exactly what she had prayed for, but it wasn't until now that she realized how much Katya's beautiful smile and large dimples brightened her days, and how much she would miss her little Zaichunook when the child finally went home.

16

Orphans, Just Like Other Kids

"Good morning!" Laura said as she and Mike walked past the Ericksons, who were seated in the restaurant having breakfast.

"Good morning," they echoed. "Please, sit here with us," Doug said as he stood up a just little and held out his hand to the empty chairs across the table.

"Thank you," Mike replied. "That sounds like a great offer. Not many people will eat with us anymore," he joked as he and Laura slid into their chairs. The Ericksons laughed as the Knights adjusted their napkins and silverware.

"Did you guys get to visit your baby girl yesterday?" Laura asked.

"Yes," Michelle replied. "Sasha took us to her orphanage and we spent the day with her."

"How was it? Did she still remember you?"

"I don't know. She was a little cold at first, but after an hour or so she warmed right up. But it was so good to see her again! I never knew how long three months could be! That was the hardest thing..." She suddenly caught herself. "Oh, I'm sorry. I shouldn't be saying that to you guys; here you are on your *first* trip. How rude of me!"

"Oh no," Laura quickly responded. "We never had any doubts that the wait would be the hardest part. Don't worry about it."

"So, how did your first meeting go?" Michelle asked.

Laura excitedly detailed the events of the visit. Everyone had to wipe tears from their eyes as she told the part about Katya hugging her and sobbing in her arms.

"Isn't it just emotionally draining?" Doug asked, more a comment than a question.

"It is!" Mike answered. "It is the most extreme in emotional highs and lows that I could ever imagine. I mean the whole process—sending in papers, re-doing papers, waiting for referrals, getting pictures, waiting for travel invitations, meeting the child, and knowing that we're going to have to leave her in a few days. Laura and I are emotional wrecks."

"We know exactly how you feel," Doug replied. "Been there, done that, bought the T-shirt."

"I think it's been worse for you guys, though," Michelle added. "Sasha told us yesterday what happened with your first selection. That must have been tough."

"It was a real heartbreaker," Laura admitted. "I mean, they send you pictures, you accept the child, you really feel like that baby is yours. Then you get the phone call. I was devastated."

"How did you deal with it?" Michelle asked.

"At first I didn't. I almost felt like my baby had died." Tears filled her eyes as she recalled her feelings, and Michelle began to cry as well. "It was Mike who reminded me that we were both sure that God had a particular child in mind for our family, one that was supposed to be in our family all along. So, if we *had* agreed to take a different child, giving up the place of the one that was intended for us, we should *expect* Him to intervene and correct the situation. Of course, that's what happened. Now, I couldn't imagine our child being anyone but Katya."

"What a wonderful way to look at it," Michelle said quietly as she wiped the tears from her face.

Doug tenderly put his arm around his wife and gently changed the subject. "So does she keep her Russian name, or are you going to change it?"

"We struggled with that one," Mike responded. "But we finally decided to give her an American first name, and keep her Russian first name as a middle name. At that point, we decided to name her Sarah Ekaterina. But it didn't flow right, so I guess the final verdict is Sarah Katerina."

"That's nice," Michelle commented thoughtfully. "Sarah Katerina. I like that."

"But Mike didn't tell you the sweet part," Laura began. "He always calls little girls 'Princess' and they just light up when he does. He has waited for years to have his own little princess; so when we finally started considering names, Mike wanted to name her Sarah. Sarah is Hebrew, for Princess."

"Oh! How sweet!" Michelle exclaimed.

"Princess Katerina. I guess we don't have to wonder if *that* little girl will get spoiled," Doug joked.

"Who could pull a little girl out of an orphanage and *not* spoil her, at least just a little?" Mike countered.

"I know. I feel the same way," Doug admitted.

"I shudder to think of our little baby girl and her daddy," Michelle chimed in. "He'll spoil her rotten."

They all laughed. "Well, enough about us; tell us about your little treasure," Laura prompted.

"Well, her Russian name is Alexandra, and they call her Sashka at the orphanage. We're going to name her Alexa Ann."

"That's pretty. Alexa Ann. I really like that," Laura added. "So how were you guys able to get hold of a young one?"

"Green ears," the couple spoke out in unison.

"Excuse me?" Mike asked. This had to be some kind of a joke.

"Well, here," Doug said while handing Mike a photograph. "This is the first picture of her they sent to us."

Laura slid closer to Mike so that she could see, too.

"Holy Cow!" Mike exclaimed. Laura kicked him hard under the table. "I'm sorry. I just…well, when you said green, I didn't think you meant bright emerald green!"

Michelle and Doug both laughed. "Yeah, we were a little startled, ourselves. It couldn't be a birthmark, especially with it being on both ears. The medical reports called it a rash. We finally figured it must have been something they were using to *treat* the rash, so we decided to move forward."

"So, is that what it was?" Laura asked anxiously.

"Yep," Michelle responded. "Turns out it was just some form of iodine! The color will go away before long. But when other people saw pictures of her, they immediately turned to other children. We like to think of it as the little mark God gave her to save her for us."

"How wonderful," Laura responded. "So are you off to see her again today?"

"Absolutely. Visiting today, court tomorrow. How about you guys? Are you visiting Katya again today?"

"We are," Laura responded. "Marik and Sasha are picking us up."

The couples sat, visiting and making small talk for another few minutes before the waiter came and took the meal coupons.

"Well, I guess we're off to get our things," Doug said while pushing back his chair and standing up.

"It was so nice visiting with you," Michelle added as she stood up and gathered her coat and purse. Enjoy your breakfast."

"Thank you," Mike and Laura replied in unison.

The four stood at the table and shook hands, and then the Ericksons left while the Knights took their seats and prepared to order breakfast.

"They said we can go into the room and play with Katya and the other children," Sasha said after returning from the security point. "This is a little unusual. Most times they don't let you interact with other children. In fact, technically, it's forbidden. This might be a good opportunity for you to see how Katya does with other children. But if you want Katya alone, we can arrange for that instead."

Mike looked at Laura and waited for her to decide. "I think we should see her around the other children," she said.

They followed Marik and Sasha down the hall to the large double doors that Katya had come through the night before. As they entered, they saw a few dozen children scattered throughout the room, involved in various activities. Laura was quite taken with the room as she glanced around. The walls were covered with murals of scenes from Russian fairytales. It was really quite elaborate, not at all what she expected.

"Mama!" Katya squealed from a corner of the room behind Mike and Laura.

Laura twirled just in time to stoop as the rushing child threw her arms around her. Laura squeezed her and then picked her up. "I missed you," she said to Katya. Sasha was right there to translate.

"She said that she missed you too."

"*Ee Papa*," Katya continued.

"And Papa," came the translation.

"Good morning, *Preens-yessa*," Mike said. He wished that he had spent more time learning a few phrases in Russian.

Katya squirmed in Laura's arms indicating that she wanted to get down, so Laura gave her a squeeze and set her on the floor. Katya immediately ran to Mike, who scooped her up and hugged her as she squeezed him around his neck. Katya began to jabber to him in Russian. All he could do was smile and wonder.

Marik chuckled. "She wants to know if you have more of the biscuits you gave her last night, so that she can share them with her friends," he translated.

"Laura, how many Rice Krispy Treats did we bring?" Mike quizzed, already knowing that it wouldn't be enough.

Laura laughed. "Forget it. But I packed several bags of the mini candy bars, you know, the trick-or-treat kind."

"That'll do," Mike replied in a relieved tone. "Marik, please tell my little princess that we don't have enough 'biscuits,' but we do have candy bars."

Laura immediately began digging through the backpack while Marik translated. The words were hardly out of his mouth before Katya began squirming to get down again. She ran to Laura, who handed her the two opened bags, then began jabbering loudly in Russian to the other children.

This was the first chance that Mike and Laura had to see the personalities of the other children. There was the obvious bully and several of his friends who pushed their way to the front. "Somebody needs some Ritalin," Laura said in a mischievously sweet tone as she handed the boys their candy. There were aggressive types, playful types, nervous types, and even one that could only be described as severely depressed. She was brought forward by one of the orphanage workers after all of the others had received their treats. The sad little girl never even looked up as Katya placed a candy bar in her hand. As the child turned to walk away, the orphanage worker stopped her. The caregiver spoke softly several times to the child, who barely acknowledged her presence. It was obvious that the worker was trying to get the child to say 'thank you.' After several attempts, the little girl finally responded: "*Spa-see-ba*" she said softly, without looking up.

"*Pah-zah-lou-sta,*" Mike responded. He had picked up that word only seconds before, hearing the response Katya was giving as the other children thanked her. He patted the sad little child's head and, for the first time, she looked up from the floor and into Mike's face. What Mike saw horrified him. The girl's blue eyes were almost hidden by her pupils. As he looked into them, he saw an emptiness that he had never witnessed before. This was not a child that was just sad or discouraged. The emptiness seemed to go clear through her soul. Without making even the slightest facial expression, she looked back down at the floor and walked away.

Several minutes later, Mike noticed the depressed little girl sitting in a chair, staring at the still unwrapped candy. Laura and Katya were busy walking around the room with the translators, getting to know the other children and caregivers. Mike walked over next to the child and touched her on the shoulder. She didn't respond.

"So, do you come here often?" he asked softly, knowing that no matter what he said, she wouldn't understand anyway. "Mind if I sit down? Can I buy you a candy bar?"

Still no response.

"Can I open that candy for you?" He asked as he reached for the bar. The child didn't move. He started to reach for the treat when she simply let it fall out of her hand into his. Mike slowly opened the candy bar for her while speaking soothingly. He pulled the chocolate from the wrapper and placed it back in her hand, but she didn't even acknowledge it was there. He even had to bend her limp fingers around the bar so that it didn't fall. The depressed little girl just continued to look off into space.

"That's good candy, Sweetheart," Mike said softly. "You should try it." He gently lifted her hand to her mouth and put the chocolate to her lips. There was still no response. She didn't open her mouth. Mike tenderly lowered her hand back down and began to stroke her hair. "I'm sorry, little one. I have no idea what you've been through, but I am so sorry. I wish I could take away the pain." He reached down and gently pulled her toward him. She flopped against him like a wet rag, still not even acknowledging his presence. Mike continued to speak soothingly to the little girl while holding her against him and stroking her hair with his other hand.

After a while, a pretty, young orphanage worker walked over to Mike and the little girl. "*Spa-see-ba,*" she said sincerely.

"*Pah-zah-lou-sta,*" Mike responded.

"Me Sofia."

"It's a pleasure. I'm Mike."

"You good man. You love childs. Katya be happy. Katya have good mama ee papa. I happy for Katya."

"*Spa-see-ba,*" Mike replied.

"*Pah-zah-lou-sta.*"

Marik approached. "The children are going out to play in the snow," he informed Mike. "Laura said she is going out with them. I guess you want to come, too?"

"Outside? You've got to be kidding! It must be twenty below outside!"

"Oh, no. It's minus eighteen, that would be about zero, Fahrenheit," Marik replied.

"Maybe on the thermometer, but those winds coming off the bay are *cold.* With wind-chill it must be minus 20."

Marik paused in thought. "Yes, with wind-chill, you might be right. Minus 20 Fahrenheit is about minus 30 Celsius. That sounds about right."

"And the children are going out to play?"

"Sure. They're used to it. Besides, this is winter camp. You don't go to winter camp to stay indoors the whole time."

"Alright," Mike hesitated. "I'm no sissy. If they're going out, then so am I."

Outside, Mike watched several boys run to a small storage shed and retrieve half a dozen eighteen-inch square sheets of old, soft vinyl floor covering, the kind that you might see in a kitchen or bathroom. The boys were immediately surrounded by other children who wanted first turn with the curious squares. Mike was puzzled. He couldn't figure what the excitement was over a few pieces of floppy old worn out vinyl.

One of the caregivers barked at the children in Russian, and though Mike didn't understand the words, it was obvious that she had told the children to gather near her at the top of a gentle sloping hill, about three meters high and stretching outward fifteen meters or so. Katya was excited, and dragged her parents toward the caregiver, jabbering quickly in Russian.

"I'm sorry, Sweetheart. I wish I knew what you were saying," Laura replied. Katya sighed in frustration. Sofia came to the rescue.

"She want her turn," she said in her thick Russian accent. "Watch, they have much fun."

About then, one of the boys put his piece of vinyl slick-side down on the snow and sat on it diagonally. He pulled the corner in front up between his legs, picked up his feet, and slid down the hill. Five other children quickly followed.

Mike laughed. While many things about the Russians frustrated him, he completely admired their adaptability, their way of making use of whatever they had. "What a brilliant improvisation," he said to Laura. "American kids couldn't have more fun with a fifty dollar sled! Who would have imagined?"

"I've got to get this on tape," she smiled back. She called back toward the building entrance. "Marik! Is it okay for us to video the children sledding?"

Marik walked over to the couple. "It is okay for you to video Katya. But it is forbidden for you to make pictures or video of the other children."

Laura dropped her head in disappointment. "However," the Russian continued, "If you accidentally got some of the other children in the video while you were filming Katya, I don't think it would be a big problem." He tilted his head toward her with a strange expression on his face; the Russian equivalent of a wink. Laura smiled as she pulled the camcorder from her bag and handed it to Mike. "Please," Marik added, "Don't be obvious." Mike hurried down the hill, tromping through snow halfway up to his knees.

By now, the first of the vinyl riders were reaching the top of the hill, sleds in hand. "*Dai-ee! Dai-ee! Meen-Ya! Dai-ee!*" The fifteen or so children at the top of the hill almost overwhelmed the riders, all trying to be the next to get a sled.

Mike filmed Katya sliding down the hill and continued to record as she raced back up to pass off her sled. Katya passed off the sled to one of the boys, and Mike pretended to be filming her at the top of the hill while he recorded the new boy coming down. As the sled reached the bottom of the hill, the six year-old orphan picked up the square of vinyl and ran straight to Mike, jabbering in Russian. Mike, still recording, stooped down and showed the little boy the orphans at the top of the hill on the camera's LCD screen. The little boy squealed with excitement. "*Dai-ee!*" he yelled, holding out his hand.

"Sorry, kid. You can't hold it," Mike replied as he stood back up. The little boy called to his friends, pointing to the camera while jumping up and down. In no time, Mike found himself surrounded by little orphans, all clamoring for a look at the fascinating high-tech gizmo. "*Dai-ee! Dai-ee! Meen-Yá! Ee-Dai-ee!*" they all screamed reaching upward for the video recorder. One even started to climb his leg. *So much for not being obvious,* Mike thought.

"Let me guess," he called over to Marik, "'*Meen-Yá*' means 'My turn' and '*Dai-ee*' means 'Give it to me.'"

Marik laughed. "You're pretty close," he yelled back down the hill. "You'll be speaking Russian in no time!"

Swarmed by a growing knot of children, Mike held the camcorder higher and looked toward the top of the hill, where Laura was now holding Katya and laughing at him. "What am I supposed to do now?" he shouted up at her.

"Sorry! You're on your own!" she yelled back, still laughing.

Then Mike had an idea. He reached up with his other hand and reversed the viewfinder on the camera to point the same direction as the lens while he directed the camera down at the orphans. The children now saw themselves on the miniature screen. *Oohs* and *aahs* now replaced the *My-turn* and *Give-me* screams. Everyone wanted to see *themselves* on the screen. He was able to get the children to spread out a little as he slowly panned the camera back and forth. Then Mike grouped the children tighter together and stepped forward, kneeling down in the middle of them. He held out the camera as far away as he could and pointed it toward the laughing group, who were excited to be on camera with the strange man from Amérika.

As he interacted with the children, he thought about how he would love to take them all out of the orphanage and give them a home. But then, he thought, the only difference would be the location of the orphanage. These kids needed reasonably sized family settings with loving parents. He began to think of all of the people he knew who had considered having one more child, but had never done it. Somewhere along the way, they crossed some vague, imperceptible line that said it was too late for them to raise another child. *If only they could look into the eyes of these children*, he thought. Maybe it was too late to start with a newborn, but it wasn't too late to start with a seven year-old. If only they could taste just a hint of what he and Laura had experienced the moment they met Katya, they would see that adoption would bring them far more joy and happiness than a few extra years of retirement ever could.

If only they could see. Parents change the world every day. Parents are the guides for those who will build the future. So much potential would go untapped as these children wasted away in orphanages.

It wasn't that the children were treated badly. Mike was amazed at how much the workers cared for the children and how much the children loved the workers. They reminded him of his kindergarten teacher, Miss Peterson, a pretty new teacher right out of college, who loved every child in her class so much that they all thought they were her favorite. All of the boys from his class fought over who was going to marry her when they grew up. But then she broke their hearts when she brought her "special friend" to class near the end of the school year. The news was devastating: Miss Peterson would become *Mrs.* Cavanaugh over the summer vacation. Mike saw the same close relationships between the orphanage workers and the children. These children knew that they were loved.

Mike turned off the camera and put it away in a deep coat pocket. There were protests, but soon the children scattered and returned to their play. Mike and Laura continued to watch Katya and the others for another fifteen minutes, then one of the workers called the children together and started herding them toward the building. Katya held out her arms to Mike and he picked her up. Laura walked alongside, holding one of Katya's hands.

"It's time for the children to eat," Marik explained to Mike and Laura. "I think that we should go in and say goodbye to

Katya. We'll come back and see her tomorrow."

Mike and Laura, though disappointed, both nodded in agreement. They entered the building and went back into the playroom, where the children began to remove their coats, hats, and gloves. But Katya noticed that her parents-to-be were not removing their coats. She didn't like that at all, so she wrinkled up her face into a sulking pout and ran to them, whining in Russian.

"Mama and Papa have to leave now," Marik explained to her in Russian. "But we will come back tomorrow evening."

Katya responded to him, still whining in Russian. "She says she wants you to stay, or she wants to go with you," he explained to Mike and Laura. They both smiled weakly and looked at each other as tears welled up in Laura's eyes.

"Give Mama and Papa a hug and we'll be back tomorrow," Marik told the little girl.

"*Nee Ha-Choó!*" She turned her back to her parents.

"Okay, you don't have to hug them. But we have to go," Marik continued in Russian as he turned his back and started toward the door.

"*Nyet! Yá Ha-Choó!*" she said firmly as she ran and wrapped her arms around Laura's legs. Laura picked her up and the two gave each other a long hug while Laura spoke soothingly in her ear.

"We'll be back tomorrow," she finally said, waiting for Marik to translate. "Papa needs a hug, too."

She handed Katya to Mike who grabbed her and held her tight. Katya wrapped her arms around his neck and jabbered to him in Russian while she hugged him. "She says she doesn't want you to go," Marik translated. "But she says that she is happy that you are coming back tomorrow."

"Ask Katya if she remembers what I promised to bring her yesterday," Mike said to Marik, who then spoke briefly to Katya in Russian. She paused momentarily, trying to remember, when all of a sudden the dimples returned.

"Chupa Chupee!"

"How many?" Marik asked.

"*DYEAS yets!*"

Mike placed Katya's feet back on the floor and reached

deep into his overcoat pockets with both hands. He pulled out all ten suckers, tucking the sticks one by one underneath the elastic belt of her skirt. Katya immediately removed one and asked him in Russian to open it, which he did before handing it back to her. Mike picked her up and sat her on one arm.

"I," he said in English.

"*Aye*" she repeated.

"Love," he continued.

"*Lub*," she mimicked.

"You," he finished.

"*Yoo*," she responded.

"Do you know what you just said?" Marik asked her in Russian. She shook her head. Marik explained to her that she and Mike had said "I love you" in English. Katya beamed. She threw her arms around Mike's neck and hugged him again and then pulled back and gave him a quick kiss on the lips.

"*Yá-Tibya-Lo-Bloo*," she said, and she hugged him again. *I love you*. Then she squirmed in his arms and held her arms out to Laura who took her from Mike.

"*Yá-Tibya-Lo-Bloo, Mama*," she said, and she leaned forward and kissed Laura on the lips.

"I love you too, Baby," Laura replied and she wrapped her arms around the little girl and held her tight for another minute. Then she put her back down on her feet. The sulking was over and the scowl had been replaced by the beautiful dimpled smile.

"*Pah-ká, Mama. Pah-ká, Papa*," she said and she turned to follow the other children to the cafeteria.

"*Pah-ká, pah-ká*," they both said in unison.

"Man, it sure is tough leaving her," Mike commented as they walked toward the exit.

"I just want to cry," Laura added.

"It's hard," Marik agreed. "But soon she will be yours."

Before they reached the outer door, Sasha entered the main hall and joined them. "Did you tell them yet?" she asked Marik in English.

"No. I thought I'd let you tell them."

"Tell us what?" Mike asked nervously.

"Oh, it's nothing bad. Don't worry. But Sasha has some information for you that you might find interesting. Let's go get some lunch. We can talk about it at the restaurant."

17

Astonishing Revelation

"So, what is this interesting information?" Mike asked as soon as the waitress gathered up the menus.

"Katya has a younger sister," Sasha replied hesitantly, not knowing how the Knights might react.

"What?" Mike asked, astonished. Laura sat silent, dumbfounded.

"Katya has a younger sister," Sasha repeated. "She's two years old. She lives at the Baby Hospital in Partizansk. In this area, all orphans under four live in Baby Hospitals. It's like a hospital and an orphanage combined. In fact, the Baby Hospital is where Katya lived until her burn healed."

"So they moved Katya away from her baby sister?" Laura asked in disbelief.

"Well, no, not exactly. Katya was taken from her mother because of her burn and other injuries. The mother was told that she needed to show some interest in the child and prove that she was a fit mother in order to get her back. But she never showed any interest. She never visited Katya, never even asked how she was doing. So the social workers began the process of terminating the mother's rights. About this time, they found out that the mother had five other children removed from her custody six years ago."

"Sad. I guess that's when they decided to remove Katya's younger sister, as well," Mike mused.

"Not right then. They didn't know about her."

"How could they not know about her?" Mike asked. "Isn't it their job to know?"

"I don't think you understand how difficult that would be. People like Katya's mother are very transient. She moved right after they took Katya out of the home, and she didn't re-register as required by law. I'm sure she did all she could to conceal the existence of the other daughter."

"Where do these parents come from?" Mike asked, not even trying to hide his contempt.

"Actually," Sasha responded quietly, "she came from the Partizansk Baby Home."

Mike turned sick. It was easy for him to sit there, self-righteously judging an unfit mother from the comfort of a typical middleclass American upbringing. But how could a person raised in an orphanage be expected to function in a family, much less succeed as a mother? Mike felt ashamed of himself for passing such hasty judgment.

"So what happened to the first five children?" Laura queried, interested in children more than circumstances.

"Four girls and an infant boy. The little boy was adopted right away, but the girls never were. They are in orphanages somewhere now. They range in age from thirteen to seven."

"What will happen to them?" Laura asked.

"I hate to say it," Sasha responded, "but most likely the same thing that happened to their mother. Russians almost never adopt children more than six months old. And Americans, as you well know, want children as young as they can get them."

"Could we adopt them?" Laura asked hastily.

"Hold on, Laura," Mike interjected, dragging her back to reality. "You're talking about adopting *six* children. Even if that were possible with our home, finances, and everything else, we're only cleared to adopt two children and we only planned on adopting one."

"Mike is correct," Sasha concurred. "You couldn't adopt the older children at this time, even if you wanted to. But that isn't what I wanted to talk about."

"The little sister," Laura said in a soft, pensive voice.

"Yes, the *little* sister."

"So why weren't we told about the little sister before?" Mike asked.

"She wasn't available. It took a while to get Katya's sister removed from the home, and, because of the six month waiting period, she was not available for international adoption until a few days ago."

"But she is available now?" Laura asked.

"Yes, she is. Would you like to meet her?"

"Of course!" Laura blurted without even really thinking. "I

mean, Mike, we do want to meet her, don't we?"

"Sure, I mean…yeah, I guess," Mike stammered.

"Okay," Sasha continued. "Her name is Luba. The Partizansk Baby Hospital is about three hours from here. Unfortunately, I have court with the Ericksons tomorrow, so I won't be able to go with you. But Marik can take you. Why don't you swing by the hotel now and pick up a change of clothes? That way you could visit Luba this afternoon and, if you're interested, stay in town and visit her again tomorrow morning. Then Marik could bring you back here in the afternoon to visit Katya."

18

Another Meeting

"I can't believe you are bringing so much for just one night!" Marik laughed as Mike hefted two full-sized suitcases into the back of the SUV.

"Marik," Mike smiled, "there are probably twenty outfits in these bags, and none of them fit me or Laura. Jeans and T-shirts, frilly dresses, sleepers and pajamas, underwear and socks, snowsuits and boots…and probably eight pairs of shoes." Mike could see the bewildered look on Marik's face. "All the clothes we bought when we thought we were adopting an infant. We'd like to give them to the Baby Hospital. Do you think that will be alright?"

"Yes, yes, of course," Marik responded. "Oksana will be very happy to get them. The orphanages can always use more clothes."

The ride to Partizansk was uneventful, and Mike found himself nodding off. Laura, the jetlag finally catching up to her, was completely asleep with her head against the window in the back seat. After a few hours they pulled off the main highway and started into town. Mike snapped awake, then yawned and stretched, apologizing to Marik for being such poor company.

"Don't worry about it," Marik said. "It's the middle of the night in Michigan."

Just then they hit a large pothole, shaking Laura from her sleep. "Are we there yet?" she joked, her eyes still closed.

"Almost," Marik replied. "We're only five minutes away."

That was enough to bring Laura fully alert. "Do they know we are coming?" she asked.

"Yes. We told the hospital that we were going to talk to you and that we might be coming down."

"Does Luba know we're coming?"

"They told her Katya's parents are coming to visit her. But she's only two and a half. We're not sure she even remembers Katya."

"Does Katya remember Luba?" Laura asked.

"Oh, of course," Marik responded. "But she doesn't talk about her very much. I think she doesn't want to risk getting too attached again. You can imagine."

The three sat quietly for the next few minutes, until Marik pulled up in front of a big building with sky-blue stucco and white window frames.

"Here it is," Marik announced, "The Partizansk Baby Hospital."

The trio stepped into the entrance of the building, where they were greeted by a pleasant, smiling woman.

"This is Oksana," Marik said. "She is the director and the doctor here at the Baby Hospital." They shook hands and exchanged a few polite words. Oksana spoke Russian for several seconds while looking at the couple and then she paused, waiting for Marik to translate. "Oksana says that she is happy that you are here to see Luba. She says that Luba is her favorite, and that she is a very smart and beautiful child. Oksana says she even thought about adopting Luba herself, but her husband has some health problems that make it impossible."

"Please tell Oksana that we are very excited to meet Luba," Laura responded. "Tell her that we just love Luba's sister, Katya, and we are sure that we will like Luba, too."

Marik quickly translated for Oksana and then listened as she responded. "Oksana says that she treated Katya's burn and broken arm when she came here. She says that she is happy that Katya is getting a family. Also, she says she is sure that you want to meet Luba now, so she will go to get her." When Marik finished, Oksana nodded politely and slipped out of the room.

The Russian doctor returned only seconds later holding the little girl, who wore a huge, shy smile. She had a very large pink ribbon tied up in her blonde hair and was wearing a blue corduroy dress with white tights, a white T-shirt, and the molded plastic sandal-shoes that all of the children in the orphanage wore. "*Prevét?*" *Hello?* Oksana coaxed her to say. "*Prevét?*"

But the little blonde girl just held her fist in front of her mouth, partially covering a huge smile. "She's a little bit shy at first," Oksana explained through Marik. "But she's a very happy and friendly child when she gets to know you."

Oksana continued to speak to the child in Russian. "She is telling her that you are Katya's mama and papa," Marik translated. "But I don't think that she understands. It seems that she doesn't remember Katya."

Oksana carried Luba over to Laura and held her out. Luba held out her arms and went to Laura smiling from ear to ear. Her perfect baby teeth were visible clear back to her molars, the smile was so big. "Oh, my goodness!" Laura exclaimed, her voice cracking as tears welled up in her eyes. "You are a little piece of heaven." Marik translated for Oksana who smiled and nodded her approval.

"Isn't she beautiful, Mike?" Laura asked as he came in close to hold her hand.

"She is beautiful," he responded. "*Preens-yessa,*" he said as he held out his hand. Luba grabbed his finger and smiled at him briefly before bashfully dropping it. She spun into Laura and laid her head on her shoulder, but she was only there for a moment before lifting her head and turning to look at Oksana.

"Mama!" Luba shouted, and she spun back to Laura and laid her head against her shoulder again. The group was surprised.

Oksana began to speak quickly in Russian. "Oksana says she told Luba that you are Katya's mother, but it looks like she might think that you are her mother, too," Marik translated.

"I'm not sure that's a bad thing," Mike commented. "How could we ever break up a pair like that?"

Oksana smiled as Marik translated. She spoke to him once again briefly and waited politely for him to explain to the Knights.

"She says that it looks like she should give you some time to get to know each other," Marik said. "She will be in her office if we need her."

"Thank you," Laura said, never taking her eyes off Luba.

"Yes, Thank you," Mike added. "Will we see you before we leave?"

Marik translated the question.

"Yaes. Aye weel taayl yoo good-bye." Oksana said in her best English. Then she nodded cordially and left the room.

"Maybe you would like to sit on the carpet and play with

her," Marik suggested. "I have never been able to figure out why you Americans like to sit on the floor, but you're welcome to sit on the floor or the couch and play with Luba. I have some other things to go over with Oksana, so, if it's okay with you, I'll leave you alone."

"Thank you, that would be nice," Mike responded.

At first Laura sat with her on the couch playing *pat-a-cake*, which Luba thought was quite fun. "Do you think that she was born with her eye like that, or do you think it's just lazy eye?" Mike asked, referring to Luba's right eye that was turned inward.

"I don't know," Laura replied. "But let's try something. Hold your hand over her left eye while I hold her." Mike covered Luba's left eye lightly with his hand and she struggled for a few seconds, but then she relaxed to look at him and see what he was doing. Her right eye immediately straightened out and focused.

"It went straight!" Mike exclaimed.

"Sounds like lazy eye. This early, it can probably be straightened out with a patch on her good eye for a few months. That's good, isn't it, Sweetheart?" she said sweetly to Luba while tickling her under the arm. Luba giggled and squirmed and stretched herself out like she wanted to get down. Laura eased her down onto her feet and she ran straight to an old worn china cabinet that ran most of the length of the room. The cabinet was filled with all kinds of toys, ranging from stuffed animals, to dolls, to battery-operated toys. Luba lifted her hand toward the top shelf and pointed to a baby doll. She grunted, squeaked, and moaned while pointing, but never spoke an actual word.

"Can I help you get a toy?" Laura asked while rising up off the couch.

"Ugh, ungh," the little girl grunted, pointing at the doll.

"I'm sure you can ask in Russian," Laura said. "What do you want? Do you want the doll?"

"Ungh, ungh, ugh," she continued.

"I bet you have a beautiful voice. Let me hear you talk."

Luba put her hand down and held both hands against her as she started to pout. She pointed her head downward, but then cast her eyes upward again to look at Laura. "Hungh, hungh, hungh," she grunted, welling up with tears as she started a little cry.

Laura reached up and grabbed the baby doll, and Luba squealed with delight.

"Can you say 'doll'?" Laura asked. "Doll? Doll?"

Luba frowned, tilted her head down, then looked back up at Laura again as she started into the same ritual of beginning to cry. "Hungh, hungh, hungh. Hungh, hungh, hungh."

Laura handed her the doll and she instantly began to smile and giggle. "Oh, you are a spoiled one, aren't you?" Laura observed. "No one makes you talk, do they?" She looked up at Mike. "She gets what she wants by being pretty and sweet and cute. That's easier than talking. Oksana said that Luba is her favorite. I'll bet that she got whatever she wanted by whining a little."

"Ungh, ungh, ugh," Luba grunted, now pointing at the toy cabinet again.

"Which toy do you want?" Mike asked while walking over to get one for her. He immediately noticed that the nicest toys were behind the glass of the two end cupboards. He grabbed the handle of the one on the left with the intent of pulling out a big stuffed pink and white bunny, but the door didn't open. On closer observation, he noticed that the two end cabinets were taped shut with clear packing tape. "I guess we don't play with those toys, Princess," he told her.

"Hungh, hungh, hungh," she began to cry. She pointed at the bunny that had caught Mike's eye. "Hungh, hungh, hungh." She cried non-convincingly, still pointing to the bunny.

"Sorry, I can't get the bunny."

Luba started into a full blown cry. She dropped the doll to the floor and started to cry louder, opening and closing her hand which was outstretched toward the rabbit.

"Oh, boy!" Laura exclaimed. "You *are* spoiled!" Once again she turned to Mike. "Just ignore it."

"Are you kidding?" he asked. "Listen to that! They'll think we're trying to kill her!"

"Don't be silly. They obviously know what she does. I doubt it will last long once she realizes that she isn't going to get her way."

Mike sat down on the couch next to Laura and the crying began to wind down. Soon the screams had returned to the former sounds before the tantrum. "Hungh, hungh, hungh. Hungh, hungh, hungh." Then it was over.

Luba picked herself up and walked over to pick up the doll. She cradled it in her arms and carried it over to Laura. Luba cooed several times at the doll and then kissed it and held it up for Laura to kiss, which she did.

"So, have you decided to be happy now?" Laura asked.

Luba smiled and cooed back at her. She had transformed back into her pleasant, charming self.

"Reminds me of the tantrums Stephen used to pitch," Mike said.

"Don't remind me."

They sat there together quietly watching the little girl playing with the doll. "I guess we have to get busy thinking of another name, huh?" Mike remarked.

"You picked Sarah's name, I thought it was my turn," Laura teased.

"Well, you obviously have one in mind. What are you thinking?"

"From the second I saw that sweet little smile, I just couldn't help but think that heaven must be like that smile. To me, she really seems like a little piece of heaven. Tantrums aside, of course."

"Of course," Mike agreed with a smile.

"Galileo had a daughter who became a nun. When it was time for her to choose a name by which she would be known at the convent, she chose Maria Celeste, Celeste being Italian for heaven. She chose that name because her father was always looking at the heavens. I think that Celeste is a perfect name for a little piece of heaven, and I would hope that she loves her papa as much as Maria Celeste loved hers."

Tears welled up in Mike's eyes. "Then Celeste it will be," he asserted. "I can't believe the emotions that you go through in the adoption process. I'm sure I haven't cried so much since I was a little kid."

"I know exactly what you mean." She leaned over and

gave him a quick kiss.

Luba smiled and giggled approvingly. "So how does that sound to you, Sweetheart? Does Celeste sound like a good name?"

Luba smiled at the direct attention, cooed and giggled and then bashfully hid her head, burying her face under Laura's arm.

"I'll take that as a yes," Laura said.

Mike and Laura continued playing with Luba for another hour before Marik and Oksana entered the room.

Luba squealed, ran for Oksana and wrapped her arms around her leg. Oksana picked the child up and began chattering to her in Russian baby talk. Luba turned in her arms and pointed at Laura. "Maw-ma!" she said excitedly. "Maw-ma!"

Mike and Laura gasped simultaneously, but Marik and Oksana seemed completely unmoved. Oksana spoke briefly to the Americans and waited for Marik to translate.

"Oksana wants to know if you like Luba," Marik translated.

"Of course we do!" Laura exclaimed, still recovering from the shock of being called Mama. "She's adorable."

Marik translated for Oksana and she nodded approvingly before waiting for several seconds for Mike to speak. When he didn't, she posed the same question to him, again through Marik.

"Oksana wants to know if you like Luba, too," Marik queried.

"Oh, I do," Mike responded. "I like her every bit as much as her sister."

"So you want to adopt Luba, too?" Marik asked before even translating, let alone waiting for Oksana to ask the question first.

Oksana tugged at his shirt sleeve, trying to get a translation before Mike responded. Marik held up his hand toward her, signaling that he was still retrieving information and could only do one thing at a time.

"Yes," Mike and Laura started, simultaneously. They laughed.

"Go ahead Mike, you talk," Laura continued.

"We wouldn't think of splitting up the sisters," Mike added. "She is a delightful child. We would love to adopt her."

"Good," Marik replied finally turning toward Oksana who was now tugging much more assertively on his sleeve.

"*Dá, dá, dá*," he responded to her tugging. *Yes, yes, yes*. He then translated all that Mike had said. Oksana smiled and began speaking even before Marik had finished.

"Oksana says that she is very happy to hear that you like Luba and that you want to adopt her. She also says that it is good that the sisters will be together. She is very happy for Luba and for Katya."

"So, is that it?" Mike asked. "We just say yes and she is ours?"

"Well, obviously, there is a lot more paperwork on our end; but when you applied to adopt, you did everything that you needed to do to adopt two children. Of course, there are additional fees for another child. The expense will be greater, but Luba is available for international adoption, and you are qualified to adopt two children. If you want her, there shouldn't be any trouble." Marik replied.

He took several seconds to explain their conversation for Oksana's benefit and then the two of them spoke back and forth in Russian momentarily.

"Oksana wants to know if we will come back and visit again tomorrow," Marik informed them. "I told her that we would be back. It is best for the court if you have visited the children at least twice; and Partizansk is so far from Vladivostok, where Katya is right now, that it is difficult to come back again. So I told her that we will be back tomorrow at ten o'clock to visit with Luba one more time."

"Please tell Oksana thank you for the opportunity to visit with Luba," Laura said politely. "We look forward to seeing her tomorrow."

"Yes, thank you," Mike followed. "It has been a pleasure meeting Oksana and a true joy getting to know Luba."

Marik passed on the comments to Oksana who smiled and began to talk to Luba in Russian baby talk. It was soon evident that she was trying to get the child to say goodbye to the

Americans. "*Pah-ká? Pah-ká? Pah-ká?*"

At first, Luba just smiled bashfully and hid her face in Oksana's shoulder. But Oksana pulled the child's head back away, teased her for a moment in Russian and tried again. "*Pah-ká? Pah-ká? Pah-ká?*"

"*Cah-ka!*" Luba squealed before burying her bashful smile back in Oksana's shoulder.

The four adults, with Oksana still holding Luba, walked out on to the front steps of the orphanage. "Oksana wishes you a pleasant and safe drive to the hotel and says she looks forward to your visit tomorrow," Marik translated.

"Thank you," Laura replied. "See you tomorrow."

"Yes, thanks. See you tomorrow," Mike added. Then they headed down the sidewalk to the SUV.

"*Cah-ka! Cah-ka!*" Luba squealed as they got into the SUV.

"So, we will stay in Nahodka tonight," Marik said as they drove away from the orphanage. "There are no good hotels here in Partizansk, so we will go there. It's only about twenty minutes away."

"Sounds fine," Mike replied indifferently.

"So, you really like Luba? You think that she will fit in well with your family?"

"Sure she will," Laura piped in. "We'll need to call the boys tonight and tell them, but they'll be excited, too. Luba and Katya will be a wonderful addition to our family."

"Good. That's good. I am happy that you like Luba. It is best to keep the sisters together. I was thinking that the judge might require it, anyway." Marik immediately knew that he had slipped and let out more information than he should have, particularly to a person like Mike. He cringed as he awaited the response.

"Excuse me? Did you say that the judge might have required it?" Mike blurted.

Marik sighed before responding. "Naturally, everyone thinks it's better for siblings to stay together. In most cases it is required for siblings to be adopted together. But, in Luba's case, where she was taken out of the home later, they didn't want to delay giving Katya an opportunity to be adopted. Once these children turn five, their chances of being adopted decrease almost by the day, particularly in the case of sibling adoptions. The social workers thought it best to give Katya a chance while she had one, rather that waiting until *after* Luba was available. I guess, in reality, we all hoped that a couple like you would decide on Katya and then agree to take Luba. In essence, this is happening exactly the way that we hoped it would, obviously, for the best of both children." Marik braced himself for Mike's reply.

"So, what you're saying is that had we not agreed to take Luba, we wouldn't have gotten Katya either," Mike replied angrily.

"No, Mike. That's not what I'm saying. The plan was for you to adopt Katya, regardless. The agency and the social workers would have done everything that we could have to make that happen, even if your decision had been not to adopt Luba. But I'm sure that it's the same in the States. The judge has the final say. It is possible that the judge would have required the sisters to stay together and if you didn't agree to adopt both, the judge *could* have made a recommendation for us to find another child for you. But Mike, let's not look at all of that. You will have two wonderful daughters. The daughters will have a home and family that most Russian orphans can only dream of. It is all working out for the best. Please try to look at it that way."

"I just feel like people weren't honest with us. We should have been told these things before we came."

Laura cut Mike off, much to Marik's relief. "Honey, settle down. It isn't going to do us any good to figure out whether or not someone should have done things differently. I'm thrilled to be able to have two little girls. Aren't you?"

"Yes. Of course I am. I just wish that…"

Laura cut him off again. "It doesn't matter. You know that we would have chosen to adopt the girls together had we known of the situation before. We both wanted a daughter as young as we could get one. Now we have Katya, who has completely stolen your heart, but also a beautiful little two-year-old. We are getting a lot more out of this than we had planned for."

"I just think that…"

"It should have been our choice rather than a leveraged deal."

"Yes."

"Okay. So maybe it should have been. Would it have changed the outcome?"

"No."

"Then swallow your pride, Mike. What matters most is that the best thing happens, not that you are in control."

It wasn't often that Mike lost in a disagreement with Laura. But this time, Mike knew that she was right.

"I'm sorry, Honey. I shouldn't get so worked up. You're right. I'm happy to get both of the girls, regardless of the circumstances."

Seeing that Mike had backed off, Laura turned her attention to Marik, who had just been happy to let Laura handle her husband. "Marik, you said that the judge might have required us to adopt Luba anyway. So, what about the older sisters?"

"The older sisters are a different situation entirely," Marik began. "The other children were removed from the home before Katya and Luba were even born. Katya and Luba never knew them. They were already separate, so they don't need to be adopted together."

Laura was relieved. "Good. Thanks for clearing that up, Marik."

The trio remained mostly silent for the remainder of the drive and soon they arrived at a small hotel in Nahodka that reminded Mike of the dark, smoky, musty hotels in Munich. He had stayed at one once, when a distributor had booked the room for him. But he, as most Americans, preferred the modern settings and amenities of the newer, American-style business hotels.

"Here we are," Marik said as they bounced through a pot hole in the ill-kept parking lot. "We should eat dinner here. They have a restaurant. I'll give you a half an hour to get situated, and then we can meet in the lobby. Then, for tomorrow, we should meet for breakfast at about nine. That will put us out to visit Luba at ten. It will be time for her to eat lunch and take a nap at noon, so then we can get some lunch and head back to Vladivostok to visit with Katya for a little while in the afternoon. If that all sounds good to you guys."

"Yeah, that sounds great," Mike said as he popped open the door to the SUV.

"Thank you, Marik," Laura said sincerely as she slid across the seat to get out Mike's door. "We'll see you in a half hour."

19

Goodbye, Luba

"Hello, Stephen," Laura greeted her son through the telephone handset. It was ten at night, Vladivostok time. The boys would just be getting up back home. "We have some good news. Are Mark and Dawn home? Is Jeff up?"

"Sure. Jeff is taking out the garbage. The others are in the kitchen," Stephen responded.

"Can you put us on speakerphone and go get them?" Laura asked.

"Sure! I'll be right back!" There was an audible click, and Laura could hear the background chatter as Stephen gathered everyone.

"We're all here!" Mark said only seconds later. "What's the big news?"

"Are you ready for this? Today we visited with Katya's sister, Luba!"

Two seconds of dead silence was followed by a cacophony of startled reactions, overlapping and tangling so that nearly no one could be understood.

"I didn't know that she had a sister!"

"How old is she?"

"Are we adopting her, too?"

"It's really exciting," Laura began, after everyone had run out of breath. "We just found out about it earlier today. Katya has a little two-year-old sister in another orphanage. We just got back from visiting with her a few hours ago. She's available for adoption. So, what do you guys think?"

The line exploded once again with everyone speaking at once, but it was clear that back in Michigan, the answer was yes.

"We thought that you'd like that," Laura laughed. "Her name is Loubov, and her baby nickname is Luba. She is really sweet. She's a beautiful blonde-haired, blue-eyed little girl and she already called me Mama."

Forty-five minutes later, everyone's excitement and

curiosity satisfied, Laura finally handed the phone to Mike.

"Hey, Mark," Mike said into the handset, "pick up, would you?"

Immediately he heard the click and the background noise dropped off dramatically.

"What's up?"

"I want to know how Mom's doing. I haven't talked to her for days."

Mike could hear his brother walking away from the crowd at home before speaking. "I don't know, Mike. It's hard to say. She claims she feels fine and that she's getting stronger every day. But…I don't know. She doesn't look right."

Mike considered the news for a moment before replying. "Maybe it's just a cold or something. I don't think it's serious. God cured her. We asked Him to cure her and He did."

"Maybe. But keep her in your prayers, big brother."

"I will," Mike said before hanging up. That night, though they were both exhausted, Laura was the only one who got any sleep.

"We need to stop here to pick up Elizaveta," Marik said as he pulled the SUV in front of a small, single-level apartment building. "She is one of the social workers here in Partizansk, and she handles the case for the Bekher girls, you know, Katya and Luba. She needs to observe you visiting with the children, and can answer any questions you have about the girls and their history."

As the vehicle stopped, they were joined by a medium-built, dark-haired woman who Mike estimated to be in her early forties.

"Eet's nice to meet yoo," Elizaveta said in her best English. The Knights responded courteously in English and Marik translated. On the ride to the orphanage it became clear that while Elizaveta had passable English, she preferred to have Marik translate both ways.

Ten minutes later the group found themselves inside the Partizansk Baby Hospital, waiting in the playroom for Oksana to bring Luba.

"I forgot the backpack," Mike said to Marik. "We brought some treats and a present for Luba. Can I go out and get them? Oh, and we have that suitcase full of clothes. Would now be a good time to bring them in?"

"Sure, now is probably the best time," Marik said as he handed him the keys to the SUV.

Mike hurried down the hall and out to the car. He retrieved the backpack and suitcase and was shutting the hatch when a thin, dirty man in his early thirties walked up and began speaking in Russian.

"*Ne po Roos-ski*," Mike replied, somewhat confident that he had just said "not in Russian."

"*Amerikányets*," the man shouted to his friend across the street. Again he tried to speak to Mike in Russian, slower this time and louder, as if somehow that would make him understand.

"*Ne po Roos-ski*," Mike repeated. "I don't speak Russian," he said in English, wondering if the man would understand that.

The man pointed to the SUV, and then gestured with both hands while talking slowly in Russian. It was obvious to Mike that he was talking about where the vehicle was parked. "*Nyet*," the man said, pointing at the SUV and gesturing at the parking spot.

"It's not my car, sport," Mike said, turning toward the building.

"*Nyet*." The man held up his hand to signal Mike to wait. The dirty man then used his finger to draw a dollar sign in the grit on the side of the vehicle and then immediately held up seven fingers. "*Okay?*"

Mike couldn't believe it. This guy was trying to shake him down for seven U.S. dollars. "Sorry, sport," he repeated. "It's not my car." Then Mike turned and walked briskly into the orphanage.

"What was going on out there?" Marik asked as Mike entered the playroom where Luba was now visiting with Laura.

Mike looked now, and noticed that Marik could have seen the whole exchange through the room's only window. "Oh, you saw that, did you?" Mike asked, clearly irritated that Marik had not bothered to come out and intervene. “Some clown wanted me to pay a seven dollar parking fee to leave your vehicle there.”

“Did you pay him?” Marik asked candidly.

“Are you kidding?”

“Sometimes it’s easier to pay the fee than to fix the car,” Marik said nervously, looking again out the window. “But it should be okay. He knows we can see the car from here. I don’t think that he’ll do anything.”

Marik then turned his attention to Oksana as began speaking in Russian while gesturing several times at the large suitcase. Oksana’s eyes grew wide and she responded to Marik excitedly in Russian.

“Oksana says that the orphanage is very happy to receive the clothes that you brought. Why don’t you open the suitcase and show her what you have for her.”

Mike carried the suitcase over and placed it on the couch. Oksana, Elizaveta, and several other orphanage workers gathered around to watch as he began to remove the clothes. He pulled out a beautiful pink snowsuit with matching boots. Elizaveta squealed and grabbed them from Mike. “*Oh Kra-see-va!*” she said, holding them up in front of her for the others to see. *How beautiful!*

Mike continued removing the other clothes. The T-shirts, jeans, dresses, shoes, socks, sandals, slippers and dresses were all removed one at a time. The Russian women looked like children at Christmas sorting through the clothes, each holding up her favorite outfit to show the others. But Mike had saved the best for last. As the women finally settled down, he removed three velvet dresses from the bottom of the case and held them up. Gasps and squeals filled the room as the women scrambled to be the first to hold the red, violet, and emerald green dresses. The women took turns passing them around and holding them up while jabbering in Russian. Finally, Oksana directed her speech, still in Russian, to Mike and Laura. When she finished, Marik translated. “Oksana thanks you for the wonderful gifts. She said the clothes are needed and will be put to good use. She also said they will use the velvet dresses only for pictures of the children to send to potential adoptive parents.

She doesn't want the dresses worn out in every day use."

Oksana waited for him to finish before politely nodding her head in approval. "Tank-yoo!" she added. Oksana then began to speak to the orphanage workers who began to gather up the clothes.

"Oksana told them to take the clothes to her office for now," Marik told Mike and Laura. "She said that they need to give you time to visit with Luba."

The workers quickly left the room, and only Elizaveta remained to observe the little orphan and her potential parents.

Laura pulled out a bottle of bubbles from the backpack and Mike grabbed the video camera. Luba danced and squealed as Laura blew bubbles into the air. Then she ran around the room chasing the bubbles and trying to catch them, surprised each time that one burst. Soon Luba wanted to blow the bubbles. Laura dipped the wand into the solution and held it up in front of Luba's face. Luba just looked at Laura and smiled. "Blow, Luba," she said. "Blow."

Luba tried, but couldn't quite get the hang of it. "Come on, Luba, blow!" she repeated.

"*Doi!*" Elizaveta encouraged her from the other end of the room. "*Doi. Doi!*"

Luba then blew hard through the wand, sending the bubbles skyward. She laughed and giggled while she chased each bubble until they were all gone. Laura filled the wand again and held it up. This time Luba knew what to do and sent more bubbles into the air. She squealed and giggled while she chased them all down again, Mike getting every bit of it on film.

"Here, Honey, you play with her," Laura said, passing him the bottle of bubble solution and the wand while taking the video camera.

Mike filled the wand with bubble solution and held it out. "Here, Luba, blow bubbles." Luba remained next to Laura. "Come on, Sweetheart, *doi!*" Luba didn't move. Mike walked over to Luba and held the wand in front of her mouth. "*Doi!*"

"*Nee!*" Luba said firmly. *No*. "Mama," she said while pointing at Laura. "Mama."

Mike held out the bottle to Luba, who took it from him and

handed it back to Laura. "I guess she showed you!" Laura quipped.

"I guess she did," Mike smiled.

"Luba only know women," Elizaveta pointed out from the other side of the room. "She not know man. It be okay later. It take some time."

"I've noticed that there aren't many men around the orphans," Mike observed.

"Yes," Elizaveta responded. "Orphans and adoption woman's work. Very few mans. Children not know mans. Later she know you. She like you. It be okay later."

"Thank you," Mike responded honestly. "That makes me feel better." He took the video camera and continued to film Laura and Luba.

After a while, Laura told Mike to get out the crayons and a coloring book. "Let's try something," she said. "Take them over to the table and start to color a picture."

Mike sat at the little table and began coloring a picture of a butterfly as Laura put the bubbles away in the backpack. "*Nee!*" Luba chirped. "*Nee!*" She tried to pull the pack from Laura's hands to retrieve the bottle.

"Let's see what Papa is doing," Laura said as she held out her hand for Luba to grab. Luba took her index finger and followed her over to the table where Mike was coloring. "Oh, look! Papa is coloring!" Laura chimed. "I want to help Papa color!" Laura knelt next to the table, picked up a crayon, and began to color on the same page as Mike.

"*Dai!*" Luba said forcefully. *Give me!*

"You have to get a crayon from Papa," Laura coaxed her. "Papa has the crayons." Mike picked up the pink crayon and held it out toward Luba.

"*Dai!*" she said as she snatched it from his hand. She then began to color on the same page with Mike and Laura. Soon the three of them were trading crayons and showing off their work to each other. Laura slowly sneaked away from the table and got out the digital camera. She shot several pictures of Luba coloring with her father. Luba looked up after the flash went off for the first picture and both Mike and Laura thought that would be the end of it, but she went right back to coloring with Papa.

Apparently, he wasn't so bad after all.

"Mike, why don't you give her the Teddy Bear," Laura suggested. "Maybe that will break the ice a little more."

Mike held out his hand for Luba to grab and she looked at him, concerned. "Come on," he said. "Let's go see what else we have in the backpack." Mike took half a step toward the pack, and Luba tentatively reached up and grabbed his hand. They walked over to the backpack next to Laura, and Luba watched with anticipation as Mike reached slowly down deep in the bag. "Let's see, what else do we have for a little princess? Oh, I think I have something!" Though Luba didn't understand the English, she was clearly excited to see what else could come out of the bag. She watched intently as Mike's hand slowly emerged from the bag until right at the end, when he jerked the pink stuffed Teddy Bear out and held it toward Luba.

"*Mishka!*" Luba squealed as she grabbed it from Mike. *Teddy Bear*. Luba hugged the bear and then held it out and studied it curiously. She buried her face in the plush toy and took several deep breaths. "*Poppy!*" she squealed. Then she planted her face back in the bear.

"Does the bear smell like Poppy, Sweetheart?" Laura asked as she placed her hand on Luba's back.

Luba looked up again. "*Poppy!*"

"Mike put his cologne on the bear and I put my perfume on a blanket, so that Luba would get used to our smells while we are away," Laura explained to Elizaveta.

"Oh, yes. This very good," Elizaveta responded while nodding approvingly.

Laura and Mike continued to play with Luba until lunch time, while Elizaveta watched and took notes. By then, though she clearly preferred Laura, Luba would let Mike play with her. She would even occasionally let him give her a little tickle under the arms, evoking loads of giggles and laughter. Mike was completely taken with the little girl by the time that Oksana returned.

"Soon it will be time for Luba to eat lunch and take her nap," Marik said. "Oksana wonders if you have any questions for her and Elizaveta."

"Yes," Laura responded. "Has Luba's eye been like that

since birth, or has it digressed over time?"

Marik repeated the question in Russian and waited for Oksana's reply. "No, she wasn't born with it like that," he translated. "The problem developed over time. Oksana says that while it is possible the eye could be trained by patching the good eye, that she really thinks Luba needs surgery. But she also says that it should be minor surgery, and it should be easy to correct. You should get an eye doctor involved as soon as you get her home. The sooner she gets it taken care of, the better chance you have of there being no permanent repercussions."

"Does she have any other health problems?" Laura asked.

"No. No other health problems."

"Allergies?"

"None that we know about."

"What about Katya?" Mike interjected. "How exactly did she get that burn on her chest?"

"We think she pulled a pan of soup over on herself," Elizaveta responded through translation. "The burn shouldn't have scarred that bad, but the mother didn't have it treated. By the time we found out about it, the skin had started to heal, but it was one big mess of infection. We brought her here to the Baby Hospital and Oksana treated her. The infection almost killed her, but Oksana got her on some antibiotics and treated the burn to the best of her ability. Finally, she healed up."

"You should get her to a plastic surgeon when you get her back to the States," Oksana informed them through Marik. "I think that they can help her quite a bit."

"Does she have any other issues?" Mike asked.

"She tested positive for tuberculosis, as you saw in her medical report. It is inactive now, but tuberculosis should always be watched. Make sure that the doctors continue to watch it. Tuberculosis can be controlled and treated, but they need to make sure that it stays inactive."

"Anything else?" Mike continued.

"Katya did have a broken arm when she came here. It had already started to mend. Fortunately, the break was healing correctly, and we didn't have to re-break and set it."

"What about family members?" Laura asked. "We've

heard that family members have to give permission for the children to be adopted. Who do we need to secure permission from?"

"There is no family," Marik relayed from Elizaveta. "Their mother grew up in the Partizansk Baby Home, so there are no grandparents on her mother's side. Neither Luba nor Katya have a father listed on their birth certificates. So legally, they have no father. It's likely the mother doesn't even know who the fathers are."

"But what if the father finds out about them and wants them back?" Laura asked.

"The laws are different here in Russia than they are in the States," Elizaveta responded. "Blood doesn't make you a father. Documents make you a father. If there are no documents confirming who the father is, then there is no legal father. But I think that you worry too much. In Russia, if the father wanted them, he would have come forward long ago. He probably doesn't even know they exist, nor would he want to know. Besides, Russian adoptions are closed. Adoptive parents are protected much better here than in the states. When you do adopt the children, the judge will order a new birth certificate showing you and Mike as the birth parents of the children. At that point, you can even request that the judge change the birth date and place of birth on the certificate so that the birth parents couldn't trace it; or for that matter, the children couldn't trace it, even if they wanted to."

"Really?" Mike exclaimed. "They actually bury the paper trail like that?"

"Yes. Russians are very skeptical about adoption. There is a very negative stigma about it," Elizaveta continued through Marik's translation. "Most Russians would not adopt children who were not related to them, unless they could conceal it. So the courts have made it possible for them to hide it so that domestic adoptions can happen. So you can see, you will have no issues securing family permission with the Bekher girls. If you want them, they can be yours."

"That's great news," Laura responded, as she went to the suitcase and removed the spare set of soft books that had been prepared in case Katya's adoption fell through and they were forced to re-select. She showed them to Oksana and Elizaveta as she explained them through Marik.

Early on during the explanation, Oksana began to speak excitedly to Marik in Russian. "Oksana is very surprised that the books are written in Russian as well as English," he translated. "She says that this will be very good to help to prepare Luba. She promises to read these books to her often."

Once they were finished, Marik spoke up. "It's time for us to go, so that Luba can eat her lunch and take her nap."

"Will we be coming back to visit Luba again?" Laura asked, already knowing the answer.

"Not on this trip," Marik responded. "There won't be time."

"How long will it be before we come back to get her?" she asked, her voice quivering.

"Usually, it's somewhere between thirty and sixty days, sometimes longer. But don't worry, the time will go fast."

Oksana, though not understanding the exchange in English, had seen this all too often and knew what was going on. She spoke briefly to Marik as she picked up Luba and handed her to Laura.

"Oksana says that we should all go out on the front steps to say goodbye," Marik said.

Mike placed the cameras and backpack into the large suitcase. Then he saw the blanket. He pulled it out and draped it over Luba's shoulders. Laura wrapped the bright quilted blanket around Luba, who sniffed it only once before burying her face in it for a deep breath. "Mama!" she squealed just before turning into Laura to smell her neck. With that, the group walked out of the visiting room, down the hall, and exited the double doors of the orphanage.

"Goodbye, Sweetheart," Laura said as she squeezed Luba, the tears streaming down her face.

Mike walked up behind Laura to face Luba, who was smiling over her shoulder. He reached around Laura and hugged Luba, pulling her tighter against his wife. "Goodbye, Princess. We'll come back as soon as we can. I love you." Mike had intentionally not faced Laura, hoping that not being able to see her cry would help him to hold back his own tears, but it wasn't enough. The tears welled up in his eyes and try as he might, he finally couldn't stop them from rolling down his cheeks.

"Come on, Sweetheart," he said after gently kissing his wife on the back of her head. "This isn't going to get any easier. We need to get going."

Laura let out a little sob before catching herself. She then put on her best artificial smile and held Luba out away from her to get one last good look that would have to last for months. "*Pah-ká Preens-yessa*," she said, trying to keep a strong voice, but only partially succeeding.

"*Cah-ka!*" Luba exclaimed and then she smiled and buried her head bashfully in Laura's shoulder.

Laura gave her one last squeeze, then handed her back to Oksana and thanked her. She reached into the pack and took out a headphone cassette player and tape that had been meant for Katya. "I made a tape of me singing some songs for Katya so that she could get used to hearing my voice. But Luba is younger. I think that she needs it more. Please let her listen to it sometimes until we come back." She handed the headphone player to Oksana and waited for Marik to translate.

"Oksana says this is a very good idea. She promises to let Luba listen to the tape."

"Thank you, Oksana," Laura said, one last time, her voice quivering; and then she hurried down the steps towards the vehicle.

"Thank you, Oksana," Mike said strongly. "I know you would anyway, but please take good care of our baby," he continued, his voice now cracking while another round of tears spilled down his face. "Take care, we'll see you in a couple of months."

Marik translated in a quiet voice, and then the two men walked off the steps to join Laura in the SUV.

The three didn't speak for several minutes as they drove away. It was Laura who broke the silence.

"You know, I've had two babies naturally. They wrapped them up and handed them to me within seconds after they were born. There is no difference between the way I felt for those children and the way I feel for Luba. There is absolutely no difference. She is my child. Now I have to leave her in an orphanage half a world away. It's too hard. I don't know how I can handle this," she said as she broke down and began to cry again. Mike didn't know what to say to comfort her.

"It is hard," Marik offered. "But Luba is in good hands."

Laura thought about that. She thought about Oksana and the others at the Baby Hospital, about the tender way each child was cared for, even with such limited resources. "I know that she's in good hands," Laura whispered, as she silently prayed for the welfare of her little girl.

20

More Fun and Games with the Orphans

"Mama! Papa!" Katya screamed as she ran across the playroom and threw herself into Laura's arms.

"Oh, I missed you, Sweetheart!" Laura exclaimed as she squeezed her little girl. Katya buried her face into her mother's shoulder and continued to hug her for a moment more, taking deep breaths to smell the perfume. Then she squirmed to get away. Laura released her and she bounded the few steps over to Mike who swooped her up in his arms.

"Poppy!" She threw her arms around his neck, hugged him tight and then gave him a quick kiss on the lips and hugged him tightly again while nuzzling up to his neck to smell his cologne.

"I…Love…You," Mike said slowly and clearly.

"*Yá-Tibya-Lo-Bloo*," she whispered in his ear, not loud enough for anyone else to hear.

"Marik, can we tell Katya about Luba now?" Mike asked.

"Sure. I think that would be good."

Mike pulled the digital camera from the backpack and turned it on so they could view the pictures in the viewfinder. Then he and Laura and Marik sat on chairs facing each other with Katya on Mike's lap. Mike scrolled to the picture of the Partizansk Baby Hospital and showed it to Katya. "Do you know this place?" he asked.

Katya scowled. She definitely remembered the baby hospital. But those weren't pleasant memories. "Your papa wants to know if you remember the baby hospital," Marik translated.

"*Dá*," Katya said firmly, deepening the scowl. Yes.

Mike, sensing the anxiety, quickly scrolled to a picture of Luba smiling at the camera. Before he could even ask, Katya squealed. "Luba!"

"Dá, Luba," Mike responded. He then scrolled to a picture of Laura holding Luba, both with huge smiles on their faces.

"*Luba ee Mama!*" Katya squealed.

"Dá. Luba ee Mama."

Katya gasped as she began to realize what might be happening. She directed the surprised look on her face to Marik and began jabbering loudly in Russian.

"Yes, little one," Marik told her in her native tongue. "Mama and Papa are adopting Luba, too. You will both be sisters in America."

Katya squealed again. Then she simplified her Russian, hoping for her parents to understand. "*Mama ee Papa ee Katya, ee Luba, Amérika?*"

"Dá, *Preens-yessa*," Laura responded. "Mama ee Papa, ee Katya, ee Luba, Amérika."

Katya couldn't stop squealing her name, her sister's name, and "Amérika" as she wriggled off of Mike's lap and danced in front of them. Then she ran around the circle hugging her parents and Marik several times.

Mike looked up and noticed that they had been partially surrounded by the throng of orphans.

"Well, what do you think, Laura? Are you brave enough to get out the bubbles?"

"Oh, I think so," she replied. Laura reached into the backpack and pulled out the bottle of bubbles. The twenty or more orphans in the room remembered how much fun Katya's parents were the day before, and they all left their play areas and gathered around. Laura pulled the wand from the bottle and blew a stream of bubbles over the crowd, which erupted with screams and squeals as they all competed to be the first to pop each of the bubbles as they floated downward. Laura only got off one more stream of bubbles before the inevitable happened. She was swarmed.

"*Meen-yá! Dai-ee! Meen-yá! Ee-Dai-ee! Ah-Meen-yá! Ah-Meen-yá!*" All of the orphans wanted to blow the bubbles. Katya was no exception, and she raced into the middle of the pack, screaming with the rest of the children.

Mike grabbed the video recorder from the backpack and filmed the children struggling to get to the front, where Laura was frantically dipping the wand and holding it in front of a different child each time. At one point, she tried to line the children up, but she finally gave up and went back to trying to be fair by positioning it again and again in different parts of the crowd.

"Now you know how I felt the other day out in the snow!" Mike teased. "Who's laughing now?"

Laura just laughed and kept dipping.

"Let's take this down a notch," Laura suggested after several minutes of the free-for-all. "Let's get out the coloring book and crayons."

"Good call," Mike agreed as he capped the lens on the recorder and turned it off. He went to the backpack and fumbled through it before finding the crayons and a huge coloring book. Mike tore a bunch of pictures from the coloring book and started placing them on the tables on one side of the room. The orphans, understanding what was going on, all found seats next to a picture from the coloring book. They seemed to be amazed at the elaborate pictures just waiting to be colored.

Mike began to pass out crayons, then suddenly realized he had a problem. He only had one set of twelve crayons. Twelve crayons, and nearly two dozen kids. So he did the only thing that he could do. He handed out all the crayons, then went back and broke each of the crayons in half. American children, he thought, would have freaked out if he had broken their new crayons. But to the Russian children, it was no big deal. That's exactly how you deal with not having enough crayons. You break them in half.

The children sat quietly coloring their individual pictures with half a crayon of a single color. After several minutes, some of the children swapped crayon halves with neighboring friends so that they could have multiple colors on their pictures. Mike was pleased to see that all of the swapping and trading was done politely and orderly. Most of the children scribbled out their pictures within five minutes, leaving the pictures at the table and scattering throughout the room to play with other toys. But one of the little girls, a dark-haired child with beautiful facial features that suggested one Caucasian and one Asian parent, sat very quietly, coloring every detail of her picture as carefully as she could. Occasionally she would get up and retrieve a crayon left on the table by another child, then return to her masterpiece. Mike watched intently as she slowly, carefully, and artistically attended to every detail.

"Mike, come here," Laura called him from across the room. Mike walked over to Laura and Marik who were sitting next to Katya and another little blonde girl with a lazy eye. "This is Anya, one of Katya's best friends," Laura told him.

"Hello, Anya," Mike said, holding out his hand for her to shake it. The little girl giggled at the funny words that he was saying and then held out her hand timidly for him to shake, which he did.

"Marik says that Katya, Anya, and Marishka are best friends. I guess that they are all but inseparable, most days. Marishka is the little girl who is still coloring over there," Laura continued, pointing subtly over to the little artist that Mike had been admiring. "Katya came up and started talking to me in Russian. Marik told me that she was asking if Anya and Marishka could come with us to live in America." Tears sparkled in the corners of Laura's eyes as she relayed what had happened. "Marik told her that we were sorry, but that Anya and Marishka still had to wait longer before they could find them mamas and papas, that it wasn't time for them yet."

Mike felt his heart sink as he sympathized with the disappointment the three little girls must have been feeling. Their friendship had to be the closest thing to family that the little orphans knew; and soon, like the last time they were in a family, this bond would end. "I'm sorry, Anya" Mike said sincerely. "But I'm sure that there are mamas and papas out there just waiting for you and Marishka to come and live with them."

Marik translated what Mike had said for Katya and Anya, and both of them smiled and began jabbering back and forth in Russian as they ran off to play.

"Man, Marik," Mike started, "what do you say to these poor kids? I mean the odds aren't good. But you can't smash their hopes with a hammer. What can anyone possibly say?"

"When they don't ask us, we tell them nothing. When they do, we tell them that we are trying to find them parents. Russians wait patiently. Getting frustrated never helps, and nothing speeds up the system here, so they try to understand. By the time they get to be seven or eight, they pretty much stop asking. They kind of get numb to it. Every once in a while one of them does get adopted, so it does give the others some hope. But when we do find parents for children like that, the children almost can't believe it. They keep waiting for something to happen to cause the adoption to fail, because a family has never worked out for them before. We have even seen kids like who try to sabotage their own adoption."

"You can't be serious!" Mike exclaimed. "Why would they do something like that?"

"I'm not entirely sure," Marik admitted. "I think it is because they are certain that the adoption will fail anyway. They just can't take the anticipation of waiting for what they believe will inevitably be a failure, so they try speeding up that failure."

Mike tried to make some sense of this as he looked across the room, where the little artist he had been observing was now tugging on his wife's sleeve.

"What, Sweetheart?" Laura asked as she looked down.

Marishka held her colored masterpiece up to Laura and began talking to her very slowly and carefully in Russian, doing her best to make sure that Katya's mother understood what she was so desperately trying to tell her.

"Marishka said this picture is for Katya." Marik translated. "She wants you to take it home with you to America so that Katya can keep it to remember her."

"Oh, my goodness," Laura said, her voice cracking as she began crying yet again. "It is a beautiful picture," she said, taking it from Marishka's hand and admiring it closely. "I will take very good care of this picture, and I will take it home to America for Katya."

Marishka smiled happily as Marik told her what Katya's mother had said. Laura carefully set the paper next to her on the bench and then picked up Marishka and placed her on her lap. "You are a wonderful, beautiful child," she told her as she squeezed her against her chest. "I'm sure that Katya will always remember you. I could never forget you myself."

Marik told Marishka what Laura had said and she smiled and gave Laura a quick hug. Laura would have been content to hold the child indefinitely, but she wriggled to get down. She had finished the present and delivered it. Now it was time to play. She ran quickly over to Anya and Katya to join in whatever they were doing.

Laura wiped the tears from her face. "People don't know these children are here," she said to Mike and Marik. "I mean, they know about statistics. They know there are orphanages, they know there are orphans. But they don't know that these are wonderful, loving, loveable, beautiful children. People need to know. People who could adopt need to know." She let the thought linger as she watched one of the caregivers call the children to sit on the floor in front of her. Soon the children were singing a song, complete with hand signs and gestures. After several songs, one of the workers suggested that maybe the people from Amérika had a fun group game that they all could learn.

Marik asked Laura if she knew any games, and she immediately thought of Duck, Duck, Goose. Marik translated as Laura circled up the workers and children, seating them on the floor in a big circle. She explained the rules through Marik, who brought up a concern.

"But I think that duck and goose are the same words in Russian," Marik said. "We just say *ootka* or *big ootka.*"

"That's alright," Laura countered. "We can play in English." Laura began circling the other participants tapping each one lightly on the head. "Duck, duck, duck, duck, duck, GOOSE!" she yelled as she tapped Katya lightly on the head. Katya bolted from her seat on the floor and chased Laura around the circle, but Laura beat her back to her place. At first, Katya frowned, knowing that she had lost the race. But the caregivers and Marik quickly explained to her that it was her turn to choose another goose. The smile and dimples returned to her face.

"Dock, dock, dock, dock, dock…" it looked as if she was going to go completely around the circle and begin again when finally, the next to the last child, Anya, was tapped on the head. "GOOOOOZ!" Katya squealed and she ran around the circle. Anya was right behind her, but not quite quick enough. Now it was Anya's turn. No one was surprised at her choice to play the next goose. Except, that was, for the goose. Sofia gasped as the child squealed "GOOZ!" as she tapped the caregiver's head.

She tried to stand up quickly to chase the child, but she had barely gotten all the way to her feet by the time that Anya was in her place.

The children all laughed as Sofia playfully scolded the child while shaking her finger at her. The young caregiver started to walk around the circle tapping people on their heads. "Gooz, gooz, gooz, gooz…"

Screams erupted from the children. "You have to say 'duck, duck, duck, duck,' then 'goose,'" Marik reminded her.

"Dock, Gooz…it's all the same," she said. The children all laughed. In Russian it *was* all the same.

The next forty-five minutes were spent playing Dock, Dock, Gooz, until everyone had a chance to be the goose at least once, and some of them several times. Sofia and Katya's parents were the favorite picks, one of them coming up every third or fourth time. But that was alright. It made it easy for them to include the children who might have been passed over.

Soon a caregiver came into the room and announced that dinner was ready. Most of the children ran for the door, but Katya stayed seated on her mother's lap. Several of the boys walked over to Mike.

"They want to know when you and Laura will come back," Marik translated. "They don't play much with men. I think they really enjoy getting a little bit of male attention."

"Tell them that we will come back and see them Friday morning," Mike answered.

Marik told the boys when they would return. Satisfied, they rushed off to eat their dinner.

"You should go eat, Katya," Laura suggested through Marik.

"*Nee-Ha-Choó*," Katya responded.

Laura remembered that phrase from the separation the day before. "I know you don't want to, Sweetheart. But you need to go eat, and Papa and I have to go back to the hotel. Marik will bring us back to visit you Friday morning."

Marik translated for Katya who immediately repeated what she had said before, "*Nee-Ha-Choó*."

"I promise to bring them back Friday," Marik told her in Russian.

"Is tomorrow Friday?" she asked.

"No. Tomorrow is Thursday. Friday is the day after tomorrow. I will bring them back the day after tomorrow." Marik promised.

"But I want them to come back tomorrow," Katya sulked as she wrinkled up her face and pouted.

"I'm sorry, tomorrow is not possible," Marik reaffirmed. "But right now, you need to go eat like your mama told you. Are you going to be a good child and mind your mother?" Marik asked.

"*Dá*," Katya responded. Then she said several more words in Russian and waited for Marik to translate.

"Katya says that she will do what you say," Marik informed Laura. "So now she must go eat."

"Thank you, Darling," Laura told her. "Now give me hugs and kisses goodbye."

Marik translated for Katya, who grinned and threw her arms around her mother's neck, kissed her on the lips, and then buried her head in her shoulder for a deep breath that would have to last until the blanket at bedtime.

"*Ee Papa*," Katya said afterwards.

Mike stooped down and lifted Katya up off her mother's lap. "Be a good girl," he said. "We'll come back and see you again on Friday."

Marik told Katya what Mike had said as they hugged each other tightly. They gave each other several rapid kisses. Then she hugged Mike, one last time for the day, and took a deep breath of his cologne.

"All right, Princess," Mike said as he placed her feet back on the ground. "We'll see you in a couple of days."

"*Pah-ká Papa! Pah-ká Mama!*" she said happily, and she took Sofia by the hand and went off to eat.

"*Pah-ká*," Mike and Laura responded in unison.

21

When the Snow Goes Away and the Flowers Come Up

"So, are you ready to go home?" Marik asked as the Knights pulled their suitcases toward him.

"We're ready to visit Katya," Mike responded. "Let's not talk about going home until we have to."

"Alright, that sounds good. Did you get all checked out of the hotel?"

"Yeah, everything is finished. We shouldn't need to do anything else except visit Katya and catch our flight."

"Okay then, let's go. I'm sure that Katya is looking forward to seeing you."

Sasha greeted them as they entered the SUV. "I wanted to see you today to tell you goodbye."

"Thanks, Sasha. You and Marik have been so kind and helpful," Laura responded. "We'll miss you when we leave."

The drive to Volny, the winter camp where Katya was staying, wasn't silent, but it was mostly filled with small talk. Everyone was consciously avoiding the subject of leaving and going home, even though it was the biggest topic available for comment.

Mike was the first out of the vehicle when they reached the two story white stucco building. He pulled the camera out, and walked away from the vehicle to get a shot of the building for the scrapbooks. He stood silently for several moments just looking and pondering after he shot the picture. It was still cold, about zero Fahrenheit, without figuring in the wind chill from the bitter breeze coming off the frozen bay. He looked around at the frost from earlier fog frozen to the branches of the trees. It was a beautiful morning with a brilliant sun in the clear blue sky, which only seemed to somehow amplify the cold. He took one last look around before taking a deep, lung-chilling breath and blowing it out slowly while he watched his breath float out on the breeze. He had decided that he didn't want Katya to see him cry. He wanted her to know that she would have a strong papa, one who would protect her and keep her safe, not a weak papa who couldn't control his emotions. But he knew it was going to be tough, if not impossible, to accomplish. Laura was right. It was heartbreaking leaving a child you had claimed as your own in an orphanage.

Sasha, Marik, and Laura sensed what was going on, and patiently waited for him to catch up to them at the door. He took another deep breath, exhaled again, and then quickly returned the camera to the backpack and hurried up to step through the door which Marik was now holding open for him.

"You know how it works," Marik said. "Wait here at security and we'll go find the kids and get permission to bring you back."

"Okay," Mike responded as he and Laura took a seat on the wooden bench. Marik and Sasha were only gone a few minutes before they returned.

"They said the children are outside playing," Marik said while faking a shiver. "We can go out and find them."

Laura took the scarf which had just been slung over her shoulder and wrapped it around her neck, folded over and buttoned the lapel of her coat, and then pulled up her collar.

"I hate the cold," Sasha said. "I'll wait in here until you come back."

Mike pulled down the flaps of his Gatsby hat, turned up his collar, then removed the gloves from his pocket and put them on. "Ready when you are," he said gesturing toward the door for Marik to lead the way.

"They told me that the children were around in back," Marik said as they rounded the corner of the building to its back side. "But I don't see them. Maybe they are over there in the… How do you call this in English?" he asked pointing toward a small, white brick building about twelve feet square and fifteen feet high.

"I don't know," Laura responded. "I don't know what it is."

"Sure you do. You have these. Mike, how do you say that in English?"

"Sorry, Marik, I don't know what it is, either."

"Sure, you will know. Come with me, I will show you. You will know what it is."

The couple's curiosity was piqued as they walked toward the little building. They rounded the small structure and Marik walked in through a regular-sized doorway without a door. Mike and Laura followed. There was no light in the room other than what streamed in through the doorway, so it took several seconds for their eyes to adjust after the reflecting glare of the sun on the bright white snow.

"There, how do you call this in English?" Marik asked again.

"Oh," Laura spoke softly. "It's a shrine."

"Yes, yes. I knew that you knew this. A shrine."

Mike removed his hat from his head and looked around the room.

"Leave your hat on," Marik told him. "It's too cold to take off your hat. You'll get sick. There's no need. Everyone knows you have to keep your hat on when it's this cold. It's not disrespectful."

"When in Rome…" Mike quoted as he placed his hat back on his head and pulled the flaps back over his ears.

"What?" Marik asked.

"Oh, nothing, it's just a silly expression." Mike responded.

"So, do the children come in here to pray?" Laura asked.

"Mostly to think," Marik responded. The workers bring them out here in a group and tell them that they should be quiet and think. Maybe some of the children pray, but mostly they just come in here for a few minutes to think."

Mike and Laura walked closer to the back of the room directly across from the door. Their eyes had adjusted enough to see well by now. There were several pictures of Christ and of saints. All of the paintings were of a very orthodox nature, reflecting the medieval artistic style prevalent in Russian Orthodox paintings. They were lined up along the wall on a ledge formed by the bottom several rows of bricks that protruded back from the wall into the room. The largest picture was a photo of a painting of Christ, about five by seven inches, bordered with a worn and beaten gold painted frame. None of the other pictures had frames. Several of them were even done baseball card style, without any text or explanation.

"So are most of the people here members of the Russian

Orthodox Church?" Laura asked.

"Everyone is Russian Orthodox," Marik responded, "but only a few of the old people attend church services. But if you ask anyone what their religion is, they will tell you Russian Orthodox, even though most of them can't tell you anything else about it."

"Are there other churches here?" Mike asked.

"Oh, sure. Since the fall of the Soviet Union, there have been lots of other churches. There are missionaries from other countries, especially the U.S., trying to convert the people to various other religions. But I think the Russian people aren't very interested. Russians don't think so much about religion. But it doesn't stop the missionaries. There are some who live by my apartment, I have seen them on the streets sometimes. You know, the ones with the white shirts, ties and black badges on their pockets."

"Oh, the Mormons," Mike responded, trying to see what Marik thought before venturing further.

"Yes, the Mormons."

"Have you ever talked with them?"

"No. I have some friends who had them visit, though."

"What did they think?" Mike asked curiously.

"He said that they were nice enough. Not strange like some people have said. Pretty normal, I guess."

"What do you mean by that?"

"They told my friend that they are Christian, and that they believe in the Bible like other Christians, but they believe in some other book too."

"I've heard people say that they have more than one wife," Mike replied, trying to get more from Marik on his position.

"I've heard that, too," Marik replied. "So had my friends, and they asked them about it. The missionaries told them that Mormon men could have more than one wife in the beginning, but that the church stopped that practice over a hundred years ago."

"Really," Mike continued. "Because I have seen stuff on TV that they still have groups of polygamists in Utah."

"My friend asked them about that, too. They said those people might call themselves Mormons, but the official

Mormon Church excommunicates anyone who is a polygamist. I guess the official church doesn't even call itself Mormon. They call themselves something else, like Saints of Christ, or something like that. Have you ever heard of that in the States?"

Mike's bluff was up. "Actually, Marik, I have. In fact, I was a missionary for The Church of Jesus Christ of Latter-day Saints for two years in Brazil. It was back in the mid 1980s, back before I met Laura."

"You're kidding!" Marik exclaimed. "You and Laura are Mormons?"

"Guilty as charged," Mike joked. "Both Laura and I have ancestors who were Mormon pioneers. Our families have been members of that church for generations."

"Wow, so Katya and Luba will be Mormons, too!" Marik exclaimed.

"They sure will," Mike responded. "Don't act so surprised."

"I'm sorry. I meant no offense," Marik added carefully. "I just never would have guessed that you and Laura were Mormons. You seem just like everyone else. I mean, not that you shouldn't. I don't know, I guess I didn't know what I thought a Mormon was supposed to be like."

"Just like any Christian who practices his religion ought to be," Mike replied. "I mean, that's what members of the church are *supposed* to be like. It doesn't always mean they act like they should."

"No, no, of course not," Marik replied. "But Mormons are just like everyone else."

"There are some doctrinal differences in teachings," Mike conceded.

"Well, yes," Marik acknowledged. "There are always doctrinal differences. If not, there would only be one church, wouldn't there? So tell me, Mike, who is right and who is wrong?"

"We're right, of course!" Mike retorted playfully. "If you really want to know, Marik, you need to get hold of those missionaries in your area. They could answer any questions you have, and you could find out for yourself."

"Oh, thanks anyway." Marik replied nonchalantly. "But

it's like I told you. We Russians aren't too interested in religion. Besides, I'm already Russian Orthodox."

"Sure, of course you are," Mike said, letting him off the hook.

"You can take the man out of the mission, but you can't take the mission out of the man," Laura joked.

They all laughed as they walked out of the shrine to continue their search for the orphans.

"I don't know where they might be if they're not here," Marik said looking in all directions. "I don't think they would go out to the bay, as cold as it is, but I don't know where else to look."

"You lead the way," Mike responded.

He and Laura followed closely behind as Marik walked out toward the bay. As they got near, they saw that the ground declined about ten feet to two sets of train tracks, then steeply down another twenty feet to the frozen bay. "We have to go down further to where we can go down a path to the bay," Marik informed them. Mike and Laura continued to follow him for another quarter of a mile along the ridge above the tracks. While they were walking, one of the passenger trains with all bright blue cars rushed past headed for Vladivostok.

"There they are!" Marik pointed out toward the bay as soon as the train had passed.

The children were standing out on the snow-covered ice of the bay and had been watching the train. They quickly spied the visitors as well, and began waving and yelling.

"Which one do you think is Katya?" Mike asked facetiously as one of the children ran from the crowd toward the shore, frantically waving hello.

"Hello, Princess!" Laura yelled. "I'm coming!"

"Mama!"

"Katya!"

Laura picked her up for a long hug. The two continued embracing until Marik and Mike finally walked up.

"Poppy!" Katya squealed as she wriggled free from Laura.

"*Preens-yessa!*" Mike yelled as he scooped her up in his arms. She hugged him tightly for several minutes. "What are you guys doing out here in the cold?" he asked.

Marik translated for Katya and then waited for a response. "She says that they are drawing pictures in the snow with sticks," he reported.

"Well that sounds like too much fun to miss," Mike said as the four of them began to move closer to the crowd of children and several caregivers. In the distance, a half mile or so away, a car was parked way out on the ice with an ice fisherman perched patiently over his hole. Katya and the three visitors had hardly reached the crowd before they were swarmed with the other children, all chattering in Russian.

"They want you to get out the camera to make pictures of them," Marik translated.

Mike laughed, placed Katya down on the snow-covered ice, removed the digital camera from the pack, and began shooting pictures of the anxious children.

Laura took Katya by the hand and wandered in the snow while Katya showed her the pictures that she had drawn. Then they went over to see the masterpiece that Sofia was working on. It was a big car complete with people smiling out the windows.

"*Ma-sheena!*" Katya squealed. *Car!*

Laura reached into her coat pocket and pulled out a cheap plastic ball point pen to use for a stick. She bent down over the snow and started to draw. Katya watched intently as did the few other children who were not in the middle of the photography session. Soon the children were shouting out guesses as to what the picture would be while Marik translated. "She thinks it's a bear. He thinks it's a truck. Now she thinks it's a flower," Marik continued.

Laura quickly finished the snow sketch and stood up. "*Bah-bawch-kah!*" Sofia said decisively.

"Yes, of course," Marik said before translating. "It's a butterfly."

"*Tsve-tok!*" Katya squealed. "*Tsve-tok!*"

"She wants you to draw a flower," Marik translated.

"Okay," Laura said as she put the pen in Katya's hand. She bent over the snow with Katya, and helped her to draw a large flower complete with stem and leaves.

The children loved it. Soon Mike walked over and took

pictures as Laura and Sofia sketched drawings in the snow at the children's requests. They drew buses, trains, dogs, cats, horses, and cows. Finally Sofia drew a picture of an airplane with Katya looking out a side window and waving, foreshadowing her upcoming trip.

Then she began to speak to the children in Russian.

"Sofia says it's time for the children to go back inside before they get chilled," Marik told the two Americans. Several of the boys started to run for the embankment, trying to be the first to scale it. The other children and caregivers started to walk, following in their footprints.

Katya stepped directly in front of Mike, turned to face him and held up her hands. "You've got it, Princess," he said as he scooped her up in his arms. He loved having this time with his little girl. Several minutes later, Katya began to speak Russian to Mike.

"I'm sorry, Princess, I don't understand," Mike responded.

"*Ah-poh-stee*," she repeated.

"I'm sorry, Sweetheart," Mike said sincerely. "I know that you're saying *apostee.* I just don't know what that means. Let's go ask Marik." Mike started back toward Marik, and Katya continued to try to get him to understand. Each time she said it slower and more clearly. It seemed to intensify proportionally to the distance they covered.

"*Ah-poh-stee. Ah-poh-stee.*"

A few seconds later Mike was standing next to Marik with Katya in arms. "Marik, what does *Ah-poh-stee* mean?"

"It means put me down. Why?"

Mike laughed and put Katya down on the ground. She immediately ran toward the group of children and caregivers who were now nearing the shrine. "She had been saying that to me for several minutes, but I didn't understand. It's funny, though. She never wiggled or tried to get down, she just kept saying it over and over."

"Well, now you know for next time," Marik said chuckling.

Marik, Mike, and Laura continued to walk toward the shrine, where Sofia and Katya had stopped and were talking.

Katya looked intently at Sofia as the caregiver stood and

spoke her best English to the other three adults. "She want go home *now.*"

"Oh, Princess," Laura said as she picked up the little girl. "I wish you could come home now, too."

Marik began to speak with Katya in Russian. Finally, after arguing for several seconds, the little girl began to cry and buried her head in her mother's shoulder.

Tears welled up in Laura's eyes as she squeezed Katya against her. "We'll come back as soon as we can," Mike said as he patted Katya on the back. Marik translated, but Katya wouldn't respond, so the small group walked solemnly together, following the others back to the building.

"Marik," Mike began as they entered the building. "We have very much enjoyed playing with the other children and seeing how Katya reacts with them. But we only have half an hour left. Would it be possible for us to meet alone with Katya, I mean alone with you and Sasha translating?"

"Yes, of course. You wait here with the others. I'll go find Sasha and ask them what room we can use." Marik hurried away while Mike, Laura, and Katya removed their coats and hats. Laura pulled a comb from her pocket and struggled through Katya's tangled hair as softly as possible. Then she pulled a barrette from her own long hair and showed it to Katya just before placing it in her hair. Katya glowed.

"*Katya kuk Mama,*" she said happily. *Katya is like Mama*.

Soon Marik returned. "They said that they are taking the other children to another room for an activity," Marik told them as he and Sasha entered the room. "We can stay here and talk to Katya."

"What do you have in mind?" Sasha asked Laura.

"First of all, we want to go over changing her name."

"Alright, we can do that. What are you going to call her?"

"Sarah Katerina. Please tell her that we wanted her to be able to keep her Russian name as part of her name, but that we wanted to give her another special name in English. Tell her that it means Princess."

"Really?" Sasha questioned. "I have heard that name in English before. Does it really mean Princess?"

"Yes, the name means Princess, in Hebrew."

"I'll be sure to tell her that. I'm sure she will be excited."

Laura continued. "We have some books that we want to leave with Katya. They have been translated into Russian and they are also in English. One tells her about her new family and home, and the other tells her about the trip we will take to get home when we come back to get her. Would you please read those to her and explain them? They're pretty short. The books are hers to keep, so she can take them back to the orphanage with her when camp is over."

"Sure, no problem," Sasha responded.

Mike picked up Katya and sat on the bench with her on his lap. Sasha sat on one side of them and Laura on the other.

"Katya, you know how everything is said differently in English than it is in Russian?" Sasha asked in her native tongue.

"*Dá*."

"Well, when you move to America, you will have a new American name."

"*Dá*."

"Your parents want you to keep your Russian name for a middle name. They think that your Russian name is very beautiful. But they have chosen a very special name for you to have for a first name. They want to call you Sarah. Sarah means Princess!"

Katya gasped as she grinned from ear to ear. Then she turned and looked at her papa and threw her arms around his neck. "*Preens-yessa*," he reaffirmed, speaking softly in her ear.

She released Mike and turned to her mother. "*Seh-la Preens-yessa*."

"Yes, Sweetheart. Sarah means Princess."

Katya lunged forward and wrapped her arms around her mother while still sitting on Mike's lap. Then she pulled back and gave her a quick kiss on the lips. The little girl was overwhelmed. Who could have ever imagined that a name could be such a wonderful gift? Then she turned back to Sasha.

Sasha opened up the first soft book and began to read to Katya in Russian. There was one page with pictures and explanations for each of the family members. Then there was a picture of each of the main rooms in the house, including the bedroom that she and Luba would share. There was a page for the horses and even one for the family dog, a Siberian Husky named Dasha, acquired several months before and intentionally given a popular Russian name to make her seem more familiar to Katya on her arrival home. Katya was fascinated reading the book of her own fairytale about to come true. Sasha kept asking her if she had any questions, but she just shook her head no and raced to each of the following pages in anticipation.

Then Sasha opened the next soft book. "When the sun goes down in Partizansk," Sasha started, "the sun comes up in Michigan!" She continued to read the book, which told of a day soon to come when Papa and Mama would come back to get her. It was filled with pictures, and it also explained that they would meet with a judge and make the judge a promise that they would keep her in their family forever. It talked about leaving the orphanage, staying in hotels, flights on airplanes, eating at restaurants, visiting Moscow and then the flight home. Sasha continued to read. "And then when it is time to leave Moscow, we will get on a very big airplane, and the pilots will fly the plane way up above the clouds until they can see the sun. The pilots will follow the sun all the way to Michigan. Then the sun will go back to Russia, to be with our friends there."

Katya grinned her biggest grin with her deepest dimples as she excitedly looked back at Sasha who was wiping tears from her face. She then spun and faced Laura who was also crying. Finally Katya turned to Mike who was still holding firm on his commitment not to let her see him cry. She kept smiling, but squealed with anticipation as she threw her arms around his neck and hugged him tightly as he hugged her.

Mike stood up and placed Katya on Laura's lap. Laura had Sasha explain to her how much she loved her and would miss her. Then she promised to return as soon as she could to bring her and her sister home.

"Katya wants to know when you will come back," Sasha translated.

"I don't know. How long will it take, Sasha?" she asked, every bit as curious as Katya.

"You know how it is," Sasha began. "There is no set time. But my guess is that it will be somewhere between thirty and sixty days. But probably closer to sixty."

Laura knew that thirty to sixty days was a little too abstract for a five-year-old to comprehend. Besides that, counting by days would seem like a lifetime to a child. "When do the flowers bloom here?" Laura asked.

"About the middle of April," Sasha responded.

"Two months from now," Laura said, more thinking out loud than making a statement. "Please tell Katya that when the snow goes away and the flowers come up, we will come back to get her."

Tears twinkled in Sasha's eyes again at the beautifully simple way that was being given to the child to help her to understand. She translated for Katya as Laura pulled a fabric marking pen from the backpack. Laura opened up the soft book on the family to the last page which was a blank white one. She held it across Katya's lap as she drew several flowers across the bottom of the page to help her to remember. Then she capped the pen to return it to the backpack.

"*Nyet!*" Katya called anxiously. She reached out and took the pen away from Laura, pulled off the cap and drew a large sun, complete with a smiling face, at the top of the page overlooking the flowers.

The two ladies cried as they realized that Katya had understood the symbolism of the sun connecting Russia and America, transporting love between those separated by the distance.

"I love you," Laura said, squeezing the child and knowing that she only had moments left before they needed to leave.

Sasha translated and Katya responded immediately.

"*Yá-Tibya-Lo-Bloo, Mama.*" No translation was needed.

Laura stood up with Katya and hugged her tightly one last time before handing her back to Mike. The tears were now streaming down Laura's face.

"*Yá-Tibya-Lo-Bloo, Preens-yessa,*" Mike said as he squeezed her tightly.

"*Yá-Tibya-Lo-Bloo, Papa.*"

Mike couldn't hold back any longer as the tears left his eyes and rolled down his cheeks. Katya just kept squeezing, even after several full minutes had passed and he tried to pull her away. She wasn't crying. She had been warned by the orphanage workers time and time again that she needed to be on her best behavior around her mama and papa. No one wanted to adopt a crybaby. But she was sad. Finally she loosened her grip on Mike and he held her back to look at her.

"Papa is crying because he will miss you," Sasha explained.

"I will miss Papa, too," Katya responded through Sasha. "*Ee Mama*." Then Katya spoke briefly to Sasha.

"Oh, she's so sweet!" Sasha said when Katya had finished. "She told me that she will miss me, too."

"I had never thought of that," Mike began. "Can you imagine how you would feel about someone who found your Mama and Papa and gave you a way out of an orphanage?"

The three adults just smiled. Sofia had returned to take Katya back to the other children, so Mike gave her one last kiss and put her down. Then he pulled the winter scarf from his coat pocket and wrapped it snuggly around Katya's neck. Before leaving the hotel that morning he had sprinkled it with his cologne. Katya noticed. She picked up the end of the long scarf, held it to her nose for a deep breath and then smiled at Mike.

Then Laura stooped down and gave her one last kiss.

Sasha spoke briefly with the Knights, telling them that the time would go quickly and not to worry. While they spoke, Katya's mind was racing. She wanted so much to give her papa a gift, but she had nothing to give him. Then she remembered the barrette that her mother had put in her hair earlier. She reached up to pull it loose, but it was stuck. Katya knew that she didn't have much time, so she pulled quickly and firmly, removing the clasp along with a small clump of hair. Then she quickly and quietly slipped it into the pocket of Mike's overcoat, undetected.

"I guess this is it," Laura said as Sofia took Katya by the hand to lead her away.

"*Pah-ká, Mama. Pah-ká, Papa*," she said as she took Sofia's hand and started out the door.

"*Pah-ká, Preens-yessa*," they replied together, and with that, she left the room.

The door remained open, and Mike and Laura watched her walk across the hall and up the stairs, holding Sofia's right hand with her left and carrying the soft books, pressed up against her body with her right. As Sofia and Katya reached the landing, half way up the stairs, they turned to go up the second level. Katya stuck her head back around the banister and squatted down for one last peak at her parents. She grinned at them for just a split second before she disappeared from their view.

Laura was still crying while they put on their coats and hats, and though Mike had stopped crying, he wasn't in much better shape. It was a solemn walk down the hall and out the big steel double doors to the bitter cold outside.

The four adults were halfway to the airport before Sasha broke the silence. "We have enjoyed having you here," she said happily. "When we read your home study, we didn't know that we would like you this much."

"We didn't show very well, huh?" Mike responded.

"No, it's not that. The home studies and paperwork are just so formal. It's hard to get a feel from them on what kind of people the paperwork represents. We thought you would be a typical family, no different than most. But you are special. We have had a lot of fun with you and the children this week. It was fun to see you with all of them."

"It just breaks my heart that we can't take more of them home," Mike responded. "I just wish they could all have homes with loving parents."

"We all wish that," Sasha concurred. "But we can only change it one family at a time."

Sasha tried to maintain the conversation to help keep the Americans from concentrating on the fact that they were leaving their children. "So, are you tired after such a busy week?"

"I'm exhausted," Mike responded. "I'll probably sleep during the entire flight to Korea. That is, if I don't cry all the way there instead."

"It's such an emotional rollercoaster," Laura said, referencing the comparison that she had used earlier in the trip. "It's not just the jetlag, or the running around. The emotional highs and lows are so extreme that I don't think I was more exhausted after giving birth."

"All of the adoptive parents go through that," Sasha

replied. "We hear it all the time. But what a lot of people don't realize is that the children go through it, too. Many times after visits, within a short period, the children ask the workers if they can go and take a rest. Within minutes they're asleep."

"The poor little things," Laura acknowledged.

"They really prepare these kids to perform for potential parents," Sasha explained. "They are told to be on their best behavior, to be polite. Not to cry, not to shout. Many times they are even told that they should not even frown. I'm sure the workers are just trying to help the children to be attractive to the prospective parents, but sometimes the poor little things are under enormous pressure."

"You know," Mike said pensively, "Now that you mention it, I hardly ever saw Katya frown! Sometimes I literally wondered if she would get cramps in her cheeks from smiling so much. Are you telling me she was parent-shopping all the time?"

"I have known Katya for almost a year now. She is a very happy child and she does love to smile. But she is a typical child. She does have days when she's not as happy as you have seen her. She is delightful, though, and she will be a wonderful addition to your family."

"It will be nice when we finally get them home and they can just be themselves," Laura said.

The couples continued to visit until they finally arrived at the airport. Marik helped Mike pull the luggage into the terminal and then he and Sasha waited in line with them until they had their boarding passes. They took them to the customs line and waited until they were ready to go through the final security checkpoint. "We can't go through the checkpoint," Marik informed them. "But you won't have any trouble beyond here. We wish you a safe and pleasant trip home, and we look forward to your return."

The Knights thanked Marik and then Sasha. Mike firmly shook Marik's hand and then they both gave Sasha a quick hug and Laura hugged Marik.

"*Desvidania!*" the couples called back and forth. And with that, Marik and Sasha walked away.

22

In Between

The boarding and takeoff from Vladivostok were uneventful. Mike and Laura were pretty quiet, replaying the events of the previous week through their heads. Finally, when the flight attendant announced that the aircraft had reached an altitude where portable electronic devices could be used, Mike pulled out his headphones and CD player. He wanted to listen to something fairly mellow. He was too tired for anything else. Mostly he just wanted to get his mind off things and take a break from his emotions. Eventually, he made his selection, snapped it in, turned it on, and laid his seat back to relax.

Mike decided to take a nap, so he pulled his overcoat out from under the seat to use for a blanket. As he did, he heard the rattle of Tic-Tacs in the pocket, so he reached in for the container. As he grabbed for the plastic box, he felt something in the pocket that he didn't recognize, so he removed it for inspection. Tears came to his eyes and immediately tumbled down his cheeks as he recognized the barrette and soft light brown hair.

"Are you alright?" Laura asked while touching his face softly and wiping away a tear.

"Yeah, I'm fine. Look at this," he said while holding out the hairpiece.

"When did that fall out?" Laura asked. "Oh, Mike, you forgot to give it back to her!"

"It didn't fall out," Mike replied. "Look," he said while pointing at the hair stuck in the clasp, "she pulled it out. She must have put it in my coat pocket when we weren't looking."

"So it was a present," Laura said, tears welling up in her own eyes.

"It appears that way. I can't believe it. Katya owns nothing in the world other than the few small gifts that we gave her, yet she felt the need to give something to us. I can't think of a gift I have ever received that I could appreciate this much," he said as he thumbed the soft light brown hair still stuck in the clasp.

Laura began crying, too. "I'm sure going to miss those two little girls," she said. Then she turned back toward Mike. "I love you," she said softly and then she kissed him gently on the lips and again on the forehead.

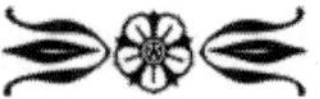

They spent the night in Seoul again, and by the next morning they were off to Tokyo, and then on to Detroit. The 747 touched down early Saturday afternoon. It took over an hour and a half to get their luggage and clear customs, and another hour and a half to drive home. They called Mark and Dawn as soon as they cleared customs and let them know they were on their way. Mark assured them all was well, that the boys were excited to see them. He also said that Dawn would have dinner ready when they got home.

"I can honestly say that was about the most eventful week of my entire life," Mike said as he turned off the red Corvette and pushed the button on the remote to close the garage door.

"I know what you mean," Laura responded just before the walk-in door burst open with Jeff and Stephen spilling through it into the garage. "It looks like it's not going to calm down just yet," she added.

"Hi, guys!" Mike called as he climbed out of the car.

"Hello, boys," Laura followed.

"Hi, Dad! Hi, Mom!" the boys called over each other.

"How are Sarah and Celeste?" Stephen asked anxiously.

"When do you go back to get them?" Jeff questioned.

"Hold on, hold on," Mike said holding up his hands. "Help me get the luggage out of the car. We'll tell you everything when we get inside."

Dinner was a flurry of questions and answers recounting almost every event that had transpired over the week-long trip to Russia. But all of the conversation really centered around one pinnacle question. "When do they get to come home?"

"Sarah asked that same question minutes before we left," Laura began. "Sasha told us it would be somewhere between thirty and sixty days, but probably closer to sixty. Now, that is what we are hoping for, but there is no set time period. It could be longer. We'll just have to see."

The family continued talking for hours, with Mike and Laura going through the details of the trip and all of the cultural peculiarities of Russia. It wasn't like it was strange to the boys. They were used to Mike traveling and he had always taught the family about other people and places. Jeff and Stephen were fascinated, and their excitement grew with the prospect of adding family members from another culture. They, as their parents, were anxious for that to happen as soon as it possibly could.

Mark had been right about Mom. She wasn't looking well at all.

Mike made the visit the day after he and Laura arrived home. He let himself into the house and found his mother in bed, watching TV. Throughout the morning she smiled and laughed and said all the right things, but Mike could tell there was something wrong; the way she winced ever-so-slightly whenever she adjusted in the bed, the way she held her breath at times, waiting for some undisclosed pain to pass.

"Mom, I'm worried about you."

"Oh, Mike. Has anyone ever told you that you worry too much?"

"Just you and Laura," Mike said with a smile.

"Well, you should listen to your wife. She's right. And not just about the worrying; she's right about everything." She held her breath again, trying to make it look like she was pausing in thought. "Laura is a wonderful mother, your new daughters are so lucky."

Mike spent the rest of the time with his mom talking about lighter things, brighter things; new hope and new life for the little Russian girls; the promise of spring; the warmth and comfort of family.

But when he left he couldn't help but feel that there were a few dark days ahead.

"Hello, Mike. This is Kristin from Miracle Child. How are you doing?"

"Oh, not bad, yet." Mike said after picking up the phone his first day back at work.

"Not bad, yet? What is that supposed to mean?" Kristin laughed into the phone.

"I have learned to leave myself a little latitude on how I'm doing when I answer a call on adoption. I've found things can go bad in a hurry."

"Boy! You can be quite the pessimist, can't you?" Kristin teased him back.

"I like to think of myself as a realist."

"Yes, okay, I guess you're right. So how was your trip?"

"It was wonderful. All things considered, we had a great trip."

"I understand that you had a pretty big surprise."

"As a matter of fact, we did. Were you in on that?"

"What do you mean?"

"If you intend for people to adopt more than one child, I really think that you should tell them up front rather than changing the plans as you go," Mike said, turning more serious.

"No, Mike. We weren't in on it. We had no idea Luba even existed. That was the coordinators in Vladivostok. We wouldn't mislead you. I'm sorry that happened."

"Oh, that's alright. It looks like everything is working out for the best. Those two little girls are darlings. Laura and I immediately fell in love with both of them. I just don't know how we're going to wait for the next 27 to 57 days until we get them."

"Excuse me? Did you say 27 to 57 days?"

"Sure I did. Sasha told us three days ago that it should be between 30 and 60 days. If my double digit math is still up to par, then that means we now have between 27 and 57 days," Mike said smugly, knowing that an absolute countdown was unrealistic, but wanting to keep the pressure on the adoption agency, anyway.

"Oh, I just hate it when our people give dates! Russia is just so unpredictable. I really don't think it's healthy to count down like that," Kristin said cautiously, hoping that Mike had been joking, but not quite sure.

"Don't worry too much," Mike reassured her.

Kristin laughed. "Alright, then. Hey, I tried to catch Laura at home; but she's not there. With the additional child, we need duplicates of all of the paperwork that we did for Katya. We can make copies, so we don't have to start over; but all of the copies have to be notarized and appostilled. We need to have this done quickly so it doesn't hold things up in Russia."

"How quickly do they need to be done?"

"I would like to have them by the end of the week. Do you think that's possible?"

"I'm sure that if I tell Laura we need to do that to keep things from being held up, she'll make it happen. I'll have her call you this afternoon so she can see exactly what we need to do."

"Alright, Mike. Thank you. I'm glad to hear things went well on your trip. We're so happy for you and your family. Have Laura give me a call."

"Sure. Thanks for keeping this moving. We'll talk to you soon."

Laura moved quickly and efficiently in accomplishing the additional paperwork. It wasn't nearly as difficult the second time, as she already knew what to do and what to expect. The days moved on slowly, but they moved on. Of course, the first full Saturday back, Laura insisted on going shopping for clothes, and the rest of the family wanted to participate. Jeff and Stephen were right there to make sure that no fashion trends were violated, so their little sisters would be cool. There were bell bottom jeans, sweaters, blouses and skirts, socks and tights, as well as all of the other necessities: shoes, little purses and bracelets, necklaces and hair accessories. Even though Jeff and Stephen saw no reason to do more than one frilly dress for each of the girls, which would only really be used for Sundays, Mike and Laura couldn't resist going overboard on attire that was a bit more formal. They finally settled on three frilly dresses each for the girls. Then there were coats, jackets, snowsuits, hats, mittens, scarves, and boots. Laura made sure that several outfits, as well as the coats and hats, matched so that she could dress up the girls together. She had never had so much fun shopping.

Then they needed toys for little girls. Baby dolls, Barbie dolls, a tea set, more stuffed animals. Laura even made sure she duplicated the pink and purple teddy bears that had been left in Russia, making the practical assumption that the orphanages would keep the ones already given to the children on the first trip. After all, that was best anyway. The original bears would be put to good use.

Even after the initial shopping spree was over, hardly a trip to the store ended without an additional purchase of a cute piece of clothing or a new toy. Mike even decided that Katya needed to leave gifts for her best friends Anya and Marishka, so he picked up two matching fluffy brown Teddy Bears. Other than the shopping, life moved on pretty much as normal. No one really talked about when the final news to travel would come. Everyone knew that speculation would do no good and would only make the time seem to move slower.

"I just spoke with Laura to see how everything is going," Kristin told Mike on the phone. "I know the waiting can be tough. She said everyone is doing fine and that you're ready."

"Yeah, we're doing fine. But each day we get a little more anxious. I thought it was tough waiting for the referral, and then for the travel plans for the first trip. But both of those pale in comparison. I just want to get them safely home, where nothing can endanger the adoption any more."

"I remember waiting for Lee. It was difficult. Hey, Laura told me that you would be able to tell me how many more days were left in the countdown."

"Negative three to 27."

"That's amazing. Did you have to look at a calendar or

something?"

"No. I always know."

"That's what Laura said. She says she doesn't like to think about it, but that you always know. I'm glad to see you were able to make the transition to the first set of negative numbers. I hope you don't have to make the next," Kristin joked.

"Yeah, you and me both. But, you know that a negative multiplied by a negative makes a positive."

"Um, yeah, but I'm not sure in this case it works that way."

"Okay, you're right. A negative minus a negative is just more negative. But I hope we don't have to go there. So, what's up? Is there any particular reason for the call?"

"Mostly I'm just checking to see how you are doing. Laura got us all of the extra paperwork we needed and we sent it off to Russia. As far as we know, everything is moving along just fine. But I also wanted to make sure you're ready. Even though it will still probably be a little longer, things could come through at any time."

"Oh, we're ready. We have all of the shopping done, and our passports are sitting at the travel agency waiting for the invitation so we can get the visas. You could tell us to be in Russia next week and we would pull it off."

"Well, hopefully, we'll be able to give you a little more time to prepare for this trip. We like to give people at least two weeks notice, but you never can tell. I guess you probably need to get back to work. I'm glad to hear everything is progressing and that you are all doing well."

"Alright, thanks for the call. Keep us posted. Goodbye."

"How many days left?" Kristin opened the conversation as Mike answered the phone.

"Negative 29 to one," he responded.

"Are you going to be able to make a transition to double negatives?"

"I guess I'll have to," he replied glumly.

"Well, I have some good news. We just got your court

date. You and Laura are scheduled for court on Thursday, April 21! You can stop counting now and you won't even have to go into double negatives! How does that sound?"

"That sounds great! Does Laura know?"

"Yes. I'm sorry. I probably should have let her tell you, but I wasn't sure if you were into the negative numbers yet or not. Laura didn't know either. Laura said I could tell you."

"Oh man, that's great. I bet Laura was excited."

"She was. She's bouncing off the walls."

"Wait a second, though, April 21. When do we need to leave?"

"Well, that's the bad news. I hoped we would be able to give you some time to prepare this time. Unfortunately, that's not the case. You and Laura need to visit the children at least once before court. With Partizansk being several hours from Vladivostok, that means that you can't visit the same day as court. Also, it makes it difficult to visit on the same day that you fly in. We recommend you arrive this Monday."

"You've got to be kidding! That means that we have to leave this Saturday! What's today? Wednesday?"

"Yes."

"This is the same as last time, but then we used tourist visas. Can we even get adoption visas that fast?"

"We have to."

"We can't do tourist visas this time. They almost threw us out last time."

"No. We never do tourist visas for the second trip."

"Well, I can get the plane tickets. That's not a problem. But the visas need to be FedEx-ed back to me by Friday. That means that the travel agency has to send them to us Thursday afternoon! It's already Wednesday? You still have to send them our invitation to travel!"

"I just sent it out by FedEx."

"So they'll get it tomorrow."

"Yes. You need to call them and tell them what's going on. You aren't the first ones that have needed a rush. I'm sure they do it all the time. Usually, there is a fee to process visas faster, but it is possible for them to get them the same day."

"This is crazy!"

"I know, Mike. This will be hectic, but it will work out. I'm sorry we couldn't give you more notice, but we can't control when Russia schedules the court date. All we can do is follow their schedule."

"What about the other flight dates? We want to bring the kids home through Moscow and spend a couple of days there with them."

"Let's see, let me look at my calendar. With court on the twenty-first, a ten day waiting period is over on Sunday, the first. It's doubtful that you'll get them on a Sunday, though, so plan on Monday, the second. You should be able to get their Russian passports and stuff Tuesday, so plan to fly to Moscow on Wednesday, the fourth. After that, it's up to you. I mean, it's possible that they'll waive the ten-day waiting period, but that almost never happens in this area, so it's best to plan that it won't. If it does, you can always change your flights in Russia."

"Alright. I'll get right on it. Thanks for the call."

"Sure. Hey, congratulations!"

"Thanks. We'll talk to you soon."

Mike immediately dialed Laura. "I'm so excited!" Laura squealed as she picked up the phone. She had recognized his number on the caller ID.

"So am I. Did Kristin tell you we need to leave Saturday?"

"No. She said that we have court on the twenty-first."

"Yeah, and in order to get a visit in with the kids before court, which is required, we have to leave Saturday."

"Well, that's a bit of a rush, but we can be ready by then."

"I'm not worried about us. I'm worried about the visas."

"Oh, my goodness! Can they be ready?"

"Only if everything goes perfectly. We don't have one day to spare."

"What do we need to do?"

"You call Jennifer and have her make the travel arrangements. Tell her that we need to leave Saturday and arrive in Vladivostok on Monday. Then we need tickets to Moscow for Wednesday, the fourth. We should try to get home soon after that, so let's plan on flying home on Sunday, the eighth."

"May eighth?"

"Yes."

"Dawn's baby is due the tenth of May. This isn't going to work for them. Should I call Mom?"

"Sure. She'll be happy to do it. Just ask her if she minds staying at our place so it doesn't mess up the kid's school schedule too badly."

"Okay. Is there anything else I can do?"

"Not for now. I'll get on the phone right now with the other travel agency about the visas, and then I'll let Jim know what's going on."

"I'll see you when I get home."

"I love you, Sweetheart!"

"I love you, too. I'll see you after work."

"Hello, Jim."

"Hi! Any good news yet?"

"Yes. I just got off the phone with the travel agency that's doing the visas. We need to leave this Saturday."

"Wow! That's short notice."

"I'll say it is. The adoption agency just FedEx-ed our letter of invitation from the Department of Education. The travel agency should get it tomorrow morning; I guess they can't start on it until then. But where yours is a tourist invitation, they can start on yours today, if you give them a call."

"Alright. I'll get right on it. Is there anything that I can do to help?"

"I don't think so. Not at this point, anyway. Laura is in the process of calling Jennifer to get the travel all arranged. So it looks like if everything works out, we'll see you at the hotel in Seoul Sunday night."

"That sounds great! I'll look forward to it! See you then."

23

Back Toward the Sunset

"Hello, Jim. It's good to see you again," Mike said while offering his hand in the lobby of the Seoul Incheon Hotel.

"It's great to see you two. It has been too long," Jim replied while shaking his hand. "And Laura, you're looking wonderful, as always." He stepped over for a long and sincere embrace.

"Oh, Jim, it's so good to see you. I miss you so much! Thank you for coming to help us," she replied, not letting go of him until she finished speaking.

"I wouldn't have missed it! I'm so glad that you gave me the opportunity." Jim was never one to acknowledge his own importance, or even his own efforts. He was always graciously shifting attention or credit to someone else.

"So, how is Patty?" Laura asked longingly. She missed her friends from Utah immensely, and while she had friends in Michigan, where they had now lived for ten years, she dearly missed the intimacy that she had with the Christensen family.

"She is doing well. She's so busy with everything she has going, I hardly see her myself. But she did ask me to send her love." Jim and Patty had always been so busy serving others that it seemed that in many instances they worked as a tag team, constantly working, but seldom in the same ring at the same time.

"How was your flight?" Mike asked.

"We had a little turbulence just out of L.A., but other than that, it was great. It was long, though. How about yours?"

"A lot less stressful than the last trip over here. At least the flights were on time this trip. We're a little stiff and sore, but all things considered, it was fine. Have you had dinner?"

"Yes. I got in about five o'clock, so I ate soon after checking in. But if you guys want to grab some dinner in the restaurant here, I could eat a bowl of ice cream. I'd love to visit."

"Sure. Let us run up to the room and freshen up a little first. Okay if we meet you in the restaurant in ten minutes?"

"That would be wonderful. Take your time."

"Sasha, this is Jim. Jim, Sasha." Mike introduced them as soon as they had exited the customs area.

"It's a pleasure to meet you, Sasha."

"Yes, for me too," she responded while offering her hand. "So, I have heard about you from Mike. You are Laura's father?"

"No, not exactly. The Knights and the Christensens have just been very good friends for a lot of years. All of their children call me Grandpa Jim."

"So, Katya will know you as her grandfather."

"Yes."

"That will be good. I was in Partizansk a couple of weeks ago. Katya was showing me your picture in her book. She is very excited to meet you."

"Well, I'm very excited to meet her, too."

"It's good to see you again, Mike and Laura," Sasha said as she stepped away from Jim and gave them each a light hug. "How was your flight?"

"Everything went very well," Mike responded. "How are Katya and Luba doing?"

"Katya was fine when I saw her, a couple of weeks ago. I haven't seen Luba for a while, but I'm sure she's fine, too."

"Are we going to see them today?"

"I'm sorry, I don't think that is possible. But Marik is planning on taking you there for a visit tomorrow. I have a meeting in a little while with a person from the Department of Education, so I think I had better drop you off at the hotel for now."

"Okay," Mike responded, the disappointment apparent in his voice. "What about trading some money? I don't have any rubles."

"There is no good place around here. But let me give you a hundred dollars worth. Then tomorrow you can pay me back."

"Thank you. That's very kind."

"Okay. So last time you stayed at the Hyundai, right?"

"Yes."

"Well, this time we have you staying at the Vlad Motor Inn. They have suites that will work out well for when you have the kids. I think you will like it there."

"That sounds good," Mike replied.

"Okay, then I guess we should go."

The threesome followed Sasha out to the car. "Oh, I forgot how much luggage you guys bring!" Sasha exclaimed. "It won't all fit in the car. Maybe we should get a taxi, too. The Vlad Inn isn't too far." Sasha hailed a cab, and the majority of the luggage was loaded into it with the lighter pieces going into Sasha's car. Jim graciously offered to ride with the luggage and let Mike and Laura ride together with Sasha. It was only a fifteen minute ride to the hotel.

"How are things going with adoptions in Russia now?" Laura asked as they drove to the hotel.

"Not so good. The media is still really against it and that makes the people against it, too."

"Is it better or worse than the last time we were here?"

"It's worse. Much worse. Remember that lady from Illinois who beat her adopted Russian child to death?"

"Yes."

"Well, you probably already know, but they sentenced her last week."

"No, we didn't know. What did she get?"

"I don't remember exactly, but it was a prison sentence of only a few years. With a chance at parole, she might not be in prison very long at all. Russians think it is not nearly enough. The media is really making a big deal about it. First, they think it took way too long for the U.S. legal system to work. In Russia, punishment would have come much quicker. Now, they think the punishment is not severe enough. There is a lot of talk that the lady got off easier because it was a Russian child rather than an American one. This is a very hot topic right now."

"How will that affect us?" Mike asked.

"Well, we had two court hearings for adoption last week. The judges were pretty harsh on the families in both instances."

"What do you mean?"

"Well, mostly they just asked them what they thought about the sentence. Then they wanted to know how the parents planned to discipline the children. It didn't seem like they were trying to stop those adoptions, but they wanted the Americans to know that they took abuse very seriously."

"So how should we handle this in court?"

"Just tell the judge you are very sorry about the child that died, and you are angry that the child was abused. The judge doesn't expect you to understand the United States legal system. But it's very important for the judge to hear you are against corporal punishment, whether you are or not."

"Oh, don't worry." Mike continued. "We don't discipline our children that way. That won't be a problem."

"How do you think that this will affect adoption in Russia in the long term?" Laura queried.

"I don't know. But things right now are very unstable."

"What will you and Marik do for work if foreign adoption is stopped?"

"I don't know," Sasha responded nonchalantly, with the typically Russian attitude of worrying about tomorrow's problems tomorrow. "But something would work out for us. Marik has an advanced degree in software engineering, so he won't have trouble finding work. For me, I have my English skills and office skills. Something would come up. But right now, adoption is still going, so we will continue to work in adoption."

Within minutes, they arrived at the hotel with Jim's taxi right behind. Sasha escorted them in and made sure they were situated, and then hurried off to her appointment.

Laura, Mike and Jim took their luggage up to their rooms and were just getting settled in when the phone rang. The lady at the front desk told Mike there was some additional paperwork that he needed to fill out, so he left Laura and went downstairs. The paperwork was mostly just contact information, and Mike was finished in just a few minutes and headed back to the room when he was stopped by a medium-built man in his mid-forties.

"Hello, I'm Craig. I'm the General Manager here at the Hotel," he said as he offered his hand.

"Hi, Craig. That's not a Russian accent. It sounds pretty American."

"Actually, I'm from Canada."

"Really! Canadian? And you're living and working here in eastern Russia?"

"That I am."

"So when's the statute of limitations up?"

Craig laughed. "Oh, it's nothing like that, I assure you. I just got a job offer to run this place that I couldn't match in Canada or the States. I can make enough money here in a few years to set myself up pretty well. Actually, I have property in New Mexico that I'm planning to build on."

"Wow, I never would have guessed."

"Yeah. Well, I think you'll like it here. They hired me to make this a place where Americans will feel comfortable. I told them I could do that. It's pretty down-to-earth here. The menu is mostly American; we do our best. Also, there is the exercise room upstairs, and the White Rabbit room."

"The what?"

"Oh, the girls at the counter must not have told you. Come on up, I'll show you around."

Mike followed Craig up the stairs. "Here is the laundry room. It's not public access, but this is where your clothes will get cleaned if you send out laundry. Over there is the exercise room. And," he said while walking around a corner, "here is the White Rabbit room."

Mike followed Craig into the room and looked around. "The drinks in the cooler are on the honor system. Just keep track of what you use and call it in to the front desk once a day. We also have a special menu for this room. The prices are significantly less than the restaurant, but the food is comparable. I just don't have the staff expense, so we're able to keep the cost down. For food up here, we ask you to pick it up rather than having it delivered to help us keep the cost down.

But, if the staff isn't too busy, a lot of times they'll just bring it up anyway. Truth be known, they like the tips."

"That makes sense."

"The pool table is there for anyone to use free of charge, and some people just like to come down to relax and watch TV. There are videos that you can check out down at the front desk for use here or in your room. For your room, you can check out a VCR or DVD player for ten bucks a day."

"That sounds great."

"So, I assume that you and your wife are here for an adoption?"

"Yes, we are."

"Boy or girl?"

"Actually, two little girls."

"Are they sisters?"

"Yes. Katya is five and Luba is two."

"Are those your first?"

"No. Laura and I have two boys at home."

"That's great. Congratulations."

"Thanks."

"We have an adoption scrapbook down at the front desk. Take a minute to look through it. It's pretty fun. Then, if you want to, leave a picture of your family along with a note for the book."

"Sounds great. We'll be sure to do that."

"Well, alright. Enjoy your stay. Be sure to let me know if you need anything."

"Alright, Craig. Thanks. See ya around."

"The restaurant here has pretty good food," Jim commented over his ham and eggs.

"The food is good," Mike replied. "I'm surprised. I've been a lot of other places more Western than Vladivostok where they claim they have American food. I'm usually at least a little disappointed; more often, amused. But this really is good American food. The buffalo wings last night were great!"

"The grilled shrimp were excellent, too," Laura interjected. "I read about other American women who claimed to have lost weight on their adoption trips for lack of food they liked. Actually, I had high hopes, but it looks like I won't be losing any weight while staying here."

They all laughed.

"So what are the plans today?" Jim asked.

"Well, as you know, Marik will pick us up at about nine. Then we go to Partizansk to see the girls. Marik mentioned that we'll be coming back tonight, but I don't know what time."

"So what do we call the girls? Do we use their Russian names or their American ones?" Jim asked.

"We told Sarah last time what her new American name would be, but so far we have only used Russian names. I don't know, Laura, what do you think?"

"I think that we should call them by their Russian names until we get them home. It ought to be a little less confusing for them that way, particularly with Celeste. She is just so young I think it will be hard for her to understand."

Both Jim and Mike agreed.

"Well, I'd like to go up and brush my teeth before Marik comes," Jim said while pushing back his chair. "So, I'll see you in the lobby just before nine?"

"That sounds great. We'll see you then," Mike replied.

"See you soon, Jim. Thanks for coming with us," Laura added.

"I wouldn't have missed it," Jim responded. "I'll see you in a few minutes."

24

The Child is Obsessed!

"I called Katya's orphanage this morning," Marik started as they pulled out of the driveway of the Vlad Inn and onto the highway. "I have some things to do tomorrow and we won't be able to visit the girls, so any visiting before court will have to be done today. That would leave little time to visit with both girls. So, I asked Katya's orphanage if we could take her with us to Luba's orphanage so we could visit with them together. Is that alright with you?"

"Sure. That sounds wonderful!" Laura responded energetically.

"While Katya was at camp on your last visit, the director of her orphanage didn't get to meet you, so I'm sure she will want to visit with you for a few minutes before we leave to see Luba. Then I thought maybe we could offer to take her, Oksana, and Elizaveta to lunch, along with the girls, of course."

"That sounds great," Mike replied. "Hey, we told Katya when we left that when the snow went away and the flowers came up, we would come back to get her. I don't see any flowers yet, so could we stop somewhere along the way and buy some for her?"

"Yes. I know a flower shop along the way. That won't be a problem."

It was about three hours from the time they left the hotel until they began to bump along the smaller residential and business roads of Partizansk. It was only another five minutes before they pulled into a yard filled with several large, orange adobe brick buildings that reminded Mike of elementary schools dating back to the thirties and forties. Three of the buildings were three stories high, with windows on all levels. The fourth building, of similar construction, was only one story high and appeared to be some kind of storage place or maintenance shop. The buildings surrounded a yard with a fair amount of playground equipment, all pretty basic, and mostly things that could be welded together from scrap pipe. But it was well kept and brightly painted. There wasn't much landscaping, but that wasn't unusual.

"Oh my goodness…" Laura spoke softly as she looked around. "Are all of these buildings filled with orphans?"

"People don't live in the little one," Marik began, "and the one over there is the school," he said pointing to one of the three story buildings. "But the other two are filled with orphans."

"How many are here?" Laura asked, all but overwhelmed at the thought of there being so many in such a small city.

"I think that Polina, the director here, said there are about a hundred and thirty."

"Plus the ones in Luba's orphanage?"

"Yes, there are another twenty-five or thirty there."

"Are those all from Partizansk, or are they from other cities, too?" Mike asked, trying to get some kind of an idea as to how many orphans there were.

"Some of these children come from surrounding villages, but all of them are from the area. Most of the cities this size have their own orphanages."

"That breaks my heart!" Laura exclaimed.

"It is sad," Marik replied. "But the children are cared for. They have clothes that fit them, they get enough to eat and they get an education. Almost without exception they are doing better than they were before coming here. But we should go in now and see Katya," he said, dragging Mike away from yet another photo session.

The three Americans followed Marik through the big steel double doors at the front of one of the three-story buildings and into a waiting room outside the director's office. Marik asked them to sit while he went in and informed Polina of their arrival.

Several moments later, Polina, a stout woman in her late fifties or early sixties, with blonde hair and dark roots, appeared at the door with Marik. She spoke quickly in Russian and made gestures welcoming them into her office. Marik translated, and asked the Americans to please take a seat and make themselves comfortable.

"Polina says she is very happy to have you here," Marik translated after all had taken their seats.

"Please tell Polina that we are equally happy to be here," Mike responded.

After Marik passed on the pleasantry, Polina broke loose and spoke for several minutes. She was very enthusiastic, and she kept pointing at the window, outside in the yard, down at the ground and down the hall where Mike assumed that the children stayed. Marik was amused at the story and kept chuckling and nodding, though he hardly got a word in. Finally, Polina finished and waited for Marik to translate the story.

"Polina says that she must be happier to see you than you are to be here. She has been very nervous hoping that you would come soon. She says that Katya is obsessed! Every morning she goes to the window and looks for flowers. When she doesn't see them, she goes out into the yard and looks everywhere, searching for any sign of a flower. Polina says that ever since the snow melted, Katya has asked her and the other workers every day when the flowers will come up. She said that she didn't know why Katya was so obsessed about the flowers until a week ago, when one of the other workers explained to her that Katya's mother told her when the snow went away and the flowers came up, she would return to bring her home. At first, Polina wasn't too worried. But then the grass started to turn green, and some of the buds started to show up on the trees. She knew that any day now, some of the early flowers would bloom and she didn't know what they would tell Katya if the flowers came up before her parents arrived!"

"I am so sorry!" Laura exclaimed. "I had no idea she would take it so literally, and count on us being here the first day that a flower bloomed. I would have never intentionally done that to you, or to her."

Marik translated for Polina, who laughed and then responded in Russian.

"Polina says that it is all for the best. It helped Katya to have something to look forward to, and, since you got here before the flowers, everything worked out very well. She also asks if those flowers are for Katya."

"Yes," Mike responded, since he was the one holding the flowers. "When we got to Russia and saw that the flowers weren't up yet, we wanted to bring these to her so she would know that there were flowers somewhere, and that we really did come when we said we would."

"You have a way with children," Polina expressed to Laura through Marik. "I saw the cloth books that you made for Katya. They are wonderful! Katya still says that you blow kisses to the sun to bring to her. She blows kisses to the sun to take to you, too. I am very happy that Katya will have a mother who loves and understands her. You are a wonderful mother."

Laura waited for Marik to finish translating before humbly thanking Polina. "I am every bit as fortunate as Katya," she responded. "I'm sure she will add as much good to my life, and to our family, as we will add to hers."

Polina responded and Marik waited until she was finished before translating. "Polina says that you understand children very well and it is evident that you feel she is needed in your family. She says this will make difficulties that arise all seem worth the trouble. She is sure Katya will be happy in your home, and her new family will also be happy to have her there. She also says you must be anxious to see Katya again. She knows Katya is anxious to see you. I guess she has been very energetic this morning while waiting for your arrival."

Polina got up and the group began following her down a hallway. They soon arrived at what appeared to be a small locker room with about 24 lockers built into a wall, each similar in size to a high school locker. Two rooms with shut doors adjoined the locker room and Polina excused herself through one of them to retrieve Katya. Marik and the three Americans stood focused on the door, waiting for Polina to reappear with Katya. Suddenly, Mike spied children leaving through the other door, down the hallway from where the Americans had come. "Marishka!" he called anxiously at the little girl who had presented them with the colored picture for Katya on their first trip. Marishka, who was walking along with the other children, looked up excitedly and waved, but she continued to move along out of sight with the other children. "Jim, Laura! Marishka just walked past with some other children," Mike blurted. "She was right over there!" he said while pointing toward the hallway.

Just as Laura looked away to see where Mike was pointing, she heard a door burst open and was all but knocked over as Katya threw her arms around her leg. Mike and Jim turned back around just in time to see Laura sweeping the child up into her arms. Katya threw her arms around her mother's neck, and squeezed her as tightly as her mother was squeezing her. She buried her face against Laura's neck and took a deep breath of the perfume scent that by now only faintly remained on her blanket. Laura and Katya continued to hug for several minutes. Finally, Katya looked up and caught Mike's eye.

"Papa!" she squealed as she wriggled to get down. Laura placed her feet down on the floor and she ran straight to Mike. He didn't even get a chance to hand her the flowers as she leapt for him to catch her and pick her up. He wrapped his arms tightly around her and fought back the tears as he spoke his favorite Russian word; "*Preens-yessa*." Katya snuggled in tightly and smelled his shoulder, taking deep breaths before finally speaking several Russian words.

"She says that you smell like Papa," Marik laughed. "I wonder what she expected you to smell like."

Mike tried to push Katya back several times so that he could look at her, but she just kept hugging him tighter and tighter. Finally she sat back on his arm and smiled her big-dimple smile. Mike lifted the bunch of flowers to her. "Since the flowers here in Partizansk aren't up yet, we brought some flowers for you."

Marik translated as Katya received the flowers and threw her arms around Mike to hug him again. She took another deep breath of his cologne and sighed.

"Hey, Princess, you need to meet *Dyedushka* Jim," Mike said as he pried her back away from him.

Katya looked at Mike excitedly as Marik translated. Mike turned her towards Jim, and Marik made the introduction.

"*Dyedushka* Jim!" she screamed while lunging towards him. It was all Mike could do to keep her from falling out of his arms while transferring her to Jim. Katya threw her arms around Jim and squeezed him just as she had her parents. Jim was overwhelmed at the reception and held her tightly. He could even feel her excited little heart beating against his chest. "She is so precious!" he said, to himself as much as to the others. Neither Katya nor her grandfather showed any signs of releasing their embrace for quite some time. All of the adults were awestruck at how quickly they bonded.

Finally, Jim put her back down and she ran to her mother again. Polina spoke with Marik for several seconds while Laura held Katya.

"Polina wants me to take some pictures of two other children who are coming up for availability on international adoption," Marik explained. "Why don't you guys sit here and visit with Katya. I'll only be ten minutes or so."

"That sounds great," Mike replied.

Laura sat down on a little wooden bench with Katya, while Jim asked questions about the other orphans and Mike filled him in the best he could.

"There are two children who keep peeking out of that room," Jim told Mike while pointing to the door where Mike had seen Marishka and the others leave earlier. Mike turned just in time to see the two children poke their heads back in the room.

"That's Dasha! The boy is Jenya! We played with them at camp last time." The children stuck their heads back through the doorway and giggled at the strangers from Amérika. "Dasha!" Mike called to her while holding out his hand. He was sure from her reaction that she remembered him. But the children only giggled and quickly shut the door. It was becoming evident that the children were not supposed to leave the room. But soon others appeared, in turn, peeking out the door. Jim waited until the door closed again, and then crept over near it and waited. Seconds later the door cracked open to reveal a nose and one eye peeking out. Jim lunged forward with a gruff growl and the door slammed shut amid squeals from the other side. The children grew bolder and began to taunt Jim, while daring each other further and further out into the locker room with Jim scaring them back behind the door amid more squeals and laughter each time. Then there was a delay. The door didn't open at its usual interval. So Jim crept up next to the doorway with his back tight up against the wall, waiting for a victim to pop out of the room. He fully intended to grab and tickle the next child through the door. He didn't have to wait long. The door popped open and the unwary victim walked through the doorway. But Jim noticed that something wasn't quite right as he lunged forward with his arms up, almost ready to produce his roar. The prey was much too tall. One of the workers had called the children back away from the door, and was now exiting the room. Somehow, mid-leap, Jim was able to stop himself and pull back without the unwary victim even knowing he was there. His eyes were like silver dollars as he turned to face Mike who had erupted into a fit of laughter.

"I almost grabbed her!" he said while walking nervously back toward Mike.

"I know you did. I watched it happen. I wondered what extremes we were going to have to go through to get you out of a Siberian prison."

"Boy, that was too close for comfort."

Mike and Jim both took turns holding Katya and visiting for the next five minutes until Polina returned with Marik.

"Polina wonders if you would like to see where Katya sleeps," Marik asked the Americans.

"Yes, of course," Laura replied.

Marik spoke briefly to Katya, who smiled and wriggled to get down. She grabbed Laura's hand and led her to the door. The Americans followed Katya into the dormitory with the Russians right behind. But the children that Jim had been playing with through the door were nowhere to be seen. They had obviously been removed to the neighboring room through the doorway at the opposite end of the dormitory.

"Look how cute!" Laura exclaimed as they walked into the room. Two windows on adjacent walls streamed light into the room. The white walls were decorated with paintings of cartoon style palm trees, monkeys, snails, clouds, and a sun. Most of the twin sized beds had bunches of flowers painted on the headboard and footboard.

Mike counted six beds in one row and seven in the other. Each of the beds had a small wooden chair next to it. The beds were made with clean sheets, pillowcases, and a blanket, and the room was immaculately clean.

"Show your parents where you sleep, Katya," Polina coaxed the child.

Katya ran to one of the beds half way down the first row, turned back toward them and placed her hand on the foot of her bed. Mike snapped a picture. He was surprised at what good conditions Katya and her peers lived in, but still heartsick over the lack of anything family-oriented. As much as everyone had done to provide for these children, the loneliness that came from lacking a family almost overwhelmed him.

As soon as the camera flash went off, Katya ran back to Mike and held up her hands. Mike picked her up, and he and the other Americans followed the Russians out of the dormitory and back into the locker room.

Polina spoke to Katya in Russian for several seconds, and then Katya hurried to one of the lockers.

"Polina told Katya to get her coat, that we will be going to visit Luba," Marik explained. "Would you like a picture of her next to her locker?" he asked as soon as Katya had her coat on.

"Sure, that would be great," Mike said while readying the camera. Katya re-opened the locker and posed for the picture. Once the coat had been removed, there was only an orange sweater on a shelf and a flannel bag that held her toothbrush and comb hanging from a coat hook. Aside from that, the locker was empty. It was evident that the extent of all her earthly belongings was the cloth bag, a toothbrush and her comb.

"Polina says we should be going so that we have time to visit. We will be taking Elizaveta and Oksana to lunch. I offered to bring Polina with us, but she apologized and said today is not a good day for her to leave," Marik explained. "So I guess we will go and meet the others."

The group said their goodbyes, and Marik escorted the Americans and Katya back out to the SUV. Katya had fun sitting with her parents in the car, but it was impossible to keep her in her seat, much less in her seat belt. She kept climbing into the front seat with Laura and then back to Mike and Jim. Clearly she had spent very little time in cars. Marik was patient. He had seen the same situation many times in the past. He finally convinced her to stay put by bargaining that she wouldn't have to wear the seatbelt if she remained in the back seat. Laura would have never allowed it, and she felt very uncomfortable. But as much as it bothered her, it was not yet time for her to make decisions for Katya.

A few minutes later they picked up Elizaveta at her apartment.

"Elizaveta says she is happy to see you," Marik said while doing up his seat belt. "She says she is glad you won the race against the flowers."

All of the adults laughed.

"Oksana said she will meet us at the restaurant," Marik told them. "I think we'll eat at the same restaurant where we ate the first time we came to see Luba, if that's alright."

"Sure," Mike responded. "Anything sounds fine."

Within minutes, they had pulled into the parking lot of the restaurant that looked like so many other small buildings in the area. They walked into the restaurant and were immediately led to a table where Oksana was already seated. "It is so good to see you again!" Oksana exclaimed through Marik. She jumped to her feet and offered warm handshakes to Laura and Mike.

Oksana then offered her hand to Jim, and spoke excitedly and rapidly to him in Russian.

"Oksana says you must be the famous *Dyedushka* Jim from the book," Marik translated.

Jim laughed and cordially accepted the hand shake. The group casually visited while Oksana made recommendations on dishes, until Katya broke in.

"Katya says that she needs to go to the bathroom," Marik informed them.

Oksana immediately offered to take her, but Katya became agitated and spoke back to Marik in a whine.

"She says she wants her mother to take her."

Oksana smiled and gave Marik directions to the bathroom, which he passed on to Laura. Then Laura took Katya by the hand and led her off to the bathroom. The toilet in the restroom had no seat, which surprised Laura, but not Katya. The truth was, Katya had never in her life seen a toilet seat. She sat right there on the rim until she was finished. Laura laughed to herself that Katya's attitude toward the lack of a toilet seat would fair well in a house full of boys who constantly forgot to put the seat back down.

Right after Laura finished helping Katya wash her hands, Katya began to speak to her in Russian.

"I'm sorry, Princess, I don't understand you."

Katya spoke more clearly and slower hoping that would help, but to no avail.

"I'm sorry, Honey, let's go ask Marik."

"*Nyet!*" Katya exclaimed. She understood that Laura wanted to have Marik translate. But this had nothing to do with Marik. This was between mother and daughter. Katya was still concerned about what her mother might think of her ugly scar. If Laura was going to reject her for it, Amérika was no place for that to happen. If Katya was going to be rejected, it needed to be now. Katya spoke slowly and intently hoping that somehow Laura would understand. Laura realized that Katya needed to talk to her alone, and hoped that with gestures, or whatever else, she would be able to understand what Katya needed her to know. Laura squatted down and listened intently while Katya spoke. Then when she was finished speaking, she pulled down the neck of her sweater to expose the huge scar that Laura had seen in the pictures late the year before. While still holding the neck of the sweater down, she gazed up in to Laura's face to see what her reaction might be.

Laura touched Katya on the shoulder and, after glancing at the scar, kissed her on the forehead. "I'm so sorry that you got hurt, Princess," she said soothingly.

Katya let go of the sweater and it sprung back up in to place. Laura wrapped her arms around the child and held her close. "I'm so sorry, Baby." She used one of her hands to cradle Katya's head against her shoulder while she continued to hug her with the other arm. "That must have hurt terribly. I'm so sorry that you had to go through that." Laura knew that Katya didn't understand the words. But it was evident that she understood the feeling. After hugging for several seconds, Katya pulled back and looked at Laura with a huge smile that didn't go away. Her mother did still love her, even though she had that ugly scar. Katya took Laura by the hand and led her back to the table where the others were sitting.

The group had a nice visit and enjoyed their lunch, but the Americans were anxious to see Luba. Even Katya asked Marik and Oksana about her sister several times. Were she and Luba really going to Amérika together? Was Luba ready? Was Luba big enough to go on an airplane? Because she could help Luba so she could come, too. The anxiety was driving Katya crazy.

As the SUV pulled up in front of the hospital/orphanage where Luba lived, the Americans noticed two young boys, not older than ten, standing there smoking with an adult man and woman.

"Is that normal here?" Mike asked Marik.

"What, the boys smoking?"

"Yes. They're pretty young for that, aren't they? I mean, I guess I understand a ten year-old stealing a cigarette and experimenting, or even picking up the habit. What surprises me is that they aren't even hiding it from the adults, and the adults don't seem concerned."

"Sadly, the adults probably gave them the cigarettes," Marik replied. "I wouldn't say that it's normal. It isn't something that you would see every day. But, unfortunately, it isn't something that is a surprise to see, either."

Mike walked to the back of the SUV with Marik to retrieve the treat-filled carry-on bag as the other adults got out. Katya ran back to Mike and threw her arms around his leg and then held her hands up to be picked up.

"Just a second, Sweetheart," he said while reaching deeper into the vehicle.

"Stó?" What?

"Papa asks that you wait for a minute," Marik explained.

Mike pulled a small roller-type carry on bag from the SUV. It was pink and purple with lots of flowers. "Please explain to Katya that this is her suitcase to take home to America," Mike said to Marik. "Ask her if she would like to practice pulling it into the building."

Marik explained to Katya as Mike pulled out the retractable handle, put the bottom on the ground and leaned it back on the wheels toward her.

"*Dá!*" she squealed. She grabbed the handle and headed quickly up the sidewalk toward the doors of the orphanage with the carry-on in tow.

"Oksana asks that we wait here in the playroom while she goes to get Luba," Marik translated.

Laura and Mike opened the carry-on suitcase and retrieved treats and toys for Luba, and prepared themselves to entertain her while Jim played with Katya. Elizaveta and Marik sat and quietly visited until Oksana entered the room carrying Luba, who was dressed in a beautiful cream-colored dress with a big matching bow in her hair.

"*Prevet?*" Oksana coaxed the child. *Hello?* "*Prevet?*" Luba just smiled bashfully and turned her head into Oksana's shoulder. Oksana continued to talk to the child with the Americans recognizing the words "Mama" and "Papa" from time to time. Finally, after a couple of minutes of coaxing and getting Luba comfortable with the situation, she took the child and handed her to Laura. "Mommy?" Oksana coaxed. "Mommy?"

"*Mama!*" Luba squealed, soliciting oos and ahs from the others in the room. Then she bashfully turned her head into Laura's shoulder. Her head was there for only a second before she sprung back, looked at Laura with big eyes, smiled and then plunged her head back into Laura's shoulder and began taking deep breaths of the perfume which she obviously recognized. Finally, she pulled back and smiled at Oksana.

"She was calling all women Mama," Marik translated for Oksana. "You know, how so many little children do. With the absence of men around here, she calls all men Mama, too. But Oksana wanted her to distinguish her parents from other adults, so as they read the cloth book or when they talk about you, Oksana calls you two Mommy and Poppy. She has been trying to get Luba to say Mommy and Poppy, but she still says Mama."

"Thank you," Laura replied sincerely to Oksana.

"You wel-cum," Oksana responded before even waiting for the translation. She then began to speak to Marik.

"Oksana said Luba has been listening to the cassette tape you made, and that she loves it," Marik translated to Laura. "She says Luba even learned how to operate the buttons and turn the tape over so she could listen to it whenever she wanted to. Oksana said she is going to get the tape player to show you."

"Thank you, I'd like that," Laura said. With that, Oksana nodded her head once and left the room.

"Do you remember Papa, too?" Laura asked Luba as she walked towards Mike. "I'm sorry, I guess it's Poppy now. Poppy? Poppy?" she coaxed as she tried to hand Luba to Mike. Luba didn't turn to look at him. But finally, Laura succeeded in handing her off.

"*Preens-yessa!*" Mike said enthusiastically as he took her. That was all it took. Luba turned toward him and smiled. "Where's my hug?" he asked as he pulled her in tight. At that point Luba, caught wind of the cologne and buried her head against his neck. She took a deep breath, pulled back to look at him and smiled.

"Poppy!" she squealed. Then she turned to Laura. "Poppy!" she squealed again while pointing at Mike.

"I guess she got your name down!" Laura exclaimed.

Mike tickled Luba several times under the arm, each time he evoked squirms and giggles. "Do you want to meet *Dyedushka?*" he asked while walking over to Jim. "*Dyedushka?*"

Jim had been busy playing with Katya until then, but he now redirected his attention. Katya was obviously put out by not being the center of his attention, and she immediately began to try to climb his leg. But Laura intervened and showed Katya a beautiful princess coloring book, and led her over to a table to help her color.

"*Dyeh-dush-ka?*" Mike coaxed directing her to Jim. "*Dyeh-dush-ka?*"

"*Deh!*" Luba squealed as she spun bashfully back to Mike.

"Sometimes Russian children use '*Dyehd*' as a nickname for *Dyedushka*," Marik explained to Jim. "It looks like she recognizes you from the cloth book."

Mike handed Luba to Jim who hugged her tight. "*Preens-yessa?*" he coaxed. "*Preens-yessa?*"

Katya was not impressed. She scowled at Luba and Jim from across the room, obviously jealous. Princess was *her* name. Mike noticed exactly what was going on, and moved to the rescue. He sat next to Katya and put his arm around her. She smiled up at him and snuggled in close. "Katya… Sarah…" he said while pointing at her.

"*Seh-lah*" she repeated.

"Sarah… *Preens-yessa*…"

"*She-lah Preensyessa!*" she repeated excitedly. She was fine now. As long as everyone realized that she was the princess, and had the name to prove it.

"She loves her name!" Marik remarked. "But I guess we can hardly be surprised. Hey, bring Katya over here. Let's see if Luba remembers her."

Mike took Katya by the hand and led her over to where Jim was sitting with Luba on his lap.

Marik asked Katya if she remembered Luba. Of course she did. He then began to speak Russian baby talk with Luba. He kept repeating her sister's name over and over while pointing to Katya. It was obvious that she didn't remember, but Marik did finally succeed in getting her to make an attempt at the name.

"*Kawcha*," Luba said before bashfully turning away yet again.

"She has only seen Katya once since she was moved into the other orphanage last August," Marik explained. "It's not surprising that she doesn't remember her yet. She will remember her, though. We see this quite often."

About then, Oksana re-entered the room carrying the headphone tape player. Luba, noticing it, squealed and held out her hand while opening and closing it rapidly. "*Dai! Dai! Dai!*"

All of the adults laughed. It was obvious that Luba loved her tape. Oksana handed her the player and Luba put on the headphones herself and pushed the play button. After several seconds, nothing had happened so she pushed the stop button, pulled out the tape, turned it over and pushed play again. Soon she was smiling as she listened to Mommy's voice singing songs.

By now, several other orphans had entered the playroom and were playing with various toys. "Marik, will you ask Katya if she will help me with the treats?" Laura asked. He explained to Katya, who was more than willing to be the big helper with the treats.

Laura opened her carry-on bag, and produced a plastic bag full of Rice Krispy treats. Katya was excited. She recognized the bright blue foil covering the biscuits from Amérika that her parents had brought on their last trip. Laura handed the bag to Katya, who walked around the room distributing the treats. All of the adults politely refused at first, but finally humored Laura when she insisted that they try them. Luba also recognized the bright blue foil wrappers and ran to get hers. The other children, realizing that there were treats, swarmed Katya. But unlike handing out candy bars to her peers on the last trip, Katya was bigger than these children. She held fast while passing out the snacks to each of the children.

"That is Annushka," Oksana explained through Marik, referring to a cute, red haired, pudgy little two-year-old girl as she took her treat. "She will be adopted by French parents. They will come for their first visit this week. If all goes well, she will go to live near Paris in a couple of months. That is Ksenya," she explained referring to a tiny little toddler girl who was barely walking. "And that is Maxim."

"Do Maxim and Ksenya have families yet?" Laura asked Oksana.

"No. Not yet. We just got Ksenya, and Maxim isn't available for international adoption for another couple of months."

By now the orphans had all run to an adult for help opening the wrappers. Without exception, the children first nibbled and then devoured the treats.

Laura, Mike, and Jim continued to play with Katya, Luba, and the other orphans for several hours, and Elizaveta faithfully took notes and wrote observations that she could use later in court.

"We need to get going," Marik announced. "We have a long drive back. I told Oksana we won't be able to come back tomorrow and that Thursday is court, so the soonest that she will see us is Friday."

Jim, Laura, and Mike all took turns giving Luba hugs and telling her goodbye. It wasn't nearly as sad this time, knowing that they would have her soon. At the prompting of Oksana, Katya gave Luba a hug goodbye too, but she acted very strange about it. Then one of the workers came and took Luba away, and the adults took Katya and walked out to the orphanage steps to say goodbye. As they stood on the steps, Katya was obviously very agitated. She kept trying to interrupt to speak to both Oksana and Marik. Finally, after being ignored with her verbal assault, she went to Marik and began tugging on his pant leg. She kept tugging harder and harder until he finally gave her his attention.

"Yes, Katya, yes!" he replied in Russian. "What is it that can't wait?"

Katya began speaking to him rapidly in Russian pointing back toward the inside of the orphanage.

"Oh, Katya wants to know why Luba isn't going with us to America," Marik translated.

Elizaveta broke in and explained to Katya that it wasn't time to go to America yet, that they still had to wait until after the meeting with the judge, and until then, that Mama and Papa would visit them at the orphanages.

"*Nyet!*" Katya screamed. "I won't go back to the orphanage!" she continued in Russian to Elizaveta and Marik. "Everyone told me that when Mama and Papa came back that I could go with them to Amérika! Now, you won't let me go!"

"Katya, I'm sorry that you didn't understand," Elizaveta explained, still in Russian. "No one ever planned for you to leave with your parents as soon as they got here. It doesn't work that way. But you will be able to leave with them soon, just not yet. For now, you must return to the orphanage."

"*Nee Ha-Choó!*" *I don't want to!*

Mike and Laura were flabbergasted at Katya's outburst. But with the entire conversation having transpired in Russian, they had no idea what was upsetting her so much.

"What's wrong?" Laura asked Marik with ample concern in her voice.

"Katya thought she was going home to America now, not back to the orphanage. Everyone told her last time that when her parents came back, she would go with them and Luba to America. Apparently, she didn't realized that there was a waiting time after you got here, but before it was time to leave. She thought that as soon as you got here that she would leave with you. It looks like coming here to visit Luba confused her even more. She thought that we were coming to get Luba, and then you would leave together to begin your trip home like the cloth book said."

"Oh, you poor baby!" Laura exclaimed as she scooped Katya up in her arms. Katya threw her arms around her mother's neck and began to sob. Laura held her, cradled her head against her and spoke soothingly, but Katya continued to sob.

"It looks like we should go now," Marik said to Oksana, "before it gets worse."

Oksana agreed, so they said their goodbyes and headed for the SUV. Laura carried Katya who was still crying and whining in Russian. *"Nee Ha-Choó Dyesky-Dome. Nee Ha-Choó!"* I *don't want the orphanage. "Ha-Choó Mama ee Papa! Ha-Choó Amérika!"*

Elizaveta tried to calm Katya by explaining the situation as Marik drove her to her apartment, but nothing helped. She continued to cry and repeated the same phrases over and over. Finally, after dropping off Elizaveta, Katya calmed to a certain extent, but she continued to cry softly while snuggled up against Laura.

Within five minutes, they had arrived at Katya's orphanage. Laura carried her in. She went willingly, but she was still crying softly.

Laura cradled Katya against her as they stood in the hallway, just inside the door. "I love you, Sweetheart. We will come back to see you soon," she said, and then waited for Marik to translate. Katya snuggled up tighter against Laura and gave her a big long hug as she took a deep breath of her perfume. Then Laura turned and handed her to Mike. Katya threw her arms around his neck, snuggled in tight and began taking deep breaths so she would remember the smell of Papa.

"I love you, Princess," he said softly. "We'll come back to get you as soon as we can."

Marik translated quickly, and then told Mike it was time to get moving. Drawing out these goodbyes never did anyone any good.

Mike hugged Katya tightly one more time, and then pushed her back to look at her. She smiled at him, cradled both sides of his face in her hands and leaned forward and gave him a quick kiss on the lips. "*Yá-Tibya-Lo-Bloo, Papa*."

"I love you too, Katya," he said as he placed her on the ground. Then one of the workers who had appeared soon after they entered the door took her by the hand, and led her back to the area where they had met her that morning.

25

All in the Same Boat Together

"There was a flyer under the door," Mike began the next morning. "It looks like someone is hosting a party for all adoptive families staying here at the hotel in the White Rabbit room tonight."

"That sounds like a great chance to meet some of the families here," Laura responded. "Do you want to go?"

"Yeah, sure. What else could we have going? We're kind of on hold until we finish with court tomorrow."

Mike and Laura headed for the hotel restaurant for breakfast and picked up Jim from his room on the way.

"How did you sleep last night?" Jim asked cordially.

"Up a little with jetlag, but pretty good, I guess, considering," Mike responded.

"So, what's the plan for today?"

"I don't know that we have one. But we never did get to a bank yesterday. We only have the rubles that Sasha loaned me. Somehow we've got to trade some money. Do you think that they do that here at the hotel?"

"It's hard to say," Jim replied. "You know hotels. Sometimes they trade, sometimes they don't and sometimes they do it at thumb-breaker prices."

"Well, let's get some breakfast. After, I'll check with the front desk and see what we need to do. Did you get a copy of that invitation to the party in the White Rabbit room tonight?"

"No. At least I didn't see anything…"

"I guess that someone is hosting a party for the adoptive families tonight. Laura and I thought that it would be a good chance to meet some of the other families and hear their stories."

"That does sound interesting. But, maybe I'm not invited. I didn't get an invitation. Maybe they only want parents there."

"Come on, Jim," Mike responded. "I'm sure that whoever is throwing the party would want everyone there."

Laura, Mike, and Jim walked to the entrance of the restaurant and were waiting to be seated when they were signaled by another couple and their little girl to come and sit with them.

"Hi, I'm Duane Lawson," the gentleman in his early forties said while rising to shake hands. "This is my wife, Shelly, and my daughter, Ashley."

"Pleased to meet you," Mike responded while shaking hands. "I'm Mike Knight, this is my wife Laura and this is a close friend of the family, Jim Christensen."

The Americans all shook hands and exchanged pleasantries for a several seconds before being seated.

"Well, you're obviously here on an adoption," Duane started. "Boy or girl?"

"Actually, two little girls," Mike responded.

"Oh! How old are they?" Shelly asked.

"Katya is five, and Luba is two and a half," Laura responded.

"Are they sisters?" she asked, directing the question at Laura.

"Yes, they are biological sisters."

"How fun! We are here to adopt Ashley's brother," Shelly announced.

"Really?" Mike responded. "There has to be a story behind that!"

"Oh, there is," Shelly continued. "Would you like to hear it?"

Various affirmative answers came from the Knight group.

"We were here almost exactly a year ago adopting Ashley, when we found out about Aleksander. I have no idea why they didn't tell us about him before we came to meet Ashley, but they didn't. After we arrived, they asked us if we wanted to adopt him, too. We were pretty surprised, so we took the night to think about it, and we decided to do it. But then, it turned out that where we had only done paperwork to adopt one child, we couldn't adopt Aleksander without going back to the states and starting over. So we told them we would take Ashley, and then start over on paperwork to get Aleksander. The agency thought that was a good idea, but when we went to court, the judge and prosecutor kept asking us why we weren't adopting Aleksander, too. We told them that we wanted to, and we asked them to allow us to take him then. But they said that it was impossible without the paperwork. Then they told us that since Aleksander was older, we should adopt him and then come back for Ashley after we did the additional paperwork. But there was no way. We told them to either let us take them both now, or we would have to come back later for Aleksander. Finally, after a lot of arguing, they allowed us to do it that way."

"We didn't know about Katya's sister until we got here either," Laura replied. "Fortunately, our agency had talked us into filling out paperwork to accept two children, even though we were only planning on adopting one. So it looks like we'll be spared what you are going through."

"You are fortunate," Duane replied. "This has been crazy. We started with the adoption plan for a little girl three years ago. It took us two years to get Ashley home, and now it's been another trying to get everything together to get Aleksander. We'll have been on this path for just over three years by the time we get home. I really don't know what we'll do after this. For us, adopting has gone beyond an adventure…it's a lifestyle."

They all laughed.

"I wonder how often they don't reveal other siblings?" Mike questioned.

"We had never heard of it before," Shelly replied. "In all of our online reading, we had never seen it. We thought that we must be the only ones. It must be quite a coincidence that we're all sitting here together."

"Are you excited to take your brother home?" Laura asked Ashley.

"Yes. Mama say Aleksander come home with us. Mama say we go home Friday."

"You've only had her for a year?" Mike questioned. "Her English is great! How old is she?"

"They learn very fast," Duane acknowledged. "Ashley is four."

"How old is Aleksander?" Laura queried.

"He is nine."

"It must be great having Ashley so that she can translate for you," Laura observed.

Duane and Shelly laughed.

"That's what we thought, too," Shelly responded. "But she won't speak Russian."

"Really?" Mike was surprised. "Does she not remember, or does she just not want to?"

"We're not quite sure," Shelly answered. "The people here at the hotel try to speak to her in Russian. Sometimes she doesn't understand them, but other times she just responds to them in English. When they ask her why she won't speak Russian, she just says she doesn't want to. She won't ever say whether or not she can, she only says that she doesn't want to."

"That's interesting," Mike replied.

"So, Ashley says you are going home Friday," Laura began, "obviously, you have already had your court hearing."

"Yes. In fact, that was a story in and of itself," Shelly replied. "The prosecutor and judge kept asking why we hadn't taken Aleksander with us on the first trip, and we kept explaining that they wouldn't let us. Then, when that was finally cleared up, they asked us why we brought Ashley with us. They said that it was too long of a trip for a child, and that it was too much for her. We explained to them that she still has separation anxiety whenever we leave, and that she's still concerned we might not come back, even when we're just gone for an evening. We told them that we thought that it would be more difficult for her if we left her than if we brought her."

"What did they say about that?" Laura asked.

"They stuck to their guns," Duane replied. "They just kept saying that it was irresponsible to bring her. But I'm convinced that if we hadn't brought her, we would have been scolded for that. I'm sure that we were 'in for it' no matter what we had done."

"Did they mention anything about that case in Illinois?" Mike asked, trying to glean practical information along with the story.

"They asked us how we punish Ashley, and we told them time-outs. Then they asked Ashley how we punished her, but she wouldn't acknowledge whether or not she understood them, so they got the translator involved. But Ashley didn't want to answer them, anyway. I think she thought that she was in trouble with the judge if she had ever done anything to warrant punishment. Finally she told them that once she had to sit on the chair."

"Oh! Poor thing!" Laura cooed. "It must have been pretty traumatic for her."

"That's what I said," Shelly responded. "I mean, these kids know that it was a judge who took them out of their first home, and now they ask her what happens when she is bad. It must have scared her to death. But I still think it would have been worse for her to have stayed at home with Grandma. She really does struggle when we aren't there, even for a few hours. Besides that, Aleksander will always remember when we all came together to get him. I think that we made the right choice, all things considered."

The Knight party agreed.

"When do you pick up Aleksander from the orphanage?" Mike asked.

"We're on our way right after breakfast," Duane responded. "We're pretty excited."

"I'll bet you are," Mike replied. "Are you guys going to be at the party tonight?"

"We'd like to, but I think that we'll be pretty busy. We have to do some shopping and we have a lot of things to do before we leave. I mean, there are all of these things to do, like getting passports for the child, medical examinations, exit interviews and everything else, but you can't do anything until you get the kids and the ten-day appeal period is over. So you sit around with nothing to do until you get the kid, and then it's a mad dash trying to get everything done to get out of the country."

"You said that you're going shopping," Laura began. "Did you do most of your meals in your room?"

"We usually eat one meal a day in the restaurant and the other two in the room," Shelly responded. "Were you guys able to get a suite?"

"Well, sort of," Laura replied. "All of the real suites with kitchenettes were gone. But we have an adjoining room with a microwave and a little fridge."

"Oh, we do most of our cooking in the microwave anyway," Shelly replied. "When you go to the grocery store, they have lots of soups in microwaveable cups. Those are so easy and that's what we make most of the time when we eat in the room."

"What else would you buy?"

"Snacks. Lots of snacks. We are almost out and we still have to make it until Friday. We don't even have Aleksander yet."

"I don't think we'll have that problem," Laura laughed. "Last time we got to play with a couple dozen orphans on several occasions. We thought it would be the same way this time so we packed over a hundred Rice Krispy treats. Also, during the last trip we found out that Katya's favorite candy was Chupa Chup suckers, so Mike bought a thousand of them off the internet. He was only able to fit six hundred in the luggage, but even after leaving a couple for every kid in Katya's and Luba's orphanages, we still have hundreds left. Maybe we can help you out on the snack situation."

Shelly laughed. "That would be great!"

"No problem," Laura replied. "Follow me to our room after breakfast and we'll fix you up. We're all in this same boat together."

"That is more truth than you know," Shelly responded. "We've been here about two weeks now, and have really gotten to know some of the other families. You cheer with them when they hear good news and cry with them on their setbacks. Everyone knows everyone else's situation. It's quite a support group. We'll miss these families when we leave."

The adults continued to talk and visit until breakfast was over. But Laura concentrated on talking to Ashley. She was trying to imagine what life with Katya would be like a year from then.

"The lady at the front desk told me that they don't trade money here," Mike explained to Laura and Jim. "But she said they have a driver we could hire to take us in to the city. I told her that would be great. We can go and trade some money and hit a grocery store. I told her we'd be ready in twenty minutes."

Laura and Jim both agreed.

The ride into downtown Vladivostok was only about ten miles, but it took over an hour to get there. The nearby bridge over the river was under repair, and what was normally a six-lane highway was bottlenecked down to two. So the driver cut back through neighborhoods of apartments, through parking lots and even driveways, picking his way through as though he had done it a million times. While the highway hadn't been too bad, the back roads were a maze of pot holes, some of them deep beyond belief.

Finally, the driver pulled onto the highway again and quickly forced his minivan between oncoming cars. Within minutes they had entered a roundabout. "What's wrong?" Mike asked as the driver started on his second trip around the circle.

"I see if other girl here. She give better price."

"What?" Mike asked. "Better price on what?"

"You trade dollar, no? She give better price. But she no here. But okay. Other girl give ok price." The driver pointed at a girl who appeared to be in her early twenties standing at the side of the road on the outside of the roundabout. She had a stack of Russian rubles in her hand, held out slightly from her hip, subtly, but it was obvious that she was soliciting business.

"I thought we were going to a bank," Mike said.

"No. Bank no pay good price. You get more ruble here. You see. You like it better here."

"Isn't this illegal? I mean, can't we go to jail for this?"

"No. You no break law. She break law. But nobody care. No one go to jail. She no take credit card, but you have dollar, no?"

"Well, yeah, I have cash."

"Ok. Then you trade money here." The driver pulled over to the side of the road and signaled the girl who stepped quickly up to the side of the minivan.

She and the driver exchanged words in Russian for a few seconds before the driver readdressed Mike. "How much you trade?"

"Can we change five hundred?" Mike asked.

"Sure. Five hundred no problem."

Mike pulled out five one hundred dollar bills that he had separated out earlier, and handed them to the girl. She held each one individually up to the sun and inspected them carefully. It was obvious that she had been trained in spotting counterfeit dollars. She took one of the bills and handed it back to Mike speaking in Russian.

"She say this one no good. This old bill. She only take new bill."

Mike pulled out his wad of cash, nervous that she could see how much he had, and took out a different, new style hundred dollar bill. The girl held it up to the sun again, and satisfied this time, placed it in a wad of American dollars larger than Mike's. Then she counted out the rubles while the driver watched.

The driver thanked the girl, and they were back on their way.

"That was crazy!" Mike exclaimed. "How does she dare stand out there like that with that much money? I can't believe she's not robbed and dead within minutes after showing up here!"

"She no there alone," The driver explained. "Men watch her."

"Where were they?" Mike questioned.

"I no know. No one see them. But them there. Anybody make trouble for girl, they come. They kill them. People no make trouble for girl. They know this."

"I guess we're not in Kansas any more!" Laura piped in from the back seat.

"You can say that again!" Jim added.

"What?" the driver questioned. "Not in Kansas? What is Kansas?"

"It's just a silly expression," Mike replied. "It wouldn't make sense in Russian."

"Ok. Now you have ruble. You need store now, no?"

"Yes, we need to find a grocery store," Mike responded.

Five minutes later they were parked in front of a large grocery store with a big glass front, like might be found in any large city. "I wait here with car," the driver told them. "It better that way. It better I not leave car. You go. Go buy food. I wait for you."

Mike, Laura, and Jim left the van and walked into the store. While it had looked grand on the outside, on the inside it reminded Mike of the grocery store in the small Idaho college town where he had worked part time while going to school. But the food supply was ample, and of reasonable quality. It didn't take them long to find the microwaveable soups, and they loaded up on them. They also bought lots of snacks like pretzels and potato chips. Then they filled the bottom of the cart with bottled water. In all, the shopping spree lasted only about fifteen minutes.

As they approached the cashier, Mike realized that he had not organized his wad of money after the rushed currency exchange in the car. He had just shoved the Russian money into his front pants pocket with the other. He would have to empty his pocket to organize the money enough to pay for the items. Pulling out that much cash right there in front of everyone made him extremely nervous. Jim and Laura walked forward, past the cashier, to wait for Mike. As the cashier finished ringing up the items, she pointed to the number on the register. Mike pulled the wad of money from his front pocket and quickly separated the American money and shoved it back in his front pocket, hoping that no one saw. But it was evident that the cashier did see, as well as the stocky woman in her mid-forties who was in line behind him. Mike fumbled through the Russian currency trying to figure out which bill to use, and then, to make matters easier, just grabbed one of the largest bills and handed it over, knowing if it would be enough.

"*Nyet*," the cashier said while shaking her head. *No*. She didn't want a bill that big, or she didn't have change for it. She reached over the counter and pointed to the stack of money. Mike fanned it out and she took three different bills, counted them in Russian, showing Mike exactly what she took and then pointed to the amount on the register. Then she counted several small coins out of the till and gave him his change as she smiled and spoke nicely to him in Russian, obviously telling him to have a nice day or something of sort. Mike was surprised at her willingness to help, and especially at her honesty. It would have been easy for her to have taken the larger bill and shorted him on change.

As he smiled and thanked the cashier in English, he felt a tug at his sleeve. Mike turned to see the woman who was standing behind him in line. She spoke to him in Russian and then pointed at the floor. There, at his feet, was a one hundred dollar bill that had fallen from the stack as he rushed to put them back in his pocket. Mike was shocked. With the way that the counter was set up, there was no way that the cashier had seen the bill fall, and with how the line was, it was evident that no one else had seen it either. The woman could have easily picked up the bill without anyone noticing. But she had chosen to help a 'rich' Amerikán who obviously didn't need the bill as much as she did. Mike stooped down and picked up the bill, looked into the woman's eyes and thanked her in English, though he tried to emphasize his sincerity as much as he possibly could with the expression on his face. The woman just smiled, nodded her head, and spoke one word in Russian. "*Pah-zah-lou-sta.*" *You're welcome.*

As Mike pushed the cartload of groceries forward his mind was troubled. Communism had not made these people selfish, evil, or criminal. The everyday people on the street were honest, friendly, and helpful. All of the articles he had read about corruption in the former Soviet States hadn't prepared him for what he found most of the Russians to be: a humble, patient, helpful, and friendly people. Russia was not corrupt, even if *some* of its people were.

"What was all that about?" Laura asked as they walked out of the store.

"I dropped some money and she showed it to me," Mike responded.

"Oh, well, that was nice," she replied.

The three Americans walked back out to the minivan and within minutes were back on their hour-long ride through parking lots, neighborhoods, and driveways to return to the hotel.

The White Rabbit room was bustling when Jim and the Knights walked in at six-thirty. Several pizzas, plates of buffalo wings, and other snacks covered the tables as adults visited and several Russian children chased and played around the room.

"Help yourself to food and drinks," Craig told them as he stood up to shake hands.

"Does the hotel do this often?" Mike asked.

"Actually, one of the adoption families is throwing the party, but they didn't want me to say who it was. The hotel is providing the drinks, though. Help yourself to soft drinks or beers in the cooler," he said while pointing at it.

"Holy smoke! A&W Root Beer!" Mike exclaimed. "I've traveled the world and I don't think I've ever seen root beer outside of North America."

"We aim to please!" Craig responded. He was happy to see that his extra efforts had been noticed. Most Americans had no idea how rare root beer was outside the U.S. and Craig had gone to efforts far beyond the call of duty to import it and keep it stocked.

Craig escorted Jim and the Knights around the room and introduced them to several couples. Then they sat down and ate. After an hour and the arrival of several more couples, someone decided that each couple should introduce themselves and give a little bit of background on their adoption.

The adoption stories were as varied as the couples. The Jamesons were a black couple in their early fifties from Louisiana. They were in Russia picking up their five-year-old son, Vladimir. He was their second from Russia, but they had three other adopted children at home. Andy, the father, was friendly but quiet. He preferred to let his wife, Allison do the talking. She told a heart-wrenching story about having two biological daughters and one of them dying as a teenager after the other had married and moved away. She told of how empty their lives had seemed until 'Jesus showed her the way.' The

Jamesons decided they needed to live a life of service, and give a home to more children. While their finances limited them in what they were able to spend on adoption, Allison had solicited friends, neighbors, their local congregation, and even local businesses to help them pay for adoption and travel expenses. The community had gotten behind them completely. First they adopted a baby from South America, and later one from Russia. Then Allison pulled out a family photo. One of the children was white. "After we adopted our first two,'" Allison explained, "I had a friend approach me and tell me that she was pregnant. She didn't want the baby. She told me that if we would agree to adopt the baby that she would have it. Otherwise, she would terminate. I couldn't have that! I knew that Jesus wanted that baby and that He had brought it to us." After things had settled down with the third adoption, the Jamesons had started on the fourth. Now they and Vladimir would return to Louisiana at the end of the week where he would meet the rest of his new family.

The Carters were a well-off family from Milwaukee in their mid-fifties. Fred held a sales position for a manufacturing company and his wife, Marci, was an executive secretary. They had thought about having a family for years, but just never got around to it. Now, at their age, they were concerned about possible health complications with pregnancy. Several years earlier, they had decided to adopt two babies, a boy and a girl. As they started into the adoption process, they decided on Romania. Soon a referral was made on a boy and a girl. But before they could get to Romania to finalize the adoption, the girl was adopted by one of the orphanage workers. Laura cried as Marci told of how hard it was to take down the pictures of her little girl. Then as they were waiting on a referral for another girl, Romania suspended all foreign adoptions, allegedly in hopes that it would increase their chances of being included in the European Union. Marci took down the pictures of her little boy, too. The heartache was too much, so the Carters went two more years before considering adoption again. But finally, under assurances from their agency that Russia appeared to be pretty stable with foreign adoptions, they started over with the attempt to adopt a pair of children from Russia.

After the year or so that it took to get themselves to the point of receiving a referral from Russia, the Carters were growing increasingly concerned about the worsening climate for international adoptions there. They were worried that they might have the same thing happen that happened to them in Romania. So when they finally got a referral on a baby girl, but still not a baby boy, they decided to move quickly. Their agency assured them that they would have the opportunity to select a little boy when they got to Russia. But on their first trip the only baby boy shown to them had severe health problems and was on a feeding tube. They decided to go with adopting the little girl alone. The Carters had their court date scheduled for the next day, an hour before the Knights. They hoped to have their baby, 'Olga,' home within two weeks.

Rick and Debbie Edinger were from San Jose, California. They had been married for several years and had not been able to have children biologically. Finally, after spending a small fortune on unsuccessful fertility treatments, they had decided to adopt. Most of the adoption expenses and travel had gone on credit cards. Rick had no idea how he'd ever pay them off. They had their court hearing in two days and hoped that the orphanage in Vladivostok City would let them bring little Jeffery back with them to the hotel during the ten-day appeal period.

Linda was a very well-to-do executive from Richmond, Virginia. She had been married once, long ago, but didn't see any reason to be married again. Linda was on her first visit with her little girl Inessa, who was in the orphanage in Ussurysk. She would be flying back home on Saturday to wait for her second trip, and would immediately make arrangements for a nanny.

Several other couples told their stories, until finally, all had finished. It was now ten-thirty and most, particularly those with children, were ready to go to bed.

"I can't sleep," Mike said after noticing Laura tossing and turning in the bed.

"I can't, either. Are you nervous?"

"I just don't know what to expect in court tomorrow. What are we supposed to say if the judge asks us about that Illinois lady's sentence?"

"I don't know. I'm worried, too."

"I mean, honestly, I don't even know the circumstances. How am I supposed to know if I agree with the sentence?"

"I know."

"Do you even know the circumstances?" Mike asked Laura while turning on the lamp on the night stand.

Laura squinted her eyes while they adjusted to the light. "A couple adopted a six year-old boy and his little sister from Siberia. Prosecutors claimed that his mother beat him to death six weeks after they arrived in the States. The defense made the argument that the child had severe emotional disorders and probably fetal alcohol syndrome. Also, that he defecated and urinated all over himself and the house. The defense was able to put forth some evidence that the injuries, at least to a certain extent, might have been self-inflicted. It happened in late 2003, but the trial just finished. The mother got twelve years, but everyone knows that she'll be out on parole before then."

"So this whole thing is about one woman who beat her adopted son to death? I mean, that's bad, but how many good adoptions are happening?"

"Well, actually, Americans want to say that it's all about this latest case, but it's not. I was recently on a web site and read that there have been twelve adopted Russian children in the U.S. who died under questionable circumstances while under the care of their adoptive parents. They died from everything from massive head injuries, to shaken baby syndrome and malnutrition. One even died from hypothermia after being locked overnight in a pump room."

"Holy cow! No wonder the Russians are concerned. How are we supposed to answer to that?"

"I don't know. Some of the Russians are saying that international adoption shouldn't be handled by private firms in the U.S., but by the Social Services arm of the government. They are saying that these adoption agencies aren't screening the adoptive parents closely enough because they only care about getting their money."

"They bring up a good point, but they obviously don't understand the Social Services arm of the U.S. government. They would never use funds for making someone's life better unless they were already American. That just won't happen."

"I know that, and you know that, but it helps to see where the Russians are coming from."

Mike shook his head. "Now I really don't know what to say in court tomorrow."

"The sad thing is that most of these children were already difficult to handle, some of them, very difficult," Laura responded. "There is help to deal with children like that. Counseling is available, so are support groups. Social Services provides all of the tools that those parents needed to deal with the situations. The parents simply didn't take advantage of the tools that were available."

Mike decided that as serious as things were, they needed a prepared statement to read when asked about their opinion of adopted children in the U.S. who were abused.

After three hours of thought, writing, and rewriting, the Knights finished their official response.

We are always deeply saddened by the loss of any child. However, we are most troubled by those losses that are caused by abuse and neglect.

There are individuals and families, who, because of life experiences or circumstances, require more specialized training in developmental and social management skills than they currently possess in order to successfully progress beyond their difficult situations.

It is a tragedy when these individuals and families are denied, or deny themselves the acquisition of these skills due to ignorance, fear, shame or pride.

No amount of legislation, litigation, or punishment will ever repair the damage done or replace the innocence and the loss of life, this most precious of gifts that is given.

We will work together with others who are also troubled by this great tragedy to help provide education, knowledge, and training, which are the only hope in preventing and eliminating such horrific abuse and neglect.

Russia and the United States have lost something that is most precious, in the loss of life of several adopted children. We deeply and sincerely regret this loss.

"I don't know what else to say," Mike said after reading the most recent version.

"Neither do I," Laura replied. "We have given them honest answers and a legitimate response. I don't know what else they could ask for."

"Alright then, let's try to get some sleep."

26

Their Day in Court

"Remember to look at the judge or prosecutor when you talk. Don't look at me. You are talking to them, not to me. I only translate. It is rude if you don't look at them while you are speaking, even if they don't understand the words." Sasha had already spent several minutes giving the Knights advice during the ride to the court house. Now that they were inside, past the guards and the metal detectors, sitting quietly on the stiff wooden bench outside the chambers, she continued to whisper last-minute instructions. "If they ask you why you chose Russia to adopt, say a friend told you. Whatever you do, don't say that you thought that adoption from Russia would be easy. It isn't easy. It is very hard. But many in Russia think that it is *too* easy. If you say it is easy, then they will make it more difficult."

Mike and Laura had heard all this before, and having Sasha go over it again and again didn't help their already jangled nerves.

"Okay," Sasha continued. "Now, always stand when addressing the judge or prosecutor. Pay attention, and I will motion to you when it is time to stand. Then you can sit back down when I do. Don't be nervous. Most of it is about common sense and respect."

Mike looked at his watch for the hundredth time. What could be taking so long? He pulled a folded page from his pocket and handed it to Sasha.

"One thing," Mike said, "we prepared a statement last night about the abuse of adopted Russian children. Here is a copy. Maybe you will want to read over it before we go in."

"Thank you," Sasha replied, as she slipped it into her own pocket. "I will keep it if we need it. But I don't think we will."

"You don't even want to read it?" Mike questioned.

"I will read it if we need to. But I think that we won't need it."

Sasha turned to Laura. "How are you doing?"

"I'm fine. I'm a little nervous, but I'm fine."

"Good. Good. You will do fine. Don't worry."

The door across the hallway opened and the Knights were invited into the court room. The room appeared more like a high school classroom than a court room. There were two long tables, one on each side of the room with chairs behind them. Mike and Laura were instructed to sit behind one of the tables and Elizaveta sat behind the other.

Mike looked up at the bench, which was just a particleboard laminate desk with three plastic swivel chairs behind it.

In front of and perpendicular to the bench were two other desks, in parallel, facing each other. Each had a wooden chair, similar to the type seen around a dinner table.

Soon a pretty young girl in a green sweater and black skirt entered and took the chair at the desk to Mike's right. "She is the court recorder," Sasha explained in a whisper.

Then an official looking woman in a medium blue uniform with brass buttons sat behind the desk facing the court recorder. "She is the prosecutor," Sasha whispered.

Then the prosecutor began to speak. "She wants to know if we have any pictures of you and the children that she can look at before the judge gets here," Sasha translated.

"Yes, of course," Laura replied, plunging into her bag. She retrieved several pictures of her and Mike with each of the girls and then pictures of the boys at home. "Oh, wait, should we show her the cloth books?"

"Do you have them with you?" Sasha asked.

"I have an extra copy of each of them."

"Sure, it couldn't hurt. Let's show those to her, too." Sasha took the soft books and pictures to the prosecutor at the front of the room and took a minute explaining the soft books, telling her that each of the girls had been presented with a set on the first visit. Then she returned to her seat.

The prosecutor took several minutes reviewing the photos before putting them down and turning to the cloth books. Mike wasn't sure, but he thought he saw a smile tug her stern face. She looked up, surprised, and began to speak to Sasha, who responded to her. The prosecutor turned back to the books.

"She is surprised that the books are also in Russian. She said that this is very good for the children. She is very impressed," Sasha whispered to Mike and Laura.

Then the prosecutor called over the court recorder to look at the books. Soon the two women were smiling and pointing and making comments in Russian as they thumbed through the books.

Suddenly, Sasha gasped quietly.

"What's wrong?" Mike whispered in his most worried tone.

"Nothing," Sasha whispered back. "Nothing is wrong. The prosecutor just said that these little girls are lucky to be going to your family. I've never seen a prosecutor act like this before a hearing."

"So this is good," Mike replied.

"Yes. Very good. Oh! Wait! Stand up!" The judge had just entered the room. Sasha, Mike, and Laura rose to their feet quickly.

The judge, a lofty woman who appeared to be in her late fifties, wore a typical black silk-like robe. She had medium blonde hair with dark roots and a stoic face.

She took her seat and then invited the others to do the same, which they did. Sasha translated in a whisper as the judge announced for the record what the proceedings were about and who they were for. Then she allowed the prosecutor time to question.

The prosecutor began by questioning Elizaveta. First, she had the social worker explain how the children had come into the possession of the state. Elizaveta explained in great detail how the children had been neglected and had not received critical medical care. She also explained that other children had been taken away from the mother for similar neglect.

Then the prosecutor queried as to whether there were other family members who might consider raising the children. Elizaveta explained that there was no legal record of the father and that any record of the father came only by the mother's indication when she gave birth. "The existence of a father was not confirmed by any document," Elizaveta said conclusively. Mike was surprised to see that this wording didn't draw a single bit of reaction from either the prosecutor or the judge. *Blood doesn't make you a father; documents make you a father.*

The prosecutor wanted to know about other family members. Elizaveta explained that the girls' birth mother had grown up in the orphanage in Partizansk. She had no family. Again, Mike was surprised. He understood that the birth mother might not have parents, but apparently, simply being an orphan meant she didn't have siblings either. *Blood doesn't make you an uncle; documents make you an uncle.*

The prosecutor then emphasized that it was the nation's desire to have Russian children adopted by Russian parents, and asked if Russians had been given adequate opportunity to adopt these children. Elizaveta explained that the girls had been available for adoption by Russians for the time required by law, and Katya had been available significantly longer. She produced several newspaper advertisements showing that they had actually advertised the availability of these two little girls in the local paper. The description of the children was there in the advertisement, along with their pictures.

Then the prosecutor wanted to know what the social worker knew about Mike and Laura. She wanted to know if they had shown interest in the children, if they had spent time with them, how they acted with them, how many times they had seen them, and what Elizaveta's opinion was of what kind of parents these people would make.

Elizaveta explained how Mike and Laura had come to Partizansk in February and had visited with Luba on two different occasions. She said that the new parents played well with the child and that every indication was that they had deep feelings for her. She told them that Luba even called Laura "Mama" and Mike "Poppy" already. Laura noticed that Elizaveta conveniently forgot to mention that Luba called everyone "Mama." The social worker explained how Mike and Laura had visited with Katya several times at camp, in February. She told her about how the parents made sure to leave Amérika early, well before their court date, so that they would have time to visit the children again. She told about how Katya had cried two days ago when she learned that it wasn't yet time to leave with her parents. Then she went over the special things that Mike and Laura had done to help prepare the children. She explained the cassette tape that Laura had left with Luba, and how Luba loved it. Then she mentioned the soft books.

The prosecutor then stopped her and began talking to the judge. Then she handed the soft books to her and continued speaking. The judge picked up the books and began to thumb through them. Unconsciously, she smiled as she went through the first several pages, then she caught herself and put her poker face back on. She continued through each of the soft books page by page until she had been through every page of each book.

Then the judge began to question Elizaveta. Most of the questions were minor variations of what the prosecutor had already asked, but Elizaveta explained the same things over again with a little more detail this time. Then the judge asked the prosecutor if she had any more questions for Elizaveta. She did not, so Elizaveta was told to be seated.

The judge then looked at Mike and began to speak in Russian. "Stand up," Sasha said quietly to Mike as she rose to her feet.

"The judge wants to know if you realize the responsibility that you will have to these children."

"Yes I do," Mike replied, his eyes fixed comfortably on the judge. "We have other children and realize that it is a lot of work and a great responsibility to raise children, but we want to do this."

Sasha translated for the judge who then spoke briefly to the prosecutor. Then the prosecutor looked at Mike and began questioning in Russian.

"The prosecutor says that you already have children," Sasha translated. "She wants to know why you want more children."

"We do have children," Mike began, "and we love them. But we have two boys. We have no girls. We always wanted to have both boys and girls, but we can't have more children biologically, so we decided to adopt daughters."

A smile tugged at the corners of the prosecutor's mouth, but then she suppressed it and sat up straight while speaking officially.

"The prosecutor says she has no further questions," Sasha translated.

But the judge wasn't about to let the Amerikáns off that easy. She had more questions. "It says in your home study that you were abused as a child," the judge said in Russian as she looked at Laura. "Is this why you want more children?"

It was all Mike could do to keep his eyebrows from furling in a scowl. What kind of question was that? Who would want to adopt kids because *they* had been abused? Fortunately, the question actually meant something to Laura, and Mike was surprised to see her nod affirmatively.

"Yes," she began. "I didn't have the life that I wanted to have in my childhood. I wished for something better. Today, I know that there are other children who wish their lives were different. Adopting is a way for me to provide that life for them. Also, though I am not the child in our family now, this is the family that I always wanted. This will make *my* childhood dream come true."

The judge smiled briefly as Sasha translated, then turned back to her stern demeanor and questioned Mike.

"The judge says that you obviously don't speak Russian and the children don't speak English. She wants to know how you intend to communicate."

"We know that this will be difficult," Mike began. "But we have bought dictionaries and picture books. We hope that by listening and referring to the dictionaries and by pointing to pictures that it will help as the children begin to learn English."

Sasha waited for the judge, who still looked very stern, to finish before she translated the comment for Mike. "The judge says she doesn't think that you realize how difficult it will be," Sasha translated.

Although it wasn't a question, Mike felt like he needed to respond. Out of the corner of his eye, he could see Sasha wince slightly.

"With all due respect, your honor, I spent a year and a half in Brazil. When I first got there, I barely understood anything that was said to me, and expressing myself was even more difficult. While I don't think this will be easy, I will understand the difficulty that the children have, and will be able to do so with true empathy."

The judge reshuffled her papers, straightening the pile by lifting it and pounding the stack on its side against the desk. She spoke gruffly. It was obvious that she was going to get the last word in, and by her body language, particularly in that she didn't even look up at Mike, it was clear that she wanted no response.

"The judge says that you will see that frustrations with a child learning a new language is more difficult than with an adult," Sasha translated as she pulled a little bit of a face, letting Mike know that he should say no more.

Mike remained silent.

The judge then continued looking at her desk while she spoke.

"We may sit down now," Sasha said to Mike and Laura while the judge continued talking.

"The judge has asked the prosecutor to make her recommendation," Sasha told them.

The prosecutor also shuffled her papers and tapped the stack on the desk to even it up while she spoke, but she couldn't help smiling just a little.

"The prosecutor recommends that the state grant the adoption," Sasha translated. "Now the judge wants to know if you have anything else to say. So stand up."

"Is this where we ask them to waive the ten-day appeal period?" Mike asked Sasha.

"If you must," Sasha replied.

Mike could tell that she really didn't want him to, but he figured it wasn't going to cost anything to ask. He looked directly at the judge and explained the situation of two nights before when Katya had been so upset that they left her. He appealed to the judge to consider all that Katya had been through with being separated from those that she loved, and asked her to avoid making her spend more time away from her parents. After all, he finished, she has no other family who would appeal the court's decision anyway. He would be forever grateful if the court could waive the ten-day waiting period for the sake of his daughter's emotions.

Sasha felt somewhat relieved. Mike had posed a legitimate concern and had done it in a way so as not to offend the judge. As she translated Mike's comments, a smile tugged at the judge's mouth. The Amerikán was clever, approaching the request from the child's perspective. But he loved the little girls, that much was clear.

Then the judge spoke briefly once more.

"The judge asks that we leave the room while she makes her decision," Sasha translated. Then she and the Americans stood up and left the room, followed by Elizaveta.

"Sorry about that," Mike said to Sasha after the door had shut behind them. "I really didn't want to provoke the judge."

"You did fine. You both did," she replied while looking at Laura.

"So do we have anything to worry about?" Mike asked.

"I don't think so," Sasha replied. "I think everything went very well." Then she turned to Elizaveta and asked her opinion.

"Elizaveta thinks everything went well, too. But it's like she says, you never know what else the court might ask for until the judge reads the decision," Sasha told them.

Mike and Laura sat quietly on the hallway bench while Elizaveta and Sasha visited a little further down the hall with another adoption coordinator they knew. They were there for about ten minutes when the door opened and they were asked to return to the court room. The prosecutor and court recorder were in their seats, but the judge was not in the room. Several seconds later, the door behind the bench opened and the judge emerged. Everyone rose to their feet. The judge sat and invited the others to do likewise.

As soon as they were seated, the judge spoke and waited for Sasha to translate. "The judge asks that we stand while she reads her decision," Sasha said while rising to her feet. Mike and Laura rose quickly.

The judge began to read the decision while Sasha translated in a whisper. "The court rules in favor of the adoption, pending a ten-day appeal period. Any party wishing to appeal the court's decision must do so and present evidence for the reason of their appeal within that time frame."

Then the judge smacked her gavel on the bench.

"Congratulations!" Sasha exclaimed just before hugging Laura and shaking Mike's hand.

The prosecutor and Elizaveta both rose and walked over to congratulate them. After the congratulations, the judge spoke briefly. "The judge wants to know if you need anything else," Sasha translated. "Perhaps you would like a picture with her?"

"Yes, please," Mike responded. "Would you ask the judge if she would be kind enough to stand in for a picture? Also if it's not offensive, I'd like Elizaveta, the prosecutor, and recorder in the picture, too."

"That shouldn't be a problem," Sasha replied just before answering the judge.

The judge smiled and waved to invite everyone up behind the bench. They lined up against the wall, with the Russian flag posted behind them. The Russian arms, complete with red shield and double-headed gold eagle, were posted on the wall above. As no one else was there to take the picture, Sasha volunteered to shoot the photo.

Then the judge congratulated Mike and Laura, as did the prosecutor and recorder, again, before they filed out of the room, leaving the Knights with Sasha and Elizaveta.

"There is a restaurant near here that has excellent borscht," Sasha said to everyone in the hall. Why don't the four of us go out to dinner to celebrate?"

Even though the beet soup was surprisingly good, Mike found himself stirring it more than eating it, until Elizaveta spoke to him.

"Elizaveta wants to know if everything is alright, Mike," Sasha translated. "She says that she has never seen you this quiet before."

"Actually, no one has seen me this quiet before," Mike joked.

Everyone laughed as Sasha told Elizaveta what he had said.

"Don't misunderstand," Mike continued. "I am very happy with the court's decision. I even understand them not waiving the ten-day appeal period. In fact, I didn't expect them to waive it. But I keep thinking about when we took Katya back to the orphanage two nights ago. She cried and cried. I just can't get it out of my mind. She is going to be so disappointed."

The group went solemn as Sasha translated for Elizaveta. The social worker listened intently, then smiled as she responded to Sasha.

"Elizaveta says that the law clearly states that during the ten-day waiting period the parents may not take possession of the children. But the law also clearly states that the social worker can do whatever she thinks is in the child's best interest. She says that she thinks it is in the children's best interest to go with you as soon as possible. If you want to, you can pick up Katya and Luba tomorrow."

Mike dropped his spoon as he looked up in amazement. Laura gasped and began crying. Mike couldn't hold back either, as tears welled up in his eyes.

Elizaveta spoke again and waited for Sasha to translate.

"There is a clause in the law" Sasha began, "giving social workers discretion. It was meant to say that if a child becomes too emotional with the parents coming and going during the appeal period, the social worker has the authority to deny the parents the right to visit the orphanage during that time. But since it literally says that the social worker can do whatever is in the best interest of an emotional child, Elizaveta is using it to do just the opposite. Congratulations."

Sasha and Elizaveta sat there, tears beginning to form as they broke into huge smiles. Impossible as it seemed, Mike's and Laura's smiles were even bigger.

27

One Last Night at the Orphanage

Minutes before the other children were sent to bed, Sofia took Katya to the dormitory. "Elizaveta called here a little while ago. Your mama and papa went to court today to see the judge. Everything went fine. Elizaveta says that your mama and papa will come to get you and Luba tomorrow!"

Katya squealed with excitement. "Did Mama and Papa promise the judge that I could stay in their family forever?"

"Yes, Zaichunook, they did," she responded. "Shall we read your soft book and see what happens next?"

"Yes, yes! I want to read the book!" Katya exclaimed.

Sofia pulled out both books and handed them to Katya. "Which one shall we read first?" she asked.

Katya hesitated for a moment, and then selected the family book, the one with the hand-drawn flowers and sun in the back. Sofia read the book to Katya one last time. As they read, they also talked about each family member and the rooms of the house. They even talked about Dasha the dog, and the horses, Porter and Macho.

Then Sofia took out the other soft book and she and Katya once more talked about Katya's trip to the fairytale land of Amérika. Sofia explained that it was still not time to go to Amérika, but that she would stay with her parents and Luba at the hotel until it was time to go. She showed Katya the picture of the hotel room in the book, just like the one where they would stay. Then they read and talked about flying on airplanes, sights in Moscow, and the elegant hotel there that even had a swimming pool. Although she had read the book a thousand times with Sofia, Katya still got excited about the swimming pool.

"But I don't know how to swim!" she exclaimed to Sofia. "Will Mama and Papa help me swim?"

"I'm sure that they will, if you go swimming, Katya."

"But they *will* let me go swimming, *won't* they? I want to go swimming!"

Sofia chuckled. "I really don't know. That's something for Mama and Papa to decide. I guess you'll have to ask *them*!"

Katya smiled but then grew pensive. "Will you come to see me in Amérika, Sofia?"

Sofia had wondered how she would handle the inevitable question. It was best to be honest. "I'm sorry, Zaichunook," she started somberly, "but that will not be possible."

"But why? I want you to come and visit me in Amérika. I want you to come and see me with Anya and Marishka."

"I really am sorry, Katya," Sofia reiterated. "But Amérika is so far away. It costs so much to go to Amérika that I'm afraid I won't *ever* have enough money to visit."

"I can ask Papa. Maybe he can help you come to Amérika."

"No, Katya. I'm sorry. But do you remember how your Mama told you that when the sun goes down in Russia, the sun comes up in Amérika?"

"Yes, I remember."

"Well, just like Mama and Papa blew kisses for the sun to carry to you when they were back in Amérika, I will blow kisses to you when you go to your new home. Every time the sun comes up, you can remember that I love you and think about you. Remember every morning that I send a kiss for you with the sun."

Tears welled up in Katya's eyes. "But I love you, Sofia. I will miss you!" The tears began to roll down her cheeks as she threw her arms around Sofia's neck. "I will miss you!"

Sofia held Katya close and her tears also began to flow. "I will miss you, too, little one. But that's the way it is supposed to be. We are supposed to miss friends when they are away from us. But we are also supposed to be happy when good things happen to our friends. Getting a family is a good thing for you, Katya, and I am happy for you!"

The child's arms were still wrapped tightly around the caregiver's neck, and Sofia could feel Katya's sobs as much as hear them. Finally, Sofia pulled her away, pushed her back and smiled at her brightly. "Now get some sleep, Zaichunook. I'll see you in the morning."

Katya wiped a tear, lunged forward, and gave Sofia another hug and then a quick kiss on the lips. She smiled bravely.

"I love you, Sofia. Good night."

"Good night, Katya. I'll see you in the morning."

28

And the Flowers Came Up

"Are you awake?" Laura asked as she felt Mike moving around in the bed early Friday morning.

"Yeah. I can't sleep. I feel like a little kid at Christmas. I wonder if Katya is this excited."

"Probably not," Laura responded. "Elizaveta was staying in Vladivostok last night. I'm sure that Katya doesn't even know yet. They probably won't tell her until they know for sure that we're coming. I'm certain they don't want to have to deal with her bouncing off the walls any longer than they have to."

"You're right, she probably doesn't even know. Maybe they should have waited to tell *me* so that you didn't have to deal with *me* bouncing off the walls."

Laura laughed. "It's five-thirty. Are you going to be able to get back to sleep?"

"I doubt it, but I might as well try," he replied.

"Let's get up and go through the clothes for the girls. I want them all laid out when they get here tonight."

"That sounds fun. It beats lying here tossing and turning."

Mike and Laura got up and began emptying the suitcases. All of the clothes still had tags, so they began removing them and stacking the clothes in two piles, one for each girl. Then there were the toys. There were stuffed animals, coloring books with crayons, bottles of bubble solution and all sorts of gadgets for blowing bubbles. "I can't believe we left the dolls at home!" Laura exclaimed.

The socks and underwear went in bundles, back in the corners of the chairs and couch, but jeans, tops, sweaters, dresses, jackets, coats, hats, mittens, scarves, cute little pajamas, and even oriental bathrobes that Mike had brought home from Korea covered the seats and backs of the furniture. Several pairs of shoes and a pair of boots for each girl were lined up in front of the chairs. Laura rearranged the layouts several times before she was satisfied.

"Don't we have to take clothes with us?" Mike asked. "I thought that we had to bring them clothes to leave the orphanage in."

"Oh, that's right," Laura replied. "I completely forgot! Come here and help me decide."

"I think their mama should decide," Mike replied, knowing he liked all of the clothes, but that Laura would want everything to be special.

"Come on, Mike, help me decide."

"Alright," Mike replied. He walked in front of the furniture and picked up the coats, hats, mittens, and scarves and tossed them in the open carry-on bag. "There you go. It's all yours from here."

Laura rolled her eyes just a little, then sighed and started looking through the clothes. For Luba, she picked up a pair of bell bottom jeans with embroidered butterflies. Then she held them up with a cute little brightly colored striped sweater. Then she put them both down. She went through the other jeans and other tops, considering multiple combinations. Finally, after exhausting just about every combination possible, she picked up the original butterfly jeans and striped sweater. "Do you think these will be okay?" she asked.

"Sure. I don't think there is a better choice," Mike replied seriously.

"You're making fun of me!" Laura exclaimed.

"No I'm not," he deadpanned. "I'm behind that choice a hundred percent."

Laura moved to the couch and began inspecting possibilities for Katya. After several minutes and multiple combinations, she finally returned to the first combination she had picked up; a pair of rhinestone studded bell bottom jeans and a long-sleeved pink pullover. "Do you think Katya will like these?" she asked holding them up for Mike.

"I'm sure she'll love them," he replied.

"Okay. Now you have to pick the shoes."

"Alright, I can do that." Mike had his eye on the little shoes that lit up when the girls walked. He walked over and picked up both pairs.

"I knew that you would pick those!" Laura exclaimed in delight. "They'll have so much fun with them!"

He placed them in the carry-on along with the other clothes. Then he grabbed the Teddy Bears that matched the ones that they had given the girls on the first trip, and splashed them with his cologne just before tossing them into the bag.

"Great idea," Laura said as she went for the two new baby blankets that Mike's mother had made. She gave them each a spray of her perfume and placed them in the bag. Mike went to another suitcase and pulled out two more stuffed bears, placing them carefully in the bag.

"Are those for Marishka and Anya?" Laura asked.

"Yep. I wanted Katya to be able to give her friends a going-away present." Mike explained. "I mean, they're her best friends in the world. Who knows what they've been through together? Now she has to leave them there in the orphanage." Tears welled up in Mike's eyes. "I know it's only a small consolation to her friends, and I can even accept the fact that they probably won't be able to keep them, at least as their own. But maybe it will help Katya to remember that the last thing she did for her friends was to give them gifts."

"You're such a good daddy!" Laura said as she threw her arms around his neck and kissed him.

"I don't know about that," Mike replied. He couldn't hold the tears back any longer and they streamed down his face. "I mean, just what are we supposed to say? Sorry, we can't have you in our family. I know that no one else is letting you into their family either, but we like Katya more. So stay here in the orphanage. But hey, here's a stuffed bear. Hope you like it. Have a nice life and good luck not becoming a prostitute when you're seventeen."

"Come on, Mike," Laura said. "It's not like that."

"No, Laura. That's *exactly* how it is." As always, for Mike, it was black and white. "I mean, I know our resources are limited. We only have so much time to spend between our children. The size of our house limits us. There is only so much we can do. But the fact is, those girls will remain in the orphanage. In fact, at their ages, the likelihood of a better life decreases every day."

"I know, Mike. It's sad. But we can't change everything."

"No, I know that," he admitted. "But someone could. There *are* enough resources in the world. There are enough families to take these kids in. But the cold hard truth is that they won't."

Laura didn't know what else to say. Nothing she said ever made a difference when Mike got like this. He would just have to take some time to figure out how to deal with it. So she hugged him tightly and gave him another kiss. "I'm sorry, Sweetheart. I love you," she said as she broke away. "I'm going to take a quick shower before breakfast."

"Mike, look!" Laura squealed as they exited the hotel. Then she burst into tears.

"What is it? What's wrong?"

But Laura couldn't speak. All she could do was point at the ground several feet in front of her.

Then Mike saw it. The little green plants that had been getting greener every day since their arrival had bloomed. These were the very first flowers of the season. There were more than a dozen bright yellow flowers scattered around the flower bed.

"The flowers!" Mike exclaimed.

"Yes! Remember?" Laura asked with her voice shaking.

"When the snow goes away and the flowers come up, we'll be back to get you," he said in a whisper. He stepped forward and wrapped his arms around his wife.

"Oh Mike, I can't believe what tender mercies God has for his children. After everything that Katya has had to go through in her young life, here is a disappointment that she didn't have to live. We made a promise, and the flowers bloomed on the very day that we are going to get her!"

Mike moved his mouth to Laura's ear. "I love you," he said softly.

"I love you, too. Can you imagine how much God loves us, though? I'll never forget this as long as I live."

"Neither will I, Laura," he said softly. "Neither will I."

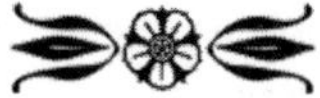

"I still can't get over all of those clothes stacked up around the room," Jim commented as they drove through the mountains on their way to Partizansk. "You should have seen it, Marik, there are clothes and toys stacked up all over the furniture for the girls. It will be like Christmas!"

"I'm sure the girls will be excited," Marik responded. "But I'm hardly surprised. I saw all the luggage that came in with the three of you!"

Jim and the Knights laughed. "I was so excited about picking up the girls," Jim continued, "that I could hardly sleep last night. I can only imagine how it must have been for you two."

"Yeah, we didn't sleep much, either," Mike responded. "Then Laura dragged us out of bed at five-thirty."

"I'm sorry," she said, though not convincingly. "I was just so excited, and I wanted everything to be just right."

"Well, everything is just right, isn't it," Mike replied. "Did you two notice the flowers this morning?" he asked Marik and Jim.

"What flowers?" they asked in unison.

Then Mike explained how the first flowers had bloomed at the hotel that morning and reminded them of what Katya had been told. Marik thought that it was a wonderful and incredible coincidence, but Jim knew that it was much more than that.

"Won't she be excited?" Jim commented. "It looks like this could be the perfect day!"

Laura thought about that as she looked out the window. The sky was overcast and gloomy, the bare trees still had not felt the touch of spring. It was a bleak, gray world out there. But not inside her heart.

"Yes," she agreed. "The perfect day."

"Polina says the workers would like to meet us," Marik translated as the director invited them into the office.

The Americans sat around a small conference table with the director and two other workers; one young and the other who appeared to be in her early sixties. Marik translated as Polina introduced Sofia, who Mike and Laura had met at the camp in February, and Támara, who had short bright orange hair and wore a leopard-skin print blouse. Everyone exchanged pleasantries.

Polina spoke and Marik translated.

"She says that you have won the race against the flowers, and she congratulates you," Marik told the Americans.

Everyone laughed, but Laura couldn't resist. "Please tell Polina we had no time to spare. The flowers at the hotel bloomed this morning."

The Russians were quite excited at this news, smiling and speculating how Katya would react seeing her first flowers of the season later that afternoon. Then Polina began to speak again, and Marik translated.

"She says that Katya is quite excited this morning. She knows that you are here to take her this time and she is anxious to go and get her little sister."

The Americans smiled and nodded.

"Well, anyway," Marik continued, "Támara is one of the workers who helps with Katya's education. Mostly at Katya's age it's speech and simple counting and things. She says that she wanted to be able to meet Katya's new parents, and also she wants to be able to answer any questions that you might have."

Támara explained through Marik that Katya was a very bright child who did very well socially. Also, that she learned quickly, showed leadership ability, and loved to dance and sing.

Then it was Sofia's turn. She told of what a pleasant child Katya was, and how happy she was that Katya was going to have a family. Sophia loved the soft books. She had read them to Katya over and over again. As Sophia spoke, Mike noticed her holding back tears and doing her best to veil what were obviously strong emotions.

"Polina asks if you are Mike's father or Laura's father," Marik translated for Jim after the director had spoken.

"Actually, neither," Jim explained. "Our families have been good friends for a long time. The Knight's boys know me as Grandpa Jim."

"Polina wants to know if you have children of your own," Marik translated.

"Yes. I have one son, three daughters, ten grandchildren, and three great grandchildren," Jim responded.

Marik translated for Polina, who spoke back while fluffing her hair with her hand. Támara and Sofia burst into fits of laughter, and then Támara also began to talk and fluff her hair. Marik laughed so hard he could barely translate.

"Polina and Támara are asking if you have a wife."

Now the Americans were laughing, too.

"Yes, I do," Jim said, taking the joke well, but still turning red with embarrassment.

"Okay," Polina expressed after the laughter died down, "we have had enough fun. I suppose that you are as anxious to see Katya as she is to see you." Then she asked Sofia to go and get the child.

A few minutes later, Sofia returned with Katya. She was wearing a hot pink pullover on top of her shirt and bright, bold-striped cable tights, along with the molded hard plastic sandals seen on most of the orphans. Today, Katya was more timid.

"*Prevet,* Mama. *Prevet,* Papa. *Prevet, Dyedushka* Jim," she said shyly as she entered the room.

"Hello, Princess!" Laura exclaimed as she held out her arms. But this time, Katya didn't run. Laura understood. It wasn't that she wasn't excited to see them. This had been her life, and there were things and people that she would miss; especially Marishka, Anya, and of course, Sofia. Katya walked slowly to Laura and gave her a hug. Laura hugged her for a minute and then picked her up and placed her on her lap. Katya smiled her enormous smile and her dimples sprung to life. But she really didn't know how to react, so she held her little fist up in front of her mouth to cover the smile.

"The Knights have brought Teddy Bears for Katya to give to Marishka and Anya as a going-away present," Marik explained to the Russian workers. "Would now be a good time to do that?"

The workers spoke for several minutes. Sofia and Támara had just put the children down for naps. It wasn't the best time. But really, there was no other time.

"Polina says the children have been put down for naps, and that they might not still be awake. We should do this now," Marik translated.

Mike softly grabbed the two bears from the carry-on bag as Marik explained the situation to Katya, whose smile broke out again when she realized that she had gifts to leave with her friends. They had already promised to find each other in Amérika when they all had new homes and mamas and papas. Perhaps the gifts would make the wait easier for Anya and Marishka.

As Katya and the adults entered the dormitory, some of the children stirred and looked up to see what was going on, though they dared not speak or get up; it was nap time. They went to Marishka's bed, and Katya presented the stuffed animal to her friend. At first, Marishka was nervous; she didn't want to get in trouble for talking during nap time. But Sofia assured her that it was alright to talk this one time, as long as they spoke in a whisper.

"Thank you for the *mishka*, Katya. I will come to see you soon in Amérika," Marishka promised.

"You're welcome. I will wait for you and Anya. Please come soon."

Sofia then led Katya over to the far end of the room where Anya slept soundly. Sofia made gentle attempts to wake the little girl, but Anya would not wake up. Sofia then shook her a little harder and even sat her up in bed, but Anya just whined and tried to lie back down.

"I'm afraid it's no use, Katya," Sofia explained sadly. "Anya won't wake up. Why don't we just leave the *mishka* here with Anya. When she wakes up later, I will tell her that you gave it to her."

Katya nodded in agreement and placed the Teddy Bear on the bed next to her friend. Sofia lifted Anya's arm up over the stuffed animal and she snuggled up next to it and squeezed it tightly while she continued to sleep. Then Sofia led Katya towards the door where her parents waited. The other orphans who were still awake stirred and partially sat up to catch one more glimpse of Katya before she was gone forever. All of them wanted to tell her goodbye one last time. But it was nap time; they dared not do it. Finally, just as Katya reached the door, one brave soul, a five-year-old little boy, decided it was worth the risk.

"*Desvidania*, Katya," he called from his bed.

The other orphans who were still awake all followed his example, though most of them in whispers.

"*Desvidania*, Katya!"

"*Desvidania!*" Katya replied to them in a quiet voice as she turned and waved goodbye to her orphanage family. *Farewell*. Then she followed Sofia out the door.

The group walked back to the director's office where they all took their seats.

"Are you ready to go, child?" Polina asked her in Russian.

Katya nodded while covering her smile with her fist.

"Very well then, it's time to change your clothes. Mama and Papa have brought you all new clothes. Would you like to see them?"

Again, Katya nodded excitedly as Mike unzipped the carry-on and removed the new clothes. He held up the jeans and pink shirt for her to look at.

"Do you like those clothes?" Polina asked her.

Katya continued to smile behind her fist and nodded.

"Those jeans are wonderful!" Polina exclaimed to Katya. "Now you can be just like Brittany Spears!" Mike understood "Brittany Spears" and mentally rolled his eyes.

Laura placed Katya down on the ground where she quickly changed into the new clothes. Mike waited until the very end before he reached back into the bag and removed the shoes. He held them up for her to look at.

"Oh, look what beautiful shoes Papa brought for you!" Sofia exclaimed.

Then Mike tapped them together and the flashing lights came to life. Katya gasped, and the adults laughed at seeing her excitement. She ran to Mike, grabbed the shoes, and quickly plopped down on the floor to put them on. Mike bent over, tied them for her, and lifted her to her feet. First she stomped one foot, then the other. Both times the lights came to life. Then she walked slowly around the office, watching the lights dance on her shoes. The adults in the room stopped her from bumping into the desk and other furniture several times as she walked around, never looking up from the shoes.

"There you go, Zaichunook," Sophia said. "You are ready. Have a wonderful trip to your new home in Amérika."

One by one, the Russian women gave hugs to the little girl, and Mike noticed that Sofia hugged her quite a bit longer than the others. He saw Sophia speak softly in his daughter's ear as tears streamed down her face. What a special relationship these two had; what a sacrifice this must be for sweet Sofia.

Mike removed the beautiful dark blue coat, with embroidered flowers and white fur trim around the hood, and handed it to Laura who helped Katya put it on. Then he removed the pink and white knitted hat and scarf.

"*Oh, kraseva!*" Polina exclaimed. *How beautiful!*

Laura placed the hat on Katya's head and wrapped the scarf around her neck as Mike pulled a new tube of cherry Chapstik from his coat pocket and hand it to Katya.

"It looks like Papa knows that you are a big girl who needs lipstick," Sofia told her. "Maybe you should put some on."

Katya beamed as she took out the tube, removed the cap and twisted the base to bring the balm up. She carefully spread the Chapstik on her lips and then rubbed them together. Then she took the Chapstik and put a dab on each cheek, rubbing it in with her finger. All of the adults laughed. It was obvious that she had seen women cheat before, using lipstick for rouge.

Now it was time.

Each of the workers gave Katya one last quick hug before Marik escorted her out of the room and down the hall with Jim and her parents. Mike had planned on carrying his daughter out of the orphanage, but instead stayed busy keeping Katya from walking into walls and doorways as she watched her shoes light up with every step.

Oksana greeted Marik and the Americans as they entered the Baby Hospital, inviting the visitors into her office to wait. Several minutes later, one of the workers entered the office carrying Luba. She was only wearing a tank top and a pair of cotton underpants. Her short blonde hair was standing on end and she was rubbing sleep from her eyes.

"I'm sorry," the worker explained through Marik's translation, "we tried to keep her awake for you, but she just couldn't stay awake any longer, so we put her down for a nap. It might take her a minute to wake up all the way."

"Oh, you poor baby!" Laura exclaimed as she held out her arms. "Did they wake you up from your nap?"

Luba held her arms out to Laura and snuggled into her shoulder. Laura sat on a chair with Luba on her lap, playing and talking for several minutes, trying to give the child a chance to wake up.

"Oksana has other things that she needs to do," Marik stated matter-of-factly, "and we really need to get on the road. We should get Luba changed."

Mike took the clothes from the carry-on and handed them to Laura, who held them up in front of Luba. She immediately came to life. Luba loved pretty clothes. She squealed as Laura held up the little jeans with embroidered butterflies and snatched them from her hands. She did the same with the sweater.

"I explained to her this morning that you would bring her beautiful new clothes," Oksana said as Marik translated. "I will truly miss this child. She is so petite, so pretty, so happy. I spent quite a bit of time with Luba this morning. We read the soft books, and I explained her trip home and what life might be like with her new mommy and poppy. I think she is a little bit nervous, but it seems that she is happy to see you."

Laura began to change Luba into her new clothes and Luba loved every bit of it. Katya was playing with *Dyedushka* Jim until she saw Mike remove Luba's shoes from the bag. She ran to Luba and began to speak rapidly to her in Russian, stomping her own feet on the ground pointing at the lights. The adults laughed.

"It looks like Katya likes her new shoes," Oksana commented.

Then Laura took Luba's hands, one shoe in each, and helped her bang the shoes together. Luba squealed with delight and continued to pound the shoes together while watching the dancing lights. Laura quickly put the shoes on Luba, then placed her on the floor. Katya again began to speak to Luba and demonstrated how to light up the shoes by stomping her own on the office floor. Luba followed suit and was soon stomping all over the office while watching the magical shoes that lit up.

"Okay," Marik said, impatient to get going, "let's put her coat on."

Laura lifted up the coat that matched Katya's, and showed Luba the beautiful embroidered flowers. Luba smiled, but turned away.

"Look at the pretty flowers," Laura said again while pointing to them. She took Luba's hand and pulled it to the coat so that she could feel the flowers.

Luba jerked back her hand and screamed. "*Nee!*" *No!*

"Don't you like the coat?" Laura asked. "It will keep you warm. We need to put it on." Then she tried to slip Luba's arm into the sleeve.

"*Nee! Nee! NEE!*" Luba continued to scream and struggled to break free while beginning to sob. Laura put her down on the floor and looked at Oksana. "What's wrong?"

Oksana shook her head with a puzzled expression. Laura attempted to put Luba's arm into the coat again.

"*NEE! NEE! NEE!*" Luba screamed as she cried and tried to break free. Again, Laura let her go. "*Mama Oksana!*" Luba screamed as she ran for Oksana and threw her arms around her leg while sobbing.

"Oh, no," Mike whispered as tears welled up in his eyes. "She knows that when she puts the coat on, it's time to go. She thinks we're taking her away from her mother."

Marik translated for Oksana, who nodded in agreement as she picked the sobbing child up into her arms. Luba wrapped her arms around her neck and clung tightly and desperately while she continued to cry and sob. Oksana continued to hug Luba while she talked to her softly. The Americans had tears in their eyes as they watched little Luba's heart break. Not only Luba's, they realized, but Oksana's, as well. Oksana continued to embrace Luba for several minutes and the two of them had a good cry together. Finally the director succeeded in getting the coat on and zipped up, and then the beautiful knitted pink and white scarf and hat. Luba continued to cry a little bit, but had settled down considerably.

"Okay, it's time to go," Marik said. "Laura, take Luba. We will go now."

Oksana gave Luba one more squeeze and then handed her to Laura, who hugged her tightly. At first it seemed that everything would be fine, but then Laura began to follow Marik out the door. Luba burst into hysterics again.

"*Mama Oksana! Mama Oksana*!" Luba lunged in Laura's arms and grasped the molding around the door frame with every ounce of strength that her little fingers possessed. Laura continued to walk and the fingers broke free. Luba's hysteria escalated as she lunged and grabbed the molding around a window in the hall. Mike looked into Luba's eyes and saw true terror. As they walked down the forty feet of hallway to the door, Luba alternated between shrieking "*Mama Oksana*" and "*NEE!*" at the top of her lungs and between sobs.

Outside, on the steps of the orphanage, Laura handed Luba back to Oksana for one last goodbye. Laura couldn't take anymore and hurried to the SUV in tears, leaving Mike to bring their daughter.Oksana held the child for just a moment more.

"*Desvidania*, Luba. *Desvidania*."

"Mike," Marik said firmly, "it won't get any better. Everyone has said goodbye. It's time to go now. Get Luba."

Oksana carefully handed the child over to Mike, and she shrieked and lunged, trying to dive to the ground. Mike held her strongly with one arm around her little legs and the other pressed up against her back, holding her tightly against his chest. Even so, she screamed and writhed, attempting to climb over his shoulder toward Oksana.

"*Mama Oksana! Mama Oksana! MAMA OKSANA!*" She shrieked louder and louder with every step toward the SUV, pleading desperately for the woman she recognized as her mother to rescue her.

Mike's heart was breaking, too. But a thought came suddenly and clearly, almost a prayer.

Oh, child. If you had any idea what awaits you, you wouldn't feel like this. There would be no panic. If you only knew what I have to give you, you wouldn't cry. And while your friends know that you are going to a better place, even they don't fully understand the life that I will give you when I take you home. Soon you will see, and you will forgive me when finally you understand. Child, I know what is best for you and I will do what is best for you, even if it hurts you now. Even if it hurts your friends and those you see as family, I will take you home.

As they approached the door to the hotel, Laura bent over, showing the flowers to Katya. In addition to the little yellow flowers that had bloomed that morning, there were also purple ones and blue ones.

"Do you remember what Mama told you when she left last winter?" Laura asked while Marik translated.

"*Dá*." She responded.

"Do you remember that she told you she would come for you when the flowers came up?"

"*Dá!*" Katya squealed as she pointed at the flowers and began to chatter in Russian.

"What is she saying?" Laura asked.

"She is excited about the flowers," Marik explained. "She says that you really did come for her when the flowers came up."

Laura smiled and held out her arms to Katya, who ran to her and threw her arms around her neck. The mother and daughter continued to hug while Marik and the other two men took the bags and Luba into the hotel.

"Is there anything else I can help you with?" Marik asked politely.

"No. But thank you," Mike replied sincerely. "Words can't express how grateful we are."

"You're welcome, Mike," Marik said. "I'm going to be taking a couple of days off. I'll call you Monday and see how you're doing. But you have my cell phone number. Don't hesitate to call if you need something."

By now Laura and Katya had entered the hotel. "Thank you, Marik," she said sincerely as she shook his hand. "Thank you for helping us to find the rest of our family and bring them together."

Marik smiled warmly at Laura, then he bent down and spoke to Katya.

"Be good for your parents," he told her in Russian. "You have a good Mama and Papa and a good *Dyedushka.* They will need lots of help with Luba, because they don't speak Russian and Luba doesn't understand. But you are a big girl and you do understand. Mama and Papa will need lots of help. Please help them as much as you can."

"I will," Katya promised him. "Thank you for giving me a Mama and Papa," she said while throwing her arms around his neck. "And *Dyedushka*."

With that, Marik gave her a quick squeeze and then stood up. He patted her on the head and then told them all goodbye one more time before walking out the door.

Mike unlocked the door to the room, and Laura carried Luba in. Jim followed closely carrying Katya. Everyone breathed a sigh of relief as they set the children down and Mike dropped the bags in the closet.

"Show them, Sweetheart," Laura said to Mike while nodding towards the furniture-covered with clothes.

"No. You go ahead," Mike replied, knowing that this was a once in a lifetime experience for Laura.

"Come on, Mike. They'll know the clothes are from both of us. I want to see them get this present from their daddy."

Mike smiled. "Thank you, Honey."

Jim and Laura stood back and watched as Mike approached the girls. "Katya." Mike called while holding out his hand. "Come here."

"*Stó,* Papa?" *What?*

"Come, here," Mike said again holding out his hands but this time wiggling his fingers to indicate that he wanted her to come.

Katya ran to him as if he was going to pick her up. But instead, he took her by the hand and led her to the couch. Mike held out his hand and moved it along slowly showing the clothes along the full length of the couch. "Katya," he said, pointing at her. He performed the same action again and then pointed at her once more and said her name.

Katya gasped. Could it be that all of these clothes were hers? She began to jabber excitedly in Russian and pointed at the clothes on the couch. She ended the jabbering with her own name and "*Dá,* Papa?"

"*Dá, Preens-yessa.*"

Katya squealed. Then she took note of the clothes on the high back chairs. She ran to them, pointed, began to jabber in Russian, and again ended the sentence with her own name, followed by "*Dá,* Papa?"

"*Nyet*," Mike replied. "Luba," he said while pointing at the clothes and then toward the younger child.

"Oh!" Katya replied. She then began to explain excitedly to her little sister that all of those clothes on the chairs were for her. Of course, she also made sure that Luba knew that the other clothes, the ones on the couch were for Katya, not Luba.

Almost at once the girls began trying on their clothes. Mike was so mesmerized by the quickness that Katya displayed—changing outfit after outfit—that he didn't notice Luba until Laura made eye contact and pointed toward the younger girl. Luba sat on the floor and was busy putting on her third pair of jeans, each over the top of the other. She also had on three shirts.

"I guess if she has them all on," Mike whispered, "then they really are hers."

Jim and Laura laughed quietly.

"You two should have some time alone with the girls," Jim said thoughtfully. "I'm going to my room to take a rest."

Mike and Laura thanked him, Laura gave him a hug and Mike walked him to the door.

"I'm sure Laura will want to give them a bath and get them cleaned up before we go to eat dinner," Mike said as Jim went to leave. "How about if we give you a call in an hour or so and we'll work out a time to meet for dinner?"

"That sounds great," Jim responded. "I'll talk to you soon."

The Knight party was the talk of the hotel as they entered the downstairs restaurant. Everyone had heard the stories, and they were excited to see the two little sisters reunited, now with a mama and papa, and even a grandpa. The waitress seated them quickly and got a booster chair for Luba.

"What do you want for the children to drink?" she asked.

"Whatever they want," Mike responded. He would soon learn that he should have known better.

The waitress spoke to the girls in Russian for several seconds before responding back to Mike. "Katya says that she will have coffee, and Luba wants tea. What can I bring for the rest of you?"

"I don't think so!" Laura blurted. "Do they let children this young drink coffee and tea?"

"Oh, I don't think it is a problem," the waitress responded. "I'm sure they had tea all the time at the orphanage. Maybe not so much coffee, but Katya probably just wants to be big. I'll put some milk with their coffee and tea. It won't be so strong then."

"Why don't you just bring them both a Sprite?" Mike recommended.

"Okay," the waitress shrugged.

Within minutes, the waitress returned with their drinks. Katya was disappointed that she didn't get her coffee, but she had fun drinking the Sprite. She would giggle as she held the glass up to her lips to feel the bubbles pop and sprinkle her face.

Katya acted surprised when the waitress asked her what she wanted to eat. At first she just stared back at her. But then the waitress started giving her choices. So many choices were overwhelming. Katya had never been asked what she wanted to eat before. Truly, she must really be a princess. Otherwise, she would be served a meal and she would eat it. Who would care what she wanted to eat, unless she was a princess? After listening to the various choices several times, Katya decided to ask for potatoes. She was even more surprised when she was asked what kind of potatoes she wanted. Finally, after several descriptions and much pondering, Katya decided that she wanted French fries. Laura ordered the same for Luba.

From that point on, dinner went the way it was supposed to go. There wasn't a lot of visiting afterwards, though. The Americans were exhausted, and so were the children. They decided to return to their rooms for the first night away from the orphanages.

Both of the girls were excited to try on their new pajamas. Katya had a pink set with a flowing princess gown which she modeled around the room after putting it on. "Mama! Mama! Katya *Preens-yessa!*" she squealed while twirling around to get the gown to flow.

"Yes," Laura responded happily. "Katya is a princess."

Luba was equally excited with her pajamas. They were a light blue velvety material with sparkling silver metallic stars all over them that made the pajamas glitter. Luba squealed as she looked down at the sparkles after Laura helped her change.

The room had two queen sized beds, so the girls were placed together in one bed while Mike and Laura got in the other one. But the excitement of the day was too much; Katya just couldn't relax. She kept teasing and playing with Luba who, in turn, refused to settle down. But Mike and Laura were exhausted. It really was time to go to bed.

"How do you say 'be quiet' in Russian?" Mike asked Laura.

"I don't know," Laura responded. "But we have the list of phrases and words that the agency gave us. I have a copy in my purse. I'll get it out."

Laura turned on the light, which made the girls even more energetic. She thumbed through the typed phrases for several minutes before finding the ones that she wanted. "*Pará Spaht*," she said firmly while pointing to the bed.

Katya, who was standing on the bed, immediately went silent and dropped to a sitting position. Luba followed her example, but couldn't stop giggling and provoking Katya. Soon Katya was wrestling with Luba.

"*Pará Spaht!*" Laura said, this time a little more sternly.

Katya again settled right down. This time, Luba stayed quiet.

"That was magic!" Mike exclaimed. "What did you say?"

"It means it's time for bed," Laura responded. "Looks like they understand."

"I hope all the phrases work like that!" Mike observed.

Laura walked over to the girl's bed and gave them each a hug and a tender kiss, which they both reciprocated. "*Pará Spaht*," she said softly one more time, and then she returned to bed herself.

The room remained silent for several minutes and then Luba began to cry. Naturally, she was afraid. She didn't remember ever sleeping anywhere but the orphanage, and she missed Mama Oksana and her own bed terribly. At first her cries were muffled, but they escalated quickly and were, of course, contagious. Within seconds, Katya was crying, too.

"Did you see how to say 'be quiet'?" Mike asked.

"It's on the same page that the other was on," Laura responded. She clicked on the lamp next to the night stand and picked up the list. After several seconds of searching while the girls continued to cry, she found it.

"*Mahl-chee!*" Laura said firmly. Katya's eyes bugged out and then both girls began to cry even harder. "*Mahl-chee!*" She repeated, to even more crying. "Katya! Luba! *Mahl-chee!*"

Luba threw her arms around her big sister and began to sob while Katya also became more upset.

Mike grabbed the list from Laura to see if there might be another way to pronounce the phrase, but it was pretty clear that Laura had said it correctly. "*Mahl-chee!*" Mike exclaimed in a stern daddy voice. That didn't help. So he moved Katya from the bed and stood her face first in the corner. Katya didn't budge, and soon became silent.

But Luba's cries escalated, so Mike placed her in another corner. It was obvious that the children had been punished like this before, since neither even attempted to move out of their corners. After a couple of minutes, both had stopped crying.

Mike took Katya over to the bed and pulled Luba out of the corner. He gave them each a hug and a kiss and put them back in bed. Each of the girls lunged forward for another hug, which he gave them, and then he laid them each back in bed and kissed them each on the forehead. "*Mahl-chee*," he said softly as he backed away. Katya gasped and Luba's eyes got big as she started to whimper, but Katya spoke to her in Russian. Luba sniffed a couple of times and pouted, but she and Katya remained silent. Mike turned off the light, got back in bed, and soon everyone went to sleep.

29

Day One

Mike had been up for an hour and was sitting on the bed reading when Luba began to stir. At first she just flopped around a little. But then she sat up and rubbed her eyes. After that, she looked over at her sister and grinned.

"Good morning, Princess," Mike said to her. Luba spun around and looked at Mike. She smiled brightly, then dove down and hid her face bashfully in the pillow. She stayed there for several seconds before peeking back out to see if he was still looking. He was, so she planted her face back in the pillow. This went on a few more times before Mike finally sneaked up and put his face right where she would peek out. When she did, Mike growled, grabbed her, lifted her up and began to tickle her. She laughed and squealed and giggled while he played with her for a few minutes. Finally, she pointed at her sleeping sister.

"Kawt-chah?"

"Yes, Princess, that's Katya," Mike replied.

"Kawt-chah!" she exclaimed as she wriggled off of Mike's lap and climbed back on her bed. Then she grabbed her older sister and began to shake her. "Kawt-chah! Kawt-chah! Kawt-chah!" She continued to try to wake her sister up.

It was clear that Katya was awake, but that she wasn't ready to get up yet. At first she tried to ignore her little sister, but Luba was relentless. Finally Katya sat up and angrily barked several words at Luba in Russian. Then she plopped back down on the bed and pulled the blanket up over her head. Luba wrinkled up her face like she was going to cry, and then just sat there pouting.

"What's going on?" Laura asked as she walked out of the bathroom and noticed Luba sulking on the bed.

"She tried to wake Katya up. It looks like Katya isn't a morning person," Mike explained. "When she couldn't ignore Luba any more she sat up and bit her head off, and then dove back under the covers."

"Oh, is that so?" Laura replied. "Okay, Katya can sleep if she wants too. But you can get dressed in your beautiful clothes." Laura picked up Luba and headed for the dresser where they had placed the clothes the night before. As she put Luba down, she stole a glance at the bed, where Katya was now peeking from under the covers, curious.

Laura pulled several pairs of pants out of Luba's drawer and laid them out on the floor in front of her. "This one, or this one, or this one?" Laura asked while pointing at each pair of jeans. Luba grabbed the pair to her right, and Laura placed the others back in the drawer. They did the same with the shirts, then Laura helped Luba get dressed while she played with her and cooed. Katya was getting jealous. Then, as Laura finished, she pushed Luba out in front of her and turned her around for inspection. "You are beautiful, *Preens-yessa!*" she said as she looked Luba over.

That was all it took. Katya lunged out of the bed. "*Luba nee preens-yessa! Katya preens-yessa!*" she said as she ran to Laura. *Luba is not a princess! Katya is a princess!*

"*Dá, Katya preens-yessa*," Laura confirmed. "*Ee, Luba preens-yessa*."

"*Nyet!*" Katya exclaimed. "*Katya kuk Selah. Selah kuk preens-yessa*." Katya was reminding her mother that it was her, not her sister, whose name, Sarah, meant princess.

"Now what do we do?" Laura asked Mike, bewildered. "You've already spoiled her with her name. She's not going to be happy if we call her sister 'Princess,' too."

"Hold on, I think I have an idea," he replied. Mike had tried to learn something of the language by observing Marik and the others. Now it was time to see if he had learned something useful.

"Katya, *preens-yessa*," he said while pointing at her.

"*Dá!*" Katya responded.

"*Ee* Luba, *preens-yeska!*"

Katya's expression changed from glowering to beaming as quickly as if a cloud had cleared the sun.

"*Dá! Dá!*" Katya exclaimed. "Luba *preens-yeska!*" Then she began to talk to Luba rapidly in Russian. Soon both girls were smiling and playing.

"What did you do?" Laura asked, amazed.

"Nothing a little knowledge of Russian couldn't take care of," he replied, obviously pleased with himself. "I told her that Katya is a princess and Luba is a *little* princess. Looks like that solved the problem."

"So how did you say that?" Laura asked. "I'll need to remember that."

"*Preens-yeska*," Mike replied.

"Okay, *Preens-yessa Katya*," Laura said to the older girl, still smiling at Mike's insight, "what would you like to wear?"

Poor Katya had never been so overwhelmed with choices. This would take some getting used to. She decided, changed her mind, and decided again four times before she finally got dressed. Then Laura took her into the bathroom to do her hair. Katya hadn't had anyone spend so much time helping her with her hair, and she decided it was kind of fun. Laura was trying to make her hair look as feminine as possible, though it was difficult, as short as it was. Finally she succeeded with the proper combinations of barrettes and bands. She lifted Katya up to look in the mirror. The little girl was pleased. Her smile spread across her face and her dimples appeared. But then she glanced at Laura and frowned. She began to jabber in Russian and then pointed at her mother's hair.

"I'm sorry, I don't understand," Laura said before realizing that she was only complicating the situation with words that Katya didn't understand. "Wait, I know," she held up her hand and then paused as she tried to remember. "*Stó?*" *What?*

Katya sighed. This time she spoke clearly and slowly while using hand gestures. She pointed to Laura's long hair and made flowing motions. Then she pointed to her own short hair and made flowing motions going down. Laura recognized the last few words; "*Katya, kuk Mama, kuk preens-yessa*." Like Mama, like a princess.

"Oh," Laura replied. "I understand. You want long hair like Mama's. Long hair like a princess." She held the end of Katya's hair and then placed her other hand out half-way to Katya's hip. "Long hair for Katya, *kuk preens-yessa*."

"*Dá!*" Katya squealed.

"Okay, Princess, we'll grow your hair long." Laura replied. "*Dá. Dá.*"

Laura placed Katya back down on the ground and she danced out of the room, sweeping her head as if she were manipulating waves of waist-long hair.

Luba's hair was more difficult. While it was well over her ears when they visited in February, she had since received a haircut, and it was obvious that an electric hair razor had been used. It wasn't just that it was short, but it was also jagged and uneven. Laura worked with it and finally found the right barrettes with little pink bows. Soon there was no doubt that Luba was a beautiful little girl.

Just as they were starting to walk out the door to go to breakfast with Jim, Luba ran to the dresser and pulled out a different shirt, starting to take off the one she had on. "Sorry, Luba, you're already dressed," Laura told her as she took the shirt away and put it back in the drawer. Luba burst into tears. Who could blame her for wanting to play dress-up with all of these new clothes? But Laura simply shut the drawer and picked up Luba, who continued to cry.

It was time to meet *Dyedushka* Jim for breakfast. Laura carried Luba and Mike started to pick up Katya after closing the door to their room behind them. "*Nyet*," Katya told him while holding out her hand signaling him to stop. "*Dyedushka* Jim," she continued as she turned to walk down the hall toward Jim's room.

"*Dá. Dyedushka* Jim *ee* Katya," Mike responded.

Katya bolted down the hallway and began to bang on Jim's door. There was no delay; the door swung open. Jim had heard them coming and was waiting for them. "*Dyedushka* Jim!" Katya squealed while throwing herself into his arms.

"Good morning, Katya," Jim said while lifting her up. She threw her arms around him for a hug and then grabbed both sides of his face and gave him a kiss. "That was nice," Jim told her. "I missed you!" Katya just smiled and sat up on his arm.

The five of them began to walk down the hall with Laura carrying Luba and Jim carrying Katya. "She has legs, Jim," Mike told him. "You don't have to carry her. She's pretty heavy on long walks."

"We're doing just fine," Jim replied. "If she gets too heavy, I'll put her down. For right now we're happy this way." Katya just smiled and continued to sit on his arm while he packed her down the stairs and into the restaurant.

Once again Katya was overwhelmed with choices for breakfast, but finally she decided to take a chance on one she didn't recognize. It sounded exotic.

"Katya says that she will have pancakes and coffee," the waitress informed her parents.

"Let's make it pancakes and apple juice," Mike suggested.

"Sure, okay," the waitress replied. "What do you want for the little one?"

"Please bring her pancakes and apple juice, too," Laura requested.

"Okay, two children's breakfasts with pancakes and apple juice."

Soon the meals arrived, but it was clear there was something wrong with Katya.

"I'm sorry," the waitress said to Mike. "Katya doesn't want pancakes now. She says she wants something else. I told her that I will bring her eggs."

"Oh, no. Let's not start this," Mike responded. "Tell her that Papa said she has to eat what she asked for."

"Really sir, it's no problem. I don't mind," the waitress told him happily.

"Thank you. That's very kind. But I don't think it's a good idea to let her think she can do that. Please tell Katya that Papa said she has to eat the pancakes."

The waitress explained the situation to Katya, who wasn't at all happy about it. After all, she was a princess. She should be able to decide what she was going to eat, and when she was going to eat it. Everyone knew that princesses could change their minds whenever they wanted to. She and the waitress spoke back and forth several times before the waitress finally translated for Mike.

"At first she said she wouldn't eat it, but I told her that she must do as Papa says. I think it might go better if we offer a reward like some fresh fruit, maybe a banana. It's pretty rare for the orphans to have fresh fruit. It's quite a treat. May I offer her a banana if she eats the pancakes?"

"Yes. That would be great. Thank you," Mike replied.

The waitress spoke to Katya again who smiled from ear to ear. It was evident that she was excited about the banana. Then she spoke quickly to the waitress and began to eat her pancakes, pulling a face when she tasted the maple syrup. Oh, well. She's the one who wanted to try something exotic.

"Katya told me thank you for the juice, but not to forget her coffee," the waitress told Mike. "Can I bring some for her?"

"No. Thanks. She's too little to be drinking coffee," Mike responded.

The waitress nodded her head cordially and walked away.

Katya had taken two bites of her pancake but now she was just poking at it. Luba, on the other hand, was already halfway finished with hers. She picked up her apple juice and took several swallows before she accidentally dropped the glass. The apple juice spilled down the front of her shirt and onto her pants. First she gasped, then she started to cry.

"I'd better take her up and change her," Laura told the men. "Please don't wait for us, go ahead and eat." With that, she took Luba from the booster chair and left to change her clothes.

Jim and Mike were finished with their breakfasts by the time that Laura and Luba got back. Katya hadn't eaten any more of her pancake, but she had devoured the banana that the waitress brought her. Luba, now in dry clothes of her own choosing, was as happy as could be. She and Laura finished their breakfasts quickly.

The waitress returned and began to speak to Katya. "She says that she doesn't feel well," she explained to Mike. "She said that her head hurts and she thinks she might throw up."

"Oh, she probably just isn't very hungry," Mike replied. "I'm sure she'll make up for it at lunch." He turned his attention to the adults. "I heard that we can walk to the beach from here. Why don't we meet in a half hour and take the girls out to the beach?"

Both agreed that it would be a good idea, so they left the restaurant and returned to their rooms.

Luba went straight to her drawer in the dresser and began looking for another set of clothes to change into.

"She's all girl!" Mike said to Laura. Laura just shook her head. In almost no time, Luba carried a new pair of pants and a shirt over to the bed and began to disrobe.

"*Nyet*," Laura told her firmly.

Luba wasn't fazed. She continued to take off her clothes.

"Luba, *nyet!*" Laura repeated as she walked over to the bed. She took the clothes back to the dresser and then returned and re-dressed Luba, who started crying. Laura let her sit on the bed and cry. It only lasted a couple of minutes, and then she was down playing. A few minutes later, Luba returned to the dresser and started looking through her clothes again. Then she took a pair of jeans and a shirt and sat them on the side of the drawer. After that, she just walked away. She went over to Laura and began to talk.

"*Peet. Peet.*"

"I'm sorry, I don't understand," Laura replied.

"Mama, *peet. Peet.*" Then she walked over to the miniature refrigerator and pointed. "*Peet. Peet.*"

Katya ran over next to Luba and began to jabber in Russian. "*Luba peet. Ee Katya peet.*" Katya opened the fridge and pulled out the bottle of apple juice.

"Oh, you want a drink," Laura observed. "Sure, you may both have a drink." Laura took two of the small juice glasses from the cupboard, and filled each halfway with apple juice. "Drink," she said while holding Katya's glass out to her.

"*Dr-ink*," Katya repeated as she took the glass.

Then Laura held out the other glass for Luba. "Drink," she said and then waited for Luba to repeat it.

"*Peet.*"

"*Peet, nyet*," Laura responded. "*Drink.*"

"*Chi.*"

"Drink."

"*Chi.*"

"I guess that's close enough for now," Laura replied. "Here's your drink."

Luba smiled, took the glass and walked into the TV area near the dresser. Katya had finished her drink and was sitting next to Mike while he went through the soft book with her, showing her the pictures of what the rest of their trip would be like.

Luba walked over to the dresser where her new clothes were still hanging over the side of her opened drawer. She turned back toward Laura and called her. "Mama! Mama! Mama!"

Laura looked up at her as did the others, to see what she wanted. "Mama! Mama! *Oi!*" and then she intentionally turned her glass of juice down the front of her. "*Oi!*"

Laura gasped. Mike hid his head so that Luba couldn't see him laughing. "She did that on purpose!" Laura exclaimed. "She tried to spill that drink on herself!"

Before Laura knew how to respond, Luba dropped the glass on the floor, picked up her new clothes and walked over to Laura. "Mama, *oi!*" she said as she handed Laura the clothes so that she could be changed.

Mike was laughing silently but energetically behind the soft book. Laura didn't see the humor. "You are not getting new clothes for that!" she said while brusquely taking them from her hand. Luba began to cry as Laura returned the dry clothes to the drawer. The child was even more surprised when her mother grabbed her by the arm and stood her in the corner. She escalated quickly from crying to screaming hysterically. But she made no attempt to get out of the corner. Within a few minutes she had finished crying, so Laura let her out. She led the child over to the dresser, opened her drawer, and pointed at the clothes. "*Nyet*," Laura said firmly while shaking her finger at the clothes. "*Nyet*."

Luba sniffed a couple of times and wrinkled up her face like she was going to cry if she didn't get her way.

"Corner?" Laura asked while pointing to the corner recently occupied by Luba. "Corner?"

"*Nee!*" Luba replied as she walked away from the drawer to look for a toy to play with.

Twenty minutes later it was time to meet Jim. Laura couldn't take Luba out in wet clothes, so she changed her. Hopefully, a stint in the corner and twenty minutes in wet clothes had taught her a lesson.

"She'll have you carry her for the rest of her life if you let her, Jim," Mike said, ten minutes into the three-quarter mile walk to the beach. Jim had picked Katya up in the hotel and hadn't put her down yet. "She has to be getting heavy. I mean, Luba is getting heavy, and Laura and I have been trading off!"

"She is getting heavy," Jim admitted. "But we're almost there. I think we can make it."

Five minutes later, they were wandering along the beach looking for small sea shells. Mike found a few flat rocks and the children were fascinated that Papa could make them skip across the water. The children were having lots of fun running up and down the beach, and Laura enjoyed capturing a few of the moments on the digital camera.

Though a little chilly, it was a beautiful spring day. A few fluffy clouds floated by in an otherwise perfect blue sky. The water was calm and lapped gently on the pebbled beach. Neither Mike nor Laura had felt this calm in months. Soon Katya dragged *Dyedushka* Jim toward her father. She began jabbering in Russian and then pointed skyward.

"Sorry, Princess. I don't understand." Then he remembered. He at least needed to put forth an effort to communicate. "*Sto?*"

Katya held up her hands indicating that she wanted him to pick her up, which he did. Again she began to jabber as she pointed toward the sky. Then she kissed her hand and blew a kiss toward the sun. "Katya *braht*," she said slowly and clearly. "*Braht Jayf ee brat Seeb*." Again she blew a kiss to the sun.

"Oh! I get it!" Mike exclaimed to Laura and Jim. "We need to blow kisses to her brothers Jeff and Steve!" Laura carried Luba over and helped her, while Mike and *Dyedushka* Jim joined with Katya in blowing several more kisses to the sun, entrusting it with a safe delivery back to America.

"*Ee Babushka!*" Katya squealed. *And Grandma.*

"*Ee Babushka!*" the adults followed blowing kisses skyward once more.

They continued to relax and wander around the beach until it was time to return for lunch. With the newness of everything, no one had even thought about Luba taking a nap, and by now she was getting quite cross. So the happy family walked back to the hotel together.

At lunch Katya, once again ordered her coffee, and Mike, once again, shut her down. Luba tried to eat her plain mashed potatoes, but her head kept nodding down and then bouncing back up as she struggled to stay awake. Halfway through her French Fries, Katya informed the adults that she was sick by saying, "*Blaugh*," and motioning with her hand thrusting from in front of her mouth.

Laura jumped up, grabbed Katya by the hand and quickly led her off to the bathroom. Several minutes later they returned.

"She did get sick," Laura said. "I wonder if she just isn't used to the food. Remember, she said she was sick at breakfast, too."

"Is there anything I can help you with?" The waitress had returned.

"Please talk to Katya and see how she's feeling now," Mike requested.

"She says that her stomach feels better now, but she says her head hurts really bad. Do you have aspirin for her in your room? If not, I can get you some," the waitress replied after an exchange with Katya.

"No, thanks, we have aspirin. Will you ask Katya if she gets headaches often?"

Again the waitress spoke with the little girl. "She says no. She says her head never hurts, but it hurts really bad now. Maybe she needs to lie down."

"Maybe," Mike responded. "Wait! Caffeine withdrawals!"

"Excuse me?"

"Please ask Katya what she would drink with her meals at the orphanage."

The waitress spoke back and forth with Katya. "Mostly she drinks tea. But she likes coffee better. She asks if I will bring her some coffee. Is that alright?"

"Tell you what. Could you bring me a can of Coke and a small glass?" he asked.

"Sure. I'll be right back."

Within minutes of drinking several ounces of the soft drink, Katya's headache was gone. Her weaning from caffeine was underway.

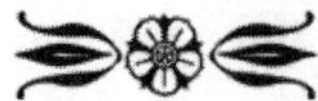

After lunch, the group returned to their rooms for a rest. After tucking Luba in, Laura sat with Katya on the couch and began to read her a story. Mike was just going over to the other bed to lay down for a short nap of his own when the phone rang.

"Hello?"

"Hello, Mr. Knight. A Mr. Mark Knight is on the phone for you. May I put him through?"

"Yes, of course. Thank you."

"Hi, Mike."

"Hi, Mark. How's it going?"

"Not so well. I just got back from the hospital."

"What's wrong?" Mike's heart raced. The last time he got a call that started like this, he was in Albuquerque and Laura was on the phone telling him that his brother, Mitch, had been killed in a work accident.

"Mom collapsed this evening at your house. Jeff called 911, and then he called me. I sent Dawn over to your house to be with the boys, and I headed for the hospital. They admitted Mom. The pain in her lower stomach is a lot worse. The doctor says that it doesn't look good. The cancer might be back. He wants to do an MRI first thing Monday morning."

"Oh, man, this isn't good. What else do you know?"

"Nothing, yet. The doctor says we won't know much until after the MRI. Until then, all we can do is wait and pray."

Laura noticed the anxiety in Mike's voice. "What's wrong?"

Mike held up his hand and shook his head. "How are the boys?" he asked Mark.

"Jeff is a little shaken. Steve seems to be okay. Jeff's older. I think he might realize what's going on."

"So, you haven't told them yet?"

"About the cancer coming back? No. I didn't see any reason to freak them out with speculation. I thought it would be better to wait until we know something."

"Yeah, of course. You're right."

"Everything okay over there in Russia?"

"Yes. We're doing fine. So you guys are staying at our house?"

"Yeah. At least until we know more."

"Thanks, Mark. I don't know what to say."

"Don't worry about it. We'll take care of things here. Tell Laura and my new nieces we said hello."

"I'll do that. Hey, please call me any time, day or night, with any information. I'll try to rent a cell phone this afternoon, so you can get in touch with us even if we're out."

"Sounds like a good idea. Get me the number as soon as you know."

"I'll do that. Thanks, Mark. Talk to you soon."

"What's wrong?" Laura gasped before Mike even finished hanging up the phone.

Quietly, Mike explained the situation.

"Oh, Mike! I'm so sorry!" Tears welled up in Laura's eyes and began to tumble down her cheeks. She felt bad for Mike, of course, but also for herself. Mike's mom was the closest thing that she had to a mother.

"It might be bad, but we can beat this thing," Mike said. "With God's help, we can beat this thing."

"Hello?" Mike said, trying to orient himself after picking up the phone in the dark.

"I'm sorry, Mr. Knight. I know it's the middle of the night, but your brother, Mark, says you wanted him to call."

"Yes. Thank you. Please put him through."

There was a soft click on the line.

"Mark. What did you find out?"

"They finished the MRI, and it's not good, Mike. Looks like they never got all of the cancer, and now it's spread. The tumors are quite extensive, and have moved on to other organs."

"When are they going to operate?"

"That's just it. The doctor says that there's not much point in operating quite yet. They want to start chemo within the next day or so, reduce the size of the tumors, and then operate later."

"How did Mom take the news?"

"Oh, you know. She thinks that if the cancer doesn't kill her, the chemotherapy will. She says if it's her time to go, she's at peace with that. She keeps talking about being ready to see Dad and Mitch again."

Mike sat on the edge of his bed shaking his head. "Are you still there?" Mark asked after a long pause.

"Yeah, I'm here. What do we do now?"

"Well, I talked privately with the doctor. With the chemo, he says they have a chance, though not a big one, of prolonging her life for years, maybe. Without it, he says she won't last long at all, definitely not more than a couple of months."

"So…what now?"

"The doctor will meet with us again tomorrow. They are giving her medication for the pain now, and they have that under control. It looks like within a day or two they'll release her. We'll need to decide whether she goes home, or comes to live with one of us."

"Yeah, but you know Mom. She'll want to be in her own home." Mike sat quietly, still trying to take it all in. "Anything else?"

"No. That's it for now. We'll keep you posted. Take care and try to get some sleep."

"Thanks, Mark. Talk to you later."

30

Groundhog Day

From the second day on, *Dyedushka* Jim would call the ten-day appeal period after court "Groundhog Day," after the movie where the main character relives the same day over and over. While everything seemed new and adventurous the first day, the succeeding days blurred one over top of the other, and the hotel room took on the feel of a prison cell. Boredom set in, even while the anxiety over Mike's mother continued to escalate.

On the third day with the girls, Luba began with her well-practiced ritual of reselecting clothes soon after Laura had dressed her. She removed her favorite pair of jeans, the bellbottoms with embroidered butterflies, along with a pink shirt, and placed them on the top of the dresser. Before Laura could walk over to make her put them away, Luba turned to face her.

"Mama. Mama! MAMA!" Luba called, making sure that she had her mother's undivided attention.

Laura stopped in the middle of the room and looked at Luba. "*Stó?*"

"Mama! *Oí!*" Then she looked down and wet herself. "*Oí!*" She said as she looked back up at Laura. "*Oi!*" Then she turned, picked up the newly selected clothes and headed for her mother.

"That does it!" Laura exclaimed as she rushed toward Luba. She took the child and whisked her off to the corner.

Luba was flabbergasted. "Mama, *oí!* Mama *oí!*" she said over and over, trying to convince her mother that it had been an accident. Laura placed her firmly in the corner and brusquely removed the clean clothes from her grasp. Luba shrieked and began to cry hysterically, though she made no attempt to leave the corner.

"Did you see that?" an exasperated Laura asked Mike.

"Yes. Yes, I did," he responded through all but silent chuckles.

Katya came quickly across the room and began to hug Laura's leg in an attempt to show her loyalty, and also to remind her mother that she was the good child. She didn't need to be punished like her sister did.

"Thank you, Katya. I love you. *Yá-Tibya-Lo-Bloo.*" Laura hugged her quickly and patted her on her head. "But please, now isn't a good time. Please, go play." She placed her hand on Katya's back and maneuvered her over to the toys. "Please play," she said while pointing at the toys. While Katya still didn't understand all of the English, she realized that such manipulation wouldn't work any better here than it did at the orphanage, so she quietly sat down and began to play with a plastic horse.

Laura turned to Mike. "What am I supposed to do now? Marik and Sasha will be here in fifteen minutes to pick us up to go shopping. I can't take her like that! But if I let her change clothes, she'll wet herself every time she wants to wear something different!"

"Well, how about not giving her the clothes she wanted? We'll have to figure something out."

By now Luba had stopped crying, but she still stood rigid, facing the corner. Laura approached Luba, took her arm and turned her around to face her. Luba stretched out her arms and moved forward for a hug. "No!" Laura said firmly. "That was naughty. I'm angry," she said as she pushed Luba back to her arm's length. "*Nyet!*" she said angrily while pointing at her wet pants. "*Nyet! Nyet! NYET!*"

Luba began to cry again and tried to move forward for a hug.

"No. That was naughty. No, No!" Laura exclaimed while pointing at the wet pants. "*Nyet!*" Then she took Luba by the hand and led her into the bathroom to clean up.

"How are things going?" Sasha asked after a little small talk in the hotel lobby.

"Oh, alright, considering," Laura responded. "We're all getting used to each other and the children are testing their limits, but that was to be expected."

"Sure. Of course. How is the communication going?"

"Pretty well, actually. Of course, they don't understand all of the English words, but with pointing and charade maneuvers, we're getting along."

"You guys have some Russian phrases that you got from the agency, don't you?" Marik asked.

"Yeah, we got them, but I don't think we say things right," Mike responded. "The first night that we got home, the kids didn't want to settle down. So, Laura got out the list and looked up 'be quiet.' Laura tried it and it didn't work too well. So I tried it and it didn't work any better. In fact, the more I said it, the worse it got."

"What did you say?" Marik asked.

"*Mahl-chee*."

Sasha gasped. "Where did you learn that word?"

"It's on the list we got from the agency," Mike replied.

"No! Really? That's not a good word!" Sasha exclaimed. "Say '*Tee-hah*' from now on."

"In English, '*Tee-hah*' would be like 'be quiet,'" Marik explained, hiding a smile. "'*Mahl-chee*' is almost like 'shut up!' It's a stern word, only used with grown-ups. The girls aren't used to having it used with them."

"Oh, great," Mike said while shaking his head. "Beautiful. I spent fifteen minutes terrorizing my new daughters, telling them to shut up!"

"I'm sure it's okay," Sasha replied. "They don't seem to be afraid of you," she said motioning to the two children in their parent's arms. "The children seem quite happy."

"Well, we're here to take you shopping," Marik said, quickly changing the subject. "What do you need?"

"Mostly just some more groceries," Laura responded. "It's getting expensive eating every meal in the hotel restaurant."

"Sure, no problem. How about clothes and toys, did you bring enough with you or should we go to other stores besides the grocery store?"

"Actually," Laura added pensively, "I would like to go to a toy store. We did bring plenty of toys, but we forgot the dolls at home. I'll bet that the girls have never been able to choose a new toy for themselves before. I'd like to give them the chance to do that."

"I'd like to pick up a few clothing items, too," Mike interjected.

"Honey, we have plenty of clothes," Laura responded.

"I know. Trust me." He turned to their Russian companion. "Marik, is there a flea market or something like that around?"

"Yes. There's a Chinese Market in town. For clothes, the quality isn't great. Are you sure that's what you want?"

"Yes. The Chinese Market would be just fine."

"I guess we're ready to go then," Sasha concluded. So they all headed out to the car.

Both girls went crazy in the toy store. Naturally, they wanted one of everything, except for the things they wanted several of.

"What do you want me to tell Katya?" Marik asked. "She is no different than the other orphans that we bring here. They are all quite overwhelmed. It takes some time for them to understand that they can't have everything. Usually, parents let them choose one toy within a price range."

"That sounds good," Laura responded. "Let's put it at twenty-five dollars each."

Marik explained the rules to Katya and Luba and showed them several toys that fit into the budget. It didn't take Luba long to snatch a baby doll from the shelf. But Katya was more difficult. The poor little five-year-old had never been so overwhelmed with choices. But when she saw the Princess Barbie, she knew that she had to have it. She squealed as she pulled it from the shelf and showed it to her new father.

Mike laughed. "A princess for a princess. I should have seen that coming. Do all of these kids view their adoption as a fairytale, Marik? Or is it just Katya, I mean with her American name 'Sarah' meaning 'princess'?"

"Katya seems to play it up a little more than most," Marik admitted. "But they all view their adoptions as a sort of fairytale. But when you think about it, how could they not?"

"Yeah, I guess they'd have to," Mike said pensively as Katya handed him the doll and began to jabber in Russian.

"She wants to know how much the doll costs," Marik explained. "She wants to know if she can have this doll."

"I'm sure it will be fine."

"I don't know," Marik responded. "Some of this stuff comes in on the black market. It can get pretty expensive. You'd better let me check." Marik took the doll from Mike, read the price tag and made a quick conversion in his head. "Just over fifty dollars U.S.," he replied.

"You've got to be kidding! Fifty bucks for a Barbie?"

"I told you, some of this stuff can get pretty expensive," Marik reiterated as he placed the Barbie back on the shelf. Then he spoke to Katya in Russian.

Katya burst into tears. "*Yá Ha-Choó Preesyessa Bárabee! Yá Ha-Choó!*"

Marik spoke with Katya trying to calm her down, but the situation only worsened. "I told her to pick another toy," Marik explained. "I told her that this one is too expensive, but that you would buy her one when she gets to America."

"Tell her that Mama will take her shopping a day or two after we get back and she can buy a Barbie."

Marik translated but Katya became even more upset. "*Yá Ha-Choó! Yá Ha-Choó! Yá Ha-Choó Preesyessa Bárabee!*"

"You know what, Marik, let's just go ahead and get it." Mike relented.

"Are you sure? That's pretty expensive. Are you sure you want to spend that much?"

Mike laughed. "When you take into account what this trip and adoption are costing, the price of that Barbie is a snowflake on Mount Everest."

Marik laughed, and then spoke with Katya who immediately ceased crying as he handed her the Barbie. She hugged the box and then threw one of her arms around Mike's leg and hugged him while she jabbered in Russian.

"Katya says 'thank you' and that she will never ask for anything else," Marik laughed.

By now Sasha and Laura had finished browsing. Laura picked up a few small, inexpensive toys and everyone headed for the checkout stand. Suddenly, Katya gasped as she shoved the Barbie into Mike's hands and ran to a small pink bicycle on display. She grabbed it by the handle bars and began to speak excitedly. Her whole face lit up with a smile and Mike had never seen her dimples bigger.

"Do you need me to translate?" Marik joked.

"No, I think I've got a pretty good idea on this one. Please remind Katya that she told me that if I let her have the Barbie she would never ask for anything again."

Marik chuckled before translating. The smile left Katya's face and was replaced by serious forehead wrinkling while she contemplated her next move. Finally she replied.

"Katya says that if you let her have the bike that she can wait until she gets to America for the Barbie."

"She's quite a negotiator, huh?" Mike replied. "She didn't talk about a trade, only that she would *wait* for the Barbie."

"It's like I told you," Marik explained. "These kids are pretty overwhelmed with choices as their lives change. They go from owning nothing and having almost no choices to having *everything,* at least everything imaginable to them. It takes them some time to learn and to adjust." Mike thought about that as Marik continued. "Before these children learn to appreciate possessions, or to share them, or even when enough is enough, they first have to learn how to *have* possessions."

Marik explained to Katya that the bicycle would not fit into the luggage and that they would not be able to take it on the plane to America. With Mike's permission, he promised her that soon after her arrival at their new home she would be given a new bike. Once again, Katya pondered before answering.

"She said to tell you thank you for the Barbie and that she can be a big girl and wait until she gets to America for a new bike."

"What exactly are you looking for, Mike?" Marik inquired as they walked through the maze of tiny storefronts known as the China Market. On the way over, Marik had taken the time to explain that the goods sold in this market were all manufactured in China. That's how it got its name.

"Just some cheap pants, shorts, and T-shirts. Luba has regressed on her potty training and we need some extra clothes for around the hotel room."

"It's quite normal for these children to take a step back in lots of areas as they leave their comfort zone," Marik explained matter-of-factly.

"Yes, but she's doing it on purpose!" Laura interjected.

"What do you mean 'on purpose'?" Marik quizzed.

Mike and Laura explained the events of the morning. "I've got to hand it to her; she's smart," Mike added. "She knows what she's doing. She just loves her new clothes so much that she wants to change them every half hour or so. But I've got a plan. If we buy her some ugly clothes and then make her change into those when she intentionally wets herself, maybe she won't do it."

Marik laughed. "The battle of wits has begun!"

Mike held Katya's hand and Laura carried Luba as they walked through the narrow walkways of small painted plywood shacks selling everything imaginable. The shacks reminded Mike of the game shacks at the fairs and carnivals that toured in the States. Katya was fascinated, and Mike had to keep dragging her forward to keep her from stopping to look at everything. Finally, it was easier to carry her, so he picked her up.

"Here we are," Marik announced as they stopped in front of a shack with all kinds of children's clothes hung from the posts and roof. "Tell them what you want and I'll translate."

Mike explained that they wanted to buy some ugly clothes for "the little girl," motioning to Luba. The man and woman standing behind a make-shift counter were confused.

"She is so beautiful!" the woman exclaimed. "You can't dress her in ugly clothes!"

Her partner agreed. "Look! We have lots of beautiful clothes," he said while gathering several T-shirts and laying them out on top of the other merchandise that was already arranged on the rickety plywood counter. "Minnie Mouse! Butterflies! Birdies!"

The sales woman cut in. "We even have shirts written in English." She placed several T-shirts marked with popular American brands next to the ones her partner had displayed. Mike chuckled, wondering how the trademark attorneys from Abercrombie, Aeropostal, and Tommy Hilfiger would feel about this.

"No. Thanks anyway. Today we're only here to buy ugly clothes." Marik translated and then explained the logic to the sales people, who laughed heartily when they came to understand the tactic. "Today is your lucky day!" Mike continued. "The clothes that you thought you could never sell, I will buy today!"

The man behind the counter laughed again as he pulled a hideous lime-green, orange, and white striped tank top from under the counter. "I am even ashamed to display this one," he joked while holding it up for Mike and Laura to see.

Luba, who had become enthralled with all of the beautiful clothes, shrieked when Laura held the ugly tank top up against her to size it. "*Nee! Nee! Nee!*" she screamed while pushing it away from her again and again.

"Sold!" Mike hollered, to all of the adult's amusement.

"*Dai-ee! Dai-ee! Dai-ee!*" Luba shouted as she pointed to the T-shirt with Minnie Mouse. But the woman handed her mother a yellow and chartreuse shirt instead. Luba continued to shriek and yell as various ugly shirts, pants, and shorts were held up to her, and she all but climbed out of her mother's arms on several occasions trying to get to clothes that were more desirable. Mike and Laura used the intensity of Luba's objections to determine their purchases, and soon the bag was filled with a wardrobe unfit for the racks at Goodwill.

"Do you think it will work?" Marik asked Mike on the way back to the car.

"Sure! Katya may like her new clothes, but Luba lives for them. She'd change her wardrobe every half hour if we'd let her. I mean, you saw her reaction to the clothes she didn't like back there. Having to wear those ought to be quite an incentive to conform."

"It will be interesting to see," Marik replied.

The boredom of Groundhog Day continued, but *Dyedushka* Jim was a great help. He and the parents took turns giving each other breaks from the children, and the children time away from their parents. During their time off, the Knights usually found themselves taking nice, long walks on the nearby beach.

"I feel like I can relax for the first time in months," Laura said to Mike on just such a stroll. "It sure is good of Jim to take the girls for us."

"It is, but I think he enjoys it every bit as much as they do."

"The girls really like him. Katya adores him."

"Really? I didn't notice," Mike joked. "I don't think I've ever carried her if Jim is around. I don't think I've even seen him make her walk more than once or twice."

"It has been an incredible experience though, hasn't it, Mike?"

"It has. I never could have imagined. I don't think that when I try to describe it I'll ever do it justice."

"Mike, do you think that the children have had any religious background at all?" Mike was surprised at the abrupt change in conversation. Obviously it had been weighing on Laura's mind.

"I don't know. I doubt it. You heard Marik on the first trip. Most Russians aren't too concerned about religion any more. I think most of the caregivers are more concerned with immediate needs, like clothing and feeding the kids."

"It's just hard though, Mike. I mean, I have no idea what Katya has been through in her life, but it's obviously been bad. I just want her to be able to have something to turn to when memories of those things trouble her."

Mike was about to tell Laura that she had parents now to turn to and that the rest would come in time. But then he realized that Laura, having come from an abusive home, knew more about the needs of such children than he ever could. "What do you recommend?"

"I brought some Bible story books with us. Do you think it's too soon to start teaching her? Do you think we have enough language skills to even try at this point?"

"I don't know, Honey. I guess we can try."

"I think I will. I think I'll try as soon as we get back."

Mike and Laura spent another hour walking along the beach, skipping stones and just relaxing. It reminded Mike of the time that he and Laura had spent together before Jeff was born, when the two of them started the family business and spent almost all of their time together. Lots of people had asked them how they could spend so much time together without getting on each other's nerves. Mike never knew how to answer that question; he and Laura loved every minute they spent together. Now that their lives had become more complicated, with children, business, and other responsibilities, they had to go out of their way to spend time alone together. But they always made time for it, and they always enjoyed it.

"Sorry," *Dyedushka* Jim explained as they walked into the room, "you're short two containers of yogurt. I know you said that they had already eaten, but they tricked me!"

"Oh, it's okay," Laura responded. "Don't worry about it."

"No! I'm serious!" Jim responded, with a measure of embarrassment in his voice. "They tricked me! Katya kept going to the fridge and showing me that she wanted yogurt, but I kept telling her that Mama said no. Finally, I put on a Disney video for the girls, and moved my chair in front of the fridge so that she couldn't get into it. That worked for a while, but then Katya and Luba stopped paying attention to the video and started talking in Russian."

It was clear that there was a story here, so Mike and Laura sat down on the edge of the bed. Mike hadn't seen Jim worked up like this in a long time, and it was kind of funny.

"So then Luba went over to play by the coat rack, just out of sight. A minute later she started crying, so I ran over to see what was wrong. Somehow she'd pulled the playpen over on herself, so I lifted it off and picked her up to make sure she was okay. It took her a while to stop crying, and after I put her down she ran over behind the counter in the kitchenette. I could hear Katya and Luba jabbering and playing back there, so I went back to watching the video." Jim paused, almost too embarrassed to continue, but then went on. "After a few minutes it seemed too quiet, so I went over to see what was going on. There they sat, the two of them, under the counter, each with a container of yogurt. It was all over their faces and Luba was eating hers with her toe. Yes, her toe!"

By now Mike was laughing so hard that tears were coming out of his eyes.

"Katya looked so guilty, but I couldn't get mad at them. It was ingenious! They planned the whole thing! I just walked away and let them finish eating. Sorry. They're too smart for me."

Now Laura joined Mike in clutching her sides, unable to contain her laughter. Jim knew the value of a good story, and soon he had the couple in stitches again as he recounted the funnier parts of the adventure, complete with pantomimed expressions of the girls' faces. After several minutes, everyone regained their composure and Jim started to get up and leave.

"NO!" Katya screamed in English as she ran past Jim to the door, trying to lock it. "*Yá Ha-Choó Dyedushka Jim!*"

Jim picked up Katya and she threw her arms around his neck as he hugged her back. "I have to go now, Katya".

"No. *Dyedushka* Jim no go." She hugged him tighter as Mike raised his eyebrows in surprise, pleased to see her beginning to use English. "*Yá Ha-Choó Samaloot.*"

"Okay," Jim responded as he placed her on the ground. "*Samaloot* one more time," he said holding up one finger.

"*Dá!*" Katya responded, her face brightening with dimples as she ran to the middle of the room.

"Katya, only one," Jim said holding up his index finger once again.

"*Dá. Wun*," Katya responded.

"What's this?" Laura asked as Katya laid down on the floor, extending one arm and one leg upward toward Jim.

"*Samaloot* is Russian for airplane," Jim explained. "We play airplane a lot."

With that, he bent over and took the extended arm and leg, and began swinging her in circles around the room. After several turns, she made a safe landing onto the bed and Jim plopped into the high-back chair to recover from dizziness.

"Whew! She wears me out!" Jim said, catching his breath. Then he stood up, gave Katya a hug and a kiss, and headed for the door.

Laura pulled the Bible storybook from a piece of luggage and took Katya by the hand to the couch, where she sat the little girl on her lap. "I want to show you a special book," she said. Katya loved to have people read to her. Laura opened the book and carefully thumbed through a few pages, allowing Katya to see some pictures and become familiar with the book before she began reading it to her.

"*Ee-soos!*" Katya squealed as she pointed to a picture of Christ sitting among children.

"What did you say?" Laura gasped.

"*Ee-soos!*" Katya squealed again. Then she began to speak excitedly in Russian. Katya knew Jesus! She rushed from page to page, pointing at pictures and chattering in Russian as she told stories about Him. Her voice went gruff as she came to a page on the crucifixion, and she acted out the swinging of a hammer as she told her mother of the brutality. But her voice became cheerful again several pages later as she pointed to Jesus appearing to Mary. Katya knew that Jesus lived again!

Tears welled up in Laura's eyes. "Do you see that, Mike?" Laura asked. "She knows!"

"Yes, she does. I didn't see that coming."

"Who do you think taught her? Her birth mother? Someone at the orphanage?"

"I have no idea. I'm just glad that *someone* taught her."

"I am too," Laura said softly, stroking her daughter's hair. "I'm glad, too."

31

Vladivostok, Farewell

Monday, the second of May. The end of the ten-day waiting period. On the record, the ten-day appeal period was there in case anyone wanted to appeal the court's decision to allow the international adoption. But in reality, it never happened. Mike wondered if the waiting period was to keep Americans in the country spending money, or if it was just the way things happened in a place so caught up in bureaucracy and red tape. This Monday was also the official observance of May Day, so all of the government offices and many businesses were shut down for the holiday. That meant a mad dash on Tuesday and Wednesday trying to accomplish all that had to be done before leaving for Moscow on Thursday.

It was Tuesday morning, and the dash was about to begin.

"This morning we will drop off the photos and forms for the girls' Russian passports at the Passport Agency," Sasha explained as Marik drove. "Then we will go to the doctor's office so that they can get their physicals. Early this afternoon, we will be able to go back to the Passport Agency to pick up their passports."

It was just after nine when they arrived at the government building. Mike followed Marik up crumbling concrete steps, past ragged landscaping consisting of clumps of uncut grass scattered around footpaths beat into the dirt and a few scraggly bushes. Marik opened the painted steel door and Mike followed him in. Immediately to the left was a wooden door with a window that served as the entrance to an office, but when Marik tried the door, it was locked. Mike noticed that no lights in the office were on either. "We should wait here in the lobby for a few minutes," Marik explained. "It's only ten minutes past nine. Sometimes they are a little late."

"What time are they supposed to open?" Mike queried.

"Nine o'clock. But it's not so rigid. If they come a little bit late, it's no big deal."

"Really? A government office with no set times?"

"Oh, they have set times. It's just that some days people are a little bit late, or sometimes they need to leave early."

Mike would never understand the Russian way of thinking, so he just sighed and joined Marik on the nearby wooden bench, watching the janitor sweep and mop the lobby floor. Finally, about nine-thirty, Marik was tired of seeing Mike check his watch every few seconds.

"I'll ask the janitor if he knows when they'll be here," he said, getting up. Mike watched Marik speak in Russian with the janitor for a few minutes before he returned. "He says they aren't working today. We'll have to come back tomorrow."

"What?! They're not working today? Why not?"

"Because yesterday was a holiday."

Mike shook his head in a quick short movement. "Okay…yesterday was a holiday. That explains why they weren't here *yesterday*. Why aren't they here *today*?"

"Yesterday was a holiday. They probably spent the day enjoying it. Maybe they had a little too much to drink. Of course, after such a day, they wouldn't be much good at work. It's better they take the day off. It's not so unusual, and it's no big deal. We'll go to the doctor today. We can come back to the passport office tomorrow."

"Will they process the passports the same day?" Mike asked.

"Sometimes, if it's urgent. But if they don't finish it tomorrow, we can pick it up before we go to the airport on Thursday. You don't leave until two o'clock, right?"

"Yeah, we fly out at two. But shouldn't we be there by twelve-thirty?"

"You're going to Moscow; it's a domestic flight. If we get there a little later, you'll still make it." Then Marik paused. "I know it's frustrating, Mike. But don't worry so much. I do this for a living. I know what I'm doing, and everything always works out one way or another. Take it easy. Let me worry about things. You just enjoy your time here."

"Alright, Marik. I'll let you do your job," Mike conceded. But it wasn't going to be that easy.

They joined Sasha, Laura, and the girls at the bottom of the stairs outside, and Marik explained Plan B as they drove to the hospital for the required physical exams. Soon they arrived, and the group walked through halls that reminded Mike of a Bronx elementary school.

"We will wait for the doctor here," Marik said while gesturing to several mismatched chairs against the wall. Mike and Laura sat with the girls on their laps. Marik and Sasha also sat down, but Katya soon got bored, so Marik walked her around, showing her different things around the waiting room and then talking with her about her trip to America and her new parents. Katya was happy to have some one to speak Russian to. It was so exhausting having to concentrate on everything that was said by her parents, trying to understand, and trying to get them to understand.

When the doctor arrived, they were ushered into a clerical office, and Mike wondered why they hadn't gone directly to the exam room. But the doctor immediately took her stethoscope out and began checking Luba. She checked her heart and lungs, pressed several places on her stomach, and checked out her eyes and nose before looking down her throat. "She appears to be healthy," the doctor announced in heavily accented English. "Have you noticed anything that would cause you to think otherwise?"

Both parents responded in the negative.

"She does have a bit of a rash on one cheek. Do you know anything about that?"

"No. I guess she has sensitive skin," Mike responded nonchalantly, seeing that Laura was suddenly worried that something so small as a rash could cause problems at the last minute. "It said something about sensitive skin in the first medicals that we got on her. Our doctor in the States saw the medical records, and said it's no big deal."

"Alright, then," the doctor responded. "Let's move on to Katya." The doctor spoke pleasantly to Katya as she performed the same brief physical that she had done on Luba. Katya was excited to tell the doctor about how she had new parents and was going on an airplane to a new home in Amérika. She told her how she would have grandparents and brothers and horses and a dog. Then she told the doctor the one thing that she never forgot to tell anyone when she spoke of her pending journey.

"In Amérika, everything has a different name than here in Russia. In Amérika my name will be different, too," she explained.

"Well, that sounds exciting, Katya," the doctor responded. "What will your new name be?"

"My new name will be Seh-lah. Seh-lah means Princess!"

"Really? How wonderful! You must be excited!"

All Katya could do was nod her head and smile her big, dimpled smile.

"Well, Katya seems to be healthy, too. Do you have the forms?" she asked Mike.

"Sure, they're right here," Mike replied while handing them over the desk.

The doctor spent several minutes filling out the pages and placing her signature in the proper place. "Okay, now I need their passports."

"That's a bit of a problem," Marik replied in English. He then explained the difficulties from earlier that morning. "We were hoping that you could just leave that section blank and let us fill in the numbers after we get the passports tomorrow."

The doctor began to speak to Marik in Russian, and it was clear that she wasn't happy. After several minutes of back-and-forth, Marik reverted to English.

"Okay," he said to the parents, "this is very difficult for Doctor Eléna. She wants to help you, but she is required by law to see the passport." Marik paused, bracing himself for the Mike-eruption that would surely come with the next bit of news. "We just pay her now, and then we come back to get the forms after we have the passports."

But Mike just rose to his feet and calmly pulled two crisp one hundred dollar bills from his pocket. He would let Marik do his job. Mike handed the bills to the doctor and cordially thanked her for her help. Dr. Eléna graciously accepted the cash and, without further ceremony, placed it directly into her purse.

Marik quickly thanked the doctor and they left the office. As they walked down the hall, Marik looked sideways at the still-calm father.

"Thank you for working with Dr. Eléna," Marik said. "Most times people work with us on things like that. But sometimes, like today, they are more rigid. But everything will work out, you will see. Everything will work out fine."

But Mike wasn't so confident.

Marik called at noon the next day to inform Mike that the passports wouldn't be ready until Thursday morning, and that things would be tight. "Please make sure that you and Laura have everything ready early in the morning," he added. "But don't worry, Mike. We'll make it."

Of course, that was the worst thing to tell Mike. It ensured that he would nothing *but* worry for the rest of the day. Worry and pace…and worry some more.

"Why don't you take a break?" Laura finally suggested, hoping for a break, herself.

"Where am I supposed to go?"

"I don't know. Jim's been cooped up in his room all morning. I'm sure he'd take a break with you. Go for a walk on the beach or something. Sitting around the hotel room isn't going to help anything."

"You're right. I'll grab Jim and take a walk."

"How's your mom doing?" Jim asked as they walked toward the beach.

"Alright, I guess, considering."

"She's started the chemo?"

"She's only had one treatment so far. Mark said that it's not too bad, but we all know that it gets worse as the treatments progress."

"What's her prognosis?"

"It's not good. The cancer has spread into several organs. Mark said that they don't want to operate now, because then they'd have to wait for her to heal to start the chemo and the doctors don't think they have time to wait."

"How's your mom taking it?"

"We can't tell."

"What do you mean?"

"In one breath she tells Mark that she has the faith to be healed. In the next breath she says things like, 'if I'm still here by then.' That doesn't sound like faith to me. How can God heal her when she's saying things like that?"

"I've known your parents for a long time, Mike. I would never question your mother's faith."

"Then what would you call it?"

"What if your mother had the faith to be healed, but didn't really have the desire?"

"Of course she wants to be healed. Why else would she agree to chemo?"

"I think that you already know the answer to that question."

"No, Jim. I don't."

"Come on, Mike," Jim coaxed. "You're a smart guy. What's the most important thing to your mom?"

"Family. I'd have to say her family."

"Okay. You mean her family here, or family that has already passed on?"

"Mom wouldn't make that distinction. Family is family."

"I agree. She cares about all her family. She knows that Mitch and your dad are on the other side, waiting for her, but waiting patiently. She knows they understand. She knows they're patient. She's not too concerned about pleasing them right now." Jim paused, letting it all sink in. "So who's left to please?"

"Her family here," he whispered, almost choking on the response as it caught in his throat.

"Think about it, Mike. This isn't easy for your mom, either. She's willing to allow things to happen as God wants. She only has one worry…those she leaves behind. This is her dilemma, Mike. Don't forget that."

Mike stopped and looked up at the gray clouds that scudded across the cold, dark sea. Across the ocean, the woman who had given him everything was torn between two worlds, not bearing to leave, not bearing to stay.

"I'll have the rest of the stuff packed and ready to go," Laura said as Mike rushed to leave the room. It was Thursday morning, and the sprint had begun. He and Marik would be gone the rest of the morning gathering the passports and medical clearances.

"Thanks, Sweetheart. See you soon." Then he and Marik headed for the car.

"Where's Sasha?" Mike asked. "I thought she was coming with us."

"She is, but she wasn't ready. She asked me to pick you up first, and then come back to get her. We live near the passport office, anyway." Marik then picked up his cell phone and called to make sure that Sasha was ready. "It looks like Sasha is having some trouble this morning," Marik informed Mike as he hung up. "Our agency in the States needs some documents translated and sent back to them right away. Sasha wants us to get the passports and medicals and then come back for her. She'll be ready by then."

Twenty minutes later they pulled into the parking lot of an apartment complex. Marik honked twice and a plastic shopping bag tied into a small bundle was thrown from a window about five floors up. It twisted and turned as it half floated, half fell to a clump of grass and dirt below.

"Just a second," Marik said as he jumped out of the car to retrieve the bag. He hurried back and tossed it to Mike as he jumped into the car.

"What's this?" Mike asked, genuinely puzzled.

"It's Katya's passport. We picked it up last night," Marik explained. "Oh, sorry, I guess you didn't know. Sasha and I live here. She wasn't dressed yet, so she just threw it down."

"So where is Luba's passport?"

"Hers wasn't finished when we got there at closing time last night, so they told us to come back and get it this morning. We'll go there right now."

Soon Mike was following Marik up the same crumbling concrete steps from two days before, and then inside the office which had been previously locked. Marik had a quick and escalating conversation with one of the workers who afterwards began rushing around.

"Come on, we should wait out here," Marik said to Mike.

"Alright. What's up, Marik?"

"They said that they thought we were coming back this afternoon, not this morning. They told me to go do other stuff and come back later. But I told them that the only thing that we have left is this, and the medical forms from the doctor, and that you have to catch a flight right after lunch. They told me to go take care of getting the medicals while they finished the passport, but I told them that the doctor wouldn't give us the medicals without the passport; that we had tried that the other day. So now they are in a big rush. They told me to wait here and they'll get it as fast as they can."

"But we'll make the flight, right?"

Marik nodded confidently, but said nothing.

Forty-five minutes later, one of the workers stepped out of the office and handed Marik the passport. Marik glanced over it quickly before thanking the woman. Then he rushed Mike out to the car. Marik drove aggressively across town to the hospital. He and Mike literally ran to the building and then walked briskly down the hallway to Dr. Eléna's office. Dr. Eléna wasn't there, but one of the clerical workers offered to go and find her. "Please tell her it's urgent," Marik pleaded.

The worker nodded, and then casually sauntered off to find the doctor. Mike sat in the chair and waited, telling himself over and over that this was Marik's profession. But as he watched Marik pace back and forth across the lobby, his anxiety went up a notch. Half an hour later, Dr. Eléna walked into the lobby. "Sorry it took so long," she apologized. "I was with a patient and couldn't get away."

"Sure, no problem," Marik said, belying the frustration in his voice. "But could we please get this done quickly? Mike and his family have a plane to catch."

"Yes, of course," the doctor replied courteously, speeding up a bit as she keyed the lock to her office. The doctor pulled the forms from her desk, carefully transferred the numbers from the passports to the medical forms, and then handed everything back to Mike. “Here you go, Mr. Knight,” she said. “Safe journey.”

“Thank you, doctor,” he said as he shook her hand.

Marik apologized for rushing, but thanked the doctor and then led Mike on a mad dash back to the car. Marik talked with Sasha on the cell phone as he rushed back across town to pick her up. “Sasha says she will be waiting for us out front,” Marik told Mike. Several minutes later they pulled into the parking lot of the apartment complex. Marik had barely stopped when she piled into the car and then they sped off to the hotel.

“So how are you, Mike?” Sasha asked politely, the calm tone of her voice seeming so out of context right now.

“I’ll be fine, if we make our flight.”

“Oh, you’ll make your flight. Marik worries too much. Sometimes I wonder if he’s American,” she joked. “In fact, we have time for lunch at the Vlad Inn. I love their pancakes!”

“Oh, Sasha!” Marik started nervously. “I don’t think we have time for lunch.”

“Sure we do! I’ll just call ahead and have Laura take the kids down and order for all of us. What do you want, Mike?”

“Um…a cheeseburger, if there’s time,” Mike responded.

“What do you want, Marik?”

Marik didn’t respond, and it was evident that he wasn’t happy about taking time out for lunch.

But when they arrived at the hotel, lunch was ready and everyone enjoyed one last meal together. “It’s like I told you,” Sasha said between bites. “Marik thinks he’s an American. He worries too much.”

“It looks like everyone is about finished with lunch,” Marik announced as he looked at his watch. “We should leave now to catch the flight. Mike still needs to confirm the flight changes and pay the fees. We don’t have much time to waste.”

Sasha led the conversation on the way to the airport, keeping it light and avoiding any discussion of the pending separation during the fifteen minute ride.

“Wait here,” Marik instructed everyone but Mike soon after entering the terminal. “I will take Mike to confirm the flight changes and pay the fees.” Then the two of them went and stood at the end of a twenty-person line. Mike knew they were on a tight schedule, but there was an hour left, so he figured that they'd be okay. But the line moved slowly, and it took twenty-five minutes for them to arrive at the counter. It took another ten minutes for the Aeroflot Airline worker to figure out the fees. For once, Marik was checking his watch as much as Mike was.

Mike's frustration was broken for a moment when he saw a sticker on the window over the counter. It was a cartoon drawing of an Aeroflot airplane with text underneath in English: "If we are not smiling, it is because we are working hard so that you can smile." *Bad service without a smile.* Whoever thought *that* was a good idea for an ad campaign?

"That will be eighteen thousand, one hundred twenty rubles," the worker informed Mike. He slid his American Express card under the glass. "We don't accept American Express," she said.

Mike pointed to the American Express sticker next to the Aeroflot Sticker on the window. "It says here that you do."

The worker simply shrugged.

"Okay…" Mike said while grabbing the card off the counter and sliding a Visa card under the glass.

"We don't take Visa, either."

"Look!" Mike blurted as he pointed at the Visa sticker right below the American Express and Mastercard stickers.

"We don't take credit cards."

"It says here that you do!"

"Today we don't."

"Look Mike, there is no time to argue!" Marik interjected. "Don't you have cash?"

"Not enough rubles. Who ever heard of an airline not accepting credit cards, anyway?"

"But you do have the cash in dollars?"

"Yes."

"Can he pay you the equivalent in dollars?" Marik asked.

"No. Only rubles. Only cash."

"Come this way quick!" Marik ordered. "There's a bank over here in the terminal." Mike ran after Marik, but halfway to the bank he shouted.

"Marik! There's an ATM right here!" He veered from following Marik, ran to the cash machine, and slid his debit card in the slot while punching the "English" language selection button. After the prompt, which seemed to take forever, he entered his PIN number. Again, after a long delay the screen flashed up a message: "Sorry, this ATM is currently out of cash. Please try again later."

"Come on, let's go the bank!" Marik ordered.

Mike snatched his card from the machine and ran behind Marik the last hundred feet to the bank office. Marik spoke loudly in Russian, asking the other customers for permission to go to the front of the line and briefly explaining Mike's time dilemma. Some ignored him, most gave a casual nod, and one gentleman stepped aside from the counter. "She hasn't started my transaction yet," he explained to Marik in Russian. "Please, come right up here."

Marik and Mike both thanked him for his kindness, and Mike handed ten one hundred dollar bills quickly to the teller. The teller thumbed through the stack carefully counting, and then she held each bill individually up to the light, checking for microfilm and watermarks. Deliberately, she handed two of the bills back to Mike and spoke in Russian.

"She doesn't like these bills," Marik explained. "Do you have better ones?" Mike jabbed his hand into his pocket and pulled out the stack of bills. He thumbed quickly through until he found two of the newest, crispest bills he had and handed them to the teller. She took them both and held them individually up to the light and then placed them in the stack with the others. She punched a few numbers into a calculator and then counted out the Russian rubles to Mike.

"*Spaseeba!*" Mike and Marik said loudly to all of the customers in line as they raced out of the bank. *Thank you!*

Mike followed Marik as they rushed back to the ticket counter. Marik, this time without saying a word to anyone in line, went straight to the window and crowded next to a woman waiting there. Most people in line seemed a little irritated, but no one voiced a complaint.

"Give me the money," Marik instructed Mike, who immediately handed over the wad he had just received from the bank. Marik spoke loudly so that the woman behind the glass, further back in the office, would hear. She was clearly irritated as she came forward. Marik simply counted out the bills and handed them to her. The woman took her time recounting, then went back and took her time reprinting the tickets and making the change. Finally she handed everything to Marik, who gave her a sarcastic "Thanks" before leading Mike off to the line for security.

He called loudly to Sasha and the others, who were still waiting where he had left them, to follow him and Mike. A few steps later, they were standing in a short line of about ten people waiting for passport control. Marik explained to everyone that they just needed to show their passports, answer a few questions and then move forward to the counter to check their bags.

"After that, you go through the metal detector. Sasha and I will wait here until you get through the metal detectors," Marik continued. "From there on, you won't have any trouble and we won't be able to see you anyway, so we will go. But in the rare chance that you have trouble, you have our cell phone number. You can call us."

It only took five minutes before they were at the head of the line. Five minutes wasn't nearly long enough for the goodbyes, as close as the friends had grown over the past three weeks and the earlier trip. But they managed. Laura was quite emotional as she said goodbye to the two people who had given her these two precious daughters. She looked down and stroked the hair of her two daughters and then threw her arms around Sasha and sobbed.

"Thank you for giving me the rest of my family," she said through her tears. Then the Knights walked forward to the agent checking passports. They were through in no time, and the woman at the baggage counter reassured them. "Don't worry," she said. "You will make the flight."

Mike thanked her, and then grabbed Katya by the hand. Laura was still holding Luba as they walked over to the metal detector. Jim and the Knights waived one last time at Marik and Sasha, feeling the weight of what they knew would be a permanent separation. Suddenly, Katya jerked her hand loose from Mike's and ran back through passport control, despite the cries from both her parents. She ran to Sasha and threw her arms around her neck as the beautiful young woman stooped.

"Thank you for giving me a mama and papa and a *dyedushka!*" she said. Then she ran back through the booths to return to her parents.

32

To Moscow! To Moscow! To Moscow!

The Moscow airport was crowded, and security was intense. Mike couldn't believe the difference between the security here and Vladivostok. In fact, in all of his international travel, he had never seen such intense security, particularly for passengers exiting the aircraft and airport. Eventually they made it through the lines with their luggage and out the double doors to the waiting area. Nika, their Moscow coordinator, was right up front holding a sign saying "Knight." The sign was hardly needed, though. She recognized the party immediately from Sasha's description.

"Hello, Mr. Knight. I'm Nika," she said while extending her petite hand.

"Hello, Nika. It's a pleasure. Please, call me Mike."

"Very well, Mike, it's nice to meet you."

Mike introduced the rest of the party. Luba was still groggy and wouldn't even lift her head off of her mother's shoulder as Nika tried to coax a smile out of her. But Katya had been revived after waking to the realization that she was now in Moscow. Nika spoke excitedly with Katya as the little girl told her of the plane ride, her new parents and grandfather, and of course, the meaning of her new name.

"Now, where are you staying?" Nika asked Mike after her discussion with Katya.

"The Marriott here in Moscow," Mike responded.

"The Marriott Grand?"

"Yeah, I'm sure that's it. It's near Red Square, right?"

"Yes, that's right. Usually, it's not *so* bad, but with the V-day celebrations, security is very intense throughout the city. Roads are shut down in certain areas. We'll hit Moscow rush hour traffic, which is always bad, but with the added difficulties, it will take a couple of hours to get to the hotel."

"Is that what's going on?" Mike asked. "I travel quite a bit and I've never seen security this intense."

"Yes. In fact, President and Mrs. Bush are supposed to be arriving at this airport later on this evening. World leaders have been arriving for days. Some are saying that there has never been a greater concentration of world leaders."

"I guess that explains it," Mike replied. In this day of conflict and terrorism, no expense would be spared to protect such a concentration of world leaders.

"Yes. Well, shall we go?" Nika asked as she grabbed the handle on one of the suitcases.

Soon they were outside the terminal and rushing to get the luggage and children situated in the old, full-sized passenger van. As their hired driver made his way through the city, Nika shared lots of information about Moscow, its history and people. But the Knights were exhausted, and Nika noticed both of them nodding off from time to time, so she ceased the tour guide narration and let them sleep.

The bellmen at the hotel unloaded the luggage onto carts and took it into the lobby, while Nika led the group into the hotel. She took Jim and Laura, who were carrying the two sleeping children, over to several formal chairs and insisted that they sit while she and Mike checked in.

"Welcome to the Marriot Grand," the beautiful young Russian woman said to Mike, in perfect English, without even the slightest hint of accent. "May I have the name of the reservation?"

"Knight. Mike Knight."

"Okay, Mr. Knight," she replied politely as she keyed the information into the computer. "Have you stayed with us before?"

"No. This will be our first time."

"Are you here on an adoption?"

"Yes," Mike replied. "That's my wife and our new daughters over there," he continued, nodding toward Laura.

"How wonderful! Are they sisters?"

"Yes. They are biological siblings."

"That is wonderful. We always give a gift to adopted children who come through," she said pulling two small stuffed bears out from under the counter. She handed them to Mike and invited him to take them to the girls while she finished checking him in. Mike left Nika at the counter and took the bears over to the girls, but found they were still sleeping.

"I'm sorry, Mike," Nika said as she walked up. "The hotel can't find your reservation."

"You've got to be kidding. Do they have any open rooms?"

"No, unfortunately not. With the V-day celebration, they are overbooked as it is. But they did check with the Marriot Royal. It looks like that is where you made your reservations."

"Oh, no! I'm so sorry! What do we do now?"

"It's alright," Nika said nonchalantly. "I'll just call the driver on his cell phone and have him come back and get us. I was planning on riding the Metro home from here, so he already left. With all of the traffic trouble, though, it will take him a while to get back. Please just relax here with the others and I will come and get you when the driver arrives."

Mike apologized again, profusely, but Nika assured him that it was no big deal and that she was happy to help.

Half an hour later the driver was back and the bellmen loaded the luggage back into the van. Because of the road closures and other security measures, it took another two hours to get to the Marriott Royal, where Nika helped the Knights check in. She then excused herself to return home after an evening that had gone much later that she planned, without even a hint of frustration or annoyance.

"I'll be here to pick you up at one o'clock in the afternoon tomorrow for our trip to the U.S. embassy, where we'll finish up the adoption paperwork," Nika informed them. "If you want to see Red Square, I recommend visiting in the morning. The news has been saying that they are going to shut down the square in the afternoon for preparation for the V-day parade."

Then Jim and the Knights thanked her once again for her help and patience, and she was on her way. Jim said that he wasn't hungry, just tired, so he went straight to his room, agreeing to meet them at eight for breakfast.

Mike and Laura took the children to their room and placed an order with room service before putting the children to bed. The food arrived quickly, to Mike's delight; he and Laura were famished. While they quickly devoured their meals, the two girls kept nodding off, eating almost nothing.

"Alright!" Mike announced. "It looks like it's time for bed. *Pará Spaht!" It's time for bed!*

"Poppy!" Katya shouted. "*Nyet!*"

"Katya, why not? What's wrong?"

Katya began to jabber in Russian while she whined incessantly. Mike tried to get her to slow down and explain what was wrong. Katya tried and tried to explain, simplifying her sentences with each attempt, finally whittling it down to two words. "Poppy, *Koh-Paht-Sa*." She repeated it again and again.

Laura grabbed the list of Russian phrases and the small dictionary that the agency had given them, but *Kopatsa* was not to be found in any variation.

"I'm sorry, Katya. I don't understand '*kopatsa*'. *Pará Spaht.*"

Then it happened, a complete and total emotional meltdown. Katya screamed and cried. Not only was she exhausted from a long day of travel, but from an entire two weeks of not being able to communicate with her parents. Laura tried to calm her, but Katya sobbed harder and harder, every once in a while mumbling the work *kopatsa*.

Finally Mike went back to one of the first things they had tried to teach her to aid in communication. "Katya, show me."

The little girl immediately ceased crying and jumped to her feet. She would be able to help them understand. She ran to one of the pieces of luggage, pulled back the zipper and began to rummage through its contents. Then she grabbed another suitcase. This time Mike helped her carefully go through the items. Finally, after opening the third piece, Katya removed one of the cloth books that had been left with her on Mike's and Laura's first visit. It was the book on her family. She quickly thumbed through the pages, looking frantically for the right one, but it wasn't in that book. She flung it aside and grabbed the other book, the one about the trip home. She rushed through the pages until she found it. She spread it open on the floor and pointed to the picture of the hotel swimming pool. "Poppy, *Koh-Paht-Sa*."

"You've got to be kidding!" Mike exclaimed. "It's ten o'clock at night! It's five a.m. in Vladivostok!"

"Mike," Laura interjected. "She doesn't understand you. She only knows she was promised that she could go swimming at the hotel. The poor little thing is exhausted. Let's just take her swimming for fifteen minutes. It has to be easier than trying to communicate. Let's fulfill the dream rather than adding another disappointment. It has to be worth fifteen minutes of our time."

Mike sighed. "Alright. *Kopatsa. Kopatsa Dá.*"

Katya squealed with delight and then began to chatter to Luba who came alive. Laura looked through the luggage until she found the swimming suits. She dressed the girls in their new suits, matching bright pink ones with accents of light blue, complete with the floating devices built in. Then she and Mike put on their suits and the foursome went down to the pool, returning an hour later after loads of fun and laughter.

"You should hurry," the receptionist at the counter explained to Jim and the Knights at nine the next morning, after giving them directions on how to walk to Red Square. "There are conflicting reports about when the square will be shut down for the V-Day parade. Some say that it will be this afternoon, but others are saying it will be sometime this morning."

Laura carried Luba, and Katya, as always, insisted that *Dyedushka* Jim carry her. They walked down the street for half a mile, when Jim pointed to a beautiful old building with columns, a fountain out front, and a life-sized bronze statue of a chariot, four horses, and the driver atop the elaborate and spacious entry way.

"That's the Bolshoi Theater. I went there when I was here in '91. It's incredibly ornate inside. The ballet that we saw was very good, but it would have been worth the price of entrance just to see the inside of the building. You two should try to go tonight or tomorrow. I'd be happy to watch the kids."

"Thank you," Laura replied excitedly. "I'd love that!"

"We'll see what happens," Mike added, buying himself more time to come up with an excuse not to go.

"That's Red Square, right over there," Jim said pointing towards the buildings surrounding it. "The gate is down here just a little further."

The plazas around the square were elaborately decorated with banners, most red with bursts of orange and yellow. Banners and posters everywhere depicted a large number "60" and the years "1945-2005," recognizing the years that had passed since victory in Europe was declared after World War II. Guards stood at almost every turn, and quite a few soldiers on horses were either riding or standing around. Mike approached two of them. "*Photográf?*" he asked as they scowled.

"*Nyet!*" the younger of the two barked. Mike simply nodded, walked away, and then used his telephoto lens from a distance.

When they arrived at the gates to Red Square, the group was disappointed to see that they were already too late. The square had never even opened that morning, and with their party scheduled to leave on Sunday, they would miss the opportunity to see what all of them, especially Mike, had really wanted to see. So they spent the next two hours walking around the plazas taking pictures.

"We should probably think about lunch sometime soon," Jim observed. "We have to get back to the hotel to meet Nika by one. Do you think we should find a restaurant around here?"

Mike looked around and then began to laugh. "What do you say? Should we turn the girls into *real* Americans?"

"What do you mean?" Jim and Laura asked simultaneously.

Mike just laughed again and pointed to the golden arches.

"McDonalds?" Jim asked.

"Sure, why not?" Mike continued to chuckle. "At least we'll understand the menu."

Laura and Jim took Luba and waited for an empty table in the open seating plaza, while Mike took Katya by the hand with him so that she could order what she wanted.

Mike ordered for himself and the others, and then told Katya to talk to the cashier.

"*Katoshka*," Katya said.

"What's *Katoshka*?" Mike asked the cashier.

"Potato," he responded while pointing to the French fries. "She want potato."

Soon the group was seated in the outdoor plaza, dividing up the order. Luba loved the food. Katya only picked at the burger, but devoured the French fries. Jim and the Knights sat back and relaxed, enjoying the beautiful architecture that surrounded them until it was time to return to meet Nika.

"Mike, I'm afraid that I have some bad news," Nika said as she walked up, even before exchanging pleasantries.

"What's wrong?" Mike asked, as Jim and Laura also stepped forward to hear.

"Last night I was organizing the documents for our meeting with the embassy, and I noticed that they have Luba marked as a male on her passport. We have to get it changed."

"Okay, fine," Mike responded. "Where do we go to get it changed?"

"The passport has to return to Vladivostok."

"You've got to be kidding!" Mike exclaimed. "I mean, we're in the capitol of this country. Obviously there is some place that we can go *in the capitol* of a country to get a passport reissued."

"I'm sorry, Mike, but it doesn't work that way here."

"No. That answer is unacceptable," Mike replied angrily. "There is obviously some *fee* we can pay to *someone* to get this problem taken care of *here. Today!*"

"Again, Mike, I'm sorry. But really, I have no control over this. The passport has to return to Vladivostok. Someone from our agency is leaving Moscow tonight for Vladivostok. I can send the passport with them. The real problem is the holiday. President Putin has declared this a two-day holiday. That means that the passport office won't be open until Wednesday morning."

"Or will it?" Mike asked sarcastically. "I mean, Wednesday is the day *after* a holiday. Don't you people take the day after a holiday off?"

"What?" Nika asked, confused.

Jim stepped in. "When we were in Vladivostok, the passport office took the day after May Day off. That was part of the reason for the big rush getting out of Vladivostok."

"Oh, I see," Nika responded, still calm and courteous. She had seen plenty of Americans lose their cool over issues like this. It never did any good to argue with them. "I can understand your frustration, Mike. I, too, was furious. Marik and Sasha should have caught this mistake. That's their job."

"No!" Mike said, the tone of his voice not weakening in the least. "There was no time for them to check. We were at the passport office the second they opened. We flew to the doctor's office for your insanely bureaucratic paperwork, and then we ran screaming through the airport trying to get past more red tape to get on to the plane. There wasn't time to catch that mistake. It's not my mistake. It's not Marik's or Sasha's mistake. It's the government's mistake. Now the government can be realistic and fix their *own* mistake at *their* inconvenience, not *mine*."

"Calm down, Mike," Laura interjected. "It's not Nika's fault. She's just trying to fix things."

"But—"

Laura cut him off again. "Please excuse him, Nika," Laura apologized. "Mike was just informed a week ago that his mother has terminal cancer. We really need to get home to see her and to help. This delay could not come at a worse time. Isn't there anything that can be done considering the circumstances?"

"I am sorry," Nika responded sincerely. "But there really is nothing that can be done. We should still go to the embassy to do Katya's paperwork. Then you will need to decide whether all of you will stay and wait for Luba, or if one of the parents will stay while the others return home."

Mike was now beyond belief. He stopped talking entirely and just walked out to the van. Jim and Laura followed with the children. Nika tried to talk to him on the ten-minute drive to the embassy, but Mike completely ignored her. Jim and Laura kept up the conversation, hoping that Nika wouldn't notice Mike's behavior, but it was painfully evident.

The Knight group sat on chairs in the embassy waiting room where dozens of families awaited their turn at finalizing all of their adoption paperwork. Nika stood, carefully reviewing all of their documentation, making sure that absolutely everything was in place, right up until the time that they were called to the window. When that happened, Jim stayed with the girls and the Knights went with Nika. She took several minutes explaining to the embassy worker what had happened, and that Luba's passport would have to be returned for correction.

"I'm sorry, Mr. Knight," the worker said. Even before Mike could respond, the worker continued. "This must be incredibly frustrating. But your coordinator is right. The passport has to go back to Vladivostok. Unfortunately, this is a Russian problem, not a U.S. problem. There is nothing that I can do to help you. The passport will have to go back to Vladivostok. Now, I will review everything else to make sure it is in order, and that there are no more delays when you come back." He then handed Mike a business card. "We are here to help Americans. That's our purpose. Now, in the course of this delay, if there are other situations that occur that we *can* help you with, please contact me directly. I'll do anything I can to help."

Mike finally felt like he was talking to someone reasonable, someone who really cared about the situation. Even though it didn't change things, he felt his rage begin to diminish. He thanked the worker and waited while he finalized Katya's documents and reviewed all of Luba's.

Nika and the driver of the rickety van drove them back to the hotel and dropped them off.

"I know it will be a tough decision," Nika said to Mike and Laura, not knowing if Mike was still ignoring her, "but we need to decide who is leaving, or if everyone is staying so we can make the proper changes with the airline. With the V-Day celebration, the earliest that Marik and Sasha can get the new passport is Wednesday. Hopefully, we can get it back here by Thursday night. That leaves us with your exit interview at the embassy on Friday afternoon. That means that tickets for those who stay should probably be changed to Saturday. Fortunately, there is an office across the street. If you want, you can go up to your room to discuss it. I'll wait here in the lobby."

"We don't need to discuss it," Mike said softly. Then he turned to his wife. "Laura, I don't want you traveling alone. You're not used to it, and you're way too nice. If one of us stays, it's got to be me. But you can't go home without Luba. She was taken away from her birth mother. Then her sister was taken away and put in another orphanage. Am I the only one who remembers taking her away from the Baby Hospital? Do you remember that child screaming in hysterics for 'Mama Oksana' to save her? We can't separate her from her mother again! To these kids, people go away and they never come back. That is the only fact they know. No. I won't let that happen to her again. Her mama stays. We all stay." Mike looked over at Jim. "I mean, Jim, if you need to leave, we'll get by, but *we* all need to stay."

"In for a penny, in for a pound," Jim replied with a smile.

"Alright, then," Nika responded. "We can change the tickets for everyone later. Maybe we'll do it tomorrow. Call me on the cell phone if you need anything."

The Knights thanked her, as did Jim, and she left. Upon returning to the room, Mike noticed the signal light on the phone flashing. He picked it up, pressed the series of keys and listened. "Oh, beautiful. Just beautiful," he said while the message played.

"What's going on, Mike?" Laura asked, the worry evident in her voice.

"That was Mark. Dawn is in labor. He took her to the hospital. Mark talked with Bob from next door and he said he'd stay with the kids at night, and they could stay at his house with their family during the day until we get back."

"What do we do now?" Laura asked.

"There's just too much going on." He sat down on the bed and cradled his head in his hands. "I don't want you to leave

Luba, but we have responsibilities at home. Mom has gone home from the hospital and really needs help, especially now, just after her chemo treatments. She has another treatment scheduled for Tuesday, and Mark and Dawn can't be there to help her. Bob and Jean can take care of Jeff and Stephen fine, but the boys need parents too, especially with what is going on with Mom. I think that you and Jim need to leave with Katya. I'll stay here with Luba."

"Is that what you think is best?" Laura asked timidly.

"It's the lesser of two evils, but I don't think we have much choice."

Laura picked up the phone and dialed Nika on her cell phone. She explained the change of plans and asked if Mike should go to change the tickets now.

"Yes, that's best," she responded. "But you know what, I want to come and help him to make sure it all goes right and that they don't change the wrong tickets. Mike doesn't speak Russian, and sometimes Aeroflot is a little bit difficult. I'd hate to have Mike have more problems than you've already had."

"I'm sorry," Laura responded sincerely. "It seems that every time we talk you get stuck with more than you planned for."

"Oh, really, don't worry about it. That's my job. I'm happy to help. I'm just at the Metro station. I'll be back in the hotel lobby in fifteen minutes. Just have Mike meet me there with the tickets."

"I'm sorry about my actions earlier," Mike said as he met Nika in the lobby.

"Don't worry about it," she replied. "You're under a lot of stress. It's understandable."

"No. I shouldn't have taken it out on you. There is no excuse. I'm sorry."

"It's quite alright. Shall we go to change your tickets?"

The two of them walked across the street and down half a block to the Aeroflot office. There was a counter with half a dozen windows, in addition to several desks lining a wall where other Aeroflot ticket agents were slowly working out issues with customers. Nika walked to a machine that had the appearance of an ATM and started pushing a series of buttons. Mike noticed there wasn't an English option.

"What's that?" he asked.

"We select what we are here for, ticket purchases, exchanges, or whatever. Then it assigns us a number." She looked around at the crowded waiting area, checked their number, and glanced at the number being served on the screen over the counter. "It looks like we'll be here for a while," she said. All of the chairs were taken, so they stood and waited.

The businessman in Mike grew frustrated as he watched the workers, though this time he was careful not to let it show. He noticed that without exception, each time agents finished with a client, having worked for ten minutes or so, they would take a five to ten minute break. While that was bad enough, each time a worker walked away from their station to take a break, they would go straight to another worker's station to talk with them, significantly reducing the amount of work being accomplished. Mike couldn't believe the regularity with which it happened. Furthermore, he couldn't believe that the Russians waiting along with him didn't act as if anything was wrong. They all just waited patiently.

Finally, it was ten minutes before five and Mike and Nika were second in line to be helped. Nika had been hopeful that they would be waited on before five, because she knew that once that hour came, the office would close, regardless of how many people were still waiting to be helped. She decided against sharing that information with Mike, hoping that all would go well so he would never have to know. Then, suddenly, there was a simultaneous moan from all of the ticket agents. One of them stood up and began to speak in Russian. People began to gather up their belongings and paperwork and leave the office.

"What's going on?" Mike asked.

"Their computer system crashed," Nika replied almost painfully as she waited for Mike to explode.

But he didn't. "What do we do now?"

"There's nothing that can be done tonight. We'll have to come back tomorrow. But if we get here half an hour before they open, we can avoid the line."

"But doesn't it take you an hour and a half to get here on the Metro?"

"Yes. It's just over an hour and a half. But I don't mind."

"So it will take you four hours on the weekend just to help me change these tickets?"

"Yes, but Mike, I don't mind. That's my job."

Now Mike was really feeling guilty for his actions earlier. Nika really would do anything she could to help him, even *after* his outburst and behavior earlier in the day. "Nika, I don't think it's necessary for you to come all the way here. Just show me how to operate the machine to get a number."

"Are you sure? I mean, I really don't mind coming in. In fact, no, I think that I should come and help you."

"No, Nika, I insist. Please, just show me how to operate the machine."

Nika hesitated for a second, but then she led him over to the machine. Mike took notes on which buttons to push, and in what order. But then she explained to him that if he stood outside the office doors half an hour before they opened, he probably wouldn't even have to take a number as he would be one of the first in line. Then she wrote a note in Russian explaining to the ticket agent what Mike needed, being careful to explain which tickets needed to be changed and which ones needed to stay the same. Then she went through the envelope containing all of the plane tickets and carefully pulled out his and Luba's from the others, paper clipping each bundle separately. She double checked all of her work, and then put all of the tickets back in the envelope along with the note.

"Thank you, Mike. Usually, I wouldn't do this. But my husband and I promised our son that we would take him to the amusement park tomorrow. I think you'll be fine, but if you have any trouble at all, don't hesitate to call me on the cell phone."

"No problem. Thanks for your patience with us anxious Americans. Sorry again for the way I acted earlier."

"Please, don't worry about it. It was nothing." She said as she reached out and shook his hand. "I'll be talking with you over the weekend to make sure that everything is going all right. See you soon."

Mike stopped at the concierge desk on the way back into the lobby and purchased two tickets for the Saturday night show at the Bolshoi. He didn't intend to go himself. He told people regularly that the closest he came to culture was yogurt. But Laura would consider this the chance of a lifetime, and he knew that Jim would be happy to take her.

"Hey, Sweetheart," Laura said as he walked into the room.

"How did it go?" Jim asked. He and Laura were watching a movie on TV with the girls.

"Not too well. We waited in line until just before five, then their computers crashed. They told us to come back tomorrow."

"I'm sorry," Laura responded cautiously, trying to gauge his frustration level.

"Nika wrote a letter telling them what needs to be done, and she said if I'm there thirty minutes before they open, I should get through pretty quick."

"What do you have planned for the rest of the day tomorrow?" Jim asked.

"I don't think we have any plans *now*." Mike responded.

"Yes. We had originally planned on spending the day seeing Red Square and all of the sites there on Saturday," Laura added. "But with everything being closed down for the V-Day celebration, I don't know what else we would do."

"Well, I have a surprise then," Jim responded. "I have a friend who has friends here in Moscow. He got me in touch with them and they have offered to take us around and show us Moscow, off the beaten tourist path. Moscow has a good zoo, too. They thought that the children might enjoy that, and it would give us translators for Katya and Luba."

"That sounds wonderful!" Laura said excitedly.

"Yeah, that sounds great, but we need to get back by six in the evening," Mike responded.

"Why? What's going on?" Laura asked.

"Two tickets to the Bolshoi tomorrow evening!" Mike replied while he pulled the tickets from the envelope and held them out toward her.

"You're taking me to the Bolshoi?" she asked excitedly.

"Well, not exactly. Jim sounded like he really enjoyed going there before. What do you think Jim, would you be interested in taking Laura to the ballet tomorrow?"

Laura looked a little disappointed, but she was hardly surprised.

"I would be happy to take her if you really don't want to go," Jim replied. "But I think you should reconsider. I'd love to stay with the girls while you two went together. You should really consider going, Mike. It's a once-in-a-lifetime experience."

"Yeah, so is performing brain surgery on yourself. Few people get a second chance at that one, either. But I think I'll pass on both."

"Alright," replied Laura, "We'll show him, won't we Jim? We'll go and have the time of our lives while he sits here in the hotel, wishing he were one of us!"

They all laughed, but everyone knew that Mike would rather sit in the dentist chair than go to a ballet.

33

Pahká

Jim and the Knights were fairly quiet during breakfast Sunday morning. The girls had still not been told of the pending separation, where Jim and Laura would return to the States with Katya, while Mike stayed with Luba until the passport issue could be resolved. The separation weighed heavy on the minds of the adults. Jim was already packed, and he returned to his room so that the Knights could have the time alone with the children for the explanation. He would meet them in the lobby just before noon when it was time to catch their ride to the airport.

Mike stopped by the front desk and explained to the receptionist the issue that they were having, and requested that a translator be sent to their room. The receptionist assured him that someone would be up within the next half hour.

"Are they sending the translator?" Laura asked as he walked into the room.

"Yes. Someone will be up within half an hour. I guess we can pack your bags until they get here."

The excitement level of the children escalated as Mike and Laura packed the bags. The cloth books had been read to them literally dozens of times since their parents first visited them. They knew what happened when the bags were packed in Moscow. "We go Amérika! We go Amérika! We go Amérika!" Katya screamed over and over again as she ran around the room.

The bags were nearly ready when the translator arrived. Mike arranged some chairs and they sat in a circle. Luba sat on her mother's lap and Katya sat on her own chair, between Laura and Mike. Even before they started talking, Laura began to stroke Luba's head and tears rolled down her cheeks. The translator started by making small talk with each of the children.

Mike explained through the translator that there had been a problem and that *Dyedushka* Jim, Mama, and Katya were going to the airport today to go home to America, but that he and Luba would need to wait a few more days.

Katya erupted. What would happen if Poppy and Luba *didn't* come later? Why couldn't they all wait and come together later? She began to cry. Soon she was hysterical. She had seen permanent family separations enough to know that they happened. People always promised that things would be all right. But family separations were never all right.

Mike choked back tears as he watched his daughter's heart break. She scrambled up on his lap and threw her arms around his neck. "*Yá Ha-Choó* Poppy," she cried over and over again.

Laura cried even harder as she watched Mike wipe the tears from his eyes before trying to pry her away to look at her. Finally, after hugging her tightly for several minutes, and lots of consoling words from the translator, she sat back and looked at him.

"Why can't Poppy and Luba come with us now?" Katya asked the translator in Russian.

"There is a problem with a document," the translator explained. Katya immediately calmed.

"So when the document is fixed, they can come?"

"Yes," the translator affirmed. "When the document is fixed, then they will come home."

"How long does it take to fix the document?" Katya asked.

"The document will be fixed in three or four days. Poppy and Luba will be home in less than a week," the translator assured her.

Katya was still frustrated, but she was no longer frantic, much to the relief of her parents.

"What did you tell her?" Mike asked, wondering what magic words had changed the situation.

"I just explained to her that there is a problem with a document and that as soon as it is fixed, you and Luba will go home."

"That's it?" Mike asked. "A five-year-old understands that documents can stop the world from turning? What kind of a place is this?"

The translator just chuckled. "I assure you, Mr. Knight, we Russians are very patient when it comes to documents."

Laura wiped her eyes one more time before speaking. "It seems that Katya understands, but Luba isn't even the least bit upset. Obviously, she doesn't know what's going on. Could you please talk to her?"

"Yes, of course, Mrs. Knight."

The translator got down on her knees in front of Laura and Luba, and began to speak baby talk. Luba giggled and cooed. Finally, after five minutes of talking with Luba, the translator stood up. "I'm sorry. She just doesn't have the language skills. She still thinks that everyone is going together."

"Thank you for trying," Laura replied. Then she picked up the little girl who was still smiling and held her against her chest as she squeezed her and began to cry yet again.

The translator, seeing that her task was finished, and realizing that they needed a little family time, quickly excused herself and left the room. Mike, trying to lighten the situation, got a ball out of the suitcase, and he and Laura played catch with the girls for another thirty minutes before they finished the last little bit of packing.

Jim was waiting for them in the lobby as they exited the elevator. "Are you ready?" he asked.

"We still have two bags upstairs," Mike explained. "I've got to go and get them."

"I'll come and help," Jim replied as he followed Mike back on to the elevator.

The bellmen loaded the luggage into the van while Laura held Luba against her and sobbed. Katya stood close by, watching. Soon Jim and Mike were back and the last two bags were loaded into the van.

Mike scooped Katya up in his arms and they held each other tightly. "*Yá-Tibya-Lo-Bloo, Preensyessa*," Mike said softly in her ear.

"*Yá-Tibya-Lo-Bloo*, Poppy," she whispered back in his. Jim and Laura were both wiping tears from their eyes as they watched the father and daughter say goodbye. Then Jim quickly kissed Luba on the forehead, told her goodbye and quickly climbed into the back seat of the van. Mike carried Katya over to the van, sat her on the seat and put her seat belt on her. "*Pahká* Poppy," Katya said as he kissed her on the cheek.

"*Pahká*," he responded as he backed out of the van. *Dyedushka* Jim began talking to Katya to keep her occupied while the others said goodbye. Laura clung to her still happy little girl and sobbed while Mike wrapped his arms around them both. Finally, he pulled back. "It's time to go, Sweetheart."

"I know," she replied. Then she sniffled and took a deep breath. She kissed her little daughter. "I love you, Little One," she said, and then she handed her to Mike.

"*Nee!*" Luba squealed. "*Dai-ee* Mama!" But she still didn't know what was going on. She was simply doing as she always did, demanding that she be held by her mother and no one else. Laura threw her arms around Mike while he hugged her with his free arm, his other holding Luba. "I'll miss you two."

"We'll miss you, too. We'll call you as soon as you get home."

"Okay. Please do. Thank you," She said, barely able to hold back the sobs. "I love you."

"I love you, too." Mike didn't know what else to say. Goodbye? See you later? With their daughters, in Russian, they had always used the less formal *Pahká*, instead of the more formal *Desvidania*. But to the Knights, as well as their children, *Pahká* had come to mean so much more than a casual "see you soon." *Pahká* had become a solemn promise of reunification.

"*Pahká*," Mike whispered in his wife's ear as he held her close.

Laura burst into tears and sobs again. "*Pahká*."

Mike and Luba walked her to the van, and she got in and shut the door. Mike had barely stepped back when the driver started away. For the first time, Luba realized what was happening.

"*Nee! Nee! NEE!*" she screamed hysterically as the van pulled away. She tried to lunge out of Mike's hold as she held out her arms, opening and closing her hands and screaming at the top of her lungs. Her screams quickly escalated into shrieks and she thrashed violently in Mike's arms.

Laura and Jim cried as they waved goodbye until the van turned out of sight. Mike pulled Luba tightly against him as he walked back into the hotel. She was still screaming and shrieking for her mother, and Mike's tears had still not stopped.

He walked straight to the elevator, but as he did he noticed several hotel workers and guests scattered throughout the lobby who were also shedding tears for the poor little girl who, for now, had lost yet another mama.

Mike sat down on the high-back chair in the hotel room with Luba on his lap. He held her tightly and stroked her head while she continued to scream, shriek, and cry for another forty-five minutes. Her head and body were soaked from sweat, and when she could finally stay awake no longer, she simply passed out in his arms. Mike could have put her to bed at that point but he just didn't want to. He sat there in the silent room with Luba in his arms for the next two hours. Every once in a while, the little body would lurch and the child would gasp and whimper. When that happened, he would give her a little squeeze and stroke her head until she would once again relax.

After two hours, Mike finally carried her into the bedroom of the suite and tucked her in. He went back out into the living room, clicked on the television and cracked open a bottle of orange juice from the minibar. He stayed there, channel surfing, until shortly before five o'clock that evening when he heard whimpers coming from the bedroom.

He put on his happiest face, hoping that would help his little girl as he softly opened the door. Luba was sitting upright in the bed softly crying. "Hello, Princess. Did you have a good nap?"

She looked at him but just continued to whimper. Mike walked over and picked her up. Luba looked at him intently and continued to whimper as she spoke.

"Poppy, *dai-ee*." Luba had only addressed him by title a couple of times since they had first met. She was always far more concerned about attention from her mother.

"*Dai-ee stó?*" Mike asked. *Give me what?*

Mike carried her into the living room and sat back down on the chair with her.

"*Poppy, dai-ee. Dai-ee. Dai-ee. Poppy, dai-ee.*" She spoke softly looking at him earnestly, begging, while she asked again and again.

"Luba," Mike replied softly, "dai-ee stó?"

"Poppy, *dai-ee* Mama."

"Oh, Princess," Mike said softly. "I wish I could help you understand. We'll see mama soon." It was time for dinner anyway, so he decided to walk past the front desk and ask someone to speak to her in Russian.

He carried her out of the hotel room and down the hall toward the elevator. "Mama!" Luba called as she caught view of the back of a dark haired woman getting onto the elevator. "Mama!"

"Sorry, Princess, that's not Mama," Mike said as they stepped in behind her.

The woman turned, smiled and looked at Luba. She took her by the hand and spoke the soothing "*ka*" and "*ska*" sounds characteristic of Russian baby talk.

"*Amerikányets*?" she asked, pointing at Mike.

"*Dá*."

"*Rooskaya?*" she asked, pointing at Luba, using the feminine form of *Rooskee.*

"*Dá*."

"*Mama ee sestra*, um, a, um, *mama ee sestra* go home, *dá?*"

The woman had heard their story. "*Dá*. Her mother and sister went home."

"Ohhh," the woman said while putting on her saddest face and looking into Luba's eyes while still holding her hand. Then she went back to speaking Russian baby talk to Luba. Though Mike still spoke no Russian, he recognized enough of the works to understand that she was telling Luba that she would be home with her family soon. The elevator arrived at the ground floor and the door opened. The woman touched Mike on the arm while she looked at him sadly. She spoke to him sympathetically in Russian and then patted his forearm twice just before giving him a quick nod of the head.

"*Spaseeba*," Mike said, nodding back just a little. Mike couldn't figure how officials in Russia could be so apathetic, when the Russian people, themselves, were so kind and sympathetic.

Luba's pep talk had already been given, so Mike carried her up the one flight of stairs to the restaurant. Luba grew excited as they approached it. Everyone always met together to eat. "Mama?" she asked. "*Dyehd? Kaw-chaw?*"

"No, Honey. I'm sorry. Mama, *Dyedushka* and Katya aren't here." Mike had never heard Luba speak so many words.

Luba quizzed the hostess as she took them to their table. "*Mama? Dyehd? Kaw-chaw*?" The hostess smiled and stooped down next to the high chair while she spoke in Russian baby talk to Luba. Then she wrapped a napkin around her neck for a bib.

"Your waitress will be right with you," she said as she walked away.

Mike had wondered how Luba would react to eating, but she quickly finished her mashed potatoes, drank her juice, and then held up her plate indicating that she wanted more. Mike ordered more potatoes for her along with another drink, which she also finished.

After dinner they spent the evening together on the laptop computer, watching the Russian Disney DVDs that they had bought in Vladivostok and eating the nuts and Pringles potato chips from the minibar.

This day, for the first time, Luba finally began to show trust and interest in her father, and Mike saw for the first time that there might actually be a silver lining to the black cloud.

34

Sun Go Amérika, Sehla Go Amérika

Katya cried most of the two-hour trip to the airport. At first, Jim and Laura tried to cuddle and comfort her, but she wanted to be left alone. "*Yá Ha-Choó Poppy*," was all that she would say as they tried to talk to her. After several attempts to console her, both of them decided to let her work through it herself.

They arrived at the airport about two o'clock, and unloaded the luggage onto a cart. The van went away and Jim led the way to the terminal with the cart, while Katya and Laura followed close behind, hand in hand. Suddenly Katya became excited and began to chatter in Russian.

"Try English," Laura said.

Katya sighed, then pondered. Then she pointed skyward. "Sun!"

"Yes, Katya. Sun."

"Sun go Amérika!"

"Yes, Katya. The sun is going to America."

"Sun go Amérika, Sehla go Amérika!"

"Yes, Katya," her mother smiled. "We will follow the sun to America." Katya became more and more excited as they got closer and closer to the terminal. Then she watched a plane roar off of the runway and catapult into the air.

"*Samaloot!*" she yelled while pointing upward.

"Yes," Laura said. "Try air-plane."

"Ay-loh-playn."

"Good. Very good."

Security was even more intense at the airport than it had been three days prior. Inside, the terminal was all but gridlocked with passengers trying to get through to their flights. Every piece of luggage was first X-rayed and then opened. Even Jim, who had spent almost all of his life in the travel industry, had never seen anything like it. It seemed that the X-raying was simply a waste of time, since each bag was moved to a table where a worker emptied every item from the bag and then re-packed it.

The Knights had packed the bags carefully to protect souvenirs and other fragile items. The items went together like puzzle pieces so that every little bit of space was used with maximum efficiency. Expanding zippers had already been expanded. As the worker loaded items back in suit cases, each time he found that when the bag was full, there was still plenty left on the table. Laura winced as, in each case, the worker would shrug his shoulders, cram the rest of the items into the bag and lay on top of it while he zipped the bulging bag shut. Laura tried to help him re-pack the first bag, but he informed her in no uncertain terms that she was not allowed to touch anything. She hoped the contents would be safe, but she was far from confident.

After the luggage check, Jim led Laura and Katya through no less than four other security checkpoints, including passport control. At the passport control window, the woman spent over twenty minutes reviewing Katya's adoption documents. By the time they got through security to their gate, their plane was boarding.

Jim gave Katya his window seat, and then jumped quickly into the middle seat to make sure that Laura could have the extra room on the aisle. Katya was as excited as she was the first time when the plane roared down the runway and up into the sky.

"Sehla go Amérika!" she squealed.

"I noticed that she has been calling herself Sarah since we got to the airport," Jim observed.

"I noticed the same thing, too. She must be ready for her new name," Laura replied.

As the engines quieted down after their initial takeoff and altitude climb, Jim leaned over to speak to Katya. "Should I call you Katya, or should I call you Sarah?" he asked slowly and clearly.

The child wrinkled up her forehead sternly. "*Yá nee Katya. Yá Sẹhla. Yá Preensyessa. Yá Amerikánka.*"

Jim began to laugh.

"I guess we call her Sarah, huh?" Laura said to him.

"I guess so. She left little doubt."

The nine-hour flight to JFK in New York was long, particularly after all of the rush and travel that had occurred over the prior four days. But what had taken the largest toll was the emotional turmoil. Laura and Jim were exhausted, and slept for a large part of the flight. Sarah slept a lot, too. But every time she would awaken, she looked out her window to the south to make sure that the sun was there and that the pilots had not become lost. They followed the sun all the way to Amérika.

Sarah was asleep when the plane made its final approach into JFK, but Jim couldn't resist. He grabbed her shoulder and shook her lightly. "Sarah. Sarah. Sarah!" The little girl opened her eyes, reoriented herself and then looked at him. "America!" Jim said excitedly while pointing out the window. Sarah lunged forward and pulled herself up to see out the window. But she was too short to see the ground, and she quickly became frustrated. Jim undid her seatbelt for her and she quickly knelt in her seat and pasted her nose and palms up against the window.

"Amérika! Amérika! Amérika!" she squealed. It was all poor Jim could do to get her back in her seat for landing.

Jim and Laura stood with Sarah in the line for Non-U.S. Citizens as they went through customs. "Adoption?" the officer at the window asked as they handed him the two blue passports and one red one.

"Yes," Laura responded. The officer summoned up another officer and requested that they follow him back to the office. A third officer quickly went through the paper work applying the proper stamps to the appropriate papers and keeping the ones to be left with customs. In all, it took only five to ten minutes. "Welcome home, Mrs. Knight," he said. "Congratulations."

Laura had never been happier to hear those words.

"We have a couple of hours before the flight to Detroit," Jim said as they left the customs office. "Shall we get something to eat?"

"That sounds good," Laura agreed.

Laura was observing the beautiful sunset outside as they walked down the hallway, looking for a restaurant. Sarah ran to the window pointing. "Sun go Rahshah now! *Pahká* Papa!

Pahká Luba!" she said excitedly, blowing a kiss after each of the last two sentences.

Tears welled up in Laura's eyes as she too lifted her hand to her lips. "*Pahká*."

Several hours later, the plane touched down in Detroit. Sarah had slept almost the entire flight and by the time they entered the terminal, it was completely dark outside. The last flight for Salt Lake City had left hours before, so Jim made arrangements to stay at the airport hotel in Detroit that night. Laura, on the other hand, would drive the two-hour trip back home with Sarah right away. Jim helped Laura retrieve her luggage and loaded it into the SUV while Laura strapped Sarah into her booster seat. Sarah had never seen a children's car seat, but she liked it. The extra height allowed her to see so much more out the window.

"Thank you for all of your help," Laura said sincerely as she wrapped her arms around Jim and gave him a big hug.

"No," Jim responded. "Thank you for allowing me to participate. It has been the opportunity of a lifetime. But more importantly, it really has been a *life-changing* experience." Laura knew exactly what he meant. No one could ever watch children go from an orphanage to a family that loved and needed them without being forever changed.

"Please call me when you get home tomorrow and let me know that you got in alright," Laura requested.

"I'll do it. Thanks again and I'll talk to you soon. Keep me posted on how things are going in Russia," he continued as he stepped up to Sarah's car seat.

"*Pahká Preensyessa* Sarah," Jim said as he kissed her on the forehead.

"*Nyet!*" Sarah yelled. Her face became stern. "*Dyedushka* no go."

"*Dyedushka* has to go home to his family," Laura explained.

"*Nyet! Dyedushka* Jim house, Sehla house."

"No, Sarah," Laura explained. "*Dyedushka* Jim doesn't live at our house."

Sarah began to sob. "*Dyedushka* Jim no go. *Dyedushka* Jim go Sehla *ee* Mama."

"Oh, no," Jim gasped. "The soft books…"

"What about them?" Laura asked.

"They mentioned me being here, but it never indicated that I would leave!" Jim leaned in and hugged Sarah. She threw her arms around his neck and squeezed him tightly while she sobbed and begged him not to go in mixed English and Russian. He let her sob and hold him without saying anything for several minutes. Then he spoke to her softly, hugged her some more, told her he loved her and that he would call her on the phone. Then he pried away from her grasp, kissed her on the forehead and shut the door between them as she sobbed, still not understanding the scope of the separation.

Sarah cried for another fifteen minutes as they drove up the freeway. Her little heart had taken almost more than she could stand over the past three weeks.

"Sarah, wake up," Laura said as she gently shook her shoulder. It was just after midnight when they pulled into the driveway. She had debated on letting Sarah sleep while she carried her in and put her to bed, but she knew that Jeff and Stephen were waiting up to meet her. Besides, she wanted Sarah to have a chance to walk around the house and become familiar with it so that she didn't wake up afraid in a place that she didn't know. "Come on, Princess, wake up. We're home," she said as she continued to shake the little girl lightly. Sarah yawned and stretched as she opened her eyes. "We're home now. Let's go in the house."

"Sehla house?" she asked excitedly as she realized now what was happening.

"Yes. This is Sarah's new house." Laura got out of the SUV and walked around to Sarah's door. She opened the door, undid the seatbelt, and lifted Sarah to the ground. The family

Siberian Husky rushed up and immediately began to lick Sarah's face.

"*Sabachka Dasha!*" Sarah squealed. *Dasha the doggie.* The fairytale was real. There really was a house and a family and even a dog named Dasha, just like in the cloth books. "*Lashotka!*" Sarah said excitedly.

"To-morr-ow," Laura said slowly. "We'll see the horses tomorrow."

"*Dá*," Sarah responded as she took her mother by the hand and walked up the steps to the back door.

Laura and Sarah were swarmed by Jeff and Stephen as they walked through the back door. Bob, their neighbor, just sat back and watched. Sarah was overwhelmed as each of her brothers had to take their turns picking her up and holding her. Sarah couldn't understand what they were saying. They spoke so fast, not slow like Poppy and Mama. But Sarah could tell that they were excited to see her and that she was home, in a family, and with people who loved her and wanted her there.

"I'll let you guys get to bed," Bob said as he walked toward the door. "You must be exhausted. But we would like to visit when you're up to it. I'll bet you have some stories to tell."

"Thanks, Bob. Thanks for taking care of our family while we couldn't," Laura told him sincerely.

"No problem. We were happy to help. Call Jean when you get situated and figure out a time when we can get together," he said as he walked out the door.

Jeff had Sarah in his arms and was walking around the kitchen, Stephen in tow. He showed her the fruit basket and the pantry so that she would know where the food was. Laura followed them into the living room where Jeff opened the cabinet and showed Sarah the big screen TV. Sarah had no idea that TVs could be that big. Then he opened the French doors to Mike and Laura's bedroom and clicked on the light.

"Mama bed!" Sarah said excitedly. It was just like the picture in the cloth book. She wriggled to get down and Jeff placed her on her feet. She wandered around the room and then opened the door to the master bath. "Sehla *kopatsa?*" she asked while pointing at the large jetted tub.

"La-ter. To-morr-ow. Tomorrow you can have a bath" Laura responded. "Do you want to see your room? Sarah's room?"

"*Dá!* Sehla loom. Sehla bed," she responded excitedly. Laura took her by the hand and led her up the stairs. Sarah gasped as she stepped into the bedroom. Two bright blue walls glowed behind beautiful lace curtains. Swarms of painted butterflies emerged from behind the headboards of the two twin-sized beds on each side of the room. Sarah ran into the room and squealed as she turned in circles. "Sehla bed?" she asked as she ran toward one of the beds covered with a purple patchwork comforter and matching pillow.

"*Dá*. Yes." Laura responded, though up until that time it had never even been discussed which sister would be in which bed.

Sarah chattered in Russian as she climbed into the bed and laid back on the beautiful covers. She pointed up at the butterflies and continued to speak her native language ending with "*Dá* Mama?"

"Bu-tter-fly," Laura said slowly.

"Bu-tel-fly," Sarah responded.

"How did you know what she was saying?" Stephen asked.

"We do a lot of guessing," Laura admitted.

Jeff wanted to talk too, but the lump in his throat hindered him. He had never seen anyone so fascinated and thankful for a family, a house, a bed, a bathtub, or even for silly butterflies painted on walls and ceilings.

Suddenly the phone rang and Laura hurried to grab it.

"Hey, Sweetheart," Mike said gently. "It looks like you made it home."

"Yes. We just walked in a few minutes ago. We were just taking Sarah around, showing her the house. How are you two doing?"

"We're okay. We just got up and we thought that we'd call before you went to bed. Luba is pretty melancholy but she seems to be a lot more comfortable with *me* now. She sure misses her mama, though. Every time she sees a dark haired woman from the back, she calls 'Mama!' and we have to chase her down to prove it's not you."

"Poor thing."

"Yeah. Maybe you should talk to her on the phone. Maybe it will help if she at least hears your voice."

"I'd love to talk to her. Put her on," Laura replied excitedly.

Mike held the phone up to her ear but Luba pushed it away. She hadn't talked on a telephone before.

"Start talking to her," Mike said to Laura. "She doesn't know what's going on."

Laura began to speak as Mike held the phone back up to her ear while saying "Mama" several times. When Luba settled down enough to hear the voice she immediately held the phone and pushed Mike's hand away. It was the voice from the cassette recorder! "Mama!" she squealed.

Laura spoke back to her and although Luba didn't understand the words, she recognized her mother's soothing voice. Mama wasn't gone forever after all! Laura sang a lullaby from the cassette tape to Luba who smiled and listened without speaking. After it was over, she tried to get Luba to speak, but the child was so fascinated hearing her voice that she wouldn't. Finally, after several more minutes, Mike took the phone away. "Can I talk to Katya now?" he asked.

"Sure. But it's only fair to warn you. She goes by Sarah now. She's an American princess. She only wants to be called by her American name."

"That sounds good to me," he replied.

"Sarah, it's Papa!" Mike heard in the background as the phone was handed off.

"Hello, Princess."

"Poppy!" Sarah squealed. Then she began to jabber, mostly in Russian, along with a little English, as she told him about her new home, her brothers and *sabachka* Dasha. Her voice turned sad as she explained to him that *Dyedushka* Jim couldn't come home with her, but that she would talk to him on the phone tomorrow. Of course Mike only understood bits and pieces of what she was saying, but tears came to his eyes. It was just so good to hear her voice.

Then he asked Sarah if she wanted to talk to Luba. "*Dá!* Luba!" she replied energetically.

Mike held the phone up to Luba's ear who quickly took it, expecting to hear her mother's voice again. She was surprised to hear her sister speaking to her. Sarah told her about the new house and Dasha and the beds and butterflies in their room. She even told her about the fruit basket in the kitchen. Luba didn't talk much, but for the first time she was beginning to understand that the family would be reunited. Soon Mike overheard Laura on the phone so he took it back from Luba and finished up the conversation.

"I'll let you get to bed. We'll go get our breakfast, watch the parade, and give you a call after lunch, when you get up. I want Luba to get used to you being available."

Laura agreed, and the phones were hung up after more than one "I love you," "Miss you," and of course, "*Pahká.*"

35

The Light at the End of the Tunnel

"Hello, Mike, it's Nika."

"Hi, Nika. I didn't expect to hear from you so soon." He really didn't. It was Wednesday morning, not even lunchtime.

"No. Neither did I. I mean, I just got a call from Sasha in Vladivostok. There's good news. Marik and Sasha were at the passport office as soon as it opened this morning. The passport office was very sorry for the problem they caused with the mistake, and they reissued the passport. Then Marik rushed the passport to the airport and paid a pilot on his way to Moscow to hand-carry it. The passport is in the air as we speak. I will go to the airport this evening to meet the flight, and I'll get it from the pilot."

"That's great!"

"There's more," Nika responded energetically. "I called the embassy. They remember you and your situation and felt sorry for you and Luba. Usually they only do adoption work in the late afternoon, but they are making an exception for you. They put you on a list of ten people who can bypass the line to enter the embassy as soon as they open tomorrow. That is a big deal, because there are usually about a hundred people in line at that time. But they said that they should be able to process Luba's paperwork in fifteen minutes or so. That means that you could catch the flight back to the States tomorrow afternoon!"

"Wow! That's incredible!" Mike responded.

"I'll come in today and help you change your tickets at the Aeroflot office."

"Thanks, Nika, but I can handle it. I still have the notes on how to get a number. There's no reason for you to take a four hour round trip for something that I can do."

"Really? Because I don't mind."

"I'm sure you don't," Mike replied. "But you'll be working late going to the airport and everything anyway. I'll take care of the tickets."

Nika thanked him, wished him luck, and hung up the phone.

Mike and Luba spent the next three hours in line at the Aeroflot office across the street. Finally, the tickets were changed and the fees, once more, were paid. Then Mike carried Luba the half mile to Red Square. They ate lunch in the patio seating at McDonalds and then headed for the gates to Red Square.

The gates were open and Mike was able to walk to the top of the small rise at the center of the square before barricades stopped his progress, far shy of the brightly painted onion shaped domes of St. Basil's and the other attractions which would remain closed until the next day. Workers were finishing the tearing down and hauling off of the pipe-frame bleachers that had been set up for the parade. Others were cleaning and sweeping. He turned in circles, shooting pictures of the barricaded sites, and then he took several pictures of Luba with the beautiful Russian features in the background.

Mike kept trying to get her to smile her beautiful smile, but she wouldn't. He tried to get her to look at the camera, but she would only stare off into the distance. Luba didn't care about culture and she didn't care about architecture. More than anything else, Luba just wanted her father to take her home. Mike put the lens cover back on the camera, placed it in its case, picked up his daughter and carried her back to the hotel.

At the hotel, Mike dialed home for one last conversation before leaving the next morning. "How's the family doing?" he asked after Laura answered the phone.

"Pretty good. Sarah is getting used to her new home, but she misses you and Luba terribly. Jeff and Stephen are doing well. They're glad to have me back, but they miss you and they're anxious to meet Luba."

"Well, I have a surprise for you. Marik, Sasha, Nika and the passport office in Vladivostok rushed everything as fast as they could. Luba's passport is being carried by a pilot from Vladivostok to Moscow. It's in the air right now and Nika will pick it up this evening. Nika also talked to the U.S. embassy here in Moscow and they have made an exception. Rather than making us wait until the afternoon, they will do our exit interview first thing tomorrow morning. I've already changed our plane tickets, so we'll be at the Detroit airport at ten Thursday night! Will you pick us up?"

"Oh, Mike!" Laura exclaimed. Then she began to cry. "We've been praying that you could come home quickly. Mom was supposed to go to another round of chemo yesterday, but she was really sick. The doctor says that she has some kind of blood infection. They admitted her to the hospital yesterday afternoon. They're trying to get the infection under control."

Mike sat down on the chair, stunned.

"Are you still there?"

"Yes. I just wasn't expecting that. How's Mom doing?"

"She's really sick, Mike. But attitude-wise she's doing great. She seems really anxious, though. She keeps asking when you and Luba will get home. She also made me promise to bring Sarah over to meet her today."

"Do you think that's a good idea?" Mike asked. "I mean as sick as Mom is?"

"I didn't even know if the hospital would allow it, so I talked to her doctor. He thinks it's a good idea, so I was planning on taking her over in a little while, unless you think I shouldn't."

"No, that sounds fine. Tell Mom I'll get home about midnight Thursday night and that I'll be in to see her Friday morning."

"I'll tell her. Are you okay?"

"Yeah. I'm fine. I'm just feeling…I don't know. We've still got to pack. But talk to Luba for a second. I should say hello to Sarah, too."

Mike began packing their belongings into the luggage while Laura spoke with Luba. Then he spoke quickly to Sarah, who was overjoyed to hear that he and Luba were coming home. He spoke once more to Laura, and then hung up the phone.

36

Calamity

Mike and Luba were both up early Thursday morning. But before doing anything else Mike booted up his laptop, located pictures of Sarah and Laura and printed off one three by five picture of each of them on his portable printer. Then he picked up Luba and carried her down to the hotel lobby. He placed her sitting on the counter as the receptionist greeted them.

"Good morning, Mr. Knight. How are you and Luba?"

"We are doing very well. We go home today!"

"Really? How wonderful. We will miss you. Everyone has been talking about your family."

"Thank you. All of you have been so helpful and supportive. It has made a difficult situation bearable."

"You are welcome. Now, how may I help you?"

"Well, I want Luba to understand that we are going home today. Would you please give her these pictures of her mother and sister and explain to her that today we are leaving to go home to be with them?"

"Oh, yes. I would love to!" The girl took Luba's hands and began speaking while Mike enjoyed listening to the soothing "*ka,*" "*ska,*" and "*shka*" sounds of Russian baby talk that would soon no longer be a part of his life. He would miss the Russian baby talk. In fact, as he thought, he would miss so much about Russia. Of course, it wasn't the United States. It was nothing like the United States. But that was part of the charm. Though he would never completely understand the culture or the country, Mike had grown to appreciate Russia and to love her people.

The girl at the counter soon finished and handed the two pictures to Luba. Luba held up the pictures, one in each hand for Mike to see. "Mama! Kawcha!" she squealed.

"It looks like she understands. Is there anything else I can help you with, Mr. Knight?"

"Thank you. No. I think that's all for now. But we will be down to check out in an hour or so. If you would have our account ready to settle, I would appreciate it."

"Certainly. I'll prepare it right now."

Mike picked up Luba and turned away from the counter. But Luba wriggled to get down. That was unusual. Luba always insisted that she be carried. But Mike placed her feet on the ground. Luba ran to a couple sitting on the couch in the lobby. "Mama! Kawcha!" she squealed as she held up the pictures. The man and woman both smiled and the woman leaned over to talk to Luba about going home. Luba listened for a moment, but then she ran to another hotel guest before the woman finished speaking. "Mama! Kawcha!" she said excitedly to her next victim. Then Luba raced to a stylish woman in her mid-forties and repeated the scene.

"You go home now?" the woman from the first couple asked Mike.

"Yes."

"Gude. Gude. We happy you go home. You, safe journey. Um, a um, yaes, um, God speed you journey."

"Thank you," Mike replied. "Have a good day." Then he raced to pick up Luba who had continued on from person to person, flashing her pictures and squealing about Mama and Kawcha over and over.

Mike swept her up into his arms and headed for the elevator. But Luba continued to hold out the pictures and squeal as he crossed the long lobby. They returned to the room and finished their preparations for leaving.

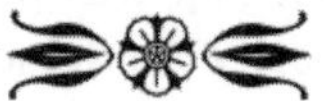

Mike had already checked out of the hotel and was standing in the lobby when Nika arrived. Luba immediately held out the pictures to explain to Nika that she was going home. Nika was kind as she took a moment with Luba, but she also seemed tense.

"Hi, Mike. How are you this morning?"

"Great! We're going home!"

"Yes, well… Have you checked out already?"

"Yes. Why?" Mike didn't like where this was going.

"I'm afraid I have some bad news," Nika responded timidly.

"Ohhh no. Not bad news. I've had it with bad news!" Mike responded as he felt his face and ears grow warm with rising blood pressure.

"I know, and I'm sorry. But anyway, there's supposed to be an ink stamp in the passport that says that Luba is leaving Russia for permanent residency someplace else. Apparently, people were in such a rush trying to help that they forgot the stamp."

"Great. That's just beautiful. Can we get that stamp and be out of the embassy in time for our flight today?"

Nika took a deep breath before responding. "I'm afraid it's worse than that. The stamp has to be done in Vladivostok. It can't be done in Moscow. Luba's passport has to go back to Vladivostok again."

"Are you crazy? This is the capitol of Russia, for crying out loud. People here can be paid to get things done. Don't tell me even for one second that it is impossible to get this stamp in Moscow. Don't tell me it can't be done, just tell me how expensive it's going to be. Then I'll tell you whether I can afford it or not. I mean how much could it cost? Just the hotel and food are over five hundred bucks a day. A 'special fee' has to be less expensive than another five days here!"

"I'm sorry, Mike. But it's impossible. If we send the passport back to Vladivostok tonight, they can have it finished tomorrow. We can have a pilot or flight attendant carry it back on Saturday or Sunday, and I think that the embassy will work with you again. Hopefully you could leave Monday afternoon. When does your travel visa expire?"

"I have to be out of the country on Sunday!"

"I was afraid of that. That creates another problem."

"What do you mean?"

"We'll have to try to get your visa extended. But it will be difficult. It usually takes more than one day, and the offices aren't open on weekends. If we don't get your visa extended, you have to leave the country on Sunday. But Luba can't leave until the stamp is in her passport."

"This is insane!" Mike spoke just shy of yelling. "What am I supposed to do with Luba?"

"I'm not sure. We've never had this problem before. Hopefully, we can get your visa extended. But we are going to need a backup plan if that doesn't work. I'd have to check with the agency, but I would be willing to take her."

"Thanks, but no thanks. We took this kid away from 'Mama Oksana' kicking and screaming. You should have seen her Sunday when her mother left. It was even worse. You guys have to start caring about these kids!" Mike unfairly generalized. "Now you're going to rip her away from me while she screams bloody murder? I won't let you do that to her again!"

"I really am sorry, Mike," Nika replied calmly, "but we need to start making other plans."

"No! I've had it. I'm done doing it your way. Do we need that stamp to get past the American embassy?"

"No. The Americans couldn't care less about this stamp. It's Russian border control where it becomes an issue."

"At the airport?"

"Yes. At the airport."

"Then take us to the embassy."

"Mike, I don't think…"

"Now!" Mike cut her off. "You take us now or I'll hail a cab."

Nika sighed. "Alright," she replied. Taking Mike to the embassy wasn't going to hurt anything. Maybe if she humored him, he would calm down and then be reasonable after finishing there.

The fifteen-minute ride to the embassy was silent, except for Luba shuffling her two pictures back and forth while she squealed "Mama" and "Kawcha." Mike's temper was flaming, and while Nika was still composed and had not taken any of his remarks personally, she felt it best to let him calm down before talking to him, even about non-related subjects.

As the van stopped outside the embassy, Mike exited with Luba and slammed his door before Nika was even completely out. But like a true professional, she didn't let her escalating frustration with Mike show.

"This way, Mike," she calmly said, resisting the urge to call him Mr. Knight. She knew that for her to help Mike and Luba, he still needed to trust her. If she acted out, like he was doing, it would complicate matters as they would be forced to work out difficult situations over the next few days.

Mike, Luba in arms, followed Nika, documents in hand, past the line of people outside the embassy to the guard station. She gave the guard the name, had Mike show him his passport, and then led him through the doors. After a security checkpoint and metal detector, Mike and Luba followed Nika through the deserted hallways and up a flight of stairs. Nika had them sit in chairs in the otherwise empty waiting area while she took the documents to the window and spoke with a woman there. Soon, the agent who had helped the week before appeared at the window.

"Hello, Mr. Knight. Ready to go home?" he asked as he motioned for Mike to come forward.

"You have no idea!" Mike replied.

"Great. Your coordinator here explained the new problem. Sorry. Sometimes paperwork gets crazy over here."

"I just can't believe it!" Mike said exasperatedly.

"Yeah, well, we've done what we need to do here. What are your plans now?"

"I'm having her take me to the airport. Maybe they'll miss it, or maybe someone there will be more reasonable. What do you think I should do?"

"You might as well try," the agent said sympathetically. "You never know if you can pull it off unless you try." He left out the part about the low likelihood of success. "I mean, what else have you got planned for the day?"

"No kidding," Mike responded, disgusted beyond belief with the situation.

"Well, good luck. I mean that sincerely. Also, I've put in a call to the Russians. We're doing whatever we can to get your visa extended, just in case."

"What are the chances of pulling that off?" Mike asked.

"Let's just say we'll do whatever we can. You work your angle as hard as you can, I'll work mine as hard as I can. One way or another, everything will work out. It always does."

Mike thanked the agent, took the documents and carried Luba toward Nika who stood up from her chair as he approached.

"What do we do next?" Nika asked him calmly.

"Take us to the airport," Mike said, not angry like before, but firmly.

Nika sighed. It wasn't going to do any good. But on the other hand, Mike had been more respectful of her time than almost any American she had ever met. He never wasted her time when he could do something on his own. She felt like she owed him the chance to try, even though she knew he would fail.

"Alright, Mike. I'll take you to the airport."

Mike and Luba followed Nika down the stairs and out to the waiting van. Nika spoke with the driver for a moment in Russian and he soon began to argue with her. It was obvious that he also thought that a trip to the airport was a waste of time. But Nika prevailed, and the van headed out into traffic for the ninety-minute drive to the airport. It didn't take too long for Nika to have Mike talking again, though she avoided any inflammatory conversation until they got close to the airport.

"Okay, Mike," she started, "do you have a game plan for when you get to the airport?"

"Yes, I do. I never proceed without a plan."

"Right. Then what's your plan?"

"Look, Nika, I've already told you my plan. Don't ask if you don't want to hear."

"Okay, Mike. I want to hear. I know it must be difficult with what has transpired. But understand. I do want to help you and Luba. Whether I agree with you or not, I am here to help you. Please tell me what you are thinking. I want to make sure that you are not going to get into trouble, particularly where we are trying to extend your visa."

"Well, first they'll check our luggage and we'll clear security. Passport control is after that. With the state of affairs in today's world, they won't send our luggage on without us. Maybe that will be a little incentive to put us through."

"Very little, I assure you," Nika responded.

"Well, there's a chance that with all of the paper work the border guard has to review on Luba, she won't catch the missing stamp," Mike added.

"The guard will catch it," Nika responded matter-of-factly.

"If she does catch it, then she has to explain to me what's wrong. I don't speak Russian, so she has to explain in English. Chances are that her English isn't the best, and I'll be the stupidest person in the world. No matter how hard she tries to explain, I won't understand. Sometimes it's easier to let someone go than to argue in a foreign language. I mean after all, this is an adoption. All of the paperwork is in place for the adoption. Everyone knows that international adoption is for permanent residency anyway. Luba will be an American after that. She will never use that Russian passport again."

"That's true. I give you a ten percent chance of that plan working. Do you have a back-up plan?"

"As a matter of fact, I do."

"Tell me about your back-up plan." Nika replied.

"The back-up plan is the kind of plan that you don't like to hear about."

"I was afraid of that. But I really need to know how you plan to do this. It's important."

"You asked for it," Mike warned her. "*If* the border guard finally convinces me that something is wrong, then I'll demand to see a supervisor. When the supervisor comes, I'll argue until they have to pull me aside to get the line moving again. Once I get away from everyone else, I'll tell the supervisor that I understand that my daughter's passport is missing a very important stamp. I'll also acknowledge that it might be very expensive to have someone else get it for us and then mail it to us in the States, later. I'll tell him that I think that there might be a five hundred dollar fee to have someone here do that for us. I'll hand him my passport to check and there will be five hundred dollars in it."

"But Mike, he won't ever send it to you," Nika said without thinking.

"I don't *care!*" Mikes responded exasperatedly.

"No. Of course you don't. Do you realize that the supervisor probably only earns five hundred dollars a month?"

"Really? Is that so? Because I was hoping I was offering him a month's salary to take care of this important stamp and mail it to me. If he decides not to keep his end of the bargain after I get home, then so be it."

"So, you are not trying to *bribe* him."

"What? No! Of course not! That would be wrong!" Mike smiled.

"Who told you that you could do this in Russia?" Nika asked.

"Don't be naive," Mike responded. "Things like that happen everywhere."

Nika paused. "Well, I never would encourage you to do something like that. But since you came up with it on your own, I guess it's worth a try. Just make sure that what you do and say is like you told me. If they construe it as a bribe, it might work, but more likely it will get you into all kinds of trouble."

"Of course."

Soon they arrived at the airport, and the driver helped them unload. Nika carried Luba and Mike pulled the luggage. Nika took Mike to the first security check point, gave Luba a squeeze, placed her on the ground, and told her to hold Papa's hand, which she did.

"Okay, Mike. I'm now giving you a fifty-fifty chance of making your flight. But now, listen to me as a friend. You might not get out today. Do you have a plan in case you don't?"

Mike smiled. "Come on, Nika! You know I always have a plan."

Nika smiled back. "Okay. But I'm curious. Humor me."

"If they don't let us through, we can still make the redeye flight back to Vladivostok tonight. We will arrive somewhere around 10:30 in the morning and then Marik and Sasha can pick us up and take us directly to the passport office. All we need is a stamp. We can get that and be back at the airport before the flight to Seoul. We might have to overnight in Seoul, but Luba will know that we're on our way home."

"That even solves the visa problem…" Nika responded pensively. "This really will work out without having to separate you and Luba!"

"It looks that way, doesn't it?" Mike replied.

"Great. That is really great. I will wait here in the lobby for you until I hear that the flight is in the air. If you are not back here by then, I'll know that you are on the flight. If you come back before then, I will help you to get your tickets changed."

"Thanks, Nika, for all of your help."

"No, not at all. I'm sorry for all of the problems. It's never this bad!"

"The problems weren't your fault. Sorry I was so tough to deal with."

"Don't worry about it," Nika told him. "You had every right to be angry." She stooped down and gave Luba one more hug and a kiss on the cheek. Then she shook Mike's hand and left him at the first security checkpoint.

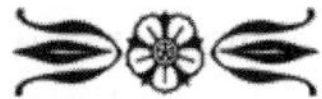

"Eet say heer der ees modder and oder geerl. Ware ees modder and oder geerl?" the border guard asked Mike shortly after he handed her the documents.

"They left last Sunday. We had to stay because there was a problem with this child's passport."

"Ware ees problem wid passport?"

"They had her marked as a male. She is a female. We had to send the passport back to Vladivostok to be corrected." The woman quickly shuffled to the proper page and checked to make sure that the mistake had been corrected. Then she spent fifteen minutes going through Luba's other documents. Mike was very nervous and it was difficult not to let it show. The only way he could think of to not be conspicuous was to play with Luba. So he talked to her about her pictures.

"Mama! Kawcha!" she said over and over. Then she pushed the photos under the window across the counter to the border guard. "Mama! Kawcha!" she said to the woman behind the glass. The woman, who had remained stoic up until that point, looked up and smiled. Then she began to speak baby talk to Luba. Luba smiled and continued to say: "Mama" and "Kawcha."

After several seconds the border guard returned to reviewing the documents. Satisfied that everything was in place with Mike's papers, she grabbed his passport and stamped it. Mike almost gasped. He was now out of the country. But Luba wasn't. Then the woman went back to looking at Luba's documents. Mike was extremely nervous now and he felt beads of sweat rolling down his back as he continued to play with his daughter.

Then the border guard picked up Luba's passport and began to examine it again. It seemed that something was missing…now, what was it? She went through the papers page by page. Wait. Where was the stamp for permanent residency? She checked again. It was missing. She looked up at Mike, who was playing with his beautiful blonde daughter, a little girl who cooed and giggled at him. The guard was about to open her mouth when the little one let out a burst of laughter and squealed "Poppy!" as she hugged him around the neck. The stern border guard looked back down and hesitated for only a second before stamping Luba's passport.

Mike, shocked but determined not to show it, looked up. The border guard handed him the documents and passports. "Safe jornee Meestor Nite," she said as he took them.

"Thank you," Mike said, and then he hurried away, still believing that she had simply overlooked the missing stamp.

Mike and Luba slept most of the flight to JFK. Clearing customs went much as it had for the others, four days earlier. Several hours later they were on the ground in Detroit.

37

Reunited

Mike and Luba were at the pick-up curb for only a couple of minutes when Laura drove up. She jumped out of the SUV and ran to them. Luba lunged from Mike's arms as she saw her mother. "Mama! Mama! MAMA!" She threw her arms around her mother's neck and squeezed while her mother embraced her with one hand and cradled her head against her with the other. Mike threw his arms around them both and squeezed them tight.

"I missed you two so much!" Laura said as tears rolled down her cheeks. Mike let them go and dragged the luggage around to the back.

"Poppy!" Sarah cried as he opened the rear door.

"Hello, Princess!" Mike quickly shoved the luggage into the back, slammed the door and rushed to open the curbside door to see Sarah. "I missed you!" he said as he dove into the vehicle and hugged her.

"I mees yoo. Ee I mees *Dyedushka* Jim." Mike didn't say anything. He just continued to hold her. After a few minutes he let her go and they gave each other kisses on the cheeks.

Mike got behind the wheel and Sarah talked incessantly for the first fifteen minutes. Surprising to Mike, much of it was in English, though heavily accented. Luba was soon asleep and Sarah quickly followed. It was a pleasant sleep that Sarah drifted into. Finally, for the first time since their separation in Moscow, Sarah felt secure.

They arrived home about midnight. But unlike Sarah, four days earlier, Luba could not be awakened upon their arrival. Lights were still illuminated in the house as they pulled into the driveway. Jeff and Stephen had waited up to see their new sister. Both crowded Laura as she entered the door, trying to get a glimpse of the little girl. Laura displayed her as a newborn, cradled in her arms, and leaned forward so the brothers could see.

"She's so beautiful!" Jeff whispered as he admired her.

"May I hold her?" Stephen asked.

"Let's wait until tomorrow," Laura responded. "She's exhausted."

Jeff and Stephen both agreed, and soon everyone was down for the night.

The boys were gone to school before Mike and the girls got up the next morning. Laura went to retrieve Luba from the bedroom when she heard her crying.

"Mama, Luba cry. Luba *bye-yoos,*" Sarah explained.

"Try English," Laura prompted Sarah as she walked toward Luba, who was still whimpering and holding out her arms to her mother.

"Luba, a, um, a, Luba scare."

"Oh. Tell her not to be scared."

Sarah spoke to her sister in Russian as Laura picked her up. But Luba wasn't looking for an explanation. She just wanted her mother. She snuggled up against Laura, turned her face toward her mother's neck and continued to whimper while Laura stroked her head and carried her out of the room.

Sarah was excited to see her father as she entered the kitchen behind Luba and Laura. "Papa!" she squealed as she ran to him and leapt into his arms.

"Good morning, Princess!" he said. He hugged her for a moment and then sat her on his lap while they ate breakfast. "I'm headed down to the hospital to see Mom," Mike said to Laura after finishing breakfast. "I have no idea when I'll be back, but I'll give you a call in a while and give you an update."

Sarah wanted to go with her father as soon as she realized that he was leaving, but Laura explained to her that he was going to visit Grandma at the hospital. If she thought that was going to pacify Sarah, she was wrong. "*Yá hawchoo* Grandma." Sarah and Grandma had hit it off at the hospital several days before and Sarah longed to spend more time with her.

"Not today, Sarah," Laura responded. "Grandma is very sick today."

"*Stó?*"

"Try English," Laura prompted.

"Oh, um, oh! What?"

"Grandma is sick. Grandma has big owies."

"Oh… Grandma big owies?"

"Yes," Laura responded. "Will you stay here and help me with Luba?"

"*Dá*. Oh, yes."

"Thank you," Laura told her. But Sarah ran back to Mike for a hug and a kiss before he left. Then he kissed Laura before heading out the door.

"How are you doing?" Mike asked his mother as he walked into the hospital room.

" Mike!" she responded excitedly. "I'm so glad that you're home!"

"I'm glad to be home. I was beginning to wonder if we were *ever* going to get here. No matter how hard we tried to make it happen, someone was standing in the way. I have never been more frustrated. Anyway, how are *you?*"

"I'm doing fine. Where are your new little princesses?"

"Oh, I left them at home. I heard that you were pretty sick. You don't need a couple of kids crawling all over you. We'll wait until you're home and feeling better."

Mike's mother turned stern. "I am just fine. The doctors here should let me go home. The least that you could do is to let me visit my grandchildren. I haven't even met Celeste! Tell me Mike, what is she like?"

"Oh Mom, she's just beautiful. Sarah is so outgoing and cute, but kind of in a tomboy way. Celeste is just fragile, delicate and beautiful, like a porcelain doll. She has blonde hair and beautiful, deep blue eyes. She's just so pretty, and she loves being pretty. She's all girl."

"She sounds so wonderful. Mike, I just have to meet her. Promise me you'll bring her to see me this afternoon."

"I don't know, Mom. Are you sure you're up to it?"

"Of course I'm up to it. The doctors don't know what they're talking about, anyway."

"Why do you say that? What are they telling you?"

"Oh, they say that I have some kind of a blood infection. They have me on an antibiotic. It should clear up in a couple of days. Then I'll be able to go home. I can't figure out why they won't let me go home anyway if the antibiotic is going to take care of the infection in a couple of days. I'm fine if I rest. I only get dizzy if I don't rest. Dawn and Mark brought little Gracie to see me last night. Have you seen her yet?"

"No, not yet."

"They only stayed for a few minutes. But I did get to hold her. She is just wonderful. I wish they had stayed longer, but they kept telling me that I needed to get some rest. I wish that people would stop telling me what I need."

"Mom, we all just want you to get better. You need your strength."

"I'm fine, just fine. It's so good to see you! I'm so glad you're back home." Mike leaned over the bed, hugged his mother, kissed her on the cheek, and then she kissed him. He looked at her for a moment and then took a seat, hunched forward on the edge of the easy chair next to the bed.

"Oh Mike, have you ever seen a woman more blessed than I am?"

"What are you talking about?"

"I just feel that God has blessed me more than anyone else in the world. I have such a wonderful family, and He has given me three more wonderful granddaughters in less than a week. Dawn and Gracie are doing fine, and you and Laura made it home safe with Sarah and Celeste. I just couldn't be more blessed."

"You certainly see the glass half full," Mike replied. "You have plenty of reason to feel otherwise."

Mike's mother scolded him for even thinking such a thing. Then they sat and visited for several hours before he decided to leave, but not before succumbing to her request for him to bring the entire family back to see her that evening.

Mike was able to speak with her doctor, briefly, in the hallway before he left. "What's her prognosis?" he asked.

"The blood infection is very serious," the doctor responded. "It isn't responding to the antibiotic the way that we hoped that it would. It looks like we'll probably start her on a different antibiotic tomorrow, if we don't see results by then."

"So, will that clear it up?"

"We hope so, but it's difficult to say with any degree of certainty. Many times a different antibiotic will get right in and clear things up. But we never know for sure. We're at a critical time right now with the blood infection, even ignoring the cancer at this point. If we don't get the infection under control, it could prove fatal in a very short time. I hate to put it that way, but it's best that you and your family understand everything."

Mike was shocked. At first he didn't know what to say. "Mom made me promise that I would bring my wife and kids back to see her tonight. Do you think that's a good idea?"

"Sure. I think limited visits are good. We have to keep her morale up. But don't overdo it. She needs rest, too."

Mike thanked the doctor, shook his hand, and then made his way out of the hospital and to the car.

Mike called Mark on the cell phone as soon as he got in to his car.

"Hey, Mike. It's good to have you back home. Have you been to see Mom yet?"

"Yeah. I just left the hospital. I'm sitting in my car in the parking lot. Mark, I just finished talking with her doctor. They're really concerned about the infection. It's not responding to the antibiotic, so unless things change by tomorrow, they're planning on starting her on a different one."

"I was afraid of that. They said the same thing last night when Dawn and I took the baby to meet her. What else are they saying?"

"The doctor said that if they don't get it under control soon that we could lose her."

"Yeah, they've been saying that since yesterday. I should tell you I called Karen and Matt last night and told them how serious this is," Mark said referring to their two siblings who both lived out-of-state. "They're flying in today to spend some time with Mom."

"Don't you think we should wait until we see how things are going to play out?" Mike asked. "Shouldn't we wait a while longer and pray and show some faith? I mean, I hate for it to look like we're sitting around waiting for a funeral!"

"How much worse do you want it to get before we take this seriously?" Mark asked. "You always have a tough time coming to accept these things, Mike. It was the same way with Dad and Mitch. I understand, and that's okay. No one is asking you to deal with it any differently. But you can't deny Karen and Matt a chance at visiting with Mom, particularly with the odds at this point."

"No, Mark, you're right. I'm sorry. I just think that we all need to show some faith. We all know that God can heal Mom. I think that we need to give Him a chance to do that."

"Sure, Mike. We will. But let's enjoy the weekend with the family together. Let's not make it any more stressful than it has to be."

"You've got it. I'm sure that everyone will be busy visiting with Mom for the rest of today, but can we get together with all of us for a meeting tomorrow morning at my house?"

"Sure, I don't see why not. It'll be good to visit with everyone. The family is so spread out that it doesn't happen enough any more."

"Thanks, Mark. See you then."

Soon after supper, Mike called his family together for a meeting in the living room shortly before taking them to visit Grandma.

"As you all know," Mike began, "Grandma is pretty sick. She has been having treatments for cancer. But earlier this week the doctors discovered that she has a serious infection. They had to stop the cancer treatments until they can get the infection under control. That's a big concern, because she needs those cancer treatments. We are going over to see Grandma in a few minutes, but I think that we need to have a family prayer together, before we leave."

Sarah sat quietly as did Stephen and Jeff, while Celestc played on her mother's lap. She didn't understand much of what was going on, other than that they were going to visit Grandma. She knew that her grandmother was sick. Mama had helped her to understand that when they visited her, but she had no idea how seriousness it was.

"We all know that God has the strength and power to heal Grandma," Mike continued. "We all need to show faith here, though. We need to believe that He can and will do this for us."

"So we're praying for God to heal Grandma from the infection and the cancer, right?" Jeff interjected. Jeff didn't take death any better than his father did. In fact, he had still not gotten over the death of his grandfather and his favorite uncle. Silently he was still angry with his Father in Heaven.

"Right now we're praying for Grandma's infection to be healed. We'll take this one thing at a time." Mike responded.

"What's the point?" Jeff asked, now even more annoyed. "Are we going to ask God to heal Grandma or not?"

"Come on, Jeff, let's be reasonable." It was at this instant, for the first time, that Mike questioned his own logic, though only briefly. Jeff just grumbled an indiscernible teenaged response and then went quiet.

Mike offered the prayer as the family knelt together. He asked his Father in Heaven to heal his mother from the blood infection and to direct the doctors in how to best help her, both with the infection and with her ordeal with cancer. He reaffirmed that they had faith that God could heal her, and he asked his Father in Heaven to manifest His strength and power by healing their mother and grandmother of her blood infection.

The ride to the hospital was quiet, but things livened up quickly as they got to Grandma's hospital room.

"Grandma!" Sarah squealed as she ran to the bed and launched herself onto it, next to her grandmother.

"Well hello, Sarah! It's good to see you!" Sarah threw her arms around the old woman who was half-sitting in bed and gave her a big hug. "Hi, Jeff and Stephen! How are you two doing?"

"Hi, Grandma," they said in unison as they both walked over to the bed. Mike and Laura stood back with Celeste for a few minutes while the other children visited. Grandma took time with each of them, finding out how they were doing in school, if they were excited for the summer vacation that would begin the next week, and telling them how beautiful and handsome they were and how proud she was of them.

"Iye luv yoo grand-maw," Sarah said as she threw her arms around her again for another hug.

"Oh! I love you too, Sarah!" she responded as she hugged her back. "I can't believe how quick they learn the language," she commented to Mike and Laura while she looked at them over Sarah's shoulder.

"She really is doing well," Laura responded.

"Sarah, is that your sister?" Grandma asked as she turned Sarah toward her parents.

"*Eta Luba*."

"Is that Celeste?"

"*Dá*. Sah-lest."

"Oh, Laura, she is beautiful, isn't she? Bring her here!"

Laura carried Celeste over to the bed and placed her sitting next to her grandma. Sarah was a little annoyed that Grandma was paying attention to someone else, but she sat quietly. Celeste took to Grandma quickly. She had never had trouble adapting to new women; living in the orphanage had got her accustomed to that. Grandma picked her up and talked to her and played with her for several minutes until Sarah jumped into the middle of them. But Grandma was happy to accommodate them both. Soon the girls were snuggled up, one on each side of her while she visited with Mike, Laura, and the older boys for the next hour.

"We had better get going so that you can have a nap before Karen and Matt get here to visit," Mike said.

To his surprise, his mother made no objection. "Okay. Thank you for coming to visit me," she said merrily.

Laura and Mike both hugged and kissed her, and then they gathered up the girls while the boys followed them out of the hospital.

"It's good to see you, Karen. It's been too long," Mike said as his younger sister and brother walked into the house. "You too, Matt. It's good to see you." Mike hugged each of them and then they sat down in the living room where Mark and Dawn waited.

"I wanted to take all of you to breakfast this morning," Mike informed them. "But I also wanted to talk a little about Mom, before we left."

"Mark has been keeping us informed," Karen responded. "This is pretty scary. Matt and I went to see her after we got in late yesterday evening. She sounds good, but she looks pretty weak. She's awful pale."

"Have we heard anything since yesterday?" Matt asked.

"I called Mom this morning," Mark responded. "I guess they started her on her new antibiotic."

"How long until we know if it's working?" Matt asked.

"Mom said the doctor told her that we should see some improvement by Monday afternoon. That is, if it works the way they hope it will." Mark replied.

"That's what I want to talk about," Mike interjected. "The antibiotic hasn't worked the way that it was supposed to. There's no telling what the new antibiotic will do on its own. But we all know that God has the strength and power to heal Mom's blood infection. I wanted to meet together this morning for a family prayer, and ask God to heal Mom of her blood infection. I believe that if we have the faith, this can and will be done."

The other siblings looked around the room at each other, waiting for someone else to respond. They all knew how Mike handled death, and they had already met earlier to discuss this very possibility. They sat in silence for several seconds before Karen finally broke down.

"Look, Mikey," she said, not condescendingly, but reverting back to the childhood term of endearment that she had used for a revered older brother, almost fifteen years her senior. "We all wish that Mom could be healed entirely. Not just from the blood infection, but also from the cancer. We want that as much as you do. But, if that isn't what Heavenly Father wants, then it isn't what is going to happen. If it's time for Mom to go, and it's inevitable, then why would we want Mom to be healed from a blood infection so that she could suffer through cancer? Mikey, please think about what's best for Mom. Should she really have to go through that much suffering only to delay what will happen shortly anyway?"

Mike's mind flashed back to the lobby of the Marriott Royal in Moscow. There, less than a week ago, he had asked essentially the same question to Nika. Why put Luba through all the suffering, when the inevitable will happen anyway? But no. That was adoption. This was different.

"You know, Mike," Mark began, directing the attention away from his younger sister and toward himself, "We can talk about faith and we can talk about God's omnipotence, but maybe we need to look at this situation another way. We also believe that when our loved ones die that they go to a better place. If we *really* believe that, should we fight it?"

Mike's mind flashed back to the hotel lobby once again, when he had silently cursed the bureaucrats who had kept him and Celeste from going home. How he had despised them for thinking that they knew what was better for his daughter than her own father did!

"Do…Do you all feel this way?" he asked as he looked around the room.

The three siblings and Dawn all silently and timidly nodded.

"Laura?" Mike asked.

"I want what's best for Mom," Laura replied. "Just like every one else in this room does. Just like you do, Sweetheart. Maybe we need to take a little bit more time to figure out exactly what that is."

The siblings all nodded in agreement. Mike could see his position crumbling. He would lose this battle. But what he feared the most was that this was more than a battle. The outcome of this battle would determine the outcome of the war. Mike hated losing battles and he abhorred losing wars. Neither happened often.

Then Mike had a sudden revelation. *Maybe he wasn't supposed to win this war. Maybe he was fighting for the wrong side.*

But he wasn't quite ready to concede. Not yet.

Peace

No one talked much on the way to the restaurant, but that suited Mike. He was deep in thought. "Why is it so wrong to ask You to show Your strength and heal Mom?" Mike prayed in his mind while driving.

"Did you show your strength at the Baby Hospital by leaving Luba there, when that is what she wanted?" The words simply came into Mike's mind. It stunned him. He couldn't even think a response. When the question went unanswered, another entered his mind. "How did you manifest your strength?"

Mike blinked rapidly, refusing to answer the question, even in his mind. Then the question came again. It wasn't accusatory, it wasn't stern. The question came with the compassion of an all-comprehending Parent helping His child to understand, by posing a question that could only be answered the right way. "How did you manifest your strength?"

"I…I took her home…" Mike spoke out loud, without even realizing that he had done so.

"What, Sweetheart?" Laura asked.

"Oh," Mike gasped, coming back to the moment. "I…nothing. I was just thinking."

After breakfast, the Knight children spent several hours visiting with their mother. Of course, she scolded them for not bringing the grandchildren, but soon she settled down and just enjoyed the rare occasion of having her children together for a visit.

That evening, after dinner, Mike told Laura that he needed some time alone. As always, she understood. She opened up the drawer where the keys were kept and tossed him the ones to his Corvette. She knew how much a long drive cleared his head.

"Have a nice break," she said. "Don't forget to take your cell phone in case we need to get in touch with you." A veiled reminder that with his mother's situation, anything could happen at any time.

Mike spent three hours driving that evening. He didn't go anywhere in particular. He didn't even play his music like he normally did. He just drove through the country with the top down, thinking about the happenings of the previous six months.

He remembered how excited he was to get the pictures of Sarah and how he longed for her to be home. He recalled how happy she was to meet him and Laura, and how she clung to them with immediate and unconditional trust. He looked back on how he felt when the two little sisters were reunited, this time in a *forever* family. Then he recalled Sarah leaving the orphanage, excited to begin the trip home, but melancholy about leaving friends and caregivers who she would never see again in this life.

He thought about taking Celeste from Oksana on the steps of the orphanage, and he vividly remembered her shrieks and sobs of horror as he took her away from the only life that she knew. Then he remembered looking back at Oksana and watching the tears stream down her face as she consoled herself in the separation by knowing that her little Luba was going to a better place. He remembered that moment, and the words came back to him.

Oh, child. If you had any idea what awaits you, you wouldn't feel like this. There would be no panic. If you only knew what I have to give you, you wouldn't cry. And while your friends know that you are going to a better place, even they don't fully understand the life that I will give you when I take you home. Soon you will see, and you will forgive me when finally you understand. Child, I know what is best for you and I will do what is best for you, even if it hurts you now. Even if it hurts your friends and those you see as family, I will take you home.

The children were all in bed when Mike got home that night, but Laura had waited up for him. "How was your drive?" she asked, as she turned off the TV with the remote.

"It was good. I feel a lot more relaxed."

"Do you feel any better about things?" she asked, giving him the opportunity to talk, but still leaving him a way out.

"Surprisingly, I do. I think I finally get it."

"Get what?"

"Death. I mean, with my religious beliefs, I always thought that I understood, even though I could never deal with it. But I was so far off. I didn't get it at all."

"What do you mean?"

"I always believed in an all-powerful God who gave us life and who would reward us in another life, if we did what He expected us to here. But now I think it's simpler than that. I keep thinking of scriptural references that refer to Him as our Father. I finally understand it. He's the perfect Father. He understands us. He wants what is best for us. He *knows* what's best for us. He loves us. He loves us *perfectly*. I finally get it."

"So, what now?" Laura asked.

"The hard part," Mike replied gently. "I have to be strong, like Oksana was on the steps of the orphanage. I have to believe that a father loves his children, and always does what is best for them. I have to believe that they go to a better place, a place far better than I can even comprehend. Then I have to let that Father do what He knows is best."

39

The Marvelous Journey Home

The next day was Sunday, and Mike spent an hour that morning alone with his mother. None of the other siblings were there at the time, and his mother kept drifting off to sleep as he talked. Finally, he decided to let her rest and he returned home.

Dinner was never a quiet time at the Knight home and this evening was no exception. But Sarah did notice that her daddy didn't say a word, and that Mama was quieter than normal. Mike didn't eat much; he just kept poking at his food, deep in thought. Laura kept looking at Mike and seemed to be worried about him, but he never looked up to meet her concerned gaze. As Stephen finished his plate, he started to slide his chair back from the table, while at the same time asking nonchalantly if he could go and play on the computer.

"Just a minute, kiddo. There's something that we need to talk about."

Sarah watched her daddy look up from his meal for the first time as he pushed the plate away and leaned his arms on the table. Stephen sat back down in his chair and urgently watched his father as his mother stood up, walked behind him and placed her hands on his shoulders. This was strange behavior at the Knight home, and it made Sarah uneasy, though Celeste continued to jabber and play with her food. Mike looked back down at his hands for a moment before taking a deep breath and looking back up at the children.

"You all know how sick Grandma has been. Well, I spent some time at the hospital with Grandma today. She is so tired, kids. I felt so bad watching her. The doctors have her on a lot of pain medicine and she can hardly stay awake.

"Now, we have been praying a lot for Grandma, and I know that I told you that if we had enough faith, she would be able to come home soon. But…" Sarah noticed that her daddy's voice started to shake. Then he stopped talking and looked back down at his hands. Sarah saw the tears streaming down her mother's cheeks as her hands squeezed her daddy's shoulders.

Then she looked down and gently kissed him on the crown of his head.

"It's okay, Mike," she said softly. Mike looked back up at the children and wiped the tears from his face, but they just kept coming.

"I think that Grandma is ready to go home to be with Grandpa. I know that she misses Uncle Mitch too. And Grandma's daddy and mama have been gone for a long time. I'm sure that she misses them. I think that sometimes we forget that we have a much bigger family beyond this life than we have here." Sarah listened while Daddy paused again, but this time he didn't look down.

"I think that Grandma's family who are waiting for her there are hoping to have her home soon. I think that they are so excited to get her back that they just can't stand it. I think that we need to change our prayers. I think that instead of praying for a miracle for Grandma to come home to us, we need to pray for a different miracle. I think that we need to pray for her to be able to go home to her other family."

Jeff's chair slammed back into the wall as he stood up angrily. "I'll have no part of this!" he yelled.

Celeste erupted into tears and began to cry loudly.

"You told us that if we had enough faith that Grandma would come home. Well I have prayed, and I have had faith. God took my Grandpa! He can't have my Grandma, too!" Jeff bolted from the kitchen and down the hall. Sarah heard his feet pound up the stairs and then the slamming of his bedroom door.

Stephen, though crying with the others, was the first to break the silence. "Why is Jeff always acting like that? He's always mad and yelling at everyone."

"It's alright, Stephen," Laura said. "Jeff just grieves differently than other people do. Most people get sad, but Jeff gets angry. We all grieve in different ways. Jeff's way is a little bit harder for us to deal with, but we need to let him work this out in his own way."

"We need to be patient with Jeff," Mike continued. "I have a feeling that this will take Jeff a long time to get over. But we are family and we will stick together. We'll be there for Jeff even when it seems like he doesn't want us to be."

"*Stó*, Mama?" Sarah had not understood the exchange. She knew that Daddy was talking about Grandma, and she knew that Grandma was sick, but she did not know what had just happened. "Why Daddy cry? Why Jayf an-gree?"

Laura took her hands off of Mike's shoulders and picked Celeste up to comfort her. Celeste snuggled into her mother and stopped crying, though whimpers continued.

"We are all sad. Grandma might die soon." Laura wished that there was a more tactful or softer way to explain it to Sarah, but her language skills were still far too weak. This was the only way that she would be able to understand.

"Grandma die *kuk* Jesus?" Sarah used the Russian word for "like."

"Yes, Sarah. Grandma might die soon, like Jesus."

"No!" Sarah started as if to cry, then stopped as a thought came to her. "Grandma go Jesus?"

"Yes, Sweetheart. Grandma will go with Jesus."

"Oh! I liyke Jesus!" Sarah said happily while wiping the tears from her face. "Grandma *ee* Jesus happy."

"Yes, Princess," Mike replied. "Grandma and Jesus will be happy." He marveled at the true, uncluttered, simple faith of little children.

But no, it was more than that. Mike found tears suddenly forming as, in a warm rush, he realized the profound truth this little girl from half a world away had taught him. All of his life he had used faith as a tool, a way of coercing his Father in Heaven. *If I believe enough, then He* has *to do what I want.* But that was not faith; that was manipulation. Faith is trust—simple, ordinary, loving trust. Why hadn't he seen this before? Why hadn't he *trusted* before?

Mike stood up, almost staggering from the weight of this new revelation, and walked down the hall to his den.

"Can I come in?" Mike asked after several taps on Jeff's door. There was no answer. Mike tapped three more times, a bit louder this time. "Jeff, I'd really like to talk to you. Can I come in?"

"Go away!" the voice yelled from the other side of the door. "I don't want to talk to you."

"Jeff, it's time for family prayer. It just won't be family prayer if we're missing part of our family."

Again, silence.

Mike hesitated, hoping for wisdom before continuing. "Son, I can imagine how you feel. But you need to know that we want you to come and be with us. I know that you don't agree, but we want you to know... *I* want you to know that you don't have to agree with me to be a part of our family. Will you please come down for family prayer?"

"Are you still going to pray for God to kill Grandma?" Jeff had a way with words and could be verbally brutal. He rarely hesitated to use this to his advantage when it helped him make his point, and tonight was no exception.

"Jeff. It doesn't have to be this way. Please come down. We can simply pray that God's will be done, if that makes you feel better."

"What do I care about *God's will*?" Jeff yelled back. "He killed Grandpa. Why would it be any different with Grandma? You and God do whatever you want, but don't ask me to be a part of it. Now leave me alone."

"Jeff," Mike said softly, "please reconsider."

This time there was no answer. Mike turned slowly and hesitated, hoping that some great wisdom would come over him and help him to know what to say. But the wisdom never came, so he started down the stairs.

"Dear God," he prayed silently as he walked down the stairs, "how is it that in order to pray for my mother, I must crush the faith of my son? How is it that You could expect me to do such a thing?" Mike hadn't really expected an answer to the prayer, at least not one so soon or so complete. But words came into his mind and filled his entire soul.

Before he was your son, he was My son; and before you loved him, I loved him. Serve your mother and those who love her who have gone on before. I will take care of My son.

Mike didn't know how; but he knew that some way, in God's own time, Jeff would be alright.

"Sarah! Celeste! Stephen! Come into the living room for prayer," Mike called down the hall.

"Are you sure that you're ready for this?" Laura asked as she squeezed his hand.

"No, I'm sure that I'm *not* ready for this. I'm just as sure that I will never be ready for this."

"What about Jeff?" Laura's voice quivered. "Will he will be okay?"

"Yes, Laura. I don't know how. But somehow everything will work out. It will take some time, but Jeff will be fine."

Stephen led his sisters into the room. Sarah walked over to Mike and held her hands up to him. He picked her up and gave her a big squeeze while Laura picked up Celeste. Then Sarah knelt next to her daddy and Celeste sat on Laura's lap while she knelt, with Stephen next to her.

"Mama, where Jaef?" Sarah asked before Mike could begin.

"Jeff just wants to be alone right now," she said soothingly. "Jeff will pray with us tomorrow. But now Jeff wants to be alone."

Mike was not so confident. He had never known a will stronger than Jeff's, and he didn't know how long it would be before Jeff prayed with the family again, much less on his own. He felt the weight of his responsibility bearing down on him as he prepared to offer the prayer, knowing full well the effect that it would have on his son, not to mention the sadness that would come from the loss of his own mother.

The Knight family prayed together often, but Sarah had never heard a prayer quite like this one. Daddy was speaking to his Heavenly Father as if he was right there. She even peeked several times to see if God was there in the room with them. Sarah didn't understand all the words, but she did understand that her father was asking God to help her grandma. It wasn't a long prayer, but she knew that God had heard the prayer, that He would listen to her daddy and that He would help her grandma.

Sarah and Stephen stood up and hugged their parents as they knelt next to the couch. They hugged for the longest time. Sarah was sad, but the big hug made her feel so warm inside. She wished that Jeff was with them so that he could feel warm and happy too.

"Off to bed, kids," Mike said. "We'll see you in the morning." Stephen quietly took the girls to their bedrooms while Mike and Laura sat down on the couch to unwind.

Mike and Laura stayed up watching TV after the kids went to bed. Jeff had not come out of his room since the exchange with Mike, and they figured that he had gone to sleep as well. About ten-thirty, the phone rang.

"Mike, it's Mark. The doctor just called me. He said that Mom isn't doing very well and that anyone who wants to say goodbye should get to the hospital pretty soon."

Mike thanked him, hung up the phone and then dialed Bob next door. He explained to his neighbor what was going on, and asked him to stay with their children. Bob was there in five minutes, assuring them that he could be there all night if need be, and that there was no reason for them to rush home.

As Mike and Laura entered the hospital room Mark, Dawn, Karen, and Matt were gathered around his mother's bed.

"What's the news?" Mike asked as he and Laura joined the circle.

"The doctor says that it probably won't be long," Mark told him. "Her breathing is pretty shallow. She hasn't been conscious all day."

Mike just nodded and looked down somberly. Laura waited for him to talk to his mother, but he didn't. So she took her turn. She leaned over the old woman and thanked her for taking her into her family. She thanked her for raising her husband, and for being such a wonderful grandmother. She told her how much she would miss her. Finally, she told the unconscious old woman not to worry about Mike, that she would take care of him. Then she hugged her, kissed her on the forehead, and stood back. The group was somber and no one spoke, but all eyes turned to Mike.

After a moment of silence, Mark spoke. "We've all taken our turns, big brother. If you need a minute alone, we can give you that."

"No. It's not that. It's not about being alone, it's about family." Mike stepped forward, leaned over his mother and hugged her. He wanted to say so many things, but he just couldn't. Then he pulled back and looked at his mother's face.

"*Pahká*, Mama," he said softly. Then he kissed her and walked out of the room.

"Wake up, sleepy head."

Sarah rolled over to see her mother smiling, but her eyes were red and her face was puffy.

"Why Mama cry?" Sarah asked.

"Oh, nothing is wrong, Sweetheart. Sometimes Mamas just cry. Are you ready for breakfast?"

Sarah was hungry. "Yaes. Sehla eat yogurt?"

"I thought that you might ask that," her mother said. "Yes, you may have yogurt. Would you like strawberries, too?"

"*Dá!* Stlawballies!" Sarah jumped out of bed and hurried off to the kitchen. Strawberries were her favorite, and she loved yogurt. Daddy and the two boys were already waiting when she pulled her chair to the table and climbed up. Mama wasn't far behind with Celeste, and soon the whole family was seated at the table.

Jeff didn't say a word during the entire meal. He ate quickly and rose from the table to leave.

"Jeff, hang on," Mike said. Jeff paused but he didn't look up at his father. "Kids, there's something that you should know. Mom and I went to the hospital last night after prayers. Grandma passed away about two-thirty." Jeff slammed his chair back into the wall even harder than he had the night before and stormed out of the house.

Celeste erupted in tears again and cried loudly.

"Why Jayf an-gree? Why Seeb cry? *Stó* Mama? *Stó?*" Again, Sarah had not understood.

Laura answered Sarah as she retrieved Celeste from her chair to comfort her. "When you were asleep, Grandma died."

"Oh, Grandma go Jesus?"

"Yes, Princess. Grandma went with Jesus."

"Oh, Sehla sad!" she burst into tears and then she began to sob. She ran to her daddy, climbed up on his lap and threw her arms around his neck. Stephen was right behind her and Mama stepped up with Celeste to be in the hug with them.

After hugging for a couple of minutes Mike stood up and placed Sarah back on the floor. "I need to get something to wipe my eyes," he said; and he walked out of the room.

"I'll do the dishes this morning," Laura told her children. "Stephen, why don't you take your sisters and play a game or read a book? But try to keep it quiet. Your daddy didn't get much sleep last night. He needs to get some rest."

Sarah and Stephen played a racecar game on the PlayStation for a few minutes while Celeste played with her baby doll. But Sarah just wasn't in the mood for games. She put the controller down and walked out of the playroom and down the hall. Sarah heard music playing in the other room. It was the kind of music that Daddy listened to, not what Jeff and Stephen liked. She liked Jeff and Stephen's music better, but she did like the kind of music that her daddy listened to, mostly because it reminded her of him. Sarah walked toward the sound of the music until she found herself standing in the doorway to the living room.

Sarah stood there silently as she watched her father slowly turn the pages of the old worn photo album. Her mother had helped her look through it several days before while they were waiting for him and Luba to come home. It was the scrapbook of pictures from when her daddy was a little boy. She loved looking at those pictures. It was hard to imagine that once her big, strong daddy was a child like her.

"Hey, Princess." Her father's voice was soft and deep. His eyes were red, though he wasn't crying any more. "Do you want to come and look at pictures with me?"

Sarah didn't answer, but she scurried across the carpet and

spun quickly up against her father as he raised his big, strong arm. He snuggled her in tightly and she hugged his stomach with her arm. Sarah loved to sit like this with her daddy. It made her feel so safe, like nothing in the world could ever hurt her. There they sat, together, slowly looking at each picture, one remembering the past with melancholy and the other actively imagining that she could see those times in her mind. They paused for the longest time on each page, oblivious to the world as the country music played softly in the background.

Mike paused as they looked at an old, faded photograph, its lower-middle class, mid-sixties origin obvious from the home in the background, as well as the clothing and hair styles. It was a picture of him with his mother and father in front of the small home that he had grown up in. The picture reflected proud and happy parents with their first child, soon before others arrived. Mike reflected on a simpler time, a time before the family became involved in patents, world travel, international awards, and red Corvettes. Somehow, none of that mattered now. The only thing that mattered was family.

Sarah felt something gently tap the top of her head. At first she didn't know what it was. But when it happened again, she knew that tears were streaming down her daddy's face. Then she cried, too. She snuggled in tighter and her daddy gave her a big squeeze.

It was at that moment that Sarah got the warm feeling inside that only comes when you've witnessed a miracle. Because Sarah Katerina understood, far better than most, the strength of a father's love and the marvelous journey that begins when he takes his child home to a better place.

Author's Note

"The Marvelous Journey Home" is a work that is known in the writing industry as "Thinly Veiled Fiction." It is based on a true story in the author's life, but not *everything* in the book happened, happened as it is written, in the order that it was written, or even to the same people, as it is told in the novel.

The idea for the book came as my wife, Amy, and I adopted three children from Russia. Late in May of 2005, we brought home two biological sisters, Katya (now Sarah, who was five and a half years old), Luba (now Celeste, who was almost three years old) and a little boy named Kirrill (now Denney, who was almost two years old.)

We had been blessed with three biological sons before we were no longer able to have more children. In our longing for daughters, we turned to adoption, as so many in our situation do.

In 1995, our first adopted child joined our family. While we had intended to adopt a girl, the agency called and told us that they had a one-month-old baby boy with Downs Syndrome (one of the special needs conditions we had agreed to accept in our application). We added Jack to our family, and decided to wait to adopt girls later. This little boy has been a joy to our home and to all who know him. Finally, when Jack was eight, we decided that he had advanced to the point where we could deal with the difficulties of parents away from home, which could be required by some international adoptions. So we decided to move forward.

As we reviewed the areas where we could find children most likely to fall within our profile, Russia stood out as the most stable for adoption. That was the primary factor in driving us that direction. Things have changed significantly since then, and sadly, now most informed people would not consider Russia a "stable" option for international adoption.

To those unfamiliar with international adoption, and particularly with the eccentricities of adoption within former Soviet States, parts of the story may seem unbelievable. However, those who have been close to such adoption experiences will testify that nothing between the covers of this book is impossible, and really, not even unlikely.

Many of the events related in this book did happen to us. And interestingly enough, some of the events which seem to be gross over-dramatizations were actually toned down in the book. For instance, Amy did explain to our daughter, Sarah, that when the snow went away and the flowers came up, we would come back to get her. Upon returning home, after our first trip, she used the same explanation with our ten-year-old son, Jack. As we returned to Russia to retrieve our children, we left home before dawn for the drive to the airport. When we arrived at the airport, we received a call on the cell phone from one of our older sons. Jack was elated that our tulips had bloomed for the first time that very morning. He knew that his sisters would be home soon. The part of the story where Sarah's director talks about her being obsessed with looking for flowers also occurred, and yes, believe it or not, the flowers at the Vlad Motor Inn really did bloom for the first time the morning that we left to pick up the girls. I must add that this truly *was* before Sarah found flowers on her own. Coincidence? You'd have a difficult time convincing our family of that. Flowers, to our family, have truly come to represent "Promises Kept."

The description of the sun carrying kisses to and from Russia was actually used with Sarah and Jack, and it helped them immensely as they restlessly waited to meet each other, and for their parents to return between trips. Our children regularly (and I must confess, their parents, from time to time) entrust the setting sun with kisses to take to their friends in Russia. We also look to sunrises and know that our distant friends still love and remember us.

The cloth books were used with great effectiveness, and the part of the story where the mother and child drew flowers and a smiley-faced sun on the back page is a true event that will remain etched in my memory forever.

With "Thinly Veiled Works of Fiction," not *everything* happens as the novel describes it. We have very little knowledge of our children's lives before we met them, or even what goes on behind the restricted scenes in the international adoptive process. Everyday life in a Russian orphanage, as described in this book is something I simply know little about. While I felt that I needed a villain for the story (and I couldn't resist the English inference of the Russian name "Nastya"), I never met one in a Russian orphanage. Likewise, I never met an orphanage worker quite as compassionate as "Sofia" (another actual Russian name, of Greek origin, where it means *wisdom*). But one thing was evident as we toured the Russian orphanages. The workers loved the children, and served them to the best of their limited resources. While we, as others, have heard horror stories, we didn't ever see them. The orphanages were clean, as were the children. The children got enough to eat and they had clean clothes that fit them (though clothes were not owned, but shared between the orphans). The workers, for the most part, reminded me of loving school teachers who made every effort to make a difference in my life. Interestingly, after Sarah began attending school here in the States, she began to refer to the workers at her orphanage as "teachers," through no prompting from anyone else.

Few people with strong religious backgrounds struggle with the death of loved ones more than I have in my life. Thankfully, I don't have a son who "is just like I am" that way. The character Jeff is based on my own reactions as I lost grandparents during my teen years. And some of the non-adoption related insight that "Mike" is given, in the novel, actually came to *my* parents as they struggled to deal with *me*, and *my* anger towards them and God, as I struggled with the loss of my grandparents.

The part of the story where Laura sits in the car and cries while Mike allows the director to say goodbye is also based on an actual event. As I carried my little girl away from the orphanage and she screamed for the woman that she recognized as her mother, I really did think to myself that if she only understood that I was taking her to a better place, she wouldn't fight going. I also believed that the director couldn't possibly understand how much better her new home really was. As that happened, for the first time in my life, I felt like I understood death. Since that time, I have viewed death as the perfect Father taking His child home to a better place. Sometimes, after particularly difficult end-of-life experiences, I actually want to cheer as the Father succeeds in wrestling His child away from this life. As I came to understand this analogy, I felt an obligation to help those with similar beliefs (that God is the perfect loving Father) to understand death a little better. That was a key reason that drove me to follow through and finish this book.

We did have to separate our party on our return trip, very much the same as it occurs in the book. But the reasons that people had to get home were different (both of my parents are alive and well as I finish this novel). It was imperative that Denney receive medical attention as soon as he possibly could, so we *had* to get him home. Celeste and I stayed in Moscow, feeling sorry for ourselves and struggling the entire time because the rest of our family had already left for home.

There is a part of the story that didn't make it into the final draft. It references orphan names scrawled and etched by little hands on bricks on the outside wall of an orphanage. It is not only true, but it haunts me every day of my life as I remember my little Russian friends, wondering when and if they ever might take their journey home. According to statistics, about two-thirds of the girls (and more than a few of the boys) who "graduate" from orphanages become destitute and often resort to prostitution as a means of support. About three-fourths of the boys live a life of crime. Somewhere between one third and half of the orphans become drug addicts. Around half end up homeless and jobless. About ten percent get jobs and contribute to society while another ten percent become suicide victims. This doesn't take into account the numbers who die on the street from sexually transmitted diseases, illness caused by poor living and health conditions, or those who are murdered.

As I worked on the end of the novel, I began to think of things that I might write to people during book signings. As I finally decided on the things that I wanted to say, I concluded I would say the same to all who read this book, the following message, from my heart:

> *May you always experience at least a little sadness, but also unspeakable joy, when you witness the Father and His child embarking on their marvelous journey home. If you cry, shed only tears of happiness. Grieve only for those of us who are left behind.*

Most sincerely,

John M. Simmons

About the Author

John Simmons was an unlikely candidate for a novelist. President of a successful engineering, manufacturing and sales business, he had already chosen a career that he loved and excelled in. Able to apply himself in areas throughout the business, he was owner of twelve U.S. patents, recipient of several industry awards, including the Dupont Plunkett award, an international award given bi-annually for the best new products designed from Teflon, and recognized for advertising within the semiconductor process equipment industry.

Through his career and other experiences, Simmons had already seen a great deal of the world. But while going through all of the many experiences involved in international adoption, he saw and learned things beyond his wildest imagination. "I had seen abject poverty before," Simmons said. "I have sat in a rat infested, one room shack made from orange crates, with no running water or electricity. I knew what poor meant." But something touched the somewhat cynical business leader as soon as he set foot in a Russian orphanage. He instantly fell in love with the children. Not just the ones that he was there to adopt, but all of them. These were beautiful children. They were as happy as children anywhere. And regardless of their chances of success (more correctly, the lack thereof), they were filled with hopes, dreams and aspirations. "These kids didn't know that they were poor," Simmons recalled. "At least, if they did, it didn't bother them. But they all knew that they didn't have a family. Against all odds, they wait anxiously for the day when a mama and papa might miraculously appear and choose *them*, to embark on a marvelous journey home."

Simmons felt compelled to share their story. He began by gleaning time wherever he could find it; in hotels, on planes, and in airports, as he began the workings of a novel. But before he could finish, as he walked away from an orphanage, carrying one of his daughters, he learned the answer to a question that had plagued him since his early teen years. The answer was so simple, yet the problem troubles so many people in so many different ways. Having received such illumination, the novel redirected, just a bit, to include this insight.

Upon completion of the novel, several of Simmons' favorite stories about their family's adoption had not fit within the book's flow or time frame. So rather than forgetting about these events, several short stories were written. *Katya's Prayer* is one of those stories. It continues on with the story of Katya's two best friends, left at the orphanage when she went home and the miraculous way that they, against all odds, eventually received their own families. *All The Little Things* is another short story based on Katya's thankfulness and amazement over every-day, commonplace things that became available as she joined her family in America. The story shows how Katya, by example, taught her family to be thankful for so many things that so many people have come to take for granted.

John M. Simmons is president and co-owner of White Knight Fluid Handling, LLC, a company that designs, manufactures and sells components for the distribution of acids and other chemicals. In addition to *The Marvelous Journey Home*, he has written several short stories, which are available from the web site; www.whiteknightpublish.com. Simmons is currently working on his next novel, a sequel to his first. "There was just so much more to tell..." he said. The author lives with his wife, Amy, and nine children in Kamas, Utah, in a small mountain valley about 35 miles east of Salt Lake City.